"That's what you'd do? You'd plead guilty to something you didn't do?" Michael Ohlig's voice is calm, as if he's conducting a survey. "Answer my question, Alex," he says with insistence. "Would you plead guilty to something knowing you're innocent?"

"If it were me, I'd plead," I tell him. "I don't see how anyone can rationally risk spending the rest of their life in jail when the alternative, although certainly difficult, is doable. It's too risky to go to trial, even if you're innocent."

He nods while I say this, as if he's actually considering my analysis. Then, with a particularly heavy voice, he says, "I don't want to have this discussion again. I'm innocent, and I'm not going to admit to something I didn't do."

"Okay," I say.

"No, not okay, Alex. Call me old-fashioned, but I need to know that my lawyer believes in my innocence. So, tell me, straight out. Do you?"

"I do," I say, and much to my own surprise, I actually still believe it.

*A Conflict of Interest* is also available as an eBook.

"Adam Mitzner combines the real world insights of an experienced litigator with the imaginative flair of a fine novelist to produce a page-turner with deeply flawed heroes, sympathetic villains, and totally unexpected twists. I loved it!"

—Alan Dershowitz

"Intriguing, exciting, and packed with suspense, mystery, and shockers you couldn't even imagine heading your way. . . . Mitzner is fresh, inventive, and original. . . . He integrates diverse and infinitely complex flawed and relatable characters into a powerful drama, delving into their lives, their emotions, and their dark sinister motivations, making *A Conflict of Interest* a deliciously satisfying read."

—themysterysite.com

"A masterfully woven suspense thriller that'll keep you reading for hours; if you're able to put the book down at all."

—*True Crime Book Reviews*

# ADAM MITZNER

# A CONFLICT OF INTEREST

POCKET BOOKS

New York London Toronto Sydney New Delhi

Pocket Books
A Division of Simon & Schuster, Inc.
1230 Avenue of the Americas
New York, NY 10020

This book is a work of fiction. Names, characters, places, and incidents either are products of the author's imagination or are used fictitiously. Any resemblance to actual events or locales or persons, living or dead, is entirely coincidental.

First Pocket Books paperback edition April 2012

POCKET and colophon are registered trademarks of Simon & Schuster, Inc.

For information about special discounts for bulk purchases, please contact Simon & Schuster Special Sales at 1-866-506-1949 or business@simonandschuster.com.

The Simon & Schuster Speakers Bureau can bring authors to your live event. For more information or to book an event, contact the Simon & Schuster Speakers Bureau at 1-866-248-3049 or visit our website at www.simonspeakers.com.

Manufactured in the United States of America

10 9 8 7 6 5 4 3 2 1

ISBN: 978-1-4391-9643-4
ISBN: 978-1-4391-9644-1 (eBook)

*To my daughters, Rebecca and Emily*

In the middle of the journey of our lives
I found myself in a dark wood where
the straight road had been lost sight of.

—DANTE

# Prologue

The first time I set eyes on Michael Ohlig I was beside my father's casket and he was standing toward the back of a group of mourners comprised almost entirely of my father's extended family. Ohlig was a good half foot taller than everyone else, and unlike my paternal relatives, his head was covered with his own hair, a shade of silver usually reserved for much younger men anchoring the evening news. He wore it a little long, almost to the base of his collar, just enough to say that he fancied himself a nonconformist. I likely wouldn't have noticed him at all if he hadn't seemed so out of place. To be blunt about it, he looked too good to be associated with that crowd.

Ohlig was twice my father's closest friend—at the beginning and the end of his adult life. As far as I know, he was my father's only friend, the thirty-some-year gap in their contact seemingly occupied only by my mother and his hardware store.

The story I heard growing up was that Ohlig and my father were playing tennis at the courts in Central Park on the same day my mother was on a good Samaritan mission to keep a girlfriend company on the train from Queens to Manhattan, so her friend could watch her boyfriend play. My parents disagreed about which one of them approached the other, but the one part that never varied in either of their renditions was that it was love at first sight. They were married less than six months later, and I arrived in November the following year.

I don't know why it never seemed odd to me that, in all the subsequent retellings, my parents provided little detail about Ohlig. I never knew what he did for a living or whether he was married or had children. If I had ever been told how he and my father came to be friends, or why they lost touch, it went in one ear and out the other. For me, he just seemed like a historical figure, no different from Caesar or John F. Kennedy; someone who I took on faith had actually existed, but who had no relevance to my life. Even when my father shared with me the coincidence of running into Ohlig at a bookstore shortly after my parents moved to their retirement community in Florida, and that he was now living in a neighboring town, I had little curiosity about Ohlig's life.

Three times Ohlig poured a shovel full of dirt on my father's casket, fulfilling the ritualistic last act of a Jewish burial. Each motion was deliberate, as if his movements were intentionally drawn out to prolong his time to say good-bye. But it was the powerful way he approached the shovel, and the force with which he yanked it from the dirt, that most caught my eye, stating unequivocally that he was not someone to challenge.

Watching this I had no inkling that Michael Ohlig would become the central thread in all that followed. Even now I can hardly fathom how it came to be that a man who had never been anything more than a minor character in the story of my life would come to dominate its plot.

Perhaps stranger still, Michael Ohlig would undoubtedly say the same thing about me.

Part **1**

## 1

Like my best closing arguments, my eulogy is short, as I think all eulogies should be, especially when delivered in the hot Florida sun to people past retirement age. I can sometimes spend a week crafting a presentation to a jury, but I didn't put pen to paper about my father until last night. The words came to me easily, however, a sign that I'd been composing my father's legacy, at least as seen through my eyes, for years.

As I knew she would, my mother smiles approvingly when I mention that my father was a man who had few close friends, and that while she had tried several times to get him to befriend the husbands of her friends, it was usually without success. "I remember one time," I tell the thirty or so mourners gathered in front of the gravesite, "my mother said he must be one of those unique individuals who didn't need anyone else. A complete unit unto himself was the phrase she used. My dad was not a man prone to displays of affection, but his eyes got moist and he wrapped both his hands around hers. Very softly, as if he didn't even want me to hear, he told her that it wasn't that he didn't need anyone; he just didn't need anyone but her."

My father died three days ago. He was sixty-seven and had never been sick a day in his life. For a man of small stature, he was freakishly strong, and while the ability to toss around boxes filled with air-conditioner units as if they contained nothing more than Styrofoam peanuts is not a contra-indicator for coronary disease, it made the shock of his death that much greater.

After the funeral, a few people accompany us back to my parents' house, which is located in a gated retirement community in Boynton Beach, Florida, about ten minutes from Palm Beach. Boynton Beach is littered with these communities, and the developers who build them must believe all elderly people secretly want to be Italian, because each project is named for someplace in Italy—Roman Gardens, Florenza Court, Venetian Islands. My parents' development is called Venezia Castle III, which means somewhere, probably within five square miles, there must exist two other "castles."

The house is much smaller than the home I grew up in, which was by no means large, and anyone with an eye for construction can see the corners that were cut—the hollow doors, the lack of molding and the cheap fixtures. In New York City real estate parlance it would be called "charmless." Despite all this, my mother has never made any secret that she prefers this place to the home where we all lived in East Carlisle, a New Jersey suburb about an hour outside of New York City. I've always thought that it's the newness she finds so appealing. In fact, other than family photographs, my mother made a point of not bringing anything from our East Carlisle house with her to Boynton.

Right before my parents moved, my mother offered all of their accumulated possessions to Elizabeth and me. We declined—already having too much furniture for our small apartment—with one exception. I asked for a framed Picasso poster. It's more of a sketch than anything else, with assorted primary colors running in jagged lines from the middle of the subject's forehead down to the base of her nose.

When I was a child, the Picasso poster was the only thing I could see from my bedroom when the door was opened the usual crack to let some light in when I went to sleep. Truth be told, it frightened me then, so much so that I used to call it the Scary Lady.

My father bought the poster for four dollars the year my parents were married because he thought the woman depicted looked like my mother. I'm not sure my mother was ever flattered by the comparison, and she would have easily parted with it, but my father overruled her, claiming a sentimental attachment. The Scary Lady now hangs in their entry hall, the first thing you see upon entering, still surrounded by its original silver frame and bright blue matte, which is completely at odds with the color scheme of the rest of the house.

"Your father thought the world of you," my aunt Joan says to me while she's spreading what looks like vegetable cream cheese on a sesame bagel. "He was just so proud of everything you had accomplished." She offers a somewhat pained smile. "How is your mother handling all of this?"

"Okay, I guess. I'm not sure the enormity of it has kicked in for her yet."

Joan nods and looks to the floor. "When Sam died,

it took a long time for me to feel like myself again. But, as they say, it gets easier. Not better, just easier."

It's my turn to nod and look away. Sam was my father's older brother, and his only sibling. He died twenty years ago, maybe more.

"And you?" Joan asks. "How are you dealing with everything?"

"Good," I say with a wan smile that by now I've perfected as the response to this query.

"Elizabeth looks great," Joan adds, nodding across the room in the direction of my wife, who is busy with her own bagel and another group of family friends. "And how's that little girl of yours?"

"Great." This I say with a real smile, my involuntary reflex whenever my daughter is the topic of discussion. "Charlotte's just wonderful."

"How old is she now?"

"She turned five last month. We didn't bring her down because we didn't think a funeral was something she'd understand."

Joan doesn't offer any insight into the fragility of the psyche of a five-year-old girl, but her face takes on a mask that suggests she's thinking about something even more frightening than a funeral would be to Charlotte. "Alex, there's actually something I wanted to—"

"Alex," my mother interrupts. "I'm sorry, Joan," she says, "I need to borrow my son for a moment."

Joan curls her lip. There's never been any love lost between her and my mother, on either side of the equation. Still, Joan knows enough not to challenge her sister-in-law with regard to my time, and so she says only, "We'll talk later."

My mother is almost twelve years my father's junior, and because of this disparity, I long suspected that she would not only survive him, but that when he died she'd still be young enough to have a second act, an opportunity to live a different life. When I tried to imagine what that other life would look like, I always believed it would be built around another man—someone very different from my father.

All of this is not to say that I ever doubted my mother's love for my father, but my parents certainly made an unlikely pair. Part of that was physical—she towered over him by a good three inches, and when she wore heels, which was not infrequently, she could be a head taller. But it was also because she was at least three points higher on the looks meter, and that spread increased as they aged.

On what my parents always referred to as a "baker's rack" is one of the last pictures they took together. It's a photo I shot at Charlotte's birthday party, which was a little more than a month ago. They're both smiling broadly, but people who don't know them would likely assume they are father and daughter, except for the fact that it would be hard to imagine my father having such a beautiful daughter.

My mother drags me by the arm over to the living room sofa. "Alex, this is Michael Ohlig," she says when we've arrived.

Ohlig stands and extends his arm. I can't help but

look down at his hand, recalling how firmly he grasped the shovel at the cemetery. Peeking out from his sleeve is a very expensive watch. It isn't flashy, not one of those clunky platinum timepieces crusted in diamonds that seemingly every one of my investment banker clients sports. It has a simple black leather band and a white chronograph face. I might not have thought it cost more than a few hundred dollars if I hadn't recently read an article in the *New York Times* about complications, the term used by aficionados to describe watches of this type, which combine several functions within a single casing. This watch, or at least one very similar, was pictured in the article, and so I know it's more expensive than a sports car.

"It's very nice to meet you," I say. "I've heard a lot about you over the years."

"I bet it's not half as much as I've heard about you," he says.

Ohlig's voice fits the man perfectly. Strong, without any sense of doubt or fear, but also conveying breeziness, as if Michael Ohlig is a man who doesn't sweat the small stuff.

The woman sitting beside him doesn't get up to take part in the introductions, but Ohlig gestures toward the couch and says, "This is my wife, Pamela."

Pamela Ohlig is the kind of woman a rich, well-preserved silver-haired man in his sixties would marry later in life, which is to say that she's my age, or at most a few years older, certainly under forty, very attractive and a little cheap looking. There's a lot that seems just a

quarter too much—the blondness of her hair, the tight-
ness of her clothes, the size of the jewels she wears.

"Yes, I'm sorry," my mother says. "Pamela, thank you
so much for coming today."

"My pleasure," she says, and then looks as if she
thought better of being pleased to be at my father's
funeral.

My mother doesn't seem to notice. Instead, she turns
back toward Ohlig and says, "Michael, Alex is a criminal defense attorney at Cromwell Altman in New York
City."

"So your father told me. Many times, in fact. If I
remember what he said, it's the best law firm in the
world, and you are the youngest partner in its ten-
thousand-year history."

I smile a bit sheepishly at the joke. My father did
have a tendency to brag about my accomplishments.

"Don't be embarrassed," Ohlig says. "It's one of the
many things I loved about your dad, the way he loved
you so. So tell me, how do you like it at Cromwell
Altman?"

Like most people, I suppose, I've answered the question—how do you like work?—so many times that my
response sounds like a prepared speech. "The cases are
always pretty interesting," I say, reciting my lines; "very
high stakes, and the people at the firm are some of the
smartest people I've ever encountered anywhere. Of
course, if you asked my wife, she might give you a different answer. I think her usual quote is that the place is
sucking out my soul."

My quip elicits the polite laughter of people who don't know me well enough to determine how much truth it contains. We go on to talk a few more minutes about nothing of substance—the astronomical price of real estate in New York City, the Florida humidity in August. At a conversational pause, my mother excuses herself to meet a new arrival, and when she's out of earshot, Ohlig turns to his wife and says, "Would you mind, dear, if I take a few moments to discuss something with Alex privately?"

"Of course," she says. "It was very nice meeting you, Alex," she adds as her husband leads me away.

"Do you mind if we go outside for a moment?" Ohlig asks, stretching his arm toward the front door as if to lead me.

My mother's postage-size front lawn has a view of a man-made canal that is narrower than a New York City side street. Without irony, she called this a "water view" when she first described the property to me.

I wait for Ohlig to tell me what I imagine is going to be some anecdote about my father that might not be suitable to be shared in front of his wife. Instead, what he says is completely unexpected.

"I'm afraid I find myself in a bit of legal trouble and need the help of a first-rate criminal defense lawyer."

He says this without the slightest trace of guilt. I'm not surprised he doesn't admit any wrongdoing; virtually none of my clients do, at least not before I learn of the evidence that leaves little room for doubt. But Ohlig doesn't proclaim his innocence either, and that is surprising.

The first credo of Cromwell Altman is never to pass up a paying client. The lesson is reinforced daily when the firm sends around the origination score-card, showing the top rainmakers. So I overlook the circumstances—my father's funeral—to pitch for the business.

"How can I help you, Mr. Ohlig?"

"Please, Alex, if we're going to be working together, and even if we're not, you have to call me Michael."

"Okay. How can I help you, Michael?"

"Thank you," he says in something of a non sequitur. "It's not appropriate to your father's memory to talk about it today. I'll come to New York next week and meet with you in your office."

"It's okay to talk about it now. I really don't mind and it will let me think about something else."

"No. It just isn't right," he says, making it clear he will not change his mind. "But, if you'll permit me one more indulgence. I don't want your mother to know about any of this. Attorney-client privilege and all that good stuff. She's got enough on her mind now without my problems adding to it."

"I understand. All representations are kept in the strictest confidence. Even from my mother."

He laughs, as if we had been talking about something other than the fact that he finds himself in criminal jeopardy. This much I've already surmised: Michael Ohlig is one cool customer. Most clients are like my daughter before a doctor's visit, requiring constant as-surance that everything is going to be all right and a painstakingly precise description of each step to follow, but not Michael Ohlig. He's heard enough.

There are really only two possibilities for Ohlig's demeanor. Either he has deluded himself into believing there's nothing to worry about, or he knows the peril he's in and sees no reason to request false promises. Even though I've only just met him, it is already apparent that Ohlig isn't the self-deluded type.

# 2

Ohlig arrives at my office at nine o'clock on the dot the following Monday. He's wearing a dark suit, a white shirt, and an expensive-looking tie. But for the fact his hair is a few inches longer than a white-shoe lawyer would find appropriate, someone passing by my office would assume I was meeting with the firm's senior partner.

"Thank you again for making time for me, Alex."

"My pleasure, Michael."

"How's your mom doing?"

"She's okay. Thanks for asking. I spoke with her yesterday. She's trying to sound upbeat, talking about the future. But it must be so hard. My father was everything to her."

He smiles softly. "She's a strong woman, your mother. She'll be okay, of that I'm sure. And you, how are you holding up?"

"Good. Again, thanks for asking."

"Good. Thanks for asking," he repeats as a gentle mock. "Have you always been so reserved in your emotions?"

The truth is that I always have been. It's something that Elizabeth finds difficult to comprehend, wondering how I can argue with people for a living and yet remain so even-tempered in my own life. "That's why," is what I normally tell her.

My father's death is my first experience with grief. I cried when my mother called me with the news, but since then I've been able to hold my emotions in check, even while eulogizing him. It was Charlotte, ironically enough, who first called me on it. Noticing how Elizabeth was crying as I told our daughter the news that Papa had died, Charlotte seemed confused.

"Papa was your daddy, right, Daddy?"

"Yes."

"Then why aren't you crying too?"

"I cried for Papa earlier, when Grandma told me the news. And I may cry for him later too. Everyone feels sad in their own way."

I told Ohlig a variant of the same thing. Like Charlotte, I don't think he bought it.

"Alex, even though I'm up here seeking your sage counsel," he says, "I may be able to offer you some advice too. I know what it's like to lose a father, and I know what a great guy your father was, which I can only assume makes it a hundred times tougher for you than it was for me when my father died because my old man was one mean SOB. I guess what I'm trying to say is that even though we don't know each other very well, other than your mother, no one knew your father better than me. So, if you ever want to talk about anything, I'm here for you."

"Thank you. I really do appreciate it," I say, meaning it.

He looks around my office. "Okay, so before we get started, you gotta tell me what's up with the Batman stuff."

It's a fair question, and one that others have posed. For the most part, my office, like much of my life, is little more than a façade with which I try to project what I think the world expects from me. In this case, that includes a sleek Le Corbusier glass table and matching guest chairs, a high-backed black leather desk chair that looks as expensive as it was, a sofa I don't believe anyone has ever sat on, pictures on my desk of Charlotte and Elizabeth that face me, and artwork I stare at for twelve to sixteen hours a day, but would be hard-pressed to identify if it were stolen.

The exception to all this high-end seriousness is assorted Batman paraphernalia. Some of it is of the expensive toy variety, like a Cobblepot for Mayor poster that was an actual prop in the 1992 Batman movie and cost nearly $2,000 on eBay, but most of it is what you might expect to see in an eight-year-old's bedroom—a Batman mug that holds my pens, Pez figures on my bookshelf, and a toy bat signal. They stand out in these surroundings much the same way I would at a partners' meeting if I dyed my hair purple.

"I like Batman," I tell him. "Think of it as my way of identifying with another defender of the innocent."

He laughs at this, but it's shallow, as if he knows my last comment was facetious.

"So what is it that caused you to come to New York City to seek, what did you call it, my sage counsel?" I say, getting down to the business at hand.

Ohlig leans forward, locking onto my eyes. It's a

stare with some power behind it, so much so that it's a struggle for me to maintain his eye contact.

"I don't know if your father ever mentioned it, but I run a boutique brokerage firm called OPM Securities. We focus on emerging companies, mainly biotech. There's a criminal investigation about some of our trading. My corporate counsel is telling me he has a conflict representing me, he's not admitted in New York, criminal law isn't his specialty, yada yada yada."

Michael Ohlig is very economical with his words. This will make him a good witness, but a difficult client. It's one thing to make a prosecutor work for every piece of information, but when your disclosures to your lawyer are on a need to know basis, there's a substantial risk that something important will be missed.

"You need to give me a little more than that, Michael. What's shared between us is privileged, so don't worry about it going any further than me. But if I'm going to represent you, I need to know everything, the good, the bad, *and* the ugly."

He smiles, a Cheshire cat–like grin. "One thing you'll learn about me, Alex, is that I'm an open book. Ask and ye shall receive."

This is something I've heard before, and like most things my clients tell me, I'm skeptical as to its veracity. "What trading, in particular, is being investigated?"

"It's in a stock called Salminol. They have this patent to produce salmonella-free eggs. So you'd go to the grocery store, and right next to the regular eggs there'd be this box that said in big letters *100% Salmonella-Free*

*Eggs—Guaranteed.* Can't miss, right?" I assume the question is rhetorical, but he comes to a complete halt, continuing only when I nod to confirm that no one would buy eggs that weren't 100 percent guaranteed to be salmonella-free.

"Here," he says and then pushes a packet of paper in front of me. It's stapled in the top corner, but it takes only an initial glance for me to recognize it as a grand jury subpoena.

A grand jury subpoena is something of a calling card, in that it's usually the first indication that the government has begun a criminal investigation. Sometimes it's difficult to ascertain what, exactly, the government is investigating, but this one leaves little room for doubt. The very first request on the subpoena reads: *All documents concerning OPM's trading in Salminol, Inc.*

When I've finished looking at the last page, Ohlig continues with his narrative. "Anyway, the company ended up being overly levered, and so it couldn't make the interest payments when the balloon came due. The insiders cleaned out whatever wasn't nailed to the floor, which sent the stock to zero. Then some blue-haired ladies complained they lost their life savings, and you know the rest, right?"

I do, actually. This is the part of the story where my clients always make some reference that no one complains when their risky investment goes up, but if it goes down they run to the government. I'm waiting for Ohlig to offer this defense, but he's silent.

"How much was the loss to the investors?" I ask.

"I don't have it down to the penny, Alex." He smiles at me, an expression that should be accompanied by a wink, I think.

"Give me your best ball park."

"A hundred and fifty million," he says without a hint of remorse.

Ohlig still hasn't offered me much, but this is enough for me to get to the first step in any representation—setting the retainer. One of my partners refers to this as meeting with the most important witness in the case—Mr. Green.

"If it were just me I wouldn't ask," I say, sounding more apologetic than I'd like, "but it's firm policy that in a matter like this we obtain a significant retainer before taking on the representation. Unfortunately, there's a very great likelihood that your assets are going to be frozen, and while there's a chance the freeze order will permit an exception for attorneys' fees, it's not a risk the firm is willing to take."

I have no doubt he's already keenly aware of the SEC's power to freeze a brokerage firm's assets, as well as the personal assets of the firm's principals. My guess is that for years he's been squirreling money away—Switzerland, the Cayman Islands, the Isle of Man—in case that day ever came.

"Conservatively," I continue, "my estimate is that, assuming there's a trial, legal fees could run a million dollars, and it might be more. So, I need to ask you for a million dollars."

He pauses, almost looking as if he's taking my

measure. "I'll wire you two million when I leave your office, and then we won't have to talk money for some time. Fair enough?"

I've negotiated with enough clients to know that someone offering twice the retainer you've requested is not something that happens every day. I pause for a moment to consider why Ohlig just did exactly that, and the only reason I can come up with is that he wants to show me that price is no object.

"It's more than fair," I say. "So, now that the money is out of the way, I suppose I should open the floor to whatever questions you have for me."

There's a joke that is often recycled at Cromwell Altman, usually when we're meeting with law students or describing criminal practice to the new associates. It's an effort to explain what white-collar criminal practice is really all about. We call it the Four Questions. At the outset of a criminal investigation, clients invariably ask four questions, in this order: *What's an indictment? What's the most jail time I can get? Does the United States have an extradition treaty with Israel? Where can I go where I* won't *be extradited?*

At the very least, I expect Ohlig to ask about jail time, which could be considerable given the amount of money that was lost. In fact, I can't recall another client who's gone this long without asking for an assessment of the worst-case scenario.

"No," Ohlig says. "I don't have any questions."

The rest of our conversation progresses along more or less standard lines. We cover the facts in slightly more detail, and I tell Ohlig the type of evidence that we can expect the government to be looking at, rattling off the usual land mines in a case like this one—trading tickets, emails, and new account documents. He confirms that OPM hasn't destroyed anything, which is the first really good news I've heard so far.

"What about taping?" I ask.

"What about it?" he says, although I'm sure he knows what I'm asking.

"Do you tape your brokers?"

"We tape the confirms. After the broker—we call them financial advisors, by the way—makes the sale, he transfers the client to the ops department to do the paperwork. Ops is taped."

Many brokerage firms tape the brokers to avoid DKs—situations where the stock goes down right after the sale and the client tries to avoid the loss by claiming he never placed the order. It stands for "don't know," as if the client is saying he didn't know the broker was buying that stock. There's only one reason for Ohlig to tape his operations personnel but not the brokers—he doesn't want a record of what his people say to sell the stock.

There must be something about my facial expression that gives me away.

"Alex, I know what you're thinking," he says, much more pointedly than any of his previous comments. "You think I'm running a pump-and-dump opera-tion. One that's in with the wrong crowd, even." He pushes his nose to the side with his index finger, the international sign for organized crime. "That I was unloading Salminol on widows knowing the stock was worthless. If that's what you're thinking, get it out of your head right now. Everything at my firm is on the up-and-up, and I don't want you thinking it isn't."

I don't say anything at first.

"Are we clear on that?" he says, in a way that reminds me of the Jack Nicholson line in *A Few Good Men*.

"Okay," I say, resisting the impulse to add, *crystal*.

"Good." He smiles, perhaps to suggest he's not really upset, despite his flash of anger, but it's too late. Although Michael Ohlig has thus far taken pains to project a nonchalant façade, it's now clear to me that below the surface lies an entirely different type of man.

# 3

Cromwell Altman rotates the position of assigning partner every eighteen months because it's the least desirable job on earth. The entire function revolves around calling associates and assigning them to cases they claim to be too busy to work on, and telling the partners that the associates they want on their cases are unavailable. Every assigning partner says he's afraid to pick up the phone if it's any of the partners, and no associate will answer the phone when they see the assigning partner's name pop up on the caller ID.

The current assigning partner is Brian Fleming, who is actually pretty well suited for the job because he's the most joyless man I've ever met. Back when I was an associate, and I'm sure the same is still true today among the current associates, his office was referred to as the House of Pain. In part, but only in part, this is because none of his guest chairs have any cushions—they are all fancy wood-carved pieces that scream that Fleming doesn't expect anyone to stay too long. His face says the same thing. When I joined the firm, Fleming wore these giant glasses that covered virtually the entire top half of his head, and a full black beard that covered the whole lower half. Twelve years later, the only difference is that his beard is now gray.

"I just brought in a big criminal case," I tell Fleming

as I shift uncomfortably in his guest chair, "and I need three, maybe four, associates. Preferably somebody senior, a mid-level, and a newbie."

Someone with social graces would congratulate me, but no one would accuse Fleming of possessing any. "So what's the case about?" he asks in a way that makes clear he really couldn't care less.

"Criminal securities fraud. Client runs a boutique brokerage firm in Florida. The loss could be as much as half a billion." I've pumped up this last figure in the hope it will earn me more help.

"Is it here or there?" he says, meaning New York or Florida. He's asking this because if significant travel is involved, some associates may not be available.

"Here."

"So, what did you get?" This is the only issue he really cares about—the size of the retainer.

"Two million."

Fleming grimaces, causing his bearded face to crinkle in the most unattractive way imaginable. "C'mon, Miller. You know the formula—two million gets you one body. You can use temps for the other stuff."

The formula is followed like the Scriptures at Cromwell Altman. About three years ago, the firm hired some high-priced consultant to give advice on how to increase profits. The consultant recommended we could improve the bottom line by—wait for it—charging higher rates and reducing expenses. The way they said we could cut expenses was to use temps for certain tasks, but bill them out at the same rate as associates.

The firm pays something like sixty bucks an hour for even the priciest temp, whereas associates cost anywhere from a quarter of a million dollars for first years up through more than twice that for senior associates when you factor in bonus, vacation, health care, and whatever perks we give them. Even though we work the associates to death, about 2,500 hours per year on average, they still cost the firm about three times as much as temps. Of course, the temps graduated from second- and third-tier law schools and can't find full-time jobs, and to be an associate at Cromwell Altman you're the type who could have had any job you wanted, so it isn't the fairest thing in the world to charge clients the same rate for vastly different legal talent, but it does boost the firm's bottom line considerably.

I look at Fleming with total defeat, which seems to brighten his mood. It's as if he thinks his job function is to break the spirit of anyone needing his assistance.

"If you're only going to give me one associate, I want someone very senior and very good," I say.

This was what I'd been angling for all along. The work of the junior people on a case really doesn't matter much being that it's usually comprised entirely of document review. Besides which, I won't have direct contact with the junior people anyway. Cromwell Altman is more hierarchical than the military in this regard. Partners deal only with the senior-most associate on the team.

"Dan's got some time," Fleming says.

"No." Further explanation is unnecessary. Dan

Salvensen was passed over for partner and is now more or less on autopilot until the firm tells him it's time to leave, at which time Cromwell Altman will find him a nice home in a client's legal department, with the understanding that he'll refer work back to the firm.

"What about David Bloom?"

"He's a fifth year, right? I need a seventh or eighth year."

A long silence follows, until Fleming looks like he's got no choice but to come clean, which in his case takes the form of his showing a glimpse of his yellow teeth. "What about Abigail Sloane?"

"If she has the time. Definitely."

"She's up for partner at the end of the year. She'll make time."

"Okay then. Abigail Sloane it is."

"You owe me, Miller," Fleming says. "Big time."

By the time I return to my office, Abby Sloane is already there. She stands beside my door frame, careful not to cross the threshold, as if my office is hallowed ground that requires special permission to enter.

"That was fast," I say. "Come on in."

Abby glides into the guest chair across from my desk and I settle in opposite her. She's wearing a very serious expression, which seems to be a fixture among associates. A yellow legal pad is in her lap, which is also standard. Virtually everything a partner says to an associate is transcribed immediately.

"Welcome aboard." My tone suggests the assignment

is some type of vacation for her, when in actuality it's going to add another sixty to seventy hours to what was likely already a fully subscribed work week.

"Thanks," she says, as if she's actually pleased to have the additional work.

This is not the first time I've worked with Abby. When she was a first year, which would have been seven years ago, five years before I made partner, we were two of at least twenty-five associates working on a large antitrust litigation. She was a document grind, one of a dozen or more who reviewed millions of pages of documents off-site at the warehouse the firm had rented, while I was on-site reviewing the thousands of pages that the ware-house people had concluded might be important.

I could remind her of that fact, but think better of it. I don't recall a single other member of the document team, and there's no reason I should recall Abby either, except that she is exceptionally beautiful. Her biography on the firm's website lists that she studied ballet, and she moves with a dancer's grace. She wears her blond curly hair loose and long, almost alone among her female colleagues, most of whom have opted for more lawyer-like styles.

"You come highly recommended," I say. "When I was in the House of Pain, I told Brian that I needed someone very good to second-seat this one, and he said it didn't get better than you."

"And when Brian told me to report to the Batcave for my new assignment, I was excited to be working with you."

I smile, surprised, but also impressed that Abby is comfortable enough to make fun of me. Most associates follow the old saw about children—they are to be seen, but not heard.

"Did you think that Brian's office was the only one in the firm with a nickname?" she asks.

"So, this is the Batcave?" I say with a self-deprecating laugh. "That makes sense. The client was here yesterday and that's the first thing he asked about. Why I like Batman."

"And what did you tell him?"

"That Batman is a defender of the innocent."

"And what's the real reason?"

I hesitate before answering. Clearly, Abby Sloane is not your typical associate.

"Why can't that be the real reason?"

"Because then you'd be a Superman guy. *He's* really a defender of the innocent. I've always seen Batman as . . . well, as a little like a criminal himself." And then, as if she fears that she might have overstepped, she adds, "I hope that's not heresy."

"No, it's actually quite perceptive. There's a view in the comic book world that you're either one or the other. You know, the way normal people divide the world up into Republicans or Democrats. Elvis or the Beatles. For comic book geeks, it's Batman or Superman."

"I see you've made your choice," she says, perusing the walls.

"Batman is much more interesting," I begin to

explain. "I know that this is now in super geek territory, but think about the two of them as literary characters. They're both orphan tales of a type. What's more traumatic, having your parents murdered in front of you or never knowing them?"

"I'm sorry, Alex," she says all of a sudden. "I should have asked about your family. The firm sent an email around last week, but I forgot about it until you mentioned parents just now. How are you doing?"

I smile, and then involuntarily chuckle to myself.

"What?" Abby asks.

"It's funny you should ask about my father because I was thinking about him the moment that you did. It's from him I get my comic book genes. Although, I have to admit, he was a Superman guy. Anyway, I'm fine. Thank you for asking." I hope my smile conveys that it's true. "And there's no need for you to apologize. I was very much enjoying talking about superheroes. I've tried getting my daughter interested, but she's all about princesses, much to my chagrin."

"How about we make a deal?" Abby pauses, as if she wants me to commit in advance to what she is about to propose.

"I'm afraid I'm too much the lawyer to ever accept any deal without reading the fine print first," I say.

"It's not that type of a deal," she says. "I'm going to do some studying up on my superheroes, and then I'll fully engage you in this Superman/Batman debate. Frankly, I feel a little overmatched at the moment. You don't know this about me yet, but I don't like to venture into areas where someone else has superior knowledge."

"If that's not the ideal trait for a litigator, I don't know what is. And I suppose I'm not going to get a better segue into talking about the facts of our little case. So, without further adieu, let's talk about everything Michael Ohlig."

I go through the basic facts of the case, explaining Ohlig's rationale for his trading position as well as the charges the government is likely considering. I also tell her about my family connection to Ohlig, adding that I didn't think it would make much of a difference given that I had just met him myself.

"The first order of business is to assemble a joint defense team," I say. Abby's been involved in enough of these types of cases to know what I mean—that I'm going to retain cooperating counsel to represent Ohlig's employees.

"Ohlig's on board for picking up the tab?"

"What's another million to him?" I say with a smile.

This is the quid pro quo of the joint defense. The main target—in this case Ohlig—will pay the legal bills for the other key people at OPM, in exchange for their cooperation with his defense. The lawyers chosen by us to receive this business are almost entirely dependent on such referrals to sustain their practices and are savvy enough to know that the gravy train comes to a screeching halt if their client turns against our client. Of course, all of this is unspoken because a lawyer has an ethical duty to represent his client zealously, regardless of who's footing the bill.

"And, while I'm doing that, I'm sorry to say, you'll be—"

"Let me guess: collecting and reviewing the documents?"

"How did you know?"

Litigation, especially as practiced at Cromwell Altman, is all about the documents. If the partners think about cases in terms of how much revenue they bring to the firm, associates categorize them in terms of how many boxes of documents to be reviewed.

"Just a wild guess," she says, showing me a smile with enough wattage to illuminate a small town. "Any idea how much?"

"I think it will be manageable, although there will probably be a lot of trade tickets. I've asked Michael to send up what he has, but I'm sure we're going to need to make a visit down to him at some point to check out the operation and make sure we've retrieved everything."

This is every associate's worst nightmare—reviewing documents when there is real lawyer work to be done. I decide to give her a ray of hope.

"I'm not looking at you to be a document grind, Abby. I really need a strong number two on this. We've got the green light to bring on as many temps as we'll need to go through the documents. I can't tell you that you won't have to review the key stuff, but when we get to trial, I'm looking to you to be operating on a partner level."

"You think there actually will be a trial?"

The firm very rarely takes a case to trial. The stakes are just too high for most clients to risk on an all-or-nothing result, be it a gamble over money or freedom, and so most cases settle. In my dozen years at the firm, I've been involved in only seven trials, and on some of those my participation was minimal.

"He says he's innocent."

By now I know Abby is smart enough not to fall for that as an answer. She doesn't disappoint me.

"Don't they all? I mean, right up until the moment you confront them with the evidence that they're not?"

There must be something in the way I react because she adds, "Are you sure there's not going to be a problem here because he's a family friend?"

"I'm sure. I just like to believe that we're on the side of the angels. You know, innocent until proven guilty and all that."

"So, you want us to get him off *and* for him to actually be innocent?" She says this with another smile, one that tells me that she's on board, regardless of her own suspicions.

## 4

Despite the fact that I've been at Cromwell Altman for most of my adult life, I doubt that there is anyone here I'd still talk to after either I or they left the firm. The one exception is Paul Harris.

Paul and I joined the firm on the same day, two of fifty-two first-year associates. Through the years, as the others began dropping away, either by relocating, going in-house, switching firms, or leaving the law altogether, it became clear that Paul and I would likely be the only two left standing. In the homestretch, we were both putting in sixteen-hour days, seven days a week, and spending a lot of our non-billable time together in the firm cafeteria. During the worst of it, we joked that we spent much more time with each other than with our wives. After we made partner, we continued the camaraderie, our horror stories about the unreasonable demands of the partners morphing seamlessly into complaints about the poor work ethic of the associates.

A few times a year, Paul and I use the expense accounts we're given to wine and dine clients to share an expensive lunch just for the two of us. We justify having the firm pick up the tab by telling ourselves we are discussing legal issues or business development, but the encounters almost always devolve into nothing more than rank gossip about firm intrigue and catching up

about our kids. Today we're at Aquavit, a top-tier Swedish restaurant about five blocks from the office.

"Sorry I'm late," Paul says as he approaches the table.
"My meeting at Taylor Beckett on that"—he looks both
ways to be sure he's not going to be overheard—"on,
you know, that merger, went longer than I'd expected."

"No worries. I just got here myself."

Paul takes his seat and tucks his tie into his shirt, an
affectation I've seen so many times I don't even make
fun of it anymore. The waiter is right behind him
and asks the usual first question in a place like this—
"sparkling or still?" I have never ordered bottled water
in a restaurant when someone other than a client or the
firm was paying. Without missing a beat, Paul tells the
waiter that sparkling would be great.

"So, how's everything going with you?" It's a reference to my father, I think.

"Okay. It's hard to know how it's supposed to feel."

"When my father died, I remember some guy telling
me that it's impossible to describe it until you've experienced it. Just the idea that I couldn't talk to him."

"I'm a little worried about my mother. She seemed
to be holding up okay, but they were married thirty-five
years."

"I could make a comment about wanting to die after
being married thirty-five years, but out of respect to
your parents, I'll refrain."

I smile, not at all offended by his effort at levity.
"Point well taken."

After the waiter has returned with our sparkling

water and taken our orders—Swedish meatballs for Paul and the smoked salmon for me—Paul announces that he has some news. My sixth sense has already alerted me to what he's about to say, but that doesn't mean I'm not hoping I'm wrong.

"Lauren and I are expecting," he says with pride. "Twins, in fact."

"That's great," I say, trying to hide my disappointment.

It's not that I'm sorry Paul and Lauren are having more children, but they are the last couple I know with a first child Charlotte's age who have not yet added to their family. Intellectually I know there are many reasons why couples stop at one, but in our case it has nothing to do with choice or ability. Without saying it aloud, both Elizabeth and I have doubts about whether our marriage can sustain the weight of another child. My reaction to Paul's news isn't a matter of misery loving company, but more that I took some solace that his presumably happy marriage provided camouflage for my marital difficulties.

"I don't know if I told you, but we had been trying for a few years and finally went to a specialist. Now we've got two for the price of one."

"That's great," I say again. "When is Lauren due?"

"March 9, but the doctor told us that second children come early, and with twins it's more likely to be late February."

"Which flavor?"

Paul chuckles a little. "One of each."

"That's great," I say for the third time. "How's Ryan taking to the idea?"

"Very excited about a little brother, but could take or leave the sister part."

I stop myself from telling Paul that this, too, is great.

"And what about you guys?" he asks.

I shift in my seat. "We're talking about it."

"I assume you know this, but given that it's been a few years since Charlotte was conceived, let me remind you that you need to do something more than talk for it to happen."

"Really? Maybe that's been our problem."

I wonder if there is too much melancholy in what I intended to be a joke because Paul segues quickly. "So, I hear congratulations are in order for you as well. Word on the street is that you bagged a big one, my friend."

"Thanks. Although I think it means a little less when you've bagged your father's best friend."

"Is his money green?

"It is indeed."

"Then it makes no difference at all." We both laugh, and before I've stopped, he adds, "But, even better than that, I hear Fleming gave you Abby Sloane."

News travels fast, apparently. I think about calling Paul on his terminology—that Fleming gave Abby to me, as if she's property—but instead I play dumb.

"And I'm to be congratulated for that why?"

"I'm sorry, but did you go blind recently?"

"And here I thought you were congratulating me because she's the best associate in the firm. If you recall, she won that insider trading case last year even though no one thought she had a chance in hell of getting an acquittal, and then she second-seated Aaron on that enormous environmental disaster thing."

"Yeah, that too," Paul says sarcastically, emphasizing the point with a roll of his eyes. "So tell me, what's the new case about?"

Paul's practice is mergers and acquisitions, which means he's more of a banker than a lawyer. He's never set foot in a courtroom or taken a deposition. My guess is he probably knows more about criminal proceedings from watching *Law & Order* reruns than from his legal training.

"The client ran a boutique brokerage house down in Florida. Apparently a hot stock he was promoting went south, and now the investors want his scalp."

"I see you've already drunk the Kool-Aid," Paul says with a laugh.

"What's that supposed to mean?"

"It means that I worked at one of those"—and he air quotes—"boutique brokerage firms between college and law school. They're the ninth circle of hell. I lasted about four months and by the time I left, I was the second most senior guy in the whole place. I swear to you, they handcuffed—actually handcuffed—some poor schmo to his desk until he made a sale. They wouldn't let him go to the bathroom or eat or anything. Sixteen hours. Imagine the worst frat house you can think of, and then imagine stealing money from senile retirees, and you're about halfway there."

"My guy says his shop wasn't like that."

"Of course not. How could I forget, all of your

clients immediately admit whenever they've done something wrong."

"Wait just a second," I say with a laugh. "He's not
just *my* client. Mike Ohlig and OPM are clients of
Cromwell Altman Rosenthal and White, which makes
them your clients too."

"OPM, huh?"

"You've heard of them?"

I'm not at all happy that Ohlig apparently has a reputation that precedes him. I had googled Ohlig, as I do
with all my clients, but the search provided only hits to
charity functions he attended and some campaign contributions. The legal databases confirmed what Ohlig
told me—OPM had only a handful of complaints
against it, and none was within the last five years, which
is a pretty good record considering how heavily securities firms are regulated and how litigious investors can
be, especially in down markets.

"Well . . . I had a college buddy who worked for
them—for three weeks—before he got the hell out of
there."

I think Paul's going to say more, but he's uncharac-
teristically silent.

"And?"

"Ohlig's a family friend, right?"

"Not really. I mean, he was a friend of my father's, but
I don't know him at all. He's just a client to me. And by
this point, I've got to know whatever there is to know
about him. So, if you've got something, let's hear it."

"Well, sorry to tell you, but remember what I said about

these guys living in the ninth circle of hell? That wouldn't apply to your guy—he's pretty much the devil himself."

"Oh c'mon. He can't be that bad. And anyway, how can you be sure it's OPM where this friend of yours worked? That was like fifteen years ago, right?"

"Not quite," he says, "more like thirteen, but I remember OPM because of the whole other people's money thing."

"Other people's money?"

"Yeah. What did you think OPM stood for?"

I'm embarrassed that it never occurred to me to ask. I'd rather not share with Paul that I've missed something so obvious, so I sidestep the question.

"Let me get this straight. You're telling me that you're sure my client is now guilty of securities fraud because, during the first Clinton Administration, a buddy of yours didn't like working at OPM, so he spent less than a month there. Do I have that right?"

"Waiter," Paul calls out, gesturing with his hands. I turn around but there's no waiter in sight, and so I realize he's playing with me. "We need another glass of Kool-Aid over here."

First Abby, now Paul. Of course, they're both probably right. It's an almost inviolate rule of criminal defense work that clients lie to you.

For reasons I can't yet articulate, however, I believe Ohlig is innocent. It's not that his story rings particularly true. In fact, it's one I've heard dozens of times before, but I take it on faith that my father's closest friend is not a criminal.

## 5

When I enter my apartment that evening, Charlotte literally leaps into my arms. I pull her close and twirl her around, as if we're dancing in some 1940s Fred Astaire–Ginger Rogers movie, and then Elizabeth comes into view.

My father claimed that on the day he met my mother he went home and immediately told my grandmother he had met the woman he was going to marry. I had no such thunderbolt moment with Elizabeth. Rather, our relationship seemed to simply evolve until I asked her to marry me. I thought I had met the one, but I couldn't say I really knew it, not beyond a reasonable doubt, anyway.

"Can you read me my story tonight, Daddy?" Charlotte asks, and then, playing the guilt card that children somehow learn very young, she adds, "You never do it and Mommy always does."

I instinctively look up at Elizabeth, who narrows her eyes and purses her lips. It's a gesture I know all too well, and it's not one of my favorites. It says— See, even your daughter knows you're never home.

"That sounds great, Charlotte," I say. "I'd love to read to you tonight."

I take Charlotte by the hand and lead her to her room, which we've christened the Pink Palace on account of the hot pink paint Charlotte selected. The wall opposite her bed is lined with floor-to-ceiling bookshelves that hold as many volumes as a small bookstore, but Charlotte runs directly to the other wall, where an open cube serves as her night table. Within the opening sit no more than three books, which she has decreed the nightly rotation for her bedtime stories.

Charlotte grabs the one on top, without looking at the others. "This one," she says, thrusting the book toward me.

"An excellent choice," I say, as if I'm the sommelier at a fancy restaurant and Charlotte has just selected the finest cabernet in the cellar.

I open the first page and begin. "Mr. Brown can—"

"Mooooooooooo," Charlotte interrupts.

"Mooooooooooo," I say back.

It continues like this through all of Mr. Brown's talents—from his tick-tock, to his knock-knock, to his soft, soft whisper of the butterfly.

"Good night, my sweet Charlotte bear," I say, pulling the blanket up to her shoulders when we're done. I kiss the top of her head, taking in the floral scent of her shampoo, and tell her that I love her.


"She loves that book," I say to Elizabeth when I enter our bedroom.

"I know. Her favorite part is the lightning sound. I can't tell you how often she says, 'But Mommy, lightning doesn't make a sound, thunder does.'"

Like most couples viewed from afar, Elizabeth and I appear to be happy. I don't think anyone would disagree too strenuously if I were to say that we're both attractive, have excellent pedigrees and a beautiful child. Of course, that doesn't differentiate us in any way from nearly all of the other parents we know, but if you asked me, I'd say that the ones who are still married are also happy, basing my opinion on exactly the same criteria.

We met at a party in Cambridge during my second year of law school. When I first laid eyes on Elizabeth, the term that popped into my mind was "stunning." She was far more than pretty, and even "beautiful" was too understated. She had fiery red hair and deep green eyes that gave her something of a feline quality. But it was her aloofness, oddly enough, that drew me in. There was something about her standing there alone that conveyed she'd be fine with or without you. For whatever reason, I took it as a challenge.

In the past few years, however, the independence I once found so attractive I have come to equate with distance. I wish that I could pinpoint what's different now, if only to prove that *something* is different. At times I hope that it's only some type of romantic fatigue, a malaise that results from the sense that everything between us is as it always will be and all that there is to look forward to is more of the same, but in darker moments I fear that it's something deeper, more fundamental than that.

Whatever the source, it often now seems that Elizabeth and I are at our best only in matters concerning

Charlotte. There are moments when I think it's still a strong enough foundation for a marriage, but at other times I fear we're less lovers than business partners, tending to the joint venture of rearing our daughter.

"How'd it go today?" she asks when I join her in bed. "You met with your father's friend, right?"

"Yeah. He's paying a $2 million retainer, so that's good."

"He's that guilty?" she says with a playful smile that was once a fixture in our banter, but now rarely appears.

"Not sure yet. At first I thought he was one of those pump-and-dump types who sells worthless securities to widows and retirees. But he swears he's on the up-and-up."

"And you believe him?"

"You say that like it's unprecedented."

"Well, isn't it? Aren't you the guy who had a fool-proof system for figuring out which one of your clients was lying to you?" She pauses for dramatic effect, but I already know the punch line. It's "whichever one is speaking, right?"

"That's a joke. I've represented people who were innocent before."

"Name one."

I'm embarrassed I don't have a name on the tip of my tongue. In fact, I'm scrolling back in my memory to before I made partner before I can recall someone who might fit the bill.

"What about that state senator? The guy who was charged in that bribery scheme. I thought he was innocent."

She laughs. "Okay, you got me. I could, of course, point out that case was a long time ago, back before you became so cynical. And, if memory serves, you thought he was innocent, but he ended up getting convicted, right?"

I laugh with her. "All that means is that I'm due for another innocent one."

"If it makes you happy to think he's innocent, then by all means. I just hope your professional judgment isn't being clouded by his almost mythical status in Miller family lore."

"I've actually been thinking about that," I say, taking on a more serious tone. "It's not as if I knew him growing up or anything. Or at least I can't remember knowing him. But when he was in my office, every time I looked at him, I couldn't help but think about my father."

"It'll get easier," she says, taking my hand. "Your father would be glad that you're helping out his friend, and he's very lucky to have you representing him."

"Thanks. I appreciate the vote of confidence."

Elizabeth keeps hold of my hand, her signal that she wants to make love. I can't recall the last time she initiated the act, and even the last time we had sex is a bit murky. At least two weeks, but maybe it's been a month, or longer. My failure to recall within a thirty-day time span is even more disconcerting than the drought itself. As if she senses my hesitation, Elizabeth leans into me, pressing her lips against mine.

When I was in college, my then-girlfriend claimed

she could tell everything she needed to know about a guy from the first kiss. I laughed and said something about her being jaded, but she held her ground. The first kiss tells you whether they are givers or takers. "Everything else flows from that, if they're comfortable or uptight, romantic, good in bed, everything," she explained.

Like so much else about her, Elizabeth's kiss has always been somewhat enigmatic to me. It is tight and off-putting at first, as if she's not sure she is fully committed. Sometimes, but not always, it dissolves into a softness that seems that much more enjoyable because of the effort it took to get there.

Our first kiss this evening has not yielded any insight, and I move toward her again. We begin to kiss more passionately, my hands moving under her pajama top.

As I kiss Elizabeth's neck, she whispers into my ear that she loves me. I know that my line is to repeat the sentiment back to her, but at first I say nothing, fully absorbed in trying to understand what Elizabeth means when she says it, and what I'll mean by saying it back.

"I love you too," I finally say.

Part **2**

## 6

Being selected as joint defense counsel is a bit like finding a golden ticket in a Wonka Bar. It creates a scenario most lawyers can only dream about—your fee is paid by an unlimited deep pocket that is not your client's.

The way it works is that the corporate entity—in this case OPM—provides legal counsel to its employees, at its expense. The theory is that the corporation denies wrongdoing, and therefore its employees, who also deny wrongdoing, are entitled to legal representation as part of their employment.

In reality, however, it's little more than a legal bribe to keep employees from admitting criminal conduct because as soon as someone in the joint defense claims something illegal occurred, the company immediately stops paying for their attorney. The company justifies this conduct on the grounds that any employee admitting guilt must either be lying or a criminal, and there's no reason for the company to pay legal bills in either case.

In the course of a year, Cromwell Altman doles out enough joint defense work to support a dozen or more lawyers. The firm keeps a roster of lawyers that are acceptable to receive this largesse, and the lucky few on that list share two main characteristics: personal connection to Cromwell Altman's managing partner, Aaron Littman, and practices almost entirely dependent on receiving such referrals. Like any good mafia don, Aaron controls when work is being distributed so as to ensure the loyalty of the recipients. As a result, the lawyers retained view Aaron as their client much more than the person they're actually representing.

For the Ohlig joint defense group, Aaron tapped George Eastman, an old-timer who's seemingly known Aaron forever, to represent Ohlig's number two, a guy named Eric Fieldston. Jason Sheffield, a former Cromwell Altman associate, was assigned Matthew Trott, OPM's head of trading. Jane McMahan represents Ohlig's secretary, Allison Shaw. And, in recognition that it was my case, Aaron allowed me one pick, with which I selected Joe Freeman, who was my college roommate, to represent OPM's chief compliance officer, Mark Ruderman.

After each of the members of the joint defense team was retained, it took ten days for us to negotiate the actual agreement that would govern the terms of the joint representation. The Joint Defense Agreement turned out to be twelve single-spaced pages but said little more than that we'd keep each other's secrets. Given that we'd all entered into dozens of such agreements before, the drafting exercise was just a reason for everyone to goose up their billable hours.

Finally, three weeks after my initial meeting with Ohlig, the first meeting of the joint defense group convenes. Every lawyer is accompanied to the meeting by an associate, all of whom are women. Quick math tells you that, with ten lawyers at a blended hourly rate north of $1,000, these meetings cost more than ten grand every sixty minutes. This meeting will last about an hour, but I'm sure everyone will bill it at two, including travel and rounding up, and then the associates will all write memos recounting what happened, which the partners will review, and then the memos will never be looked at again. All in, this meeting will cost Ohlig about $40,000.

Over the past three weeks, we (and by that I mean Abby and the temps) had begun the process of collecting OPM's documents, uploading them onto our system, and segregating them into different piles. In litigation-speak we refer to the piles as "buckets"—one for key documents, one for documents that may become key documents, one for documents required to be produced pursuant to the grand jury subpoena, one for documents that probably aren't important, and a final category for documents we didn't understand. Often a single document falls into more than one bucket, which increases by a factor of two or three the total number of documents in the case.

Even without the duplication, we retrieved more than two million pages of documents from OPM. More than half are trading tickets, which, thankfully, will be analyzed by an outside support firm that will give us summary information about what they mean. As for the remaining million pages, the bucket designations will ultimately yield to a different system of classification: the key documents will be winnowed to about ten thousand and put in "hot doc" binders. In time, the hot docs will be reduced to the less than a thousand that will become our daily working file. Half of the working file will make it into the trial binders as likely exhibits, and then less than 10 percent of those will actually be introduced at trial.

The facts we've learned so far through the documents are not in dispute. OPM bought 185 million shares of Salminol at between a dime and a quarter a share, for a total investment of about $35 million. Before OPM started selling it, Salminol shares had dropped to ten cents, which would have resulted in a loss to OPM of more than $26 million. However, by aggressively finding buyers for the stock, OPM drove the price up, until buyers were paying just under $2 a share. The litigation support team will calculate the total profit to the penny, but my back of the envelope analysis is that Ohlig was right on—OPM earned about $150 million. When OPM was completely out of the position, no one was touting the stock any longer, and the price plummeted to zero, wiping out the investment of the poor saps who bought it from OPM.

Those facts, however, do not a crime make. The line between a bad investment and criminal fraud is breached only if Michael Ohlig knew Salminol was worthless at the time he instructed his brokers to sell it. Ohlig has assured Abby and me that was not the case, but I told him, as I have told many clients through the years, documents don't lie, and financial fraud prosecutions are built on emails in which statements of bravado become smoking guns. Ohlig's response was only to say that OPM employees never communicated by email.

That leaves the prosecution with two options—present a circumstantial case in which they show to the jury that Ohlig must have known that Salminol was a dog stock based on the financial statements underlying the company, a daunting prospect if ever there was one, or flip someone to testify that Ohlig said he knew Salminol was worthless.

Our top priority, therefore, is keeping everyone who can hurt Ohlig in line. As the saying goes, you want everyone in the tent pissing out.

Protocol for the joint defense meetings is that we can't actually get down to business until the breakfast needs are met. The lawyers line up along the back of the conference room as if they are waiting at a buffet station at a wedding.

"Alex, who do I talk to about the bagel toppings?" asks Matthew Trott, a known schmoozer.

"It already looks like a deli counter in here," I joke back.

"C'mon, Ohlig can afford to spring for some lox," he says.

"Or at least some whitefish salad," Joe Freeman adds.

"You guys and your smoked fish," George Eastman says. "Take it from an old Irishman, we should meet later over some whiskey and we'd actually get stuff done."

After the smoked fish discussion has been tabled and everyone is seated, I call the meeting to order. I'm at the head of the table. Abby is to my right and will be taking notes. The other associates sit beside their partners and will also serve solely as scriveners.

"Let's get down to it," I say. "I'm happy to report that, aside from the subpoena, we still haven't heard anything from the U.S. Attorney's Office. We'll be in a position to produce our documents next week, so maybe that will cause them to contact us."

"How do the docs look?" Jane McMahan asks.

McMahan is a former clerk for a U.S. Supreme Court Justice, which is the highest credential you can have as a practicing lawyer. It also means that she's the smartest of the group, a fact of which we're all well aware, I'm sure. Ironically, she's representing the lowest-level employee, Ohlig's secretary. Aaron Littman knows McMahan because he also clerked on the Supreme Court, and he made the call to have McMahan represent Shaw because, as he said, "It's the secretary, and not the CFO, who can do the most damage."

"So far, so good," I say. "Since it's been radio silence from the U.S. Attorneys' Office for us, I thought we should go around the room and see what contact any of you have had."

McMahan goes first. "I'm a little deeper into it than you, Alex," she says. "The AUSA called me last week. A guy named Christopher Pavin. Anyone know him?"

"I think I've heard his name before," Sheffield says, "but I haven't encountered him on a case yet."

By their silence on the issue, the others indicate that they also haven't heard of him. This surprises me, but in a good way. I would have thought that Ohlig's case was high profile enough to justify someone with significant tenure in the office leading the prosecution team. That no one in this group has heard of Pavin is a pretty good indicator that he's new to the office, or at least to the securities division, which handles these types of cases.

"I'll tell you," McMahan continues, "he didn't sound too sure of himself. There was a lot of cliché talk, like he's playing a prosecutor from the movies. When I asked him what he could tell me, he actually used the term 'one-way street' and said the government wasn't going to lay out proof of anyone's guilt until legally obligated to do so."

"Did you ask him about your client's status?" Eastman asks.

"Subject," McMahan says, with a smile of relief.

In Department of Justice parlance, being a subject means the government doesn't have a present intention to indict. It's the second best of the three designations. Defense attorneys want to hear their clients are witnesses, which means the prosecutor has no suspicion of culpability.

"If Ohlig's secretary is a subject, that pretty much means the rest of us are probably subjects too," Trott says.

"I hope that's the case," Eastman retorts, never one to be an optimist. "Some of our guys may be targets."

I know that Ohlig is a target without asking, and

I'm of two minds as to how I want the others to be viewed. If they're targets then they are, at least in the first instance, more inclined to deny any wrongdoing, or else they would be incriminating themselves. It's a fine line, however, because targets are in greater the legal jeopardy and therefore are more incentivized to cut deals and save themselves, and I have absolutely no doubt that the prosecutor won't give a plea deal unless it's in exchange for testimony he can use against Ohlig.

"Did Pavin invite your client in?" I ask McMahan.

"No. It was a little strange, actually. I don't really know why he called. He said he was introducing himself and that a grand jury had been convened. I already knew about the grand jury, but I wasn't going to let him know that, so I just played dumb. And that was pretty much it. I told him I was just getting up to speed on the facts, and he said he was too, and he'd be back in touch. I haven't heard from him since."

This is the dance of criminal defense, at least in the pre-indictment stage. It's like a mini-trial except that your adversary is also the judge. The game-within-the-game involves defense counsel trying to get information from the prosecutor without giving any up, while still presenting the veneer of cooperation.

"So, can I take it that none of you are going to let your clients talk to him?" I ask.

I scan each lawyer's face, looking for a clue as to whether anyone is considering a plea in exchange for leniency. It's common knowledge that the AUSA doesn't need more than one insider to prove the case against everyone, and it's right out of the playbook to start at the lowest rung of the food chain and work up. I'm sure Pavin will offer Allison Shaw immunity if she has anything incriminating on Ohlig. If she's not so inclined, he'll go up the seniority ladder, offering a similar deal until someone bites. Investment bank or mafia family, a criminal prosecution follows the same script.

"I think we're all with you," Eastman says. "My guy tells me that everything was on the up-and-up, and he should know, he's the number two after all. He says that Salminol was a bad investment, but selling a dog stock isn't a crime."

# 7

I've heard airline pilots describe their jobs as hours of boredom interrupted only by moments of terror. Criminal defense fits that bill too.

After the prosecutor served a subpoena on OPM, nothing happened for more than a month. We used the time to collect documents and meet with the joint defense group and, mainly, wait for the other shoe to drop.

It dropped at 5:45 in the morning, and I learn about it because Ohlig is shouting something into my cell phone that I can't quite understand, seeing as I'm still half asleep. "What?" I say, still groggy.

"I'm standing in front of my office, and there's a padlock on the front door. Some type of list is taped to it, I think of my files."

"It means that the government has executed a search warrant."

"Can they do that?"

"If they got a judge to authorize it, they can," I say, going into lawyer mode. "I'll be on the next flight down. In the meantime, go home. Send an email to the employees telling them the office is closed and that they'll get another email later when it opens. Michael, this is important. That's all the email should say. No explanations. Just that the office is closed. Understand?"

He speaks more quietly now. "There's never going to be another email, is there?"

"Not likely," I say.

"Who was that?" Elizabeth says when I roll over to return the phone to the holder.

"Ohlig. They've executed a search warrant at his office in Florida. I need to get down there right away."

"Have you told your mother that you're representing him?"

"No."

"Don't you think you should, especially if you're going down there?"

Elizabeth is an honesty-is-the-best-policy type of person. That outlook works well in her chosen vocation: Elizabeth is an artist, a talented painter, to be specific, though she hasn't actually painted anything since Charlotte was born. I used to joke with her that I never understood how someone with her worldview could possibly have ended up married to a lawyer. Her standard response was that she didn't marry a lawyer; she married a man who practices law when he's at the office.

"He's asked me not to," I say, and leave it at that, sparing her the blather about how my professional obligations trump any notions of honesty that exist in the non-lawyer world. "I'll just tell my mother that I'm down there on a case. She never asks about what I'm working on."

"Are you leaving now?" Elizabeth asks, as I roll out of bed.

"As soon as I can," I say. "Go back to sleep. I'll call you from Florida tonight."

I walk into the kitchen and fill the coffeemaker before dialing Abby from my BlackBerry. She answers on the third ring. I can tell that I've woken her.

"Michael Ohlig just called. The FBI has apparently executed a search warrant at his office. I told him to close up shop and wait for the cavalry, and by that I mean you and me. Can you call the office and have someone book us on the earliest flight we can make to West Palm, and get us rooms at the Four Seasons?"

"Sure," she says, the standard associate response. "How many nights?"

"One should do it, I think."

"Okay."

Despite the fact that we've already produced more than a million pages pursuant to the subpoena, the government executed a search warrant because they still think Ohlig is holding stuff back. It's an odd anomaly about discovery in a white collar criminal prosecution—the stakes couldn't be higher and the accused is the accused because the government believes he doesn't follow the rules, and yet discovery is still governed, for the most part, by an honor policy. When the prosecution can persuade a judge that they have probable cause that documents have been improperly withheld, they can do the collection themselves via a search warrant.

"Do you think there's something we didn't turn over?" I ask Abby.

A foolish question. If she thought there was

something we hadn't turned over, she would have asked Ohlig for it and then she would have produced it to the government. In essence, I'm asking her to tell me if she knows of something she didn't know.

"Not unless he was holding back on us," she says.

"I suppose that'll be the first question we ask once we're down there. Email me ASAP with the flight information. I'll meet you at the gate."

"Mind if I ask a stupid question?"

"Is this when I'm supposed to say that there's no such thing as a stupid question?"

"What are we going to do once we're down there? I mean, if they've already executed the search warrant, what can we do about that now? It's a little like closing the barn door after the horse gets out, isn't it?"

"We're putting in a personal appearance to tell Michael Ohlig that everything is going to be okay. Even though we know it's not."

# 8

I've been in more than my share of clients' twenty-million-dollar Hamptons estates and duplex apartments on Park Avenue, so I'm somewhat jaded when it comes to ostentatious real estate. New York money, at least in my experience, tends either to be old money or to try to look that way. Even the guy who struck it rich yesterday more often than not ends up buying a pre-war apartment and a country home that was built by robber barons in the 1920s, or that's brand new construction designed to look like it was built by robber barons in the 1920s.

Ohlig's house doesn't fit at all within this paradigm. The exterior is starkly modern, glass and steel coming together at harsh angles. It reminds me more of an airport terminal than a residence, and Abby makes the somewhat obvious joke about whether he throws stones.

"Welcome," says the tall, thin man who opens the large front door. He's dressed in what must be the tropics version of a butler's uniform—a tan suit, white shirt, and black tie. "My name is Carlos," he tells us. "Mr. Ohlig asked me to bring you to the study. He will join you there momentarily. Coffee is already out, but please tell me if there is anything else I can get for either of you. Some breakfast, perhaps?"

"Thank you," I tell him. "I'm fine."

"Me too," Abby says.

Carlos leads us past the entry hall and through the living room until we arrive at what he announces is the study. The room overlooks the Atlantic through large picture windows on two sides, while the far wall is lined with a floor-to-ceiling bookcase. The room's center is dominated by a long white marble table surrounded by eight black leather chairs. Like all the other rooms I've seen so far, this space reminds me of the lair of a Bond villain.

I'm about to make a joke about whether the chairs are equipped to deliver electric jolts when Abby says, "Do you have a bat pole behind the bookshelves in your apartment?"

I laugh. "I do, but when I slide down it, instead of a mask and cape, it puts me in an Armani suit."

She laughs too. Unlike most beautiful women I've encountered, including my wife, Abby has a way of making you feel as if she is happiest when in your company. Somehow she conveys that every gesture is for you, and you alone. Her laugh is no exception.

"What's so funny?" Ohlig says from behind me. Despite this morning's turn of events, he looks like a man without a care in the world.

"Nothing," I say. "An inside joke." I turn to Abby. "Michael, this is—"

"The one and only Abigail Sloane," he interrupts. He's wearing a particularly wolfish grin. "I'm so glad to be able to put such a beautiful face to the voice."

For a moment I'm startled, forgetting that Abby's been talking to Ohlig more than I have as of late. She's been the point person haranguing him about documents or asking him what something means. Ohlig most likely looked Abby up on the Cromwell Altman website, so he knew to expect that she is attractive, but the picture is a headshot only, and it doesn't do her justice.

"Thank you," Abby says, smiling broadly. She doesn't seem offended; rather, it seems clear to me that Abby is well aware of the effect she has on men and considers Ohlig's remark to be par for the course.

"You seem to be holding up well," I say. "All things considered."

"It's not like you didn't warn me this might happen."

"I called the guys right after your phone call." The "guys" is the shorthand we use for the lawyers in the joint defense group. "So far, not a peep out of the U.S. Attorney's Office. Jane McMahan said she might reach out to the Assistant U.S. Attorney handling this case, but I asked her to wait a few days to see how everything shakes out."

"Who do I pay her to represent?"

"Your secretary. Allison Shaw."

Ohlig doesn't show much emotion at my disclosure that Shaw may soon be breaking bread with the government. "Anything we have to worry about there?" I ask.

"I've told you before, no. Allison and I are not—" He looks at Abby, and then, apparently thinking better of the term he was initially going to use, says, "We're not romantically involved. And as for the business, she doesn't know much, but she knows enough to know I've done nothing wrong."

"Okay, good. I expect some of the other lawyers will also go in and meet with Pavin. I'd prefer that there be a total cone of silence, but so long as it's only the lawyers going in, we'll be okay. Besides, it will give us some idea of what they've got."

"I want to meet with him," Ohlig says matter-of-factly.

"That just isn't smart, Michael. A prosecutor ready to indict is simply not going to be persuaded by you telling him that you're innocent. The only beneficiary of such a meeting is him—he gets to hear your defense and locks you into a story. And, to make life that much better for him, he could easily charge you with the felony of lying to him in the interview."

"I can explain what happened in a way no one else can," Ohlig says, as if he hadn't heard what I just said. "They're not going to drop this unless they're convinced I'm innocent. The only way that's ever going to happen is if I do the convincing."

"We'll have our opportunity to put on our defense. It's just that now is not the right time."

"And when is the right time?"

"When you take the witness stand at trial. And not a second before that."

Ohlig again shakes his head at me, this time seemingly more in disgust than disagreement. "So you've already conceded an indictment?"

"Michael, part of my job is to be realistic about the state of play. It doesn't mean I don't believe in your innocence."

A look of utter contempt comes over him, and for a moment I actually think he might lose his temper completely. Then, as if somewhere he's flipped an internal switch, he smiles broadly instead. "What are the odds?" he asks.

"The what?" I say, not understanding his question.

"You believe I'm going to get indicted, right?"

I nod.

"So, what are the odds I won't be? What are the odds I walk on this? No indictment."

I hate giving a client odds of any potential occurrence. Odds always reflect a likelihood of an event happening or not, and in reality it happens or it doesn't. Tell a client the odds are 90 percent of something occurring and then it happens, he says you were too conservative in your estimation. And God forbid you tell a client that there's a 60 percent likelihood and then it doesn't occur.

"Haven't we been over this already?" I say. His expression tells me that I'm not going to get off that easily, and he wants to hear it again. "As we've discussed, the U.S. Attorneys' Office in New York loves to prosecute bankers. So, you're a very attractive defendant for Pavin to go after. In addition, these things often take on a momentum of their own. Once they devote the resources to review millions of pages of documents, if they don't indict, it's like it was a wasted effort. All of that, I'm afraid, makes it far more likely than not that they're going to indict you."

Ohlig looks like I've insulted him. "I know it's *likely* I'm going to be indicted, Atticus Finch. What I'm asking you is, what are the odds that I *won't* be? Ten to one? Hundred to one? Million to one? Give me your best guess."

"Fifty to one," I say, only fixing the odds there because I think any worse would sound as if I'd lost all hope.

A canny smile comes to Ohlig's face; he's gotten from me what he wanted. "Fifty to one," he repeats. "You and I both know you think the odds are more like fifty thousand to one, right? But you're the house for our purposes here, and you say fifty to one, so I'll respect that. Okay. I'll put up ten grand that I'm not indicted. But you owe me half a million if I walk."

My discomfort with this line of discussion must be obvious. I want to look over at Abby to see how she's reacting to this showdown, but I'm pretty sure I know.

"I'd love to take your action," I tell him, "but I don't have that kind of money."

He chuckles, a condescending gesture if ever there was one. "Two minutes ago, my getting indicted was as certain as the sunrise. But now, when you've got something at stake, you're suddenly not so sure."

"I'm sorry, Michael. I think I missed your point."

"It's actually pretty simple," he says, all evidence of good humor having vanished. "Nothing is certain when you're the one at risk."

# 9

My mother is waiting for me on her front lawn. The guard at the front gate must have called her when I passed that checkpoint, even though my name is on the permanent "let through" list.

"This is such a wonderful surprise," she calls out as I walk up to greet her.

"I called you this morning to say I was coming," I say, embracing her.

"I know, but before you called, I wasn't expecting a visit from you until Thanksgiving. So it's still a surprise. Are you here on a case?"

"Yes. I told you. I have a client down here."

My mother leads me into her house, the first time I've been back since my father's death. Oddly, it seems larger than the last time, although that may be because it was filled with people then, and before that it had always been occupied by my father too.

It's strange to be back. I can't shake the feeling that any moment my father will emerge from the bedroom wearing his red and blue pajama nightshirt, which was more of a dress, actually, and was his standard uniform at home, not unlike the one Scrooge wears.

"Have you eaten dinner?" I ask. "I'll take you out."

"Oh, thank you, but I just had some pasta. I can make you something if you'd like."

"That's okay. I'll just have some cereal."

We reassemble in her kitchen, me with a bowl of Frosted Flakes, while she has a glass of chardonnay.

"Are they stale?" my mother asks.

"No. They're fine. I don't think there's an expiration date on Frosted Flakes."

I take a visual inventory of my mother's condition. She's a very attractive woman, always has been and, likely, always will be. She's tall, five-nine she tells people, but I suspect she's an inch or maybe two taller than that. Her hair is now blond, but it suits her, not at all brassy looking, and her only wrinkles are the crow's-feet at the corner of her eyes, which most people think make her look more attractive. She's always been extremely fit, even without adhering to any type of exercise regimen, so much so that she sometimes looks too thin, although she would say there's no such thing.

There's a part of me that would like her to appear more bereaved, but then I realize I'm being unfair. After all, I look the same as I normally do too, and it doesn't mean that I'm not still in mourning.

"So, what's your case about?" she asks.

The question surprises me. As I told Elizabeth, my mother almost never asks about my work. I hesitate for a moment to see if she's going to say something to reveal she already knows Michael Ohlig is my client. When she doesn't, I assume I'm just being paranoid and proceed to answer her question, although with as little detail as possible.

"It's a stock trading case."

"Did the guy do it?"

I laugh dismissively. "Sorry, no exception to the attorney-client privilege for moms."

"Who am I going to tell?"

"That's not the point. Let's talk about something that won't get me disbarred. Okay? So, how have you been?"

"I'm hanging in there. Everyone says you've got to take it one day at a time. So that's what I'm doing."

"Can't argue with that advice. What are you doing each day at a time?"

"Same thing as always. Luckily for me, there always seems to be something to do. I play bridge with these other ladies on Wednesdays and Fridays, and I was just asked to help plan the Halloween party at the clubhouse. So, I'm keeping busy. I sometimes wonder how your father would have been without me if I was the one who died first." Her eyes roll down and to the right, which I learned in a deposition seminar is a sign of engaging in an internal monologue, but then she gives her head a slight shake, pushing whatever she was considering out of her mind.

"I know, Mom. I think about Dad all the time. Every time Charlotte does something, I can imagine how happy it would have made him, and then I feel this wave of sadness because I can't tell him."

"I just wasn't prepared. Not that you're ever prepared, but . . ." She chuckles, more to herself than to me. "You know, I don't even know how to pump gas. That's something your father always did."

"I'll show you," I say, even though I know that wasn't

her point. "I know it doesn't feel like this now, but you have a lot of life ahead of you. Dad would want you to be happy, to do the things you want to do."

"Like what?" she says, almost as a challenge.

"You always said you wanted to travel, right? So, now you can."

It was a constant complaint of my mother's during my childhood—that she could never get my father to take a vacation. He was a one-man operation in the store and claimed he couldn't trust anyone else to run it, even for a few days. Vacations were put on hold until "someday."

My mother sits there, staring into her glass for a long time before finally saying, "Alex, do you think your father was happy?"

"Yes," I say, out of reflex more than anything else. In truth, I always felt that my father was a difficult man to read. Some of that I attributed to sons never truly knowing their fathers, but her posing the question means that she also found him to be something of a mystery.

"No, really," she presses me.

I sigh, signaling that I'll take the question more seriously, although I'm still going to answer it the same way. "I know without a shadow of a doubt that he loved you very much. And me, too. He often said that was all that mattered in life. Loving your family. So, on the measure that he deemed most important, he was the happiest person I know."

She shows a wan smile.

"I'm glad you think that," she says.

"It sounds like you disagree."

"I just don't know. Can you imagine anything sadder than that? I was married to the man for more than thirty-five years, and I don't know if he was happy."

For a moment I wonder if Elizabeth would say the same thing about me, and then an equally jarring thought strikes me—I'd say the same thing about her. I really have no idea if Elizabeth is happy.

"He was," I say, as if my father's happiness is a fact not open to dispute.

"Did you know that when your father was a boy, maybe ten years old, your grandparents sent him to foster care because they couldn't afford to feed him?"

"Uncle Sam too?"

"No. Can you believe that? They decided that they could feed one of their sons, but not the other, so your father pulled the short straw. I'm not sure how long he was there, but at least a year."

"How could I have never heard that before?"

"You did," she says, smiling. "Your father referred to it as going to camp. He thought of it as an adventure. He got out of the Lower East Side, spent some time in the country. Made new friends. If your father could convince himself that being sent to foster care—which back then probably looked pretty grim—was camp, I always thought he could delude himself about anything."

"I don't think he was deluded about loving you, if that's what you're getting at. You could see it in his eyes, Mom. He would light up when you entered the room. Did I ever tell you what he said to me right before Elizabeth and I got married?" She shakes her head no. "It was at the rehearsal dinner. If you remember, Dad had a little more to drink than he usually did. We were talking in the corner and he said that his greatest hope was that I'd found someone I could love as much as he loved you. I said that I thought I had, and all of a sudden he seemed concerned for me. He said, 'With your mother, I don't think it, I live it. Every single day I can't believe how lucky I am to be with her.'"

My mother's eyes are moist. At first I thought they were tears of joy, but now I'm concerned that I've upset her.

"I'm sorry. I thought you'd be pleased that he felt that way," I say.

"No, I'm okay. That was a very nice story."

# 10

I enter the Four Seasons lobby at nine-thirty, and see Abby sitting at the bar. A nearly empty glass of scotch rests in front of her.

She's changed out of her suit and is now wearing blue jeans and a black top, which stretches across her breasts. I've never seen her in jeans before, and even with her sitting down, I can tell that she looks good in them.

"I was hoping you'd find me here. How's your mom?"

"She's good. A little weepy at times."

"It must be hard for her to suddenly be all alone."

I chuckle. "I think so, but when I told Paul Harris that my parents had been married for thirty-five years, he joked that my father must be enjoying the solitude."

"Do you think that's true?"

She says this with a serious stare, which shames me, although I'm sure that wasn't her intent. "No. If there's a heaven, I'm sure my father won't think he's in it until she's with him."

"That's sweet," she says, now with an inviting smile, "and also as it should be. No wonder your mom is lonely."

"The funny thing is that I never thought the feeling was totally mutual. I know she loved him, but he always had this gaga thing in his eyes over her.

Sometimes I think she felt like she got a little bait-and-switched by him."

"How so?"

"When they got married, she was not even twenty, and still living at home, and he was thirty-one, working on Madison Avenue, and had his own apartment in Manhattan. My mom is the type who's impressed by that sort of thing. If you saw them together, you'd know what I was talking about. Everyone says that back then she was model beautiful; they say it now too, and even being charitable about it, my father wasn't much of a looker. My father used to joke that everyone thought that she married him for his money, until they found out he didn't have any."

She laughs. "I guess I don't have to ask which side of the family you favor."

"Should I take that as a compliment?"

"Take it however you'd like."

The way she says this, unabashedly flirtatiously, makes me wonder how many drinks she's already had. When I took my seat at the bar, I assumed she was on her first, but it now occurs to me that she could be working on her second. Given that Abby can't be more than 115 pounds, two scotches likely puts her well above the legal limit.

"Regardless how you meant it, it was a running joke in my family. My mom would always say that I'm all Greene—the only thing Miller about me is my name."

"I'm sure your dad loved hearing that."

I chuckle. "He actually agreed. It was kind of hard

for him not to. I'm about half a foot taller than him and have most of my mother's features and coloring."

"Who's responsible for the dimples?"

Now I know she's flirting. "Mom again."

"Pete," she calls to the bartender, a guy with a shaved head, and then she turns back to me. "I peg you as a scotch man. Am I right?"

"Scotch would be great," I confirm.

"Pete, a scotch for my boss. Single malt, of course," she says, laughing.

"Of course. And shaken, not stirred," I add, but only for her ears, not Pete's.

"Here you go," Pete says a moment later. "Another one for you, Abby?"

"No, I'm going to wait for the boss to catch up."

We make small talk about how the meeting with Ohlig went while I work on my drink. I haven't even returned the glass to the bar after taking my final swig before Pete's back, asking if we'd like another round.

"Absolutely," Abby says.

"Take it easy on me," I say. "I hardly ever drink anymore."

"You're only a few years older than me," she laughs, "so don't act like you're such an old man."

The bar begins to fill up. Midway through my second drink, two men and a woman begin to set up their instruments, along with some speakers, in the corner. Pete makes his way over to us after servicing a loud group of Asian businessmen on the other end of the bar.

"Another round?" he asks.

I still have a finger's width left in my glass, but Abby's glass has been empty since my first sip.

"Yes," she says. "For both of us."

"I do believe that you're trying to get me drunk, Ms. Sloane."

Her response is that high-wattage smile. Then she turns away from me and says, "Pete, we're going to move to a table, if that's okay."

"I don't blame you," he says. "The band can get pretty loud. I'll bring your drinks."

Abby leads me to a table for four in the corner of the bar, the spot farthest away from the band. She takes the seat against the wall, and motions for me to choose the chair to her immediate left, rather than the one across from her.

"This way we won't have to talk so loud when the band starts up," she says by way of explanation.

Pete brings over our drinks, but I'm now acutely aware that the scotch is not the most intoxicating part of this evening. Not by a long shot.

It's been nearly a decade since I've been in such close proximity to a new sexual encounter, and the thrill of that feeling overwhelms me. I wonder, if push came to shove, if Abby told me that she was mine for the offering, whether I would be able to resist.

The very fact I'm considering this issue is more than enough of a warning that I shouldn't be here. Nothing good ever comes from ordering a third scotch. But the high I'm feeling is too strong not to want it to continue. I won't let it get too far, I tell myself, pushing out of my mind that the mere utterance of such a phrase is a clear sign that it's already gone too far.

It's not just my marriage that concerns me. I know that the firm will consider my sexual involvement with a subordinate—especially a subordinate coming up for partner—to be a capital offense. I've seen us counsel too many Fortune 500 companies to sack high-ranking people over office affairs to think that there'd be any leniency shown to me.

Rather than listen to my inner voice of reason, I raise my glass. "To . . ."

"To Batman," she says with another one of her smiles.

"To Batman," and I touch my glass to hers.

"So, how do you think I'd be as a superhero?" she asks.

"Am I now supposed to wonder what your super-powers are?"

"I'll leave that to your imagination. But I will tell you that, as for the costume, I see a lot of spandex and knee-high red boots."

"Now there's an image. But what about your secret identity?"

"I don't think I need one. I'd just be Abby Sloane, superhero. I mean, I never understood why Super-man ever pretended to be Clark Kent in the first place. Think about it, if you were Superman, why would you pretend to be a loser?"

"Oh no," I say, as if I'm about to impart critical information. "You have it all wrong. Superman isn't pretending to be Clark Kent. That's really who he is, deep down, at his core. He knows Lois Lane is in love with Superman, but to him that's like when a woman wants you for your money. Superman wants Lois Lane to love the real him, and that's Clark."

"I should have known better than to get into a comic book discussion with you. So, are you also going to tell me that Bruce Wayne is who Batman really is at *his* core?"

"Since you're asking," I say with a smile because I know she's not really interested in the answer, "no. In fact, it's actually the opposite."

"How so, professor?"

"Well, the Batman dichotomy is a crazy vigilante—that's the Batman side—and the rich playboy, who is Bruce Wayne. No one *pretends* to be a crazy vigilante who fights arch criminals. If you go into that line of work, you're pretty much a true believer. Which means that, at his core, Bruce Wayne is *really* Batman. The Bruce Wayne persona is the real disguise."

Abby laughs out loud. Now she clearly seems drunk to me. She leans back in her seat, causing her long hair to cascade around her face.

"This is way too existential a discussion to comfortably follow given my current state of inebriation," she says. "But riddle me this: Which Alex Miller is with me now? The real one or the secret identity?"

It's a good question, one that I'd thought about before, but without ever coming to a satisfactory answer. When am I really me?

## 11

We leave Florida the next morning, booked on a 10:00 A.M. flight. Although I'm sure Ohlig is sorry to see Abby go, he points out that he has a wife and friends who do not charge him a thousand bucks an hour for the pleasure of their company.

After clearing security at the West Palm airport, I excuse myself from Abby for a moment and call home, even though there's no reason for me to be checking in. I called Elizabeth from the car last night on the way back from my mother's house and told her I was going to sleep when I got back to the hotel. But my evening with Abby has shaken me, and I feel the need to be pulled back into my real life.

Elizabeth answers the phone sounding concerned. "Everything okay?"

"Yeah. Everything's fine. I'm at the airport. I'm going to go straight into the office today, but I'll be home tonight."

"Oh, I was worried. You usually don't call me during the day. I don't know, I thought maybe something was wrong with your mother."

"No. She's good. I didn't mean to worry you. I was just calling to say hello."

"Well, hello to you too then," she says cheerfully. "Want to talk to the cannoli?"

She means Charlotte, a long-standing joke, a line

from *The Godfather*. When Charlotte was a baby and we travelled, I'd always say to Elizabeth, "I'll take the bags, and you take the cannoli."

"Hi Daddy!" Charlotte screams. I sometimes think that Charlotte believes I won't be able to hear her unless she shouts into the phone.

"Hi baby. How are you today?"

"Good," she says, and then demonstrates just how much of her mother's daughter she is. "Daddy, why are you calling? We talked last night."

"Just to say I love you."

"Oh. I love you too, Daddy. Here's Mommy."

Elizabeth takes the phone back. "I think you worried her too," she says, laughing.

For me, however, it's hardly a laughing matter. My father worked long hours, the necessity of which I never questioned growing up, but now I see it more as a choice he made. It's not my place to judge him for it, at least not without all the facts. I don't know if the store could have survived without him putting in such long hours, and it would certainly make me a hypocrite to criticize him now when his work put me through college and law school. But the fact remains that my daughter will someday think about my choices in the same light and wonder if I really needed to be at the firm all that time, or if I was avoiding something at home that I didn't want to face.

On the flight home, it's business as usual between me and Abby. I'm a little fuzzy on how things precisely ended last night, but I'm sure that there was no inappropriate contact. I recall being in the elevator together, but somehow when I got out, she didn't. I wonder if Abby would have followed if I'd asked, but now I'm grateful I'll never know.

Despite the fact that nothing untoward happened, she has begun calling me "boss." I'm concerned that it's an effort to set boundaries, but vaguely recall that the practice began early last night at the bar, and so I conclude she's just doing it to be funny.

At least I hope that's it.


The flight ends up being delayed and we don't land until two. As we're taxiing to the gate, I send an email to the joint defense team, asking them to meet us at Cromwell Altman at three. Even with the short notice, everyone emails back that they'll be there, a further testament to how beholden this group is to future referral business.

We hit traffic on the way back from JFK, and all the members of the joint defense team other than Charles Eastman are already in the Cromwell Altman reception area when Abby and I arrive. I make a quip about being late to my own party, and they each chuckle politely, the way I do when Aaron Littman makes a joke, more out of deference to his power over me than because I think it's funny.

The receptionist is telling me that we're in Conference Room E when Eastman comes off the elevator. "Are we going to meet here?" he says with a chuckle, and then looking down at Abby and my luggage, he adds, "This isn't one of those two-day meetings, is it?"

The group gives him a more sincere laugh than I got.

"We just came in from visiting with Michael," I say. "Follow me to the conference room and we can get started right away."

As we assemble, there are the usual gripes about the food (cookies, fruit, soft drinks, and coffee are the Cromwell Altman selections after 2 P.M., but the cookies are oatmeal raisin and the consensus among the joint defense team is that chocolate chip should be included for the next time). When everyone has filled their plates and is seated, I begin the meeting just as I had the previous one, by going around the room asking for any new developments. This time Joe Freeman goes first, and when I call on him he thanks me, as if he's been given the floor to make a wedding toast.

"I called Pavin earlier in the week," he says. "After some phone tag, I reached him on Wednesday. I think we sent an email to everyone about that call." He turns to his associate, a woman whose head is buried in her legal pad as she scribbles furiously. "Michelle, we sent everyone an email, right?"

Michelle looks up for a second and nods. "Okay," Freeman continues. "So you all know what happened. I did the usual dance, telling Pavin that my guy is a Boy Scout and I'd hate for the government to get the wrong idea, so if he had any questions or legal theories that he could discuss with me, I'm all ears. This guy doesn't just follow the book, I think he's memorized it. Just like he said to Jane, he told me, quote, It's a one-way street, closed quote. Then I offered to come in myself and give him the lay of the land. He wasn't too interested in that either."

Matthew Trott breaks into Freeman's narrative. "Pavin told me that's now the Office's policy." Former AUSAs, as Trott and McMahan both are, refer to the U.S. Attorneys' Office simply as "the Office." Sometimes, when the non-AUSAs of the group want to be especially annoying, one of us will ask if they plan on taking the issue up with Michael Scott in the Scranton branch. "They don't allow attorney proffers anymore," he adds.

"Proffers" is one of those terms of art that lawyers bandy about but is almost never used in the real world. It's about telling the prosecutor what happened. Of course, lawyers prefer that they do the telling, because that way the government can't use what's said as evidence later on against the client—which is exactly the reason the government frowns on the practice.

The group looks to Eastman for confirmation that he, too, was not given permission to make an attorney proffer. "Same here," he says, realizing we're going out of turn. "Pavin said he only wanted to hear the client's story directly from the client's mouth." Eastman pauses, chuckling. "Actually, what he said was that I'd be wasting my time with anything else."

With that, everyone's eyes swing back to Freeman for the completion of his report. "So Pavin then tells me I should bring Ruderman in. He was offering the full Queen, and making it sound like it was immunity."

We all speak this shorthand, so we know Freeman's referring to a "Queen for a Day" agreement, the unfortunate nickname given to what the U.S. Attorneys' Office officially refers to as client proffer agreements. A Queen for a Day agreement prohibits the government from using anything said to them in their case in chief; translated into normal-people speak, that means that it forbids testimony about what was said during the meeting when the government puts on its evidence. But as always, there's a catch: the government reserves the right to use the information any way it wants to during its rebuttal case or in cross-examination. Meaning that if your story at trial differs from the one you told the government during the Queen interview, there's no stopping Uncle Sam from using what you said in the interview however it pleases. And most importantly for the other members of the joint defense group, a Queen doesn't at all limit the use of the information against other people—so, if someone starts pointing fingers, which often happens, everyone's risk of indictment goes up.

"I told Pavin thanks, but no thanks," Freeman continues. "Get this—he actually said that if my guy was really as innocent as I claimed, he'd jump at the chance to clear his name. I told him this was my call, not the client's, and it would be malpractice for me to let him go in if Pavin isn't willing to show me his first."

Freeman looks at Jane McMahan when he says this, not meaning to, I think. He must have belatedly realized his phrasing was less than politically correct.

"What? You think I've never used the expression?" McMahan says. "Let me assure you, I've seen a lot more of theirs first," she adds, eliciting laughter from the rest of us, and smiles from the associates, who are too busy scribbling to take time out to laugh.

"I put it a bit more bluntly," Eastman says. "When Pavin pulled that crap with me, I told him this isn't my first rodeo. I just don't bring clients in anymore. I didn't tell him this, but about five years ago, an AUSA who shall remain nameless—Larry Ames—screwed me over something fierce. I brought my guy in because I was told he was a witness, nothing to worry about, the whole song and dance. So my guy goes in, everything goes great, and then I get a call two weeks later from the prick Ames that they're going to indict my guy. I say, 'What the fuck? He didn't lie to you guys.' And Ames tells me that my guy said something that, I swear, he never came close to saying and he's going to charge with a 1001. So, I said, 'Look, we have notes of the meeting, that's not what he said and he never lied to you guys, so there's no basis for a 1001 charge.' And Ames says, 'We don't rely on defense counsel's self-serving notes; we'll use our own, thank you.' As if his notes aren't self-serving. Long story short, client fires me, and now he's a long-term guest of the government. So ever since then, I follow a blanket rule—no client proffers. If the client wants to do one, he's not doing it with me as his lawyer."

This is the greatest danger to agreeing to talk to the prosecutor. It is a federal crime—set forth in section

1001 of the U.S. penal code—to lie to a federal officer, even if that lie is not under oath. The result is that a 1001 charge is the prosecutor's ace in the hole, a way of imposing criminal liability even if he can't prove any other criminal conduct. That's how the government got Martha Stewart and Scooter Libby; when they couldn't prove the underlying offenses, they alleged a 1001 violation.

After Eastman's war story, Trott concurs that he got the same offer to bring his client in, and he makes a point to tell us Pavin also delivered the "one-way street" line to him. And like the others, Trott says he told Pavin to pound sand.

"I suppose that leaves me," I say, "and I, unfortunately, have a problem. Our mutual benefactor, Michael Ohlig, is *insisting* on going in. I keep trying to talk him out of it, but he says he can make this whole thing go away."

"If he's got those powers, maybe he can explain some stuff to my wife," Trott cracks. "There's no way. Just no way."

"Seriously, Alex," Eastman says, "I assume you've explained the facts of life to him?"

"I have. He completely believes that, one, he did nothing wrong and, two, he can persuade Pavin of that. I think his exact words were that I was underestimating his ability to be charming."

"Look, all of our clients are absolutely one hundred percent not guilty," Sheffield says, channeling O.J. Simpson with a heavy side of sarcasm. "That doesn't mean we let them just hand over the defense to the government."

"You're preaching to the choir," I say. "I told Ohlig I would share his views with the group, and we wouldn't make a decision until after I'd heard your objections and discussed them with him."

"Where should we start?" Eastman says. "Forgive me if I'm out of line here, but I've got the most gray hair of the group, so I hope you'll take this in the spirit with which it's intended. If your guy goes in, he doesn't just kill himself, he hurts all of us."

"That's right," McMahan says quickly. "My gal is the least culpable. She's a secretary, for God's sake. But if the head honcho is going in, I've got to revisit my thinking on keeping her out."

"I'm with Jane," Trott says.

"Me too," is Freeman's input.

"Alex," Eastman says, using his Dutch uncle voice, "all clients want to go in, and they all want to testify at trial. And although no one likes to tell a client he's full of it, the quicker you tell Ohlig that, the better—not only for him, but for you, too."

# 12

Right after the meeting breaks up, I call Ohlig.

"Counselor," he says, as he always does when I call, "to what do I owe this pleasure?"

"Your favorite guys and I just sat down and broke bread."

"Let me guess—they think you're right and I'm wrong about talking to the prosecutor."

"That doesn't even begin to address their feelings on the subject."

"Well, forgive me if I'm not surprised that a group of lawyers tend to think alike."

"Michael, they were, to a person, adamantly opposed to your going in. When the prosecutor invited their clients in, each one of them told him to screw himself. They all think it's absolutely crazy for the target of the investigation to talk to the government."

"How many times do we have to have the same discussion, Alex? I mean, is that what happens when you get paid by the hour? You feel the need to plow the same ground over and over again?"

"Michael, you need to listen to me. Going in is a mistake. Period. End of discussion. There's no way they're not going to indict you, and so you accomplish nothing by going in except weakening our defense at trial. There's a reason none of the others are going in, you know."

"None of the others are going in because they're assuming the weight of this is going to fall on me, and they're hoping to ride this out by hiding in the tall grass. But I'm the guy with a bull's-eye on his back."

"If you go in, one of the likely side effects will be that they'll go in. Otherwise it looks like they've got something to hide."

"So?"

"So, whatever they tell the government will be admissible against *you* at trial. That's one of the reasons you're paying for everyone's defense—so we could get them counsel who are smart enough to keep them away from the U.S. Attorney."

"Alex, now *you* need to listen to me. I'm going in. Period. Call him right now and set it up. End of discussion."

And then he hangs up.

Pavin answers his phone, "Assistant United States Attorney Christopher Pavin."

"Christopher, it's Alex Miller here."

"Just the man I was about to call," he says, which is never a good sign.

"What about?"

"Nope, you dialed the phone, you go first."

This is only the second time I've spoken to Pavin. The first was right after I was retained. During that call, he gave me the same song and dance as he did the other members of the joint defense group—uttering the one-way street line and saying that if my client really had nothing to hide, he'd come in under the Queen for a Day. I told him I'd consider it and get back to him.

"I actually called you to set up a time for the Queen for a Day," I say.

"Is that so?"

At first I don't think he expects a response, but his continued silence tells me to say something. "Yeah, that's so" is what I come up with.

"The grand jury just handed up a true bill."

He means that Michael Ohlig has been indicted for securities fraud.

Pavin says this as if it should be of no surprise, and on one level it isn't. The prosecutor's power to influence the grand jury is so complete that it is a commonly told joke among lawyers that he could get the grand jury to indict a ham sandwich. But Pavin must know I had absolutely no sense an indictment was imminent, and the timing is troubling, indicating that he may just have uncovered new evidence.

I decide to go fish for the explanation. "What happened to giving my client the option to come in and provide you with evidence of his innocence?"

"First off, I made the offer to come in more than a month ago. I took your silence as evidence of a lack of interest. But look on the bright side, I'm actually doing you a favor." The smugness the others had mentioned about Pavin is manifested by his not finishing the thought. He's going to make me ask.

"How do you figure?"

"I'm saving Mr. Ohlig the problem of a thousand one count in the indictment."

Translation: he's preventing Ohlig from lying to his face and getting prosecuted for it afterward.

"Thanks," I say, as sarcastically as possible. "I'll be sure to pass that on to him."

"It's not all bad news. I'm willing to allow your client to surrender voluntarily, so long as he does it by eight tomorrow morning."

In this respect, Pavin is being generous, eschewing a splashy arrest with the obligatory perp walk for the media, but that doesn't mean I shouldn't try to buy Ohlig some time. "Mr. Ohlig will, of course, be happy to voluntarily surrender, but he's currently in Florida—"

Pavin doesn't let me finish the thought. "Offer expires right now. I need your commitment that he's showing up at our office at eight tomorrow morning or I'm sending the federal marshals down to his house right now to arrest him, and that'll guarantee he shows up tomorrow morning at eight. I checked; there are flights out of West Palm until ten, so he's got plenty of time to get up here tonight."

So that's that. We both know I have no leverage in this fight, and so there's no point for me to posture.

"With an offer like that, I'll make sure my client is on the next flight up here. We'll surrender tomorrow morning at eight."

"Good. And more good news is that I'm not going to kill you on bail. I just need enough so it means something. Fifteen million was the number I had in mind. And I'm going to need a travel restriction, of course."

"He's going to need to go back to Florida, but we can live with a New York-and-Florida-only restriction."

"That's fair. He'll have to surrender his passport, of course."

"That's not a problem."

"What about the money?" Pavin asks.

I could try to negotiate it down a bit; Pavin probably offered fifteen million thinking that we would agree on ten. In this case, however, I'd prefer not to give Ohlig any unnecessary incentives to head to Venezuela.

"Fifteen million is fine, so long as he can put up the bond equivalent."

"It sounds like we have a deal then."

After hanging up with Assistant United States Attorney Christopher Pavin, I take a deep breath, then call Ohlig.

"That was fast, counselor."

"Bad news, I'm afraid. Pavin said he was just about to call me when I called him. The grand jury just issued an indictment."

I expect Ohlig to blame me for not letting him meet with Pavin sooner to head this off, or maybe just for him to curse Pavin's name. I then flash on Eastman's story about being fired after a prosecutor bait-and-switched him, and wonder if Ohlig is about to say that he's going to find new counsel. He doesn't say anything, however, so I continue. "I told Pavin we wanted to take him up on the Queen for a Day offer, but he said it was a good thing we didn't because he would have added a count to the indictment for false statements."

Ohlig still doesn't respond. I wonder if he's in shock, but by this point I know he doesn't shock this easily. He isn't saying anything because he knows nothing he'd say would serve any purpose.

"The good news is that we've agreed on a bail package," I go on. "I can't guarantee the judge will sign off, but you'll likely only have to post a bond, and you'll be spending tomorrow night in your suite at the Pierre."

This is the point when clients ask how much money they'll have to post, or get me to swear that there's no way they'll be going to jail. Some inquire what happens if they don't show up.

Ohlig is still silent.

"You need to fly up tonight and be at my office tomorrow by seven A.M. We'll go down to the FBI together. After you've gone through processing, they'll take you in for arraignment, at which time you'll enter a not-guilty plea."

"Do you like steak?" Ohlig says.

"What?"

"Do you like steak?"

"I guess."

"I'll meet you at Peter Luger's tonight at nine."

"You're kidding, right?"

"If there's any possibility on earth I'll be spending tomorrow night in jail, I want to make sure I get one last good meal in me."

"Okay," I tell him.

"Bring Abby too," he says, and then hangs up.

# 13

Peter Luger's is a New York tradition, consistently ranked as the best steak house in the city, if not on earth, despite the fact that the decor is little more than old tables paired with barely comfortable chairs, the lighting is too bright, they take only cash or their own credit card and, worst of all, it's in Brooklyn. Despite this, the place is always jammed, as it is tonight.

The waiter comes over and hesitates for a moment, catching each of our eyes before handing Ohlig the wine list.

"I don't even need to look," Ohlig says, pushing the list back at him. "Do you have an Amarone?"

"We have several, sir," the waiter says.

"Whichever is the best one, we want it."

The waiter quickly returns. He shows the bottle to Ohlig and after Ohlig nods, the waiter pulls the cork out and pours Ohlig a taste.

The wine is a deep purple, and its legs stick to the side of Ohlig's glass when he swirls it. After taking a sip, he pronounces it exceptional, and directs the waiter to fill our glasses.

While the pouring occurs, Ohlig orders dinner for all of us. The steak for three, "Pittsburgh," which he explains afterwards means charred on the outside but rare on the inside, with sides of hash browns "burnt to a crisp," and, at Abby's insistence, asparagus.

After the waiter leaves, Ohlig leans toward Abby. "Has Alex told you I knew his parents before he was born?"

"He's mentioned it," she says, "but I'd love to hear more."

It's a bit of a Rashomon moment for me. Ohlig's version sticks to the script I've heard before, although he claims it was my father's challenge that brought them to Central Park, whereas my father tells it the other way around. Ohlig also incorporates my mother's claim about how she didn't want to go at all, but was talked into it by a girlfriend who wanted company on the train.

Then he adds something I'd never heard before.

"We'd been playing for about a half hour, when on one of the changeovers I say to Alex's dad, 'Have you noticed that girl over there?'" For most of this story Ohlig has been holding Abby's stare, but now he looks at me. "Your dad was a great guy about a lot of things, but about women he was a little bit clueless. So he says to me, 'What girl?' And I point to your mother and say, 'Look, you're getting killed on the court, you should try to salvage the day somehow. Go talk to her.'"

Ohlig has my rapt attention. I look over at Abby and see she has the same mesmerized expression, the way Charlotte stares at me when I'm reading her a bedtime story.

"I don't mean to embarrass you, Alex, but your

mother was one of the most beautiful women I'd ever seen. She looked just like Ali MacGraw. Do you young'uns even know who that is?"

I nod that I do. Despite Abby's prior comment about me being not much older than her, Ali MacGraw must be before Abby's time because her head moves the other way.

"She was a movie star," I say, "in the early seventies. She starred in *Love Story.*"

"She wasn't just a movie star," Ohlig corrects me. "She epitomized female beauty at the time. She had these amazingly long legs, and dark hair, and she was Steve McQueen's girlfriend to boot."

Abby takes a long sip of her wine. She's barely placed the glass back on the table before Ohlig's filling it again.

"Were you involved with someone then?" she asks Ohlig.

"What do you mean?"

"I mean, why didn't you go after Alex's mother?"

He pauses, as if he's deciding between several different answers. "That's a question I asked myself for many years. And then I met Pamela." He shrugs and takes a sip of wine. "We all find the person we're destined to be with in the end."

After dinner, the three of us cram into the back of a Lincoln Town Car, with Abby taking the middle seat. During the ride over the Brooklyn Bridge back into Manhattan, I'm acutely aware of our legs touching, noticing her other leg is in contact with Ohlig's. When we reach midtown, Ohlig places his hand on Abby's knee, but even after several glasses of wine he seems to realize he should remove it quickly.

The doorman at the Pierre opens the car door and addresses Ohlig by name. For a moment Ohlig doesn't move. I suspect it's because he's contemplating whether he can get away with kissing Abby good-night. Thankfully, he makes the right decision and doesn't try.

"Good night, you two," he says, peering into the window once he's alighted. "I don't mind telling you I'm a little concerned about having the only people who stand between me and prison traveling in the same car." He straightens up and turns to the driver. "Make sure these two get home safely. My freedom depends on it."

"Our next stop is going to be 80th and Park," Abby says to the driver, giving him my address so he can drop me off next.

"No," I say. "Go to 88th and Riverside," which is where Abby lives. "Then you can go through the park to drop me off."

"That's completely out of the way," Abby says to me, not to the driver. "We're already on the East Side." But by this time the car has already turned west.

"I just want you to know that chivalry is not dead."

"Tell that to Bob Ralston," she says, referencing a mid-level litigation partner. "I had a case with him last year and he made me carry the bags."

I laugh, and then we fall into a comfortable silence. In a way, it makes the back of the car more intimate.

We continue west on Central Park South, and then

north up Central Park West. The car turns west at 72nd Street, just in front of the Dakota, and proceeds toward Riverside Drive.

After we turn east on 88th Street, Abby says, "This one on the right," when the car approaches a Victorian brownstone with a stoop front. It's the kind of place where a twentysomething struggling artist would live in a television sitcom. In reality, the monthly rent can only be afforded by hard-charging types in banking or law.

The car stops in front of her house, which is on my side of the car. Although Abby could easily exit on the street side, I open my door and get out first.

We're standing face-to-face, neither of us moving. I wonder if she thinks I'm going to kiss her, just as I'm wondering if that's what she'll do.

"Good night," I finally say, when I'm thinking clearly enough to prevent something from happening. "Tonight was fun, probably a lot more than tomorrow will be."

"Sleep tight, Alex," she says, and then flashes that smile of hers before turning around and walking up the stairs to her front door.

Elizabeth is watching television in the bedroom when I get home. "So, how was it?" she asks as I begin removing my suit.

"Good. A little weird, actually. The guy is going to be arraigned tomorrow and he acts like it's somebody else's freedom that's in jeopardy."

"Maybe he just has supreme confidence in his lawyer."

"I truly don't think that's it. Although he does seem to like Abby a lot."

"I guess that tells me all I need to know about her."

"Be nice."

"Have I ever met her?"

"I don't know. Maybe at one of the firm parties. She comes up for partner this year and everyone thinks she's going to make it, so I'm sure you'll meet her at the new partner reception in February."

Elizabeth is the least jealous person I know. I could say it's because she trusts me, but it's something more than that. It's almost as if she thinks that merely recognizing the possibility that I could find someone else diminishes her, and she'd rather not even consider the possibility.

I lean over to kiss Elizabeth, and as I do so I feel a pang of guilt that my passion is fueled largely by my close proximity to Abby this evening (plus the three, or maybe four, glasses of wine), but somehow I've also convinced myself that my restraint at Abby's door entitles me to a reward.

"You smell like smoke," she says.

"I should only smell like wine."

"Either way, I'm tired, Alex."

And she rolls over away from me.

# 14

The FBI's offices are housed in what is perhaps the ugliest structure in the entire city. It's a squat brown stucco building attached to the facility that temporarily houses inmates when they have court appearances. The joke is that the inmates have the more luxurious space.

Ohlig, Abby, and I arrive half an hour early. The last thing I want is to be late and have Ohlig declared a fugitive from justice.

The guard in the lobby tells us to go to the sixth floor. Once there, I try the knob of the windowless metal door next to the elevator, but it's locked. On the adjacent wall is a phone with a handwritten note taped to it telling visitors to dial 0 for assistance. I do as directed and a woman's voice tells me she'll be right out. We wait five minutes before a small, African-American woman carrying a large gun in a shoulder holster appears.

"Good morning," she says cheerfully. "I'm Special Agent Erica Cole."

"Good morning. I'm Alex Miller and this is my colleague, Abigail Sloane, and, of course, this is Michael Ohlig."

"Nice to meet all of you," Agent Cole says, "but I'm only interested in you, Mr. Ohlig. Will you please follow me?"

"I'd like to accompany my client through booking,"

I say, even though I told Ohlig only minutes before that wasn't going to happen.

"Afraid not, counselor. Booking is one of those things that's done alone."

"Like death," Ohlig says.

Agent Cole smiles at Ohlig's quip and presses a buzzer that unlocks another steel, windowless door of equal size and depth as the one we entered through. When they're out of sight, the door slams shut, making a loud clanking sound.

Twenty minutes later, Ohlig emerges back into the reception area, a different FBI agent now accompanying him. This one is a man, but just as short as Agent Cole, if not shorter.

As usual, Michael Ohlig looks completely unfazed, so much so it takes me a moment to realize he's now handcuffed.

"Mr. Miller," the FBI agent says to me, "I'm Special Agent Gregory McNiven. You can have a moment to talk to your client, but you'll have to stay in the reception area. Mr. Ohlig is now officially in federal custody. We'll take him down to Part One when the judge is ready for us. You can meet him there."

"Can you take the handcuffs off, Agent McNiven?" I ask.

"Sorry, it's policy. We'll take them off when we're in the courtroom."

"Seriously?" Ohlig says, despite the fact I told him it was going to go exactly like this.

"Seriously," McNiven replies, and you've never heard the word spoken like that until you've heard it from an FBI agent.

The Part One judge handles arraignments and other matters that are not yet assigned to another judge, such as discovery disputes from cases pending in other jurisdictions and emergency matters in cases not yet filed. The judges rotate in the position, and although they're each supposed to take a turn, it always seems to me that a judge on senior status has the job whenever I'm making an application.

The Part One judge today is Milton Liebman, a barely living symbol to both the Constitutional framers' wisdom and shortsightedness in bestowing lifetime appointments on federal judges. In his day, Liebman was one of the finest minds in the federal judiciary and the author of several seminal opinions protecting Constitutional liberties. It's very possible that without the guarantee of lifetime tenure, Liebman wouldn't have felt free to stake his job on the backs of such unpopular causes. On the other hand, Liebman is now over ninety, nearly completely deaf, and can barely hold a pen to sign an order.

There isn't a specifically designated Part One courtroom, so the venue rotates too. Just like Air Force One's the call sign for whatever plane carries the president, the Part One courtroom is wherever the Part One judge sits.

As the oldest member of the court, Judge Liebman

has the courthouse's ceremonial courtroom. It's a massive space, capable of seating over two hundred spectators, darkly paneled, and boasting a double-height ceiling with stained-glass windows. Some of the most celebrated trials in American history have occurred in this room, but now it's mainly used for citizenship ceremonies, and on the rare occasions when Liebman is on the bench.

Pavin walks over to our table and hands me a sheaf of papers. "The indictment," he says casually.

This is the first time I've actually seen Christopher Pavin. Based on the fact that no one had heard of him, I'd assumed he was only a few years out of law school, but he's clearly older than me, and likely more than forty. He moves with a military bearing, and I seize upon that as the explanation for where he spent the period between college and law school, even though I know that's probably not the case. Nevertheless, he certainly looks like a former military man—broad shoulders, short-cropped sandy colored hair, and a strong chin. He's handsome, which is never good for the defense, with clear blue eyes and an easy smile.

"Thanks," I tell him, and immediately regret it, like you do when you thank a cop for handing you a speeding ticket.

The indictment is over twenty single-spaced pages. From my quick perusal, it seems that aside from listing the statutes the government claims Ohlig violated—which are the same seven counts that I would have guessed they'd go for—the indictment doesn't give any clues as to the evidence they have on him. It's based solely on Agent McNiven's "information and belief" that the criminal statutes listed have been violated, which means that, based on the evidence McNiven's reviewed—which is likely limited to the documents we produced and interviews with low-level OPM employees—he's concluded Ohlig violated the law.

Out of the corner of my eye, I see Ohlig enter the courtroom. Agent McNiven is a half step behind him, but because his head barely reaches Ohlig's shoulder blades, I don't realize he's there until they're both well inside the room.

I've always thought you can tell a lot about a man by the way he wears handcuffs, especially in public. Some appear like snarling animals, as if the moment they're unshackled they're going to go right for the throat of their captor. Others look exactly the opposite, like broken men; restrained or not, they couldn't muster the strength to be dangerous.

Ohlig acts as if he's entering a charity benefit with the handcuffs as some exotic yet elegant accessory.

As promised, McNiven uncuffs Ohlig as soon as he delivers him to counsel table. A second FBI agent—one much younger and much larger—is going to stand behind us during the proceeding. He's the one charged with making sure Ohlig doesn't try to escape. McNiven takes his place next to Pavin at the government's table.

The judge's courtroom deputy, a man who looks a little like Eddie Murphy, knocks hard three times on the wood molding of the door leading to the judge's chambers. "All rise," he commands.

I had forgotten just what a little man Judge Liebman is. In his robe, he looks like a kid wearing a Halloween ghost costume, except for the fact that he's cloaked in black and as wrinkled as a shar-pei. It takes him longer than I can ever recall a judge taking to walk the fifteen feet from the doorway to his chair. When he's finally sitting, he allows everyone else to do the same.

The deputy bellows: "The United States of America v. Michael Louis Ohlig. Counsel, please state your appearances, starting with the government."

"If it pleases the court, Assistant United States Attorney Christopher G. Pavin for the United States of America. With me at counsel table, your Honor, is Special Agent Gregory McNiven of the Federal Bureau of Investigation. Thank you, your Honor."

Judge Liebman nods in my direction, signaling it's my turn to rise. "Good morning. My name is Alexander Miller of the law firm Cromwell Altman Rosenthal and White. I am joined here today by my colleague Abigail Sloane. We represent Michael Ohlig."

"Very good, counsel. Please, both of you be seated. And welcome, Mr. Ohlig." Judge Liebman speaks in a squeak that makes him almost impossible to hear. "Waive reading?" is what I think he says next.

The defendant has the right to have his charges publicly aired, but all defendants waive reading of the indictment as a matter of course. The very idea of sitting through the clerk reading aloud a five-thousand-word document is about as unbearable as any torture I can imagine.

"The defense is willing to waive reading of the indictment," I say.

"Mr. Miller, would your client like to enter a plea at this time?" Judge Liebman asks next.

Ohlig rises and we're standing shoulder to shoulder. It's time for him to say the only words I told him he could utter at this proceeding.

"Your Honor," Ohlig says in a strong voice. "I am not guilty."

Judge Liebman shows no reaction to this, nor would I expect him to. "Would the government like to be heard on the question of bail?"

"We would, your Honor." Pavin has a very formal way about him in court, which is not surprising given he's very formal out of court too. He ends nearly every statement with the phrase *your Honor,* which is just as annoying as ending every phrase with the name of the person you're addressing. *I agree, Bill. We'll meet at two, Bill. At that restaurant on Madison, Bill.*

"The government has discussed the issue of bail with defendant's counsel, your Honor, and we jointly make the following recommendation: that your Honor impose bail in the amount of $15 million, to be satisfied by a bond of at least ten percent cash or its equivalent in real estate. Mr. Ohlig has agreed to surrender his passport and we request your Honor impose, as a condition of bail, that he not be permitted to travel outside his home state of Florida, other than to come to New York to meet with his counsel. Thank you, your Honor."

"What's that, Mr. Paylin?" Judge Liebman squeaks.

Pavin doesn't correct the judge's mispronunciation of his name, and instead goes through the same speech as before, nearly word for word, which tells me he's the kind of lawyer who doesn't leave much to chance in the courtroom, right down to scripting what he's going to say. I don't say that as a criticism; I do the same thing.

"Is that acceptable to the defense?" the judge asks in my direction after Pavin finishes his repeat performance.

"It is." I deliberately leave off calling him your Honor to make Pavin's sucking up seem more pronounced.

"If you're both happy, then I'm happy. Thank you, gentlemen."

I look over at Pavin and he's looking at me. I make a gesture to indicate that he should be the one to tell Judge Liebman that he's forgotten to pull a name from the wheel, and he either understands it or reaches that conclusion on his own, because he's standing again.

"Your Honor, I believe you need to assign a trial judge," Pavin says.

"Oh, I thought we'd done that. We haven't? Okay." Liebman looks over to his deputy. "Rod, could you please spin the wheel?"

I'm sure no one intended for the selection of a United States district judge to resemble the lottery drawings on television before the evening news, but that's exactly what it looks like. There's a big wire mesh case with a crank on the side and inside are thirty-six white tiles, each about the size of a domino, with a judge's name written in black.

The wire mesh case makes several turns around before coming to a stop. Rod reaches in and pulls out a single tile. "The Honorable Nicole Sullivan," he calls out, and holds out the tile for everyone to see.

"Good or bad?" Ohlig asks in a loud whisper.

"Bad," I whisper back, much more quietly. "Very bad."

Part **3**

# 15

Just like the dormancy between the convening of the grand jury and the indictment, the month after the indictment has also resembled a calm before the storm. Nothing of note happened until the date the government was ordered to turn over its Brady material.

So named for the Supreme Court decision *Brady v. Maryland, Brady* material is the evidence the government has collected that could be considered exculpatory, plus any statements given by witnesses who the government intends to call at trial. As with all procedural rules, there are ways to end-run it so that it's quite often the case that the *Brady* material contains very little the defense doesn't already know.

Had that been the case here, I would have been supremely relieved.

No such luck, however. That's why I summoned Ohlig up to New York to meet with us. He's perfected his Mr. Cool persona to such an extent that he didn't even ask why.

"I can't believe the Four Seasons in this city charges eight hundred bucks a night and the rooms are like shoeboxes," Ohlig says. "You know who I blame for this, don't you?"

I know the answer—he blames me. After the indictment, I told him to sell the three vacation homes he owned. He protested, of course, but ultimately relented when I explained that a jury would not feel any sympathy for a guy who owns homes all over the world. He found a buyer for the pied-à-terre at the Pierre Hotel almost immediately, but claims the market is such that he can't give away the ski chalet in Vail or the villa in Turks and Caicos.

"I.M. Pei?" I say with a straight face.

"Who?" he asks, momentarily thrown from his punch line.

"I.M. Pei. He's the architect who designed the Manhattan Four Seasons. I'm assuming that if you have a problem with your room's proportions, he would be the guy to blame."

Ohlig laughs, the good laugh, the one that says he means it. "Very good. Okay. Yes, I blame I.M. Pei. And I'll tell you another thing, I'm not too happy with what he did with the Louvre either."

This causes me to laugh with him. "Why don't we continue our discussion of modern architecture in a conference room," I say, reaching over to dial Abby's extension. "That way Abby can join us."

"Sure." Ohlig wears a wide grin, his usual reaction whenever he's told Abby will be joining us.

I pick up the receiver to take Abby off speakerphone before she can say anything I wouldn't want Ohlig to hear. "Abby, it's Alex. Michael is here and I thought we could meet in the conference room on 57 to talk about the tapes."

"Tapes?" Ohlig says as I put down the phone. "Are we going to listen to some Tony Bennett today?" His quip notwithstanding, I can tell by the obvious effort it takes him to hold his smile that he knows this is no joking matter.

"Sorry, no such luck. It's going to be your greatest hits, I'm afraid." Now I've got his undivided attention. "For the last three months of OPM's existence, the government had wiretaps on your brokers."

Ohlig's only response is to narrow his eyes, as if he's running through his mind what he's about to hear. After a few moments of thought, he says, "Shall we?" with his trademark grin, and begins to rise.

Abby is already in the conference room when we arrive. A yellow legal pad sits on the table in front of her and she's wearing her game face.

In the past month, I've spent, on average, sixty hours a week in Abby's company. Although I've managed to stay true to my marriage vows, I've done so only in the most literal sense. In every other way I'm engaged in a full-fledged affair. Abby and I are in each other's offices three to four times a day, and our IM exchanges are virtually non-stop. We have all of our meals together in the "war room" (which is actually a windowless conference room filled with boxes that is now the command center for our battle against the government), but once a week or so we go out to dinner somewhere expensive, which also means romantic, on Ohlig's tab. And I begin and end my day dialing into my voicemail, where there is almost always a message from Abby, more often than not having nothing to do with work.

At first I thought I could compartmentalize Abby separately from Elizabeth, the way I do one case from another. Of course, that has turned out to be impossible. My time with Elizabeth is spent counting the hours until I can go back to the office.

Elizabeth hasn't mentioned anything, at least not directly. From time to time she'll make a comment about how I seem distracted, and I'll tell her I'm thinking about the case or about my father, which is sometimes true, but more often than not is a lie. She accepts my explanation without further inquiry. She's seen me work non-stop before, so that may be the reason she hasn't cross-examined me further, but if I were a betting man, I'd wager she knows that my distance is the result of something else entirely, and that she hasn't asked about it because she doesn't want to confirm her suspicion.

"Michael, help yourself to some coffee or breakfast," I say when we enter the conference room. "You too, Abby."

A buffet of coffee, pastries, and fresh fruit lines the back of the conference room. Ohlig makes a beeline for the food. Abby stays put.

"I figure if I eat enough pastry, I can break even on your bill. How many of these guys do you think I need to put down?" He holds up a mini chocolate croissant.

I don't respond. By now I'm more surprised when he doesn't make a joke about the bill. When Ohlig returns to the table, his plate full of food, I say to Abby, "I've told Michael that the government has produced some audio tapes."

"Give it to me straight, Abby," Ohlig says, leaning into her and locking onto her eyes.

This is something else I'm quite used to. When we meet one-on-one, I'm the recipient of Ohlig's charm, but as soon as Abby enters the room, it's as if I don't exist anymore.

"Most are defensible," Abby says. "The same type of hyperbole all brokers use. We've got a problem with one guy, though. His name is Kevin Gates."

Ohlig shows no hint that he recognizes the name. "What's this Gates-guy saying?" he asks.

"Take a listen," she says and then reaches over to her laptop. A couple of clicks later we hear static, followed by an authoritative voice.

"This is Special Agent Gregory McNiven of the Federal Bureau of Investigation. The conversations on this tape will be from the phone number area code 561-555-7597. This tape recording is pursuant to warrant."

"Hello," says a man's faint voice on the tape. You can tell instantly he's over eighty.

"Mrs., oh I'm sorry, Mr. Rudintsky." From the sound of his voice, Kevin Gates's age clearly falls on the other end of the spectrum; he sounds barely old enough to have a job.

"Rudnitsky," the old man corrects.

"Rudnitsky. Sorry. Listen, I know your time is valuable, as is my own." Gates runs his words together, indicating that he might be working off a script, even though Ohlig swears that wasn't the way OPM's business was conducted and, so far at least, we haven't seen anything to contradict him. "Allow me to introduce myself. My name is Kevin Gates. I'm a Senior Vice President in the wealth management department at OPM Securities, located right here in beautiful Palm Beach, Florida. I was provided your name by a colleague who told me you were an experienced enough investor to know that when an opportunity comes along, you either grab it or wish you had. So, let me give it to you straight.

"My company has permitted me to offer to a select few qualified investors a stock called Salminol at a very attractive price. Salminol is a publicly traded security, and the company holds a certified United States patent for completely eliminating salmonella in eggs. Now I'm sure you're aware that salmonella is one of the leading causes of death in certain parts of the world, and a major problem here at home too. And you must have heard about the dangers of eggs. I mean, it was all over the news; about a billion of them had to be recalled. Well, this company is going to make all of that a thing of the past. Imagine, you go into your grocery store and sitting there on the shelf are two boxes of eggs. One is the regular kind, you have no idea where it comes from, and right next to it is a box that says right on the box, in big bold letters, *100% Salmonella-Free—Guaranteed*. I mean, it's a no-brainer, right? Everyone's going to buy the salmonella-free one.

"I know what you're thinking. There's a catch, right? Like my daddy always told me, if it sounds too good to be true, it is. So, here's the catch. These eggs are being sold in parts of Canada and sales there are through the roof. But the company needs to expand its distribution and its market penetration. They've got to be global, right? It's a global economy out there. So here's why their problem is good news for you. To raise money so they can go global, the company is selling—for a short time only—a limited amount of its stock in a private offering. Now, I'm sure you've heard of IPOs and you know that usually only the big shots get in on them— CEOs, hedge fund managers, Hollywood types—and they clean up. But my company does its bread and butter with sophisticated but lower net-worth investors such as yourself, and so this time we decided to share the wealth a little and let our investors get in on something big. I mean, the stock's gotta go to the moon, between the product being can't-miss and with the company likely going to buy back some stock at a premium—hold on, I'm not sure I'm allowed to say that, so forget I said that, okay?

"Anyway, the bottom line is, I can put aside seven thousand shares. The current ask is a buck, but it might end up being a little more because this thing is on the uptick even as we speak. But if you put up, let's say, ten grand, I guarantee you triple it in less than a month."

During this pitch, for the most part, Abby, Ohlig, and I have been staring at the computer, as if there was a person actually inside it delivering these words. Hearing Gates make a guarantee—which results in an immediate license revocation by the SEC—causes me to look up at Ohlig. His expression back doesn't contain even the slightest bit of concern.

"What's your name again?" the old man on the tape asks.

"It's Kevin, Kevin Gates. Hey, hold on for a second, I'm on an important call with Mr. Rudnitsky, the man I told you about." Gates must have said this pulling his mouth away from the phone, as if he's talking to someone else, because this part sounds more muted. "Yes, yes, I'll call him right back. I understand he's about to get on the jet, but I have another client on the phone now. I promise, three minutes. No, I can't guarantee it's going to be the same price as I quoted this morning. Yes, I know he wants to buy a million shares, but it's going up every minute. I'm very sorry about that, Mr. Rudnitsky," Gates says, now more loudly. "Can I put you down for fifteen thousand?"

"I don't know. I normally discuss any type of investment with my wife. You know, we're on a fixed budget and—"

"I totally understand where you're coming from, and if your wife makes all the decisions in your house, that's fine. But here's the thing. When you call back, I'm not going to be able to offer you the same deal. Look, even though I shouldn't be telling you this, I'm sure you've already figured it out. My other client is going to buy a million shares as soon as I get off the phone with you. That's going to move the price at least a buck. So, you can pretty much double your money just by getting in ahead of him. If after that your wife wants to sell, God bless, and you'll have enough in profits to take her on a cruise around the world. Not bad for ten minutes' work, right? And, if you want to keep going, who knows how much you'll make. Imagine if I was calling you about Microsoft before anybody had heard of it. What would your wife be saying if you told her you passed?"

"Well—"

"Yes, yes, I know," Gates says to whom I imagine to be the pretend person standing in his office. "I'm going to do this right now. Tell Mr. Windsor to hold. I'm sorry, Mr. Rudnitsky, I have to take this other call. The guy simply can't wait when money's on the line, and he's afraid it's going to cost him another million because it's ticking up. But, look, I live by the credo that a client is a client, and I'm not judging based on how fat their wallets are. So, you're the client I have on the phone now, and if you give me the go-ahead, you're in."

"Okay, I suppose I can swing—"

"Great, I'm going to transfer you to one of my assistants, and she'll do the paperwork. For twenty thou. If you have any questions, just give me a call. You've made a great decision. Gotta run now—"

The tape goes silent.

I'm about to say something, when Abby interrupts. "Hold on, this is the part I really wanted you to hear."

Gates's voice comes back on the tape. "Thanks B-man, I thought he was going to croak before I could wrest the fucking twenty grand out of his hand. Wait till he tells the wife he invested twenty grand in a steaming pile of dog shit. Ohlig better give me that bonus he promised for selling out of this mofo before it hits zero."

"Gates apparently didn't realize he hadn't disconnected the line after transferring the client to ops," Abby says, stating the obvious.

She and I now wait, looking at Ohlig to provide some explanation. Apparently, Ohlig doesn't think he has to add anything to what we've heard, even though he's smart enough to know that this is a major problem.

"We need to find Gates," I say when it's clear Ohlig isn't going to say anything.

"Gates isn't even the guy's real name," Ohlig says. "It's Popowski. He thought customers would be more trusting if they thought he was rich, so the idiot decided to call himself Gates. Anyway, the guy worked for me for less than three weeks. I found out that he was pulling this crap and he was out on his ass."

"That makes it pretty clear he's not going to be helpful to us on the stand," I say.

"Look, I can see that you're troubled by this, so let me put you at ease. I never said that I thought it was going to zero. That's just him blowing smoke." Ohlig shakes his head. "But it's all beside the point because there's no way they're going to put him on the stand." Ohlig says this with an authoritative air, as if he's fully versed in prosecutorial decision making. "The guy's a known liar. At least ten people will testify to that."

"They've got to put him on the stand," Abby

responds. "Without Gates, or Popowski, or whoever he is, they won't be able to get the tape into evidence."

"Really?" Ohlig asks.

"Don't kill him yet," I joke, "but Abby's right. The tape would be inadmissible. They might be able to figure out some other way to authenticate it, but usually you do it by having the person on the tape testify."

"What about the FBI guy?" he asks.

"That wouldn't work. Maybe Judge Sullivan lets in the sales pitch through the agent, but she'd never allow him to testify about the part where he says you knew it would go to zero. That's Hearsay 101." I turn toward Abby. "Have you heard any other pitches like this?"

"No," she says.

"Like I've been telling you guys," Ohlig says, "it's all legit. You know, we're salesmen, so we sell. That's what we do all day. But I tell my guys, it's got to be the truth, and if I find out differently, you're gone. No second chance. Zero tolerance. I mean, how many calls did they tape and all they got is this one guy. Doesn't that say something?"

He has a point, but I know that it will be lost on the jury. "It doesn't work like that, I'm afraid," I tell him. "Unfortunately, for most jurors, a single incriminating statement on a thousand hours of tape isn't much different than if the statement stood alone. Either way, it shows a crime has been committed."

He shakes his head, as if the act itself repudiates my opinion. "Abby," he says with the lascivious cadence that usually accompanies his invocation of her name, "did they tape any of my phones?"

"No. Just the salesmen."

"Are you sure my office wasn't taped?"

Abby looks in my direction. I know what she's think-ing, but she's waiting for me to confront him about it.

"Michael, is there something we should know? Any discussions you're concerned about?"

"No. Nothing like that. I just wanted to be sure I'm safe making my heavy breathing calls to Abby."

Whatever concerns he had moments before about his private conversations being served up for public consumption have apparently been assuaged. He flashes the smile he has come to rely on when the pressure mounts.

The one that says things couldn't be going any better.

# 16

I'm already wearing my coat when the phone rings. If it were any number other than Aaron Littman's I'd ignore it.

"Hi Aaron," I say, picking up the phone.

"It's actually Kathleen, Alex." Kathleen is one of Aaron's two secretaries. "He wants to see you. Now, if you can."

The timing couldn't be worse. Charlotte's autumn concert is tonight. For some reason they start these things at 5:30, even though I'm sure that no one who can afford private school tuition has the kind of job that they can comfortably leave by five. I promised Elizabeth that I'd be at Charlotte's school concert no later than 5:15, but that was going to be doubtful even if I left this minute, and a detour to Aaron's, no matter how brief, means I'll miss the beginning of the concert. On the other hand, an invitation to see Aaron Littman isn't really a request.

"I'll be right up," I say.

If I did a year-by-year analysis of who in the world I wanted to be, the eighties would have been dominated by Bruce Springsteen, the nineties by Jerry Seinfeld, and the last ten years or so by Aaron Littman. It's not that I think Aaron's life is better than, say, George Clooney's; it's just that it makes more sense to wish you could be someone you may have a chance of actually being someday. And, ever since I was in law school, Aaron Littman has been universally regarded as the finest trial lawyer of his generation. He has a client list that reads like a virtual who's-who of billionaires, high-ranking government officials, and movie stars. On top of that, he looks the part: six foot two, same weight as he was when he rowed crew at Yale, dark hair speckled with grey, and always attired in five-thousand-dollar custom suits.

When I arrive, Kathleen is nowhere to be found. "Is the great man around?" I ask Regina, Aaron's other secretary.

Regina is in her mid-fifties, and on the dowdy side. Most people would say she has a pretty face, but beyond that she does little to attract men, which might be the reason she's never been married. She's been with Aaron since the day he joined the firm, and I've been told by more than one person that she didn't always look the way she does now. As one of the senior partners once told me, "Back in the day, we would come to Aaron's office just to look at her. Imagine the same size breasts as now, but fifty pounds less everywhere else."

"He's here somewhere," she tells me. "He's in about three different meetings at the moment. Your best bet is probably Conference Room B, but he might be in with David Bloom down on 52. He also said something about stepping into that takeover Jim Martin is handling. You're welcome to wait here if you'd like."

This is typical Aaron. At any given time he is

shuttling between various crises. More than once I've seen him walk into the middle of a meeting in which twenty lawyers have been negotiating for hours, offer a resolution to the impasse in about three minutes, and then leave to let everyone else iron out the details.

Aaron isn't gone long. "Sorry I'm late," he says a few moments later, making me wonder how many times a day he must utter that phrase. He asks Regina if anyone's been looking for him and she playfully rolls her eyes. "Anyone looking for me who I need to call back before I talk with Alex," he clarifies.

The answer, for the moment, is no.

Aaron leads me into his office, directing me to take a seat on his sofa. His office has always seemed to me more of a museum than a place from which to practice law. It's enormous—three times the size of mine and that of every other partner (except for Sam Rosenthal, whose name is on the letterhead and who has an office of equal size), and the walls are lined with pictures of Aaron standing with a litany of A-listers. My favorite was taken at *Time* magazine's gathering of the most influential people of the twentieth century, in which Aaron is sandwiched between Muhammad Ali and Mikhail Gorbachev.

"Thanks for coming by," Aaron says, acting as if I had an option not to answer his invitation. "I just thought we'd chat about how your case is shaping up."

Since I'd already anticipated that this was the reason I was being summoned, I was ready with a response. My thought was that short, without too much detail, was the way to go, peppering my conclusions with plenty of caveats, in case things ultimately turned out differently than I was reporting now.

"It's still early," I begin, "and we just got in some tapes that I haven't heard yet, so things could change, but so far I think we're in pretty good shape. It's largely going to be a state-of-mind case—did Ohlig know Salminol was worthless when he sold it to investors? The experts will cancel each other out and the case will boil down to whether the jury believes Ohlig or not."

"I take that to mean you plan to have him testify?"

Whether the defendant is going to take the stand is the key strategy decision in any case, as well as the best indicator to whether the lawyer thinks the client is innocent. Most lawyers will tell you that no matter how gifted a liar a client may be, the lie can't be sustained against a good cross-examiner. Something inevitably trips them up.

"Barring something completely unforeseen like an admission on the tapes," I say, keeping with the caveats, "I don't see how I'll be able to keep him off the stand."

"Don't let the inmates run the asylum," Aaron says with a parental note of disapproval. "It's your case, and you're much closer to it than me, but I wouldn't open with even the suggestion that Ohlig's going to testify. Stick to an attack of the government's case, with a heavy emphasis on reasonable doubt. If you promise your guy is going to testify, and then think better of it, you're screwed. Juries just won't forgive that kind of bait and switch. On the other hand, there's no problem if your opening doesn't address the issue, and then you later decide to put him on."

Aaron's strategy is the textbook approach, especially when representing a guilty client. But I continue to believe in Ohlig's innocence. More than that, as I'd told Aaron, this is a state-of-mind case, and I can't imagine a jury voting to acquit without Ohlig taking the stand. As the adage goes, *If you don't talk, you don't walk.*

I'm about to explain this to him when he abruptly changes the subject. "So, how's Abby working out?" he asks.

The question throws me for a moment. I can't help but wonder if there's gossip around the firm about Abby and me, even as I console myself with the thought that there's really nothing to gossip about.

"She's great," I say. "Very smart and hard working. Ohlig just loves her."

Aaron smiles but is too politically correct to say what I imagine he's thinking about Ohlig's interest in Abby. "So, I take it you'll be supporting her when she comes up for partner?"

"I don't see why not. But the more important question, of course, is whether you'll be supporting her."

Aaron deflects the tribute with a shrug of his shoulder. "You know that your vote is just as important as mine."

I'm surprised he can say this without laughing. Although he's technically correct that each partner has a single vote and majority rules, Aaron's power at the firm is so unchallenged that his backing is all it takes. Since

I've been a partner, every partnership vote has been unanimous, both for or against, much the way political conventions always nominate by acclamation, regardless of how contentious the primary battle. Once the result is a foregone conclusion, there's no reason not to side with the winners. At Cromwell Altman, Aaron's vote makes the result a foregone conclusion.

"But to answer your question, yes, I'll be supporting her," he says.

## 17

Last year during the holiday season, Elizabeth and I dragged Charlotte to ten of the city's most elite private schools, begging them to allow us to pay more than $30,000 a year for her to attend their kindergarten. The process involved Charlotte being tested by a child psychologist; multi-page applications, complete with essays written by us addressing the type of school environment in which we believed Charlotte would most thrive; "private interviews" with Charlotte and the school admissions directors; "play groups," which enabled other school admissions officers to watch Charlotte as she interacted (or didn't) with peers; and interviews of Elizabeth and me with the schools' headmasters to see if there was the "right fit," a euphemism that applied to everything from our religion to how much we could be expected to contribute to the school beyond tuition.

On February 15, known as D-Day to those involved in what is called the "independent school admission process," we received a letter from each of the schools, only two of which contained enrollment contracts. Charlotte was deemed worthy by Hamilton, a co-ed K-8 that is more than 150 years old, and an all-girls establishment called The Hewson School, which was trying to shake its reputation as a finishing school and become a more rigorous academic institution. We picked Hewson because Elizabeth fully bought into the whole pitch about the benefits of a single-sex education—that girls are more mature and can learn more quickly in the earlier years, are apt to be distracted by boys in the classroom in middle school, and are able to thrive in math and science and take leadership roles in a single-sex high school.

Hewson is housed in a double-wide brownstone just off Fifth Avenue in the seventies, which is about as expensive as real estate gets. Townhouses in the area routinely sell for well over $5 million, and apartments of similar square footage in the white glove doorman buildings can go for twice that. With the marquee address, however, comes a shortage of space, which requires that all full-school events be held at the Presbyterian church around the corner.

As predicted, my detour to Aaron's office has made me late. The concert started twenty minutes ago. If Charlotte's kindergarten class went on first, I might as well have not shown up at all.

At school events like this, the seniors wear long white dresses so as to differentiate them from the sea of glen plaid that is the official school uniform—jumpers for the girls in K–6 and skirts paired with white blouses for grades 7–11. Not all of the seniors are required to sing, and those who aren't in the choir work as ushers. As I enter the church, a senior with long, dark curly hair hands me today's program. On the cover it announces that *Autumn Is Here* and features a drawing of a tree surrounded by birds that is attributed to Olivia

Regan, Grade 2. The inside page lists the order of performance, and to my great relief the kindergartners are up last.

Elizabeth is sitting on the left side of the church, near the back. She's saved me a seat next to her, on the end of the pew. After I've settled in beside her, I lean over and kiss her on the cheek. Her expression does not say that she's glad to see me.

On the stage, a group of girls is singing a song I've never heard before. I peg them to be fourteen or so, which means I've missed the seniors and juniors, and quite possibly the sophomores as well.

"Thank goodness she's last," I whisper to Elizabeth.

"Kindergarten always is," she replies, as if this is a written rule somewhere that I should have known about. After a short pause, she adds, "I suppose I should thank you for showing up at all."

"I'm sorry. Aaron needed to see me at the last minute."

"What if you had already left? Or told him that you'd see him tomorrow?"

At moments like this, I can't help but wonder how different my life might be with Abby. We speak the same language, whereas there are times with Elizabeth when I feel the need to translate what she's said in my head before it makes sense. Some of it is simply work-related. Abby understands what I'm talking about when I use legal shorthand, and she knows that Aaron Littman is not someone you push off until the next day, be it for your daughter's kindergarten concert or because you're in need of major surgery.

"I said I'm sorry." Then, placing my hand on Elizabeth's, I add, "After the Ohlig trial everything will return to normal."

Elizabeth looks at me with a different expression, but one that also needs no further articulation to make its point. *What's normal to you?*

What *is* normal to me? I'm thirty-five years old, the youngest partner at a world-renowned law firm, with a beautiful wife and a healthy daughter, earning more every year than my father did in a decade, and yet I'm unhappy.

Forty-six minutes later (with me checking my watch after each performance), the school's headmistress finally utters the words I've been waiting for. "Parents, for our final performance of the evening, the kindergarten is going to sing 'Trees Are Our Friends.' Now, I know that you're not going to be able to control yourselves from taking pictures, but please don't wave to your daughters. It distracts them."

She is halfway through her little schoolmarm speech when the first of Charlotte's classmates enters the sanctuary through a door at stage left. Like clockwork, two people whom I assume to be the girl's parents rise and begin to wave. The little girl doesn't seem too distracted as she waves back, a wide, toothy grin on her face. The ritual is repeated with every girl, and when Charlotte finally appears, about midway through the processional, it's Elizabeth's and my turn to disobey the headmistress's request.

# 18

The Constitution provides every criminal defendant with the right to a speedy trial. The original intent was based on the belief that someone charged with a crime would want to erase the stain of accusation at the earliest possible time. The reality of criminal practice now has it completely the other way around, however. The prosecutor is far more eager than the defendant to get to trial because by the time an indictment is issued, the prosecutor has already completed his investigation, but the defendant is just learning what the evidence looks like and has to play catch-up.

The Ohlig case proves the point. In the five weeks since the indictment, we've barely made a dent in understanding what the prosecution's case is really going to look like. Even though they have Popowski, since he's not part of OPM management, he likely won't be able to get them all the way to a conviction. They're still going to need to rely primarily on the trading tickets to put together the story of how OPM took a worthless stock, jacked up the price, and then reaped more than a hundred and fifty million dollars in profit before it cratered to zero. The government has already done this analysis, but for us to review those tickets will take at least another month.

Ohlig flew back to New York last night so he could

be at this morning's scheduling conference, the sole purpose of which is to set a trial date. Initially Ohlig wasn't going to attend because I told him that these types of calendar calls are not very substantive, explaining that Pavin would throw out an unreasonably early date, we'd counter with an unreasonably late one, so as to put off the day of reckoning for as long as possible, and then Judge Sullivan would pick one in the middle. That would likely mean we'd start trial in March or April of next year.

Yesterday Ohlig changed his mind and insisted on being here. I should have asked him why, but I just chalked it up to his wanting to be part of his own defense. Then, on our way to the courthouse, he tells me the real reason.

"I want you to ask for the earliest possible trial date," he says matter-of-factly.

"What?"

"I want to get this over with as soon as possible. Tell the judge that the first available trial date is when we want to go."

"That . . . that just makes no sense, Michael. We've already talked about the benefits of delay, and I thought we were in agreement. Is there some reason why you think an earlier trial is all of a sudden to our advantage?"

"The sooner it's tried, the sooner I'm acquitted."

"If only that were always the case. The truth is, the sooner you're tried, the less likely you'll be acquitted."

"Do you still work for me, Alex, or have I missed

something?" He says this with his trademark smile, but by now I know it belies a deadly seriousness.

"I do," I tell him, wondering if he has the judicial equivalent of a death wish.

"The earliest possible date," he says, ending the discussion.

Judge Sullivan is known around the courthouse as the Love Judge. Rumor has it that she worked as a model to put herself through law school, but it's not part of her official judicial resume. She's in her early forties and has been on the bench for four or five years. For the most part, she's known to be a smart, no-nonsense jurist, with a reputation for being particularly tough on defense counsel, so much so that some among the defense bar refer to her as "AUSA Judge Sullivan" because she can make it feel like there's another prosecutor in the room. To make matters worse, she's ambitious, which, almost by definition, makes her pro-government for the simple reason that no one has ever been disqualified from achieving higher office because they were too hard on criminals, whereas many a judicial career has been derailed by the beneficiary of a lenient sentence who returns the favor by going on to murder or rape—or, in Ohlig's case, defraud unsophisticated investors like Mr. Rudnitsky—again.

"Good news, everyone," Judge Sullivan announces upon taking the bench, a spark in her voice that sounds like she's about to tell us she has just saved a lot of money on her car insurance. "Another case that was scheduled to go to trial has just settled. I can put this matter down for November 29. That's the Tuesday after Thanksgiving. Does that work for everyone?"

The federal courthouse in New York does not permit electronic devices in the building, including cell phones or BlackBerrys. It's a post-9/11 development, although the state courts don't follow the prohibition and most other federal courts just ask you to turn off your phone. As a result of the ban, the lawyers—at least those who are not technologically impaired—can't access their schedules when a judge asks for availability. Even without my BlackBerry, however, I know that the twenty-ninth is a little more than two weeks from today. There's no way we can be ready by then, even with Abby and me working our usual fifteen-hour-day, seven-days-a-week schedules.

Pavin stands, buttoning the top button of his suit jacket. "Your Honor," he says, looking surprisingly grim-faced, "the government respectfully requests you set a trial date for some time after the first of the year."

Judge Sullivan's suggestion of a trial date two weeks out was surprising, but Pavin resisting it really throws me. It's a usual point of pride with the U.S. Attorney's Office that the government is always ready.

"Do you have a conflict in another court, Mr. Pavin?" Judge Sullivan asks.

"No, your Honor."

"Then what's the problem with the twenty-ninth? I would think that you wouldn't have brought an indictment unless you were ready to proceed to trial. Frankly,

I expected some pushback from Mr. Miller, but not from the government."

As a former assistant herself, Judge Sullivan's one pro-defense characteristic is that she can be counted on to give prosecutors a hard time whenever she believes that they are not living up to her lofty standards. This is seemingly going to be one of those times.

Pavin glances over at counsel table to Agent Mc-Niven. It looks to me like McNiven nods his assent.

"Your Honor, we have a missing witness, I'm afraid. We need some time to track him down."

"Who is it?" she asks. When Pavin looks reluctant to answer, Judge Sullivan adds, "Mr. Pavin, the parties have exchanged witness lists, am I correct?"

"You are, your Honor," Pavin confirms.

We had exchanged witness lists with the government as part of initial discovery, but both our lists were virtually worthless. Ours had 115 names and theirs more than that, listing every employee of OPM and every purchaser of Salminol, as well as every member of Salminol's board of directors. Both sides knew that almost none of those people would actually be called as witnesses. They were included as a combination prophylactic measure, just in case they were needed, and to hide the real witnesses in plain sight.

"In that case," Judge Sullivan says, "the defense already knows everyone you're likely to call, so I don't see the problem in sharing with us which witness you're having trouble locating. In fact, I have a problem with them thinking someone is going to testify for the government who, in fact, is not going to testify."

"Your Honor," Pavin begins, this time sounding even more sheepish, "one of the government's key witnesses is a man named Kevin Popowski, although he went by the alias Kevin Gates when he worked as a broker at the defendant's firm. The government has interviewed Mr. Popowski, several times in fact. We have a sworn statement from him that Mr. Ohlig knew that Salminol—the stock in question in this case—was worthless, and to avoid a catastrophic loss for his firm, Mr. Ohlig ordered that it be pumped up and dumped on unsuspecting investors, mainly the elderly. Unfortunately, when we attempted to make contact with Mr. Popowski earlier in the week, we were informed that he'd moved out of his apartment and did not leave a forwarding address. We suspect Mr. Ohlig has hidden him."

Even before I could say anything, Judge Sullivan does it for me. "Does the government have any proof of that?"

"Not yet, your Honor."

"I'll take that as a no, then. And I suggest you not raise those kinds of allegations when you don't have any proof." She then looks in my direction. "Mr. Miller, even though I won't permit unsubstantiated allegations in my courtroom, please be advised that if your client is hiding a witness, I will not hesitate to hold him—and you, for that matter—in contempt. The crime of obstruction of justice is one that is ongoing, and so if you know where Mr. Popowski is, you have a duty as an officer of this court to so inform the prosecution, or you'll be aiding and abetting the obstruction. That's a long way of saying that the attorney-client privilege does not apply here, so act at your own peril."

"I have absolutely no idea where he is," I tell Judge Sullivan, thankful that Ohlig was smart enough not to involve me in this scheme.

"Okay, then," she says, and then swings her gaze back to Pavin. "While I sympathize with your predicament, Mr. Pavin, the speedy trial rules are in effect, and if Mr. Ohlig wants a fast trial, a fast trial he will get. Lucky for you that you have the FBI at your disposal to track down your missing witness. I think two weeks should be enough time because if you can't do it by then, you're probably not going to be able to find him no matter how long I give you."

"Your Honor, we won't have to find him if we're simply permitted to introduce the tape."

"I bet Mr. Miller's going to have something to say about that, aren't you?"

I take this as an invitation to state my piece. "We would object to that. Without Mr. Ga—Popowski to authenticate it, the tape recording is hearsay."

"Not necessarily, your Honor," Pavin says. "We can put Special Agent McNiven on the stand to testify the tape was on Mr. Popowski's phone, and we have Mr. Popowski's sworn statement that it's his voice on the tape."

"Your Honor . . ." I say, but she waves her hand.

"No need, Mr. Miller. Mr. Pavin, it's not going to fly.

Anyone could have used the phone, and the affidavit is hearsay too, so that can't be used to corroborate another piece of hearsay. I wish you well in your search for the elusive Mr. Popowski. Now, Mr. Miller, do you want to be heard on the issue of the trial date?"

The fact that the government temporarily lost Gates-Popowski gives me a reason to support Ohlig's desire for an early trial. Given time, the FBI will eventually track him down.

"The twenty-ninth of November is fine for us," I tell her.

"Very good," she says, now looking down at some papers, most likely for her next case. She turns her gaze toward us again. "Gentlemen, and you too Ms. Sloane, I will see you all here on Tuesday, November 29th. Have a happy Thanksgiving, everyone."

We are all silent as we leave the courtroom and during the elevator ride downstairs. It's an unspoken rule of court—like not talking to your pitcher if he carries a no-hitter past the sixth inning—that you don't comment on a court proceeding until you're safely out of the building. It's more than just superstition. Anyone who overhears what you say could be a member of the press or the judge's law clerk or someone from the U.S. Attorneys' Office.

"What?" Ohlig says to me when we've made it to the bottom step outside the courthouse. Even though it seems like he's trying to keep a straight face, he can't, and he breaks out a wide grin. "What I heard is that

Popowski came into some unexpected money, and headed south, somewhere remote."

It doesn't take a genius or having the FBI at your disposal to narrow down the possibilities regarding Popowski's sudden disappearance. He's either dead or in hiding.

On the bright side, I don't think he's dead. Pavin expressly stated they had evidence he was in hiding and was asking for time to find him. But if Popowski's dropped out of sight, he's either afraid to be found or fulfilling his end of a bargain. I reject fear as a motive out of hand. In my limited experience with these matters, killers don't threaten to kill witnesses—they just kill them. Besides which, whatever else he might be, Ohlig's not a killer, he's a money guy. So the far greater likelihood is that Ohlig paid for Popowski to take a long vacation to someplace warm, and without an extradition treaty.

"I don't want to know, Michael," I say, shaking my head. "And just so you know, it's not only because of what Judge Sullivan said about my becoming a co-conspirator. I'm still holding on to the idea that I'm representing an innocent man."

## 19

Abby and I go to dinner that night at Michael's, a well-known power scene for the media set. Like many midtown restaurants, getting a table for dinner is much easier than securing a spot for lunch.

"I'm going to have a glass of wine," I say, "so feel free to imbibe as well."

"Thanks, Dad," she says with deserved sarcasm.

"Should I order a bottle?"

"You should if you're going to drink most of it. Some of us are going to have to go back to work."

We each order by the glass. White for Abby, who orders the sea bass, a cabernet for me to go with the lamb chops.

"Are you still going to go to Florida for Thanksgiving?" she asks me after our entrees have arrived.

"I don't think so. As it is, I don't see how we're going to be able to get everything ready by the 29th. There's no way that's going to happen if we really have to be ready to go the Wednesday before that."

"What are you going to do then?"

"I don't know. We'll probably end up going to Elizabeth's family in Fairfield. It's not a great situation because I don't want my mother to be alone."

"You should invite her up."

"Yeah, I will, but I don't know if she'll come. She's going to complain about the travel and the cost—even though I'll pay, she'll still complain about it. It was one of the funny things about my parents. My dad, you could be sticking pins in his eyes and he wouldn't say a word. But my mom, if the temperature in a restaurant was two degrees warmer than she liked it, she'd tell the waiter she was sweltering. Don't get me wrong, I love my mother, but she's the kind of woman who can just suck the air out of a room."

"Well, you know what they say, Alex?"

"No, what do they say, Abby?"

"That boys marry their mothers."

I laugh. "Not me. If anything, I married my father. I suppose it's just further proof of what my mother says—I'm exactly like her, right down to picking the same type of spouse."

"I've seen your wife, and I'm pretty sure she doesn't look anything like your father. Unless he was a knock-out too."

"That's funny because Elizabeth just asked me if you two had ever met, and I told her that I didn't think you had."

"I don't think we were ever formally introduced, but I've checked her out at different events. You don't go unnoticed by the female associates, Alex, so I was curious about the type of woman you chose to marry."

"Really?"

"Yes, really. But enough flattery for your pretty little head; tell me more about how you married your father. This seems like the kind of stuff that could keep a shrink employed for some time."

I feel myself becoming choked up at the thought of my father. I wonder if he ever felt tempted by someone else the way I feel about Abby. For a moment I wish that he were alive so I could ask him, but even if he were, I know I wouldn't ever raise the issue, nor could I expect him to truly give me an honest answer, any more than I would tell Charlotte about my infatuation with Abby twenty years from now.

"It's not that she's like my father, per se," I begin to explain, "it's just that she . . . I'm not quite sure how to say this without it sounding bad, and I don't mean it to sound bad, but she's . . . distant like he was. Hard to read. You know, when I saw my mother when we went down to Florida, she asked me if I thought my father was happy. I told her I thought he was, but she said she had absolutely no idea, and then was going on about how sad that was because they were married forever and she didn't even know if he was happy. And the whole time I'm thinking, I would say the exact same thing about Elizabeth."

"Why do you think I'm still single?" she laughs, a lovely sound.

"That's actually a question I ask myself a lot." She gives me a serious look, and I worry for a moment that I'm out of line, but then she laughs again.

"I'm sure that's what you spend your days thinking about."

"Seriously, how is that you're not spoken for?"

"Maybe it's because I prefer to do my own speaking." Now I give her a look, prodding her to answer. "Okay, if you want a reason, I'll give you one, but I'm afraid it's not very interesting. In fact, it's probably the oldest tale known to womankind. Focus on work to the exclusion of all else, and then one day you're thirty-two, about to make partner, knock on wood"—and then she knocks on the table—"but alone."

"Well, I'm sure you're not destined to be single forever, and take it from an old married guy, when you do take the plunge, make sure it's with someone who understands what the life of a partner at Cromwell Altman is like."

"Why, Alex, I'm not sure which of the unspoken parts of that sentence interest me most."

I laugh. "Well, I think it's dangerous for me to go into any of them too deeply. But I will tell you that I had a recent discussion with Aaron about you, and things are looking very good."

"Really?"

"Really. So, even if Michael Ohlig goes down in flames, you won't."

"Well, let's hope I make it and he's acquitted. And, speaking of Michael, I wanted to ask you, do you still really believe he's innocent?"

"What do you mean?"

"Today you told him that you wanted to continue to believe we were representing an innocent man. But after the whole Popowski thing, you can't really believe that, can you?"

"I take it from the question that you don't."

"Don't tell me you think he's not behind Popowski's disappearance."

"No, but I don't think he killed him, if that's any consolation."

"Sending a witness into hiding isn't exactly the conduct of an innocent man."

"I don't know. I can envision a scenario where Ohlig feels like he's being persecuted, and he's trying to improve his hand. He figures he's innocent, so the ends justify the means. If Popowski was a rogue broker, he's going to lie under oath that Ohlig put him up to it. Who's obstructing justice more in that scenario—the government by giving Popowski immunity in return for his lying under oath, or Ohlig by paying for his vacation?"

Abby stares at me for a moment before saying, "Wow. You can just about convince yourself of anything, can't you? Batman would be very proud."

# 20

Elizabeth's expression is one that I've become all too accustomed to seeing lately. She's disappointed in me. I shouldn't be surprised this time—I've just told her that, with the trial starting right after Thanksgiving, we're not going to be able to spend the holiday with my mother in Florida as we had previously planned. So far she's kept her thoughts unspoken, apparently deciding that neither of us needs to articulate what we both already know.

I'm not so disciplined, however. "I know you wanted to go, and I wish we could, but there's just no way I can take four days off—or even *one* day off—right before trial. It's not fair to my client."

I shouldn't have said the last part, which revives the struggle we've been having for years—Elizabeth telling me that my devotion to work shortchanges her and Charlotte, and my countering that it's not as if she doesn't spend the money I earn. It's a battle that I know I'm on the wrong end of; Elizabeth would be very content with a simpler life than the one we lead.

"Alex," she says with a heavy sigh, "it's not so much that I wanted to go. I'm more than happy to spend Thanksgiving with my family in Connecticut. But think of it from your mother's point of view. It's the first Thanksgiving without your father."

"I know. I'm going to invite her up here. She can come with us to your parents'."

"It's not the same thing. She's not going to have any fun up here. Thanksgiving will be nice, but then on Friday you're going to run to the office and she's going to be stuck with me for the rest of the weekend. As it is, I'm probably going to want to go back up to Fairfield and spend some more time with my family, so she'll end up in Connecticut all weekend and not see you at all."

"I really don't have any choice," I say.

"Oh, please. Don't give me that. You always have a choice, Alex."

I call my mother the next day from the office. I don't know what my parents thought my work life was like, but neither of them ever called me at the office, and whenever I called them from work, it seemed to alarm them more than anything else. True to form, my mother's immediate reaction is to ask if anything is wrong. I tell her we're all doing fine, and then proceed to tell her what's wrong.

"The reason I'm calling is because the judge in one of my cases just threw us a curveball. I have a trial that's going to start right after Thanksgiving. The fact that it's been moved up like this means I can't take any real time off over Thanksgiving because I need to stay here to prepare. I'm going to take Thanksgiving day off, and we're going to go to Elizabeth's parents' house in Connecticut. I'd like you to come up here so we can still all be together. I'll buy a ticket for you, and you can fly up on Wednesday and then go back whenever you want."

My failure to tell my mother that the client in question is Michael Ohlig is intentional. Seeing that I've already put in an appearance in open court, the attorney-client privilege no longer bars me from telling her, or anyone else for that matter, that I represent Ohlig in a criminal case. But Ohlig specifically asked me not to say anything to her, and so I still have an obligation to my client to keep my mother in the dark.

"Thank you for the very generous offer," my mother replies, "but I haven't been feeling that well lately. I don't think I'm up to traveling on Thanksgiving weekend and the cold weather I could do without."

I want to remind her that *I* had been ready to travel Thanksgiving weekend, and I would have had a five-year-old in tow to make the trip that much more difficult, but I let it go. I'm now more concerned about my mother's health.

"You haven't mentioned not feeling well before, Mom. What's wrong?"

"Maybe I'm getting the flu." My mother's usual go-to illness, no matter what symptoms are actually present.

"Do you have a fever?"

"No, at least I don't think so. I'm just feeling blah. I've been having trouble sleeping, and I'm a little achy."

"Mom, it's pretty common for people to get depressed around the holiday and Dad's death has got to be wearing down on you."

"I don't mean to worry you, Alex. I'm going to be fine. As they say, this too shall pass."

"You should do what's best for you, but traveling won't be that bad and neither will the weather. I've traveled on that Wednesday and my flights have always been on time. I'll have a car pick you up at JFK. The whole trip, door-to-door, won't even take four hours."

"You know, I'd really like to see you, and the little one too, but I'm just not up to it right now."

"It's an open invitation, Mom. And if we don't see each other for Thanksgiving, we'll definitely come down there for Christmas."

There's silence on the line for a few moments, then I ask: "Are you sure everything is all right, Mom?"

"I'm fine," she replies. "Don't worry about me."

## 21

"This is Assistant United States Attorney Christopher Pavin," he says when I pick up the phone.

"I've got a case with a guy who has exactly that same name." My witticism is apparently lost on Pavin because all I hear is dead air. "What can I do for you, Christopher?"

"Classy move you and your client pulled with Popowski," he says, "too bad it didn't work."

Damn. He must have found Popowski. That makes things ten times worse than it was before. The old Watergate cliché—the cover-up is worse than the crime—is truer in criminal law than in politics. Even if Ohlig is innocent of the securities fraud charges, evidence that he was involved in Popowski's disappearance will earn Pavin a conviction on everything. Jurors think the same way Abby did—innocent men don't obstruct justice.

"I don't know what you're talking about," I say.

"We have a witness who's going to testify that your guy knew that Salminol was a dog stock, and he directed the sales force to pump it and then dump it, and that's a direct quote."

Pavin has overplayed his hand. Enough at least that I feel justified retaking some of the moral high ground.

"Be serious," I say. "Popowski was there for what, all

of two weeks? No one's going to believe a word that guy has to say."

"It's not Popowski," Pavin says calmly. I can tell he's been savoring that information, hoping to drop it on me for maximum effect, which is just what he's done. "I'll give the devil his due—Ohlig's hiding Popowski but good. But I'm not an all-my-eggs-in-one-basket kind of guy, no pun intended. Let's just say I've got someone who worked at OPM way more than two weeks."

"Who?" I ask, but already know the answer I'm going to get.

"When you get serious about taking a plea, I'll lay it all out for you. If not, you'll find out at trial. Have a good day, Mr. Miller."

"How's my favorite gravy train?" Joe Freeman asks.

"I'm good. My colleague, Abby Sloane, is with me and that's why I've got you on speaker."

"Okay. Let me bring in Maria if this is going to be a business call."

After Freeman's flunky joins us, I get down to brass tacks. "I hear there may be some dissent brewing in our joint defense club. Our mutual best friend, Chris Pavin—"

"You mean Assistant United States Attorney Christopher Pavin," Freeman says, laughing.

"Yes, that's him. He's telling me he's got a witness from inside OPM."

"He must have had FBI agents staking out every

beach in the Caribbean to find Popowski," Freeman says, chuckling again.

"He says it's not Popowski, but a real insider."

"I can tell you it's not Ruderman, if that's what you're asking."

"That's what I'm asking. I didn't think it would be your guy, but stranger things have happened."

"Trust, but verify. I get it."

"So, have you heard anything?"

"Nada."

"Be sure to tell me if that changes, okay?"

"Will do. Hey, when are you going to let me take you out to lunch? I'd like to thank you for sending the work my way."

"Out to lunch? I thought with what you're billing Ohlig on this thing, you'd buy me a car."

"It's my strict policy that on the first referral—no matter how large—all you get is lunch, but it'll be at a nice place. It's the second client when you get into automobile territory." Freeman laughs again. "Don't even ask what I do for the third one."

After Freeman, Abby and I go down the list of the other lawyers for whom Ohlig's footing the bill. Next comes Sheffield. "Not my guy," he tells us with some conviction. "He's as loyal as the day is long."

George Eastman's assistant tells me that her boss is on another line. "Ask him to call me back," I tell her. "It's about his client Eric Fieldston. It's important that I speak with him right away."

Our last call is to Jane McMahan, Allison Shaw's

lawyer. Based on Ohlig's leering at Abby, I had a pre-conceived notion of the type of woman Ohlig would hire as his assistant. McMahan has already confirmed my suspicions, at least in part. *Take what you're thinking and double it* was the way she put it after her first meeting with her client. But McMahan also told me that Allison Shaw swore the relationship was always absolutely professional.

After I explain the purpose of my call and McMahan conferences in her associate to participate, I'm assured that Shaw remains firmly in the tent. "I don't know what Ohlig's either giving her or holding over her, but unless something dramatically changes, Allison is the least of your worries. She's going down with the ship on this one."

As I'm hanging up the phone, my other line rings. It's the long buzz indicating an internal call. The caller ID tells me it's Aaron Littman.

I pick up the receiver. Aaron's not the kind of person you answer on speakerphone.

"Hello Aaron. How are you?"

"I just got a call from George Eastman."

My stomach drops. It makes sense that Eastman would reach out to Aaron first. He probably owes 70 percent of his practice to referrals from Aaron, and he's doing whatever he can to explain that he had no choice, in the hope that Aaron forgives him. It's ironic, actually. Aaron's quip about secretaries being more dangerous to the defense than CFOs notwithstanding, I knew from the outset that Fieldston was the guy who could hurt us the most if he flipped, and Aaron figured that Eastman was our best bet to prevent that from happening given his dependence on Aaron for work, and his well-known distrust of the government.

Aaron is now calling to tell me that he was wrong.

"I hope you're not calling with bad news," I say.

"You already know, then?"

"Pavin told me someone had gone to the dark side, so I've been calling the most likely suspects. When I called George Eastman, I was told he was on the phone. You call five minutes later, and so I figure it's not a co-incidence."

"He wanted to give me a heads-up first."

I mouth to Abby "It's Fieldston," and then say into the phone, "What did he say?"

"Usual B.S. He had no choice. He'd be disbarred or at least sued for malpractice if he didn't allow a client to take a get-out-of-jail-free card. He'll try to get his guy not to hurt us too badly, but now he's got almost no control since his client is taking his marching orders from the prosecutor."

"Did he tell you what his client is going to say when he testifies?"

"I didn't get into the particulars because I knew you'd need to hear it from him. Call George. He's waiting for your call."

When we reach Eastman's assistant the second time, she puts us right through.

"I just got off the phone with Aaron," Eastman says.

"Yeah, me too. But it's my case, George, so I need to hear it directly from you."

"Pick up, Alex. No offense, Abby."

I remove the handset from the cradle and turn off the speaker button. "Okay, go ahead."

"Thank you. I want to do this one-on-one."

"So tell me."

"Before we get into it, my client wants to express to your client that he's very sorry about this. He said I should tell you, and that you should tell Ohlig, that he knows Ohlig has always treated him and his family very generously and—and this is a direct quote—it breaks his heart to have to do this."

"Then why is he doing it?"

"He has no choice. Pavin was really turning the screws on him. Eric's got three young kids, and his wife is sick. She's got some type of woman's cancer or something. The stress of a trial, the prospect that his wife would die, and he'd be in prison . . . it was just too much."

"So he's going to commit perjury to save his own skin?"

As soon as the words leave my mouth, I know I've made a mistake. I should be treating Eastman like a hostile witness—kid gloves at first, so I get the information I want while he still thinks we're friends—and then hit him with the accusations at the end. Throwing a punch right out of the gate is just going to cause Eastman to shut down.

"You know I'd never let him lie on the stand. He

tells me it's the truth, and I have no reason to believe otherwise."

I start to backpedal in the hope that I can repair the damage. "I know this isn't your fault, George. I would have done the same thing if Pavin offered my guy immunity to testify against your guy. But give me a nibble here. What's Fieldston going to say?"

"Sorry," he says in a world-weary tone. "Pavin told me no-can-do. I actually had to get special dispensation from the Holy Pavin just to have this call with you right now, and he relented only when I told him you'd figure it out anyway when I stopped taking your calls, so the least he could do was to allow me to try to keep what was left of my professional reputation."

"Witness tampering if we do it; the word of God if Pavin does it."

"Something like that." Eastman's voice is heavy, as if he knows how unfair all of this is, although it isn't clear to me whether he feels most sorry for Ohlig or himself, knowing full well that I will do everything I can to get Aaron to cut off Eastman's referral spigot for this kick in the teeth.

After we've hung up, Abby asks, "So, what's he going to say?"

"On the advice of Christopher Pavin, George Eastman's taken a vow of silence, I'm afraid."

"Great."

"It doesn't matter. You know what Fieldston's going to say?" She's already nodding. "Whatever Pavin tells him to."

"So, what now?"

"We get Ohlig here tomorrow morning and start talking to him about a plea."

That evening, as I'm getting ready to go home, I call Abby. It's been our routine as of late for me to tell her before I leave for the day. At first they were status calls, talking about what we needed to do the next day, with a little small talk at the end. The last couple of weeks, however, the percentages have shifted the other way, and more recently I've been saying good-bye in person. The irony isn't lost on me that I used to call Elizabeth to tell her I was coming home, but now I usually don't.

"I'm heading out for the day," I say.

"What, no personal visit? Now I'm just a phone call?"

"Do you have a lot of stuff still to do?"

"Is that a trick question?"

"Want to share a ride home?"

"Can you give me a half hour? If you can't wait, that's fine. But I need to get an email out tonight or my boss is going to have my head."

"Your boss really sucks," I say, and then agree to meet her downstairs in half an hour.

After six, Cromwell Altman has a car service that maintains a lineup of Lincoln Town Car sedans, like a taxi stand at the airport. You just get in the first one and tell the driver where you're heading, and he hands you a voucher so the client is charged for the ride.

Abby and I pile into the back of the first car on the line. It's as telling as anything else about where we stand with each other that Abby doesn't ask why I'd want to share a car home with her given that we live on opposite sides of the park.

"Two stops," I tell the driver. "The first is to Riverside and 88th. Then you'll go crosstown to take me home to 80th and Park."

The feeling in the back of the car reminds me of that evening after Peter Luger's. I'm specifically conscious of my hands, so much so that, not knowing what to do with them, I clasp them in each another. Abby is apparently suffering from the same dilemma because her hands are in the same position.

The car pulls up to Abby's building. Just like before, I get out of the car first. Unlike the last time, however, I extend my hand to help her out of the car.

We stand face-to-face, still holding hands. I feel almost as if a magnetic force is pulling me closer to her. *Only one kiss, and that's it,* I tell myself, although even as I think it, I know it's a lie. Once we kiss, I'll want more.

"Good night," I finally say, somehow able to get the words out before acting on my impulse.

"Good night," she replies, smiling as if she heard everything that was in my mind.

I must have the worst poker face on earth because the moment Elizabeth sees me, she says, "Someone looks very happy."

"Just glad to be home," I say. "A tough day."

She's sitting up in bed, reading, and looks at me suspiciously. "What happened?"

"For starters, the one guy we knew could bury us—Ohlig's second in command—has cut a deal with the prosecution. So, we're pretty much dead in the water now."

"I'm sorry, Alex. I'm sure you'll figure something out."

"I don't see how. The guy's going to say that Ohlig is guilty. It's pretty hard to come back from that."

"What does Ohlig say about it?"

"I haven't told him. I called him and asked him to come up tomorrow so we can talk face-to-face. You know, he doesn't even ask me what's going on. It's the weirdest thing. I can't figure out if he's just super cool or delusional."

"Do you think he's going to take a plea now?"

I smile at her, impressed at her understanding of trial strategy. "I don't know. I'm going to recommend it, but he's been swearing he's innocent from day one, and I think he's so far out there that there's no coming back."

# 22

"So, you've called me into the Batcave," Ohlig says as soon as he's settled into my guest chair. "And now I'm here. Will Batgirl be joining us? Or is Abby more like Robin?"

"I thought we should do this just the two of us," I say, ignoring his attempt at humor. I also leave out that the reason it's just me and him is because Abby's presence immediately brings out Ohlig's Mr. Happy-Go-Lucky persona.

"Okay, you've built your suspense. What's so important that the phone is no longer an adequate means of communication?"

"Fieldston's flipped."

Ohlig gives a weak smile, an attempt to show this is nothing he can't handle, I suspect. Then, in keeping with that theme, he says, "I had my money on Ruderman. I always thought that guy was a weasel."

With his punch line delivered, the smile that's the usual fixture on his face recedes, replaced by the expression that defines most people in Ohlig's circumstances—the grim sadness of someone confronting his mortality for the first time. Ohlig looks away from me, his focus directed over my shoulder, somewhere out the window.

"I just can't believe it," he says, now more in regret

than in anger, and not really to me as much as into space. "I mean, Eric was like family. I know that people say that all the time, but I've known the guy for twenty-five years. He came to work for me right out of college. I taught him this business. I paid for him to get an MBA, for Christ's sake."

I shake my head in sympathy. "Don't be too hard on him. If Pavin had offered you immunity to turn on Fieldston, I would have told you to take it."

"But I wouldn't have."

I assume Ohlig's saying that he wouldn't lie to save his own skin. But it could be that he wouldn't betray someone to save his own skin even if it required only that he tell the truth. It's one of those pronouncements that's easiest made when it's not going to be tested, however.

"This changes things," I tell him.

"No, it doesn't," he tells me.

"Michael, we need to focus on reality for a moment. All that stuff about the presumption of innocence they teach you in fifth grade—you can forget it. It just doesn't exist. Jurors assume the same thing you do when someone's arrested—that they're probably guilty. Pavin's going to show them that you made more money than they can even contemplate exists, and in the process that you destroyed the life savings of thousands of people, most of whom were widows and retirees. And then, to top it all off, Eric Fieldston—the person at OPM you most trusted—will swear under oath that although he loves you like a father, his conscience requires that he tell the truth, and the truth is that he knows for a fact that you knew Salminol was a total sham."

Ohlig shakes his head. It's a soft gesture, suggesting he absolutely can't fathom how it's come to this.

"I thought Salminol was the real thing," he says without emotion. "That's why I bought it for myself, and that's why my company was selling it." His words get stronger, picking up some speed as he works his way through a speech I get the sense he's delivered before. "My business is not selling blue chip stocks, it's finding the next big thing. We were selling Microsoft before anybody. I remember the questions. 'Windows?' How can a computer have windows in it, so you can reach inside?' That is actually what they would say, no joke. You want to know how many of them retired early because we sold them Microsoft? Okay, so I was wrong on Salminol. I never claimed to be able to predict the future."

"Michael, with all due respect, your company bought Salminol at a dime and was selling it at ten times that much. Then when the position was completely sold, the market dried up, and the stock crashed to zero."

"Ah, now that sounds like the government talking, not my lawyer. What actually happened is that the price kept going up, and we sold at the ask. I know we were a large seller of the stock, but that's not unprecedented for us. You forget, I was still personally holding four million bucks of the stuff. I was waiting like all the investors for the secondary. Then, literally out of nowhere, the company files for bankruptcy. Everyone tried to get out, which is why we couldn't sell the clients out of it. We tried. There were just no buyers. I went down the tubes with every other investor."

I'll say this, Michael Ohlig can sell it. He looks as sincere as I can imagine a person could be. It reinforces just how strong he'd be as a witness in his own defense.

"A jury is not going to be sympathetic. It's going to look to them like you're just fulfilling the company's motto—getting rich on other people's money."

"Motto? Where'd you get that from? OPM stands for Ohlig, Pamela and Michael."

I don't say anything. I've believed in Ohlig's innocence when no else did, and I'm wondering if my suspicions now are a fleeting lack of faith or the moment when I come to realize what Abby has thought now for weeks.

"Hey, I need you to level with me, Alex. Your father knew me for more than forty years, and never once questioned my honesty. You and I have been working together for what, three months? Have I ever said anything that turned out not to be true?" I still don't answer. "Answer me, goddammit. The tapes all show I'm telling the truth."

"Not all of them."

"Popowski? C'mon, you know that's bullshit."

"And now Eric Fieldston."

"More bullshit. Fieldston is lying to save his own ass."

"At this point, Michael, only you and God know for sure whether you're innocent. Besides which, the truth doesn't really matter anyway. A trial isn't about whether you're actually innocent or guilty, but about what twelve people who aren't smart enough to get out of jury duty believe. And trust me, the two are not the same thing by any stretch of the imagination. Even before Fieldston flipped, an acquittal was, at best, a fifty-fifty shot, and that might have been too generous in our favor. Now with Fieldston against us, the reality is that our odds of an acquittal are considerably longer." I pause, allowing this to sink in, before hitting him with the stuff that's really going to sting. "I've never dwelled on the worst-case scenario with you because, frankly, you never ask, and I've always thought you'd consider my bringing it up as a sign that I lacked faith."

"Just spit it out, Alex," he says, looking as if the last thing he wants to hear is any more of this speech.

"Okay . . . here it comes. If you're convicted, given the amount of money involved and our misfortune in pulling Judge Sullivan, who's nothing if not tough on white collar crime, you'll probably get at least twenty years. Even if by some stroke of luck Judge Sullivan takes pity on you, she's still going to sentence you to somewhere between seven and ten years. Either way, it would feel like a life sentence."

I expect him to say something. Another protestation of innocence, or maybe that he intends to live much longer than ten years. Anything. But he's silent. It's as if he wants me to say everything I have prepared before he commits to a position.

"Pavin doesn't have a whole lot of experience in front

of a jury," I continue, "and he's never been in a high-profile case before. That leads me to believe that he'd be more than happy to have you take a plea rather than run the risk of losing his first big case. I think I'll be able to get him to go down to five years, maybe four. The bottom line is that you can either spend three years in prison and then some time in a halfway house, and then enjoy your retirement, or run the risk you'll very likely die in jail."

I've had more than a few clients cry at this point, the moment when they realize it's all over and they're going away, thoughts of rampant sodomy filling their heads. Some start talking about suicide and one or two have fired me on the spot. I have no doubt Ohlig will not fall into any of these groups.

"That's what you'd do? You'd plead guilty to something you didn't do?" His voice is calm, as if he's conducting a survey.

"Let me start a discussion so we can see where Pavin's bottom line is on this."

"Answer my question, Alex," he says with insistence. "Would you plead guilty to something knowing you're innocent?"

It's an occupational hazard of a criminal defense lawyer to put yourself in your client's shoes. Every client's knee-jerk reaction is to claim that he would never—*never*—falsely admit guilt, even if it meant avoiding jail. The wisdom of adhering to that principle is reinforced by the movies and on television because when it's scripted, justice always prevails. Real life, unfortunately, has a way of sometimes ending the other way around. As a result, I've long ago considered the practice of criminal law to be less about the pursuit of justice, and more about risk management.

"If it were me, I'd plead," I tell him. "I don't see how anyone can rationally risk spending the rest of their life in jail when the alternative, although certainly difficult, is doable. It's just that simple. It's too risky to go to trial, even if you're innocent."

He nods while I say this, as if he's actually considering my analysis. Then, with a particularly heavy voice, he says, "You disappoint me, Alex. I thought we were more alike than that."

I have no earthly idea why he thinks we share any similarities. We have disagreed on most every decision I've made so far. If anything, he should be surprised if we were in accord about his decision to head to trial, despite its risks.

"I don't want to have this discussion again," Ohlig says. "I'm innocent and I'm not going to admit to something I didn't do."

"Okay," I say.

"No, not okay, Alex. Call me old-fashioned, but I need to know that my lawyer believes in my innocence. So, tell me, straight out. Do you?"

"I do," I say, and much to my own surprise, I actually still believe it.

# 23

I had been hoping to sleep in a little on Sunday, but wasn't too surprised when that didn't happen. I try to get out of bed without waking Elizabeth, but she stirs, and then realizing that I'm awake, she becomes concerned that I'm going back on my promise to spend the day with her.

"You're not going to work," she says, "right?"

"I told you that I wouldn't. I'm just going to make some coffee."

"Stay in bed. It's your birthday. I'll make breakfast. Or we can go out."

"It's still early, Elizabeth. You sleep. I can make coffee myself. And I promise, I'll still be here when you get up."

"Happy birthday, sweetheart," she says, and then turns to go back to sleep.

As soon as I'm out of the bedroom, I reach for my BlackBerry. I don't have any emails, but I have a voicemail. I can feel myself smile and my heart rate picks up. I speed-dial my voicemail, cursing to myself when I can't get a signal and the call fails. On the second try, I'm in, and after typing in my PIN, I hear the electronic voice confirm that the unlistened-to message is from Abby's extension.

She actually sings "Happy Birthday," the full song.

When she's finished, she says in a serious voice, "Alex, I really hope you have a great birthday. I also hope that I get to see you today sometime. I understand if you decide to take the day off, but that doesn't mean that I'm not going to try to bribe you. I have a little present for you and brought in some candles and two white-and-white cookies, which I know are your favorite. If you can't come in, at least give me a call so I can wish you a happy birthday in person," she chuckled. "Or at least over the phone in person. Guess where I'll be. Bye."

White-and-white cookies have become just one of many inside jokes Abby and I now share. They are the classic black and whites, made famous by that Seinfeld episode, but without the chocolate side. Abby and I have gone to the coffee shop downstairs so often that she claims she's going to need to schedule an intervention to get me to kick the habit.

I listen to the message a second time, and then press the prompt to allow me to leave a return message. "Hi," I whisper, so Elizabeth won't hear, even though I'm certain she wouldn't be able to hear even if I spoke in my normal voice. "Thanks so much for your message. I'm definitely going to try to come in today. Probably before dinner, maybe four-ish. I won't be able to stay long, but, as you know all too well, I can't resist a white-and-white cookie. Bye."

I make coffee and read the paper, enjoying the quiet at home, which I rarely experience. It is somewhat short-lived, however. Even though Charlotte went to bed late last night, she's up by a quarter after eight. Thankfully, she goes straight into our bedroom to crawl into bed with Elizabeth.

At eight-thirty, Charlotte comes bounding out of the bedroom screaming, "Happy birthday, Daddy!" Elizabeth is a few steps behind her, undoubtedly having just reminded Charlotte.

"Can I give you your present now, Daddy?"

"Let's do this, Charlotte," Elizabeth answers. "Why don't you watch some television in Mommy's room, while Daddy and I have coffee. Then, when it's time for breakfast, we'll do presents."

This is more than a fair compromise for Charlotte and she runs into the bedroom. Elizabeth and I share a laugh, and then Elizabeth goes to the coffeepot.

"Can I warm yours up?" she asks.

"Sure."

When Elizabeth walks over to pour my cup, she kisses me on the top of my head. "Happy birthday, Alex. I'm so glad we're going to spend the day together."

I take a deep breath, which Elizabeth knows is a non-verbal cue that I'm withholding. I'm sure she also knows that it means I'm considering going into the office, but she pretends otherwise.

"What?" she asks.

"Nothing. We're going to spend today together, but I'm going to have to go into the office for a little bit. That's all."

"You promised, Alex."

"I promised that I'd spend the day with you and

Charlotte, and I will. It's not going to matter if I show up at the office for an hour. I'll meet with the team, make sure that they're not doing anything that's a waste of time, and then I'll come right home."

Now it's her turn to sigh deeply. I understand what she means, just as clearly as she did with me. She can't believe that I'm going to go into the office today, and she knows that she's not going to be able to change my mind.

I take advantage of the momentary silence to change the subject. "Last week, it was James Winters's fiftieth birthday," I say. "He's a partner in the real estate group, and the firm had a little party for him. When I wished him a happy birthday, I told him that it was my birthday in a week, but it wasn't a big birthday like fifty—instead I was only turning thirty-five. He looked at me and said, 'I'll let you in on a little secret. Thirty-five is the only birthday that really matters.' I laughed and asked him why, and he said, 'Because after you're thirty-five, people expect you to know what you're doing.'"

Elizabeth smiles politely at the punch line, which I'm sure she anticipated from the beginning of the story. "So, do you think what he said is true?" I ask.

"I don't know, Alex. I guess I'll find out in two years if people expect me to know what I'm doing."

"Fair enough."

"I'll tell you one thing, though."

I know by the fact that she's requiring me to ask her what the one thing is that I'm not going to like the answer.

"What?"

"If the first few hours of your thirty-sixth year are any indication, I don't think you know what you're doing yet."

When the phone rings, Elizabeth says I should let it go to voicemail. I check the caller ID before answering. It's not Abby, but it's still a call I need to take.

"It's my mother," I say to Elizabeth, and then, after picking it up, "Hi Mom."

"Happy birthday."

"Thanks. How are you?"

"Not so good."

"What's wrong?"

"Well, I just heard some very disturbing news."

"What?"

"I just heard from a friend that Michael Ohlig is about to go on trial for securities fraud, and that you're his lawyer. Alex, how could you keep something like that from me?"

"I'm sorry, Mom. He asked me not to tell you."

"Alex, I'm your mother."

"I know. But I've got professional obligations, and one of them is that I can't break a client's confidences. I thought about turning the case down, just so I wouldn't have any secrets from you, but I thought you'd be more upset if I did that. And, even if I didn't represent him, I still wouldn't be able to tell you about his situation. Besides, I thought that it would make Dad happy that I was doing it and, in a weird way, it makes me feel closer to Dad when I'm with Michael."

"I'm very hurt that you didn't tell me, Alex."

"I'm sorry. Please don't be mad at me about this."

"When my friend told me about it, she was just flabbergasted that I didn't already know. I felt like such a fool."

I wonder how many times I can say "I'm sorry" in one conversation, but I do it again.

There's enough silence for her to get her point across that she's still upset, and then she says, "I don't want to fight with you, Alex. Especially on your birthday. I can't believe it's been thirty-five years. When did that happen?"

"It certainly goes by quickly. I can't believe Charlotte's in kindergarten already."

"How is she?"

"She's great. She just gave me a bunch of pictures she drew as my gift."

"That's nice. What did Elizabeth give you?"

"Nothing yet. We're going to lunch today at this place we all like, especially Charlotte. It's kind of a birthday tradition and we all order milk shakes. And then we may go to the movies or something. There's a new Disney movie Charlotte wants to see." I chuckle. "It actually won't be that different than Charlotte's birthday, come to think of it."

My mother doesn't say anything in response and so there's another long period of silence. "I miss Dad," I say. "I miss him every day, but it's sad not being able to talk to him on my birthday, you know?"

"I know. I get so mad at him sometimes because he

should have taken better care of himself. I begged him to see a doctor and he just never would."

"I'm not sure it mattered in the end. I mean, what could an annual physical have done for him anyway?"

"I know. That's what I tell myself too. That once someone's gone, it really doesn't matter why, right?"

"Right," I say. "So, have you reconsidered about Thanksgiving? You can still come up. It's not too late, although by Thursday it will be."

"No . . ." And then her tone changes, back to anger. "You know, Alex, I'm such an idiot. I just put it together. It's Michael Ohlig's case that's keeping you in New York, isn't it?"

"It is," I say with a sigh. "The trial starts a week from Tuesday. He's going to be in New York on Monday to work with us this week, but we're definitely going to take off Thanksgiving."

"Is Michael going to be with you for Thanksgiving?"

"No. It's just Elizabeth's family. And you, of course. Anyway, I think he's going back to Florida to spend it with his family."

"Can you do me a favor, please?"

"Sure, Mom."

"Don't tell him that I know. He obviously didn't want me to know, so I don't want to upset him. I imagine he's got a lot on his mind right now."

"Okay. I won't tell him. We'll invoke mother-son privilege."

"Thanks," she says with a weak chuckle. "Do you think he's going to go to jail?"

Most people ask if my clients are innocent. My mother is much more practical, I guess.

"I hope not," I say. "It's my job to make sure he doesn't."

"No, really. Do you think he will?"

"Really, I don't know, Mom. I think he's innocent though, if that matters."

"If he's convicted, will he go to jail?"

There's no reason to lie to her. "Yes," I say flatly.

"For how long?"

"I don't know."

"Will it be like a year or a long time?"

"A long time."

The day plays out almost exactly as I told my mother. We go out to lunch to EJ's, a diner (although it proclaims itself a luncheonette) near our apartment that Charlotte calls her favorite restaurant in the entire world. And we all order milk shakes—black and white for Charlotte, peanut butter and jelly for me (which actually isn't as bad as it sounds), and strawberry for Elizabeth.

Then on to the Disney movie, which turns out to be a Pixar film. I doze off slightly in the middle without missing any of the story, which has something to do with secret agent rodents and a plot to destroy all the cheese in France.

After the movie, Charlotte asks when we're going to have cake. Elizabeth says she still needs to get it, as well as "some other things," which I can only assume also includes a birthday gift for me.

"This sounds like a good time for us to separate then," I say. "Why don't you both run your errands, and I'll put in a quick appearance at the office, and then we can meet back at the apartment. No later than six," I add.

Elizabeth still doesn't look happy about this plan, even though it's clear she has an hour or so of things to do that I cannot attend, but I understand that she'd prefer I sit in the apartment and watch television rather than go to the office. "Okay," she finally relents.

I call the war room from the cab and tell Abby that I should be at the office in ten minutes.

"Let's meet in the empty conference room next to the war room," she says. "That way none of the temps will bother us and there's no chance we'll destroy something."

"It sounds like this is going to be a messy celebration," I say, clearly flirting.

"You never know," she says in a similar tone.

I find her in the war room. She tells me to go next door while she gathers up some things.

When she walks into the conference room, she closes the door behind her. In one hand is a brown paper shopping bag and the other holds a wrapped gift about the size of a cell phone.

"First," she says, reaching into the bag, "a toast."

She pulls out a full-sized bottle of champagne.

"La Fleur," I say. "Fancy."

"Only the best for you, Alex. You know that." She

hands me the bottle to open. "This was the part I thought might get messy," she says, nodding at the champagne bottle. "I don't know what you were thinking, Mr. Mind-in-the-Gutter."

I laugh. "You would think my mind was in the gutter only if your mind was in the gutter."

The champagne bottle opens with a loud pop, but I catch the cork without allowing it to shoot across the room. I'm not able to stop the champagne from spilling out of the top, and Abby grabs the bottle from my hand and drinks the overflow.

"Nice catch," I say.

"I hate when even a drop goes wasted."

She reaches back into the bag and pulls out two plastic champagne flutes and hands them to me. After I pour each of us a glass, she raises hers to eye level and says, "To the birthday that changes everything."

I told Abby about Winters's comment right after, maybe even during, the party. "You remembered?" I say.

"Of course I remembered. What, you don't think I'm listening to you when you talk?"

I touch my glass to hers, and we both take a sip.

She pulls out two white-and-white cookies along with two candles—one in the shape of the number 3, and the other in the shape of the number 5. Then she pushes the cookies together, so that they form a figure eight, and places a candle in each cookie.

"I have to tell you, I was a little worried about running afoul of the fire code if I went all out with the candles, so I thought that this would do the trick. Oh, I forgot . . ." She reaches back into her bag a second time and pulls out a lighter.

She carefully lights both candles and then favors me with a full-on smile. "Get ready now because I'm going to sing again." She sings "Happy Birthday," this time channeling Marilyn Monroe, and when she's finished I'm applauding as if I've never heard anything so beautiful.

"Time to make a wish and blow," she says. "You know how to do that, right?"   *Lauren Bacall*

I'm tempted to tell her that she's morphed from Marilyn to Mae West, but I'm preoccupied by the request. My normal go-to wish is the health and happiness of my family. Perhaps I should include myself in the equation this year. Maybe I should wish that thirty-five is when I finally do know what I'm doing. Then again, part of me just wants to wish that Abby and I make love soon. Without consequences, of course.

I don't settle on any one wish but blow out the candles anyway. "But wait, there's more," she says excitedly, like the infomercial barkers. "The present."

The box is light, and I have no idea what it might be. "Can I open it now?" I ask.

"Of course."

They're cufflinks. But more than that, they're cufflinks in the shape of the Batman symbol.

"I love them."

"Really?"

"Really. I now know what I'm wearing on the first day of the trial."

We eat the cookies and finish the champagne in our glasses. Abby begins to pour me another glass, but I stop her.

"I can't go home drunk. I told Elizabeth that duty called, which is why I was coming in."

"That means we're still going to have to celebrate your birthday for real. Okay?"

"Okay," I say.

"Promise?"

"Yes, I promise."

My day ends in bed with Elizabeth. "Did you have a nice birthday?" she asks.

"I did. Thank you."

"No need to thank me, Alex. Not until I give you your present, anyway."

She reaches under her pillow and hands me a tie box with the Barney's logo on the front, and a white satin ribbon around the corners. Inside is a blue and white striped tie.

"I thought you could use a new lucky tie for the trial," she says. "I didn't want to get you anything too flashy. I hope you like it."

"I do," I say to her, but can't help thinking that I like the cufflinks more.

# 24

The Wednesday before Thanksgiving, Cromwell Altman lets everyone go at 2 P.M. to get a jump on the long weekend. Michael Ohlig, however, had another idea. It's now close to five, and Abby and I are still in the war room with him, no end in sight.

Some clients don't want to be involved in their defense and treat their lawyers the way they do their auto mechanics—they don't need to know what's broken or how to fix it, so long as when they get the car back everything runs properly. Others want to be active participants, talking over strategy, scribbling questions during cross-examination.

It came as no surprise to me that Ohlig fell into the latter camp, but he brought it to an entirely new level by demanding to hear my draft opening statement. I've done it twice already this afternoon, with Ohlig offering critiques on everything from the word choice to the cadence of my voice.

Some of this makes sense, given that cases are often won and lost during opening statements. Jurors are like quick-drying cement. Most make up their minds prior to seeing a single piece of evidence or hearing from any witnesses, and then they conform the evidence to their already made-up minds about the verdict, dismissing as unreliable whatever contradicts their initial determinations.

For the defense, and especially for a defendant who is adamant about testifying on his own behalf, it's therefore imperative that the jury wait for this testimony. Usually the only way to do that is to promise them during the opening that the defendant will take the stand. The risk, however, is precisely what Aaron warned me about. If you commit during opening statements to having the defendant testify, he better damn well end up testifying, or the jury is left believing you've lied to them, and like women scorned, jurors who have been deceived demonstrate considerable fury when it comes to rendering verdicts.

"One more time," Ohlig tells me.

I look at my watch, more for effect than to see the time. "This is going to be the last time. And I'm just doing the last part again."

"That's my favorite part anyway," Ohlig says, winking at me, or more likely, Abby.

I stand as if I'm in court, clear my throat, and then take a deep breath. "Ladies and gentlemen of the jury, I know what you're thinking. You wouldn't be human if you weren't. It's the question on each and every one of your minds. Is the man sitting here"—and then I point—"Michael Ohlig, guilty of these crimes? I'm going to tell you the answer." Dramatic pause. "He is innocent. And I'm not the only one who thinks so. Judge Sullivan thinks so. Even Mr. Pavin thinks so. And, by law, every single one of you *must* think so. And that's because Mr. Ohlig is innocent until proven guilty, and at this point there has been no proof of Mr. Ohlig's guilt.

"Over the next few days you're going to hear various witnesses, but not one of them—not one—knows what was in Mr. Ohlig's mind. They can speculate after the fact about whether Salminol was a good investment, but they can't tell you the only thing that matters in this case—whether at the time OPM was selling Salminol, Michael Ohlig knew it was a worthless stock such that he was intentionally defrauding his investors.

"It will be only at the end of this trial that you will hear from the one witness who knows the truth." Another dramatic pause. "And that is Michael Ohlig himself. He is going to take the stand in his own defense, place his hand on the Bible, and swear before God and all of you that he is completely innocent of these charges. We—Michael Ohlig and I—ask you to remember that until he has the opportunity to deny these charges under oath, you *must* believe he is innocent. If you do that, we have no doubt that *after* he testifies you will reach the only verdict that is reasonable in this case, and that is that Michael Ohlig is not guilty."

"Bravo!" Ohlig shouts.

I bow in an exaggerated fashion, my hand stretched out in front of me, like a Broadway actor taking a second curtain call. Even Abby is clapping, although I'm sure it's to join in the theatrics of the moment and not because she finds the closing flourish particularly praiseworthy, or at least not any more than it was the other times I did it this afternoon.

All of this cheering is quickly drowned out by the ringtone of Ohlig's BlackBerry, which, aptly enough, is to the tune of Sinatra's "My Way." He immediately breaks eye contact with me, and he reaches for the device on the table beside him. He answers it right before Sinatra can lament about the few regrets he's had.

"I've got to take this," Ohlig says. He gets up and walks to the back of the room, going as far away from us as he can, which still isn't more than fifteen feet.

I look across the table at Abby, and she rolls her eyes at me. I know what she means—Ohlig's been keeping us here, and now he's making us wait.

"I'm sorry too," Ohlig whispers into the phone. "Yes, I'll be home tonight."

All of a sudden I go from being annoyed that he has interrupted our meeting to feeling uncomfortable about listening in on his call, which I assume is with his wife, in part because I can't imagine Michael Ohlig apologizing to anyone else. He gestures that he'll be only a minute more.

Ohlig looks around the room and I can almost read his mind. He wants to find a place where he can have some privacy for this call.

"Michael," I whisper, "would you like us to leave you alone for a few minutes?"

His eyes open more widely, a signal of his exasperation, and then he says, sotto vocce, "Would you mind? Just for a few minutes?"

Abby and I leave him with his call, stepping out into the hallway and shutting the door to the conference room behind us. "I'm glad I'm not married," Abby says, laughing.

"He's a braver man than me," I reply. "It's the busiest travel day of the year and he still hasn't made his way to the airport. No wonder his wife is pissed."

I'm about to say more when Ohlig peeks his head out of the room. "I gotta go," he says. "Pamela is concerned that my flight is going to be overbooked or cancelled or something and I won't make it home before Thanksgiving."

"I'll call you a car," Abby says.

"Thanks, but it will be quicker if I just grab a cab."

"Okay," I say, "but it might be tough getting one in midtown at this time."

"Don't worry about me." He flashes the trademark smile that says that he's not worried, so no one else should be.

Not five minutes after Ohlig's left the building, I ask Abby if she's ready to call it a night as well.

"Might as well," she says. "Meet you downstairs in five?"

Since the first time we shared a car home together, it has become our daily routine. Once Abby asked if I had concerns that the firm's car service would show that we shared a car each night, but I told her that I was sure Aaron Littman didn't review the taxi slips to see if the lawyers were taking the most direct route home. "Besides," I said, "it's cheaper for the client than two cars. Everybody's a winner."

"I'm going to miss you tomorrow," Abby says to me when the car turns onto the West Side Highway.

"Me too," I say. I can't remember the last day we didn't see each other, now that we're pulling seven-day weeks. "Promise me you'll be back in the office on Friday?"

"I promise," she laughs. "But that begs the question. How will I survive a day without you, Alex?" She says this with a mocking chirp to her voice, but I don't think she's joking. Then, again, maybe I'm projecting because that's how I feel.

# 25

I wake up shortly after sunrise on the day after Thanksgiving, following an evening when I had difficulty falling asleep. I was hoping the extra helping of turkey might give me a break from my recent insomnia, but no such luck.

Elizabeth has recently begun suggesting I see someone about my sleep problems. So far I've dismissed the idea by saying I don't have the time to be on a shrink's couch, and by pointing out the professional benefits for me to be awake for twenty hours a day leading up to the trial. Besides, I know all too well the source of my inner turmoil.

As soon as I've finished brushing my teeth, I'm dialing into my voicemail, as I do every morning. I have a message, which causes me to smile as if it were an involuntary reflex. The message turns out to be the same one from last night, which I've already listened to, more than once, actually.

It's from Abby, of course. She says she was just calling to say goodnight and hoped I had a happy Thanksgiving. She ended the message saying, "Thank God we're going to see each other tomorrow. I feel like I'm going through Alex withdrawal." I should erase it, but I like to keep Abby's most current message, just so I can hear her voice at will.

I could go right to the office, but it's going to be a late night and Abby won't be arriving until at least ten. Most likely because I'm feeling guilty about being so happy to see Abby, I decide to make breakfast for Elizabeth and Charlotte. That inner turmoil thing again.

It isn't long after I've started mixing the pancake batter that I hear Charlotte's soft patter coming from her room. She's wearing a pink nightgown with Sleeping Beauty on the front and holding by the ears the stuffed toy rabbit that is her usual bedtime companion.

"Good morning, sweet Charlotte bear." I struggle for a moment to recall the bunny's name. "And good morning to you too, Belle."

"What are you doing, Daddy?"

"I'm making pancakes."

"Why?"

"Because I thought you and Mommy might like pancakes for breakfast."

"Can you make a smiley face on them with chocolate chips, like Mommy?"

"Okay," I say, fighting the impulse to tell her that chocolate chips for breakfast isn't the most nutritious start to the day. "Does Belle want some pancakes too?"

"No," Charlotte guffaws in a low voice that I love. "Belle's a baby bunny. She doesn't eat pancakes."

"Well, maybe she'd like to try them," I continue. "Or should I serve up some carrots?"

"Daddy," Charlotte says, now sounding a bit annoyed with me, "Belle is pretend. She doesn't eat anything."

"I'm sorry, sweetie. I didn't know."

Charlotte doesn't acknowledge the apology. Instead, apparently satisfied her first basic need of existence— food with chocolate—will be met this morning, she proceeds to her second basic need and asks if she can watch television. When I tell her yes, she runs into the living room.

I am pouring the last of the batter into the pan when I hear Elizabeth giving Charlotte her good-morning hug and kiss. "Mommy, Mommy," Charlotte exclaims, "do you want to watch SpongeBob with me?"

"Let me say good morning to Daddy first, okay?"

"Okay," Charlotte says, sounding disappointed.

"Am I still dreaming, or are those pancakes I smell?" Elizabeth says when she enters the kitchen.

"They are indeed. I've been thinking that the quality of my life should be defined by the quality of the pancakes in it." This is a line from a movie we saw on television a few weeks before.

"An excellent idea," Elizabeth answers. "You should eat pancakes all the time if you want," she says, continuing the reference.

"Charlotte requested hers with chocolate chips for the eyes, nose, and mouth. Is that the way you want them too?"

Elizabeth laughs. "No, I'll just have mine with some coffee, if that's okay."

Ten minutes later the pancakes are ready. "Charlotte, breakfast," I call out. "There's a pancake here with your name on it."

Charlotte runs into the kitchen and stares disappointedly at her pancakes. "It doesn't have my name on it. It just has a smiley face."

I instinctively look at Elizabeth and she has done the same toward me. "It's just an expression," Elizabeth says before I can. "It means that this pancake is for you."

"But if you'd like, I can put your name on a pancake," I add.

Charlotte doesn't answer, but Elizabeth is more polite. "These are great, Alex. Didn't Daddy do a good job making the pancakes, Charlotte?"

"Yes," Charlotte responds on cue. "These are the best pancakes I've ever had."

Elizabeth laughs. "It isn't going to get better than that."

*No,* I think to myself. *It isn't going to get better than that.*

As a thank-you for my cooking, Elizabeth offers to do cleanup, but I tell her that I'm happy to finish the job. When I'm done and come out into the living room, Charlotte is standing before the toy easel we bought her for her birthday. She is wearing one of my old T-shirts, which is what she uses as a smock, and it looks like Elizabeth is wearing one too.

My father used to say that you could tell the difference between a tennis player and someone who plays tennis by the way they hold a racquet. Those who were more than recreational players had a way of making it appear that the racquet was an extension of their arm.

I was a tennis player, my father told me on many an occasion, whereas he merely played tennis. Sometimes he also mentioned that Michael Ohlig was a tennis player too.

Elizabeth holds a brush in that same way, leaving no doubt that she's a painter, and not just someone who paints. But since Charlotte's birth, it's a sight I've rarely seen. In fact, I don't think Elizabeth's painted other than with our daughter since she was born. The last time I asked Elizabeth about it, which was more than two years ago, she said that she was just too busy, pointing to Charlotte as Exhibit One.

I excuse myself to take a shower. I've been under the water for only a few minutes when I hear a hard knock on the door.

"What?" I yell after turning off the water.

"Honey, open the door," Elizabeth says.

"I'm in the shower."

"I know. You need to get out of the shower and open the door, please." She says this forcefully, like when she commands Charlotte to take a time-out.

I pull the door open a crack and poke my lathered head through the small opening. "What? Can't I shower in peace?"

"Alex, there are two policemen here to see you," she says, looking frightened.

I'm done in thirty seconds. I dry off and put on a T-shirt and jeans to walk out to our living room, where I see that one of the policemen is actually a policewoman. She is much younger than her partner; so young, in fact, that I wonder if she might still be in training.

I wait, saying nothing for an awkward moment, assuming one of them will explain their presence. The female officer finally does the honors.

"I'm Officer Kenney and this is Officer Michaud. We've just explained to your wife that we received a call from the Palm Beach Sheriff's Department. Apparently they had your address, but no phone number. They want you to call them as soon as possible. You're supposed to ask for a Deputy John Gattia."

She hands me a business card, with the back facing me. On it, in red pen, someone has written *John Gattia—561-555-4242—Palm Beach*. I expect one of them to tell me why I should call the Palm Beach Sheriff's Department, but they act as if their mission is complete.

"What's this about?" I finally ask, although I might as well have said, *What did Michael Ohlig do now?*

"We honestly don't know, sir," the male officer replies.

I go into the bedroom and shut the door behind me. Looking at the back of Officer Kenney's card, I dial John Gattia's phone number.

"Hi, is this Officer Gattia?" I say to the first person who answers.

"No. Who may I say is calling?"

"This is Alex Miller. I got a message from the New

York City Police Department that I was to call this number and ask for Officer Gattia."

"Yes, sir, please hold."

A click, a moment of silence, and then I hear, "This is Deputy Sheriff Gattia," in a smooth-sounding voice.

"Officer Gattia, my name is Alex Miller. I was told by the police in New York City to call you."

"Thank you, Mr. Miller. Are you the son of Barbara Miller?"

All of a sudden it feels like I've been punched in the gut. I don't say anything, unable to fathom the change of direction. This isn't about Michael Ohlig at all.

"Mr. Miller? Mr. Miller, are you still there?"

"Yes," I finally say, although it sounds like little more than a squeak. It is apparently loud enough for Gattia, however, as he keeps talking.

"I'm very sorry to inform you of this over the phone. Your mother's body was found this morning washed up on the beach. We believe she drowned."

I take a deep breath before saying anything. I'm consumed with the mental image of my mother washing up on the sand, like in a movie. I can almost see her face, tinged in blue. But then another thought hits me, one equally disturbing. "What do you mean you *believe* she drowned? What else could it be?"

Now the silence is on the other end of the line. More time elapses than I think should be necessary given that Officer Gattia should have anticipated this question.

"That's the most likely scenario. But until we conclude the autopsy, there's no way to know for certain the exact cause of death."

I wait for him to say more, but he doesn't.

Elizabeth enters our bedroom and says she heard me crying. I'm still sitting on the bed. The phone is next to me. Even though Elizabeth must know that the only news from Palm Beach that would cause me to break down would be something terrible happening to my mother, she doesn't ask.

"My mother is dead," I say to break the silence.

"Oh my God, Alex. I'm so sorry. What happened?"

"I don't know. The police officer just said they found her body washed up on the beach."

"Your mother was in the ocean?"

That was also my first thought. My mother hated the ocean. Whenever we'd come to visit, we'd make a point to take Charlotte to the beach, but my mother never came. Even though the town was called Boynton Beach, she often joked that she didn't even know there was an actual beach.

"I've told you everything I know," I say.

Despite my statement, she asks another question. "When?"

"I don't know, Elizabeth. I assume yesterday. When did I last speak to her?"

"Did you call her yesterday?"

"I did, but I left a message. I assumed she was already at the Thanksgiving dinner at the clubhouse."

"Do they have any idea how it happened? It just doesn't make any sense."

"I don't know. I don't know if I'll ever know."

I take a very deep breath, the kind that fills your lungs completely and makes a noise when it's exhaled. With nothing more to say, I walk over to my closet and pull out my weekend bag.

"You're going to go down there today?" Elizabeth asks.

"Yeah. I'm going to have to make the arrangements."

"What can I do?"

"Nothing."

I'm now throwing underwear in the bag along with my dress socks. I pull my darkest suit out of the closet, a three button that I wore to my father's funeral, and throw it on the bed.

"Is it tacky if I wear the exact same thing as I did at my father's funeral?"

"Alex, could you please stop just for a moment? Talk to me. Please."

I nod, and walk over to the bed. Elizabeth is sitting beside my half-filled overnight bag, and I take a seat next to her on the edge of the bed. As soon as I sit down, she puts her hand over mine.

I sniffle, but it doesn't hold back my tears, and so I wipe both my eyes. "There's one thing you can do for me, Elizabeth. It would mean a lot."

"Okay."

"Please bring Charlotte to Florida. She doesn't have to come to the cemetery if you're still concerned about it being too scary, but I really want her to come down."

This was something of a bitter fight we had in the aftermath of my father's death. Elizabeth was adamant that Charlotte not make the trip to Florida, and I argued the other side just as vehemently.

"If it's really that important to you, Alex, I'll bring her down."

"It is," I tell her. "Thank you."

# 26

On my way to the airport, I call Abby.

"Boy, you really are a slave driver," she says without saying hello. "I was just about to head into the office. Why don't you come across the park and pick me up?"

"Can't. I'm actually on my way to Florida."

"Florida? What did Ohlig do now?"

"It has nothing to do with him. My mother died last night."

"Oh my God, Alex. I'm so sorry."

"Thanks."

"Is there anything I can do?"

"Unfortunately, yes. You're going to need to call Pavin and see about getting an adjournment. Get as much time as you can out of him. Once you've agreed, send a letter to Judge Sullivan."

"How?"

I know what she means, of course, but I want to show her that I'm not so grief stricken that I can't still banter. "How do you send a letter to a judge? You stick it in an envelope and then put it in the mailbox."

"Very funny. No, I mean, how did your mother die? Unless you don't want to talk about it. I don't mean to pry."

"You know I don't keep any secrets from you, Abby. It appears—the police say nothing's for certain until after an autopsy is conducted—that she drowned. The ocean," I add.

"I'm so sorry," she says again. "Are you sure there's nothing else I can do? Can I help with any of the arrangements?"

"Thank you again, but I've got it under control. I'm going to meet with the Palm Beach sheriff tomorrow and then I'll make all the arrangements. With any luck, the funeral will be on Sunday and I can come right home."

"Can I come down for the funeral . . . or would that just be too weird?"

"I don't think it would be weird," I reply. The truth is I'm sure that Elizabeth would find it quite strange for Abby to spend a thousand dollars to fly down to Florida and stay overnight in a hotel just to attend her boss's mother's funeral. How would I explain that one? "But it isn't necessary. What I really need is for you to hold down the fort here. Judge Sullivan may want to hear from you in person."

"Okay. I could come down today and then come right back, if you want." Before Elizabeth arrives, I assume she means. "Just so you're not doing all of this alone."

I wonder why Abby thinks I'm doing this alone. I suppose it's because I've called her from the cab, something she knows I wouldn't do with Elizabeth sitting next to me. It's another one of those little tells that indicates that Abby, too, knows our relationship is over the line.

"Thank you, but stay there and deal with Pavin and Judge Sullivan. I'll call you tonight, as soon as I get in, and we can talk more."

"Okay, but remember, the offer doesn't expire. Just ask."

While I'm waiting in the airport, I call Ohlig.

"Good morning, counselor," he says, sounding as cheerful as ever.

"Not exactly. I'm sorry to have some bad news—my mother died last night."

"What?"

"The police came to my house this morning and told me to call the Palm Beach sheriff's office. They told me she had drowned. In the ocean."

Neither one of us says anything for a good twenty seconds. Then, he breaks the silence.

"I'm so sorry, Alex." He sounds shaken; something I didn't think was possible. "I just don't know what to say. Is there anything I can do?"

"Thank you, but no. I'm flying down now to make some arrangements. The funeral will most likely be on Sunday. And don't worry, Michael, Abby is making an application to get more time from Judge Sullivan. I know you wanted to start the trial and soon as possible, but—"

"Alex, please don't concern yourself with my problems today. Take as much time as you need."

"Thank you. That's very nice of you to say, and I do very much appreciate it."

"She was swimming alone in the ocean?"

I stop to consider that same question again. I assumed she had been alone if only because no one had reported her missing, but then a far worse possibility enters my mind. She could have been with a friend who was also swept up in the current or whatever caused her death, and whose body just hadn't been found yet. As tragic as that would be, it would at least make more sense than my mother swimming alone. But wouldn't that other person have a family or someone who would have reported her missing by now? Then again, I hadn't realized my mother was missing and wouldn't have for at least a few more days. I was going to call her this weekend, but if she wasn't home I wouldn't become concerned for at least two days after that. Maybe there's a son somewhere who has no idea his mother has died.

"I don't know the circumstances," I tell Ohlig. "I didn't ask many questions. I was pretty stunned."

Confronted with how much I still don't know about the final moments of my mother's life and the realization that she must have felt so alone in the water, I begin to cry, my sadness coupled with embarrassment that Ohlig is a witness to this breakdown.

"I'm sorry, Michael, you'll have to pardon me," I say, sniffling back tears.

"Alex, no apologies are necessary or appropriate. I can't imagine how terrible this is for you. I mean, we're all still reeling from the shock of your father's death, and now this. I'm . . . words just don't capture it, but I'm so very sorry."

Whenever I work past Charlotte's bedtime, which is most nights, I call at around eight o'clock to say goodnight.

Charlotte, however, has little interest in talking on the phone, so it's our family routine for Charlotte to ask Elizabeth to find out if I have a message for her. After Elizabeth repeats the query, I ask Elizabeth to tell Charlotte that I love her. The message received, Charlotte then asks Elizabeth to tell me that she loves me too.

Elizabeth has dismissed any meaning in this ritual, claiming it's nothing more than a manifestation of Charlotte's enjoyment of word games. I'm not so sure. There's something about it that seems like an effort to hold Elizabeth and me together, the way Charlotte is able to get us to say "I love you" to each other.

When Elizabeth gets on the phone this evening, we talk about the travel plans. She tells me she's on a flight tomorrow afternoon and should arrive by dinnertime. Then she revisits the same discussion we had before I left.

"I know you asked me to bring Charlotte, and I will if you really want me to. I just wanted to tell you again that I'm worried that it's going to be very upsetting to her."

I sigh into the phone. "It's going to be upsetting for everyone, Elizabeth."

"I know, but she's five."

"Please, I don't want to argue with you about this. It's very important to me. I let you win when it was my father's funeral, and I regretted it. Please."

It is a cliché that married people have the same fight over and over, but clichés become so for a reason, and in Elizabeth's and my case, for the better part of the last half decade, our most passionate disagreements have had much less to do with the issue at hand than they were referendums on the state of our union. This one is no different. I do not believe Elizabeth's resistance to bringing Charlotte is solely because she believes that it will give our daughter nightmares, although that may be the case on the conscious level. Subconsciously, I suspect, her opposition is rooted in the hope that if it's just the two of us, even if only for a weekend, and even under such sad circumstances, we might remember how happy we once were. At times it seems like we're both grasping to understand what we had then, so we can recreate it now. As if the love we once shared was lost, like car keys, and might be found simply by retracing our steps.

I wish it could be that easy. And it's not as if I haven't tried over the past months to pinpoint where or even when we went off track. Perhaps it's just the life of a lawyer, the hours that keep me away from home, but that would be too much of an oversimplification, just as it would be to point to the stress of rearing Charlotte as the prime culprit. No, if anything, I think Charlotte has brought Elizabeth and me closer, not pulled us apart. Which is why I'm so insistent on having Charlotte there. It is less because I *want* her there, and more because I *need* her there, fearing that without my daughter's presence I will be denied what, at times, seems to me to be the only reason Elizabeth and I are still together.

## 27

Mr. Miller?" asks the man who is approaching me in the reception area of the Palm Beach Sheriff's Department. He does not fit at all with the voice that told me my mother was dead. The image in my mind was more Ricardo Montalban—tall, graying at the temples, distinguished looking. This man does not seem capable of commanding the immediate respect of the public. It's not only his slight physical stature, probably not more than 125 pounds soaking wet, but his age, mid-twenties, I'd guess.

"Officer Gattia?" I say, having it sound more like a question than I had intended.

"That's me," he says, "except down here it's Deputy." He's much too chipper for the circumstances at hand. As if he realizes that his tone is off, his expression changes and his eyes look to the floor. "I'm very sorry for your loss, Mr. Miller."

"Thank you. And thank you for meeting me on a Saturday. I greatly appreciate it, because I'd like to be able to hold the funeral tomorrow."

"I understand. I know that in the Jewish religion burials are held as soon as possible, and so I'm happy to meet with you today. Besides, it's not like the police station closes on the weekend."

He leads me back through the stationhouse, past the

array of desks that reminds me of the cop shows I've seen through the years. We finally arrive in a small, windowless room. Gattia asks me if I'd like any coffee, but I decline.

Through all my involvement in the criminal justice system, I've never actually been in a police station before. It's common for me to become involved in a matter before an arrest has been made but, like with Ohlig, I usually deal with the prosecutor, not the police or the FBI. As a result, the whole interrogation room scene— the one-way mirror and bad coffee—is not something to which I've ever been privy.

"Mr. Miller," he says after we've both sat down around a badly nicked wooden table, "it turns out we won't need for you to make a formal identification. We were able to match your mother's dental records. Of course, if you want to see her body—"

"No. That's okay."

"All right then. Let me give you your mother's personal effects. We found her handbag on the beach."

He walks over to a filing cabinet in the corner of the room, locked by one of those blue combination locks that I used in gym class in the seventh grade. After a few turns of the dial, he's holding my mother's handbag and a small, brown box, no larger than a shoe box.

He hands me the bag. It was a birthday gift from me a year or two ago. It's one of those fancy designer things that everyone in New York had to have at the time, emblazoned on the front with the designer's logo.

Inside are the expected items: a brush, makeup and lipstick, her wallet, which still had seventy-three dollars in it, and a book, the most recent paperback by an author who churned out detective stories that always made the bestseller list. The bookmark indicates that my mother was about two-thirds through it. Otherwise, aside from some sand inside, neither the bag nor its contents seem any worse for wear.

"Was anything removed?" I ask, not because I suspect anything has been, but because I think I should ask something.

"No. Is something missing?"

"I don't think so, but I don't really know what my mother kept in her handbag."

"That's all there was. By the way, we found her car in the beach parking lot and it's been impounded. Whatever was inside was inventoried and should be in the box."

When I catch his eyes, he looks away.

"Forgive me for saying this," he says, still avoiding eye contact, "and I hate to raise this even as a possibility, but we need to consider whether your mother took her own life. I assume you didn't receive a suicide note or anything else that would lead you to that conclusion?"

The words are as jarring as when I first heard that my mother was dead. Suicide never even entered my mind. My mother was always a glass-half-empty type, but I never thought she was distraught in that way. Even after my father's death, I didn't think she was any more upset than was situationally appropriate. Did I miss the signs?

"We didn't find a suicide note in your mother's house," he says.

"You've been to her home?"

"It's standard operating procedure in a case like this." He must be able to tell that I'm upset about the intrusion. "Remember, Mr. Miller, we found a purse and a body, but we weren't even sure they were connected for several hours. We entered your mother's home to ensure there was no evidence of foul play."

"Of course. I'm sorry."

"No need to apologize, sir. But I still need to ask. Did your mother say anything that might lead you to think she was suicidal?"

"No." And then, realizing that I'm not a witness who should answer as narrowly as possible, but someone seeking the police's help, I add, "My father died unexpectedly in September. But I thought she was handling it all right. She was sad, but not more than anyone else would be under the circumstances."

"Just this past September? Three months ago?"

I nod. "Closer to four months," I say, fully knowing that the extra thirty days is insignificant to the issue at hand.

His expression, a kind of pity, makes me question my own emotions, which is foolish, I know, because I'm the one who's suffered the loss of both my parents in quick succession, not Deputy Gattia. And then I realize something that, up until then, I had truly not connected. It was shortly after my father's death that I started working with Abby, and much of my time since then has been spent in her company. Just like a broken heart is easily healed when you find a new lover, it seems that the same is true of the sense of loss that accompanies the death of a parent.

I pull the rental car up to the Venezia Castle security booth. "I'm Alex Miller," I tell the woman wearing one of those rent-a-cop uniforms. "My mother is Barbara Miller at 7501 Turino," realizing too late that I'm using the present tense.

"ID, please," the woman says, and I hand her my driver's license.

She reaches over to the phone, the usual protocol. "No one's going to be home," I tell her. "My mother died."

"Oh, Barbara Miller." She says this without any condolence in her voice and puts down the receiver. "Yeah, they told me that someone had died and I'm supposed to let you through."

"Thank you," I say, as she raises the gate. I want to be angry with her over her insensitivity, but I immediately realize that she must get this a lot, considering Venezia Castle's median age.

Like the uniformity of the communities along the highway, within Venezia Castle every house is precisely the same. Not only do they share the same design— small, single-level box homes with the two-car garage taking up more than 50 percent of the exterior—but under the Venezia Castle bylaws, all houses must be painted white with black doors, and repainted every five years. The result is that there isn't even any difference in the signs of aging among the structures.

The Scary Lady is the first thing that greets me when I enter my mother's house. She's hanging on the wall immediately adjacent to the front door, still bordered by the same ugly metal frame and blue matting.

Even though Deputy Gattia told me that the police had already searched for a suicide note, I've come here to look myself. I begin in the bedroom, rummaging through my mother's possessions the way a burglar might look for hidden jewelry, running my hand through my mother's underwear drawer, looking behind books, and then proceeding through the other concealed spaces in the room.

When I open my father's night table drawer, I see a manila envelope marked *Personal* and wonder if this could be it. Inside, however, are only old photographs.

A few pictures in, after some shots of my grandparents, is one of my father at the beach. The feathered hair on the girls in the background screams that it was taken in the mid-1970s. My father would have been, at most, in his early thirties. The man with his arm around his shoulder is Michael Ohlig, who displays the same look of utter confidence that he wears today.

I continue for another fifteen minutes, but to no avail. I'm not sure how, exactly, to react. A note would have given some meaning to her death, but it would have been one to which I'd rather not ascribe.

I return to the living room, taking a seat across from the Scary Lady. "How did she die?" I say aloud.

The Scary Lady does not answer.

# 28

Most of the same people attend my mother's funeral as did my father's, and many of them appear to be wearing the same clothing, as am I. The service, too, has an eerie familiarity to it, the listing of Elizabeth, Charlotte, and my names as loved ones left behind, the recitation of the story about how my parents met.

Before the service I met briefly with the rabbi. At first he didn't remember presiding over my father's funeral, but when I reminded him his eyes widened and I could tell he'd found the theme of his eulogy—that my mother died of a broken heart.

After I place the shovel of earth on the casket, others follow suit, and a processional arranges itself to offer condolences to me. I'm thanking yet another of the residents of Venezia Castle for coming when I see Michael Ohlig out of the corner of my eye. The square-shouldered way he approaches the shovel, the methodical sweep of his arms as he performs his service to my mother, as smooth as a professional golfer's swing, provides yet another experience of déjà vu.

When it's Ohlig's turn to shake my hand, he instead throws his arms around me, pulling me tight. My father was not a very demonstrative man and, to my surprise, I find Ohlig's embrace comforting.

"I'm so sorry," he says into my ear.

As I emerge from Ohlig's arms, I notice Pamela beside him. "We both are," she says, and then looks at the ground.

"If there is anything—anything—that either of us can do, Alex, please don't hesitate to ask," Ohlig says.

"Thank you. I appreciate it."

They are about to take their leave, and I should let them go, especially considering that the line behind them has now grown to be about six people deep, but I pull Ohlig closer.

"Can I ask you something?"

"Of course, Alex. Anything."

"The police said my mother might have committed suicide, and I just can't get the thought of it out of my mind."

"That's ridiculous. She didn't commit suicide." He says this with authority. Placing his hand on my shoulder, he adds, "She had too much to live for to do that. Your father's death was hard on her, no doubt about that. They'd been together for a lot of years. But she loved you and she loved your little girl."

"Did she say anything to make you think she might be depressed? Was there a change in her mood recently?"

He takes a deep breath, and then looks to his wife, as if she's more suited to answer. "I'm sorry, but, well, you know what I've been doing with my time the last week or so, cooped up in your conference room. The last time I spoke to your mother was about two weeks ago;

you know, it may even have been longer than that, I'm sorry to say." He smiles at me. "After all you've taught me about answering the question directly, here I'm giving you a non-answer. Let me try again. I didn't notice anything different about her. I thought that, given the circumstances, she was doing well."

"Thank you so much for coming, Michael. And you too, Pamela. It means a lot to me."

"No need to thank me," he says. "That's what family does for each other."

"It's like we were just here," says one of my mother's neighbors whose name I can't recall, after we've returned to my mother's home where bagels and appetizers are once again arranged. I've heard the same sentiment at least twenty times today. He seems well-meaning, but then he asks about my plans for my mother's home, and I realize the conversation has run its course.

"Excuse me. I need to talk to my wife about something."

Elizabeth is holding Charlotte, no longer an easy feat since Charlotte crossed the thirty-pound threshold. Our daughter has my strong chin and the beginnings of the dimples Abby mentioned that night at the Four Seasons, and Elizabeth's mysterious emerald eyes and red hair. When Elizabeth was pregnant and we joked about which of our features we wanted our daughter to inherit, it went exactly like that.

"How are you doing?" I ask Elizabeth.

"Probably better than you."

She puts Charlotte down, but my daughter's feet don't touch the ground for more than a second before she's leaping into my arms. I'm happy to have her there and kiss the top of her head.

Elizabeth and my mother never got on very well. They each put a good face on it, neither ever disparaging the other, at least not to me, but they were different types of women. Even people who knew my mother only superficially described her as a force of nature. They meant it as a compliment, but the phrase always conjured an image in my mind of a hurricane, with my mother pulling everything into her orbit. By contrast, Elizabeth is much more a repellant force. That first sense I had when seeing her at that party in Cambridge has turned out to be right. She has few friends, and doesn't seem driven to be surrounded by others.

"My father was easier to eulogize." I laugh.

"It's not a competition."

"It's not?"

"Okay, for your mother maybe it was."

"How are you holding up, Charlotte bear?"

"Good," she says.

"You sure?"

"It's sad that Grandma's dead. I wish she were alive. And Papa too."

"Me too, sweetie. Me too."

"Do you think they're together now in Heaven?"

"I do," I tell her, although in truth, I do not. I've never been a big believer in any form of afterlife. "What do you think of that picture?" I say to Charlotte, pointing to the Scary Lady.

"The lady with the colors on her face?"

"Yes. I'm going to take that back to New York with us and put it up in our apartment. Papa bought it for Grandma before I was even born."

"It must be really old," Charlotte says, without any sarcasm.

"Papa thought it looked like Grandma. Do you think it does?"

"No." Charlotte scrunches up her face the way she sometimes does when she's thinking about something really hard. "It looks kind of like a witch, I think. Or maybe a clown, because of the colors on her face."

"When I was a little boy it frightened me. I called her the Scary Lady."

"Why do you want to hang it in the house if it's scary, Daddy?"

Elizabeth laughs, but I can see in her eyes that she agrees with Charlotte.

## 29

We leave West Palm on Monday at three-thirty, but it isn't until we've arrived back at JFK that I tell Elizabeth I need to head to the office. There was no point in our fighting for the entire flight, I figured.

"Alex, please just give us one more night," Elizabeth begs.

"Abby only got a two-week extension from the court. We've got to start the trial on Monday."

"So because Abby sucks at her job, she gets you for the night and your family suffers?"

"Abby isn't *getting* me. And she doesn't suck at her job. I'm just going to work."

I go straight to the war room, without even stopping at my office first. Abby's there, reviewing our witness binders, looking almost exactly the same as she did five days ago when I last saw her.

I feel myself exhale. Finally, I can relax.

"I was hoping I'd see you today," she says. Her eyes are bright and her smile is ear-to-ear.

"I missed you," I say, even though I know I shouldn't be so . . . honest.

"I wish I could have come to the funeral."

Abby looks down at the table. At first I think it's to express further condolence, and then I realize she's looking at my hand. I wonder if she's going to put her hand on top of mine. I wait, but she doesn't move.

"Look at this," I say, and pull an envelope out of my briefcase. "I found it in my mother's house. It was in my father's night table. It's him and Ohlig, when they were about my age, maybe a little younger."

Abby studies the photograph. "I see you're not a victim of male pattern baldness," she says.

"My father was a cue ball well before thirty," I reply, running my hand through my own full head of hair. "As I've told you, my mother always said I'm all her."

Abby looks at me sympathetically. Her eyes are telling me it's okay if I want to talk about my mother. I accept the invitation.

"I'm trying to figure out how she died. It just doesn't make sense to me."

"What doesn't?"

"She wouldn't go in the ocean by herself. It just wasn't like her. And on Thanksgiving morning? The police said they looked for a suicide note, but didn't find one. Apparently that's standard operating procedure in drowning cases." I shake my head. "I never should have left her alone for the holiday."

"You're being too hard on yourself," she says. "You couldn't go to Florida for Thanksgiving. You had a professional obligation to keep your client out of jail, a man who was your family's oldest friend. And you did the only thing you could—you asked your mother to come to New York for the holiday. It was her decision not to come. You didn't keep her away."

I feel my eyes becoming moist, and I look away from Abby. She moves from the far side of the table until she's sitting next to me, and then gently places her hand on my shoulder.

"Alex, your mother did not commit suicide. There wasn't a suicide note. Doesn't that settle it?"

"Not necessarily. Apparently lots of people commit suicide without leaving notes." I give her a shrug. "I googled it."

Neither of us says anything for a moment. Finally I remark: "She died all alone. That's the part I hate most. I keep imagining her in the water, alone and scared."

Abby places her hand on mine without saying anything. When I caress her hand she caresses mine back, as if to say that I'm not alone and so I shouldn't be scared.

We sit like that in silence, well past the time when one of us should have withdrawn, or said something. I'm focused solely on my thumb, which is massaging the top of her hand, the space between her thumb and index finger. The moment hangs in the air, as if it's not really of this time or place.

As if I'm awakened from a dream, I notice that the conference room door is open. Not completely, but enough that someone would enter without knocking. Abby seemingly can read my mind because she realizes that I'm suddenly concerned that someone will find us here, holding hands, and takes her hand off mine, but while doing so smiles at me to confirm that she wishes she didn't have to.

"I should go home," I say. "I was only allowed to come in because I promised Elizabeth I wouldn't stay long."

"You didn't have to come in at all, Alex. You should be home with your family."

"I really did miss you," I say, and at that moment believed with all my heart that if the door was closed just a little more, I would have kissed her.

I am still thinking about the softness of Abby's touch when I enter our apartment, and so I am immediately ashamed of myself when I see what can only be described as pure joy. Charlotte is sitting on Elizabeth's lap, receiving a manicure. As if they are puppets on the same string, both of their heads move up in unison, and their faces adopt the same broad smile when they see I'm home.

"Daddy!" Charlotte screams. "Mommy is painting my nails. Guess what color?"

There is perhaps nothing in the entire world I can be as sure of as the color Charlotte has chosen to paint her fingernails, yet I consider it my paternal responsibility to allow her to surprise me. "Blue?" I say.

"No!" She says this with a squeal, the delight of having knowledge I lack. "Guess again."

"It must be red."

"No! It's pink."

"Pink?" I say, continuing to play my part. "You're having your fingernails painted pink? What color were they before?"

Charlotte tilts her head slightly, as if she's considering this question. "I don't know. What color was it?" she asks her mother.

"It was a different shade of pink," Elizabeth says, and then Charlotte repeats it for me, in case I didn't get it the first time.

I put down my briefcase, hang up my coat, and make my way over to the couch to inspect Elizabeth's handiwork. "It's absolutely beautiful, Charlotte. I really love the color you picked." I lean over to place a kiss on the top of my daughter's head, and then do the same to Elizabeth's.

"I thought you'd be at the office much later tonight," Elizabeth says. It is about as sad a commentary on my life as I can imagine, but Elizabeth is more surprised when I come home before midnight than when I'm out past that time. She smiles at me and says, "I'm glad you're home."

"I'm sorry about going into the office. I was a little freaked out by the judge refusing us a reasonable extension. But everything seems under control, so I figured I should make sure all was good at home."

"I'm not sure your priorities are properly sequenced," Elizabeth says, "but all's well here."

I immediately become defensive. "I had to go in, Elizabeth."

"I'm not criticizing," Elizabeth says softly, highlighting that my tone was uncalled for. "I'm just stating a fact. I realize that you have this trial, and that it's important. But after this one there'll be another one.

And another after that. Et cetera and so on. Remember when you joined the firm you had to establish yourself, and then you were up for partner, and then as a junior partner people were looking to see whether you'd ultimately take a leadership role in the firm, and now you've got this trial."

"Elizabeth—my mother just died, can't you cut me a little slack?"

"No, Alex, that's precisely why I shouldn't. Your mother's death should be a wake-up call for you, and not another excuse to bury yourself in work. Life is just too short."

"What's that supposed to mean?"

"Do I have to spell it out for you? You know what I'm saying."

"I really don't, Elizabeth," I say, although the better answer is that I hope I don't.

"The short version, Alex, is that this"—and she waves around the room—"is your life. Me, Charlotte. And it's right now. Not *someday* or *later*. But now. Is this really the way you want it to be? Because it's getting damn near the point where that decision is going to be irrevocably made."

"Is that a threat?"

"No, " she says with a sigh, as if I've missed the point entirely. "It's my greatest fear is what it is."

## 30

The red light on my phone is blinking when I arrive at the office. I assume it's Abby, and eagerly punch in my password, but when I access my messages, it's a much different voice that I hear.

"This is Assistant United States Attorney Christopher Pavin calling about the United States v. Michael Ohlig matter," his message begins, as if we've never met. "Mr. Miller, it is extremely important that you call me back as soon as possible. Thank you."

When I call Pavin back, I get his voicemail. "This is private attorney Alexander Miller of the law firm Cromwell Altman Rosenthal and White. I received a voicemail message from Assistant United States Attorney Christopher Pavin to call him on a matter of extreme importance. By this phone message, I hereby return his phone call. The time of this call is nine-thirty-five in the a.m. The date is Friday, the fifth of December."

Pavin calls me back less than five minutes later. "I liked your message," he says. "You're a funny guy."

"You're the one who can't just say, 'Alex, it's Chris, call me,'" I respond, trying my best to act unconcerned that the prosecutor has left a dire message on the eve of the trial.

"Alex, it's Chris," he deadpans back. "Before getting

to the reason for my call, I wanted to express my sincere condolences about your mother."

"Thank you. I appreciate that you didn't take a hard line with Judge Sullivan on the extension. Not that it mattered very much."

"She wants this trial to go. That's for sure."

Our small talk complete, I wait for the purpose of the call. He's at least experienced enough not to make me wait very long.

"I've got something important to talk to you about."

"Okay. Shoot," I say, still trying to convey there is absolutely nothing he could say that would shake my belief in Ohlig's total innocence.

"We had considerable internal discussion on this issue and we ultimately concluded we needed to focus you on something, in case you didn't realize its importance."

"That's very kind of you." Although Pavin's preface is condescending, I know better than to turn down free discovery.

"You need to listen to tape number 17 very carefully," he says gravely. "I think it would be inappropriate for me to say more at this point, but if you have questions after you've listened to it, feel free to call me."

"Well, you certainly have piqued my interest, Assistant United States Attorney Christopher Pavin. I'll take a listen and get back to you. Thanks for the heads-up."

He says nothing for a moment, then, "I've never encountered this type of situation before and, truth be told, no one else in my office has either. We really didn't know what to do, so we decided to err on the side of caution." If this were not tantalizing enough, Pavin adds, "Just so I'm clear, when I say you need to listen to it, I mean *you*, Alex. Don't have Abby Sloane or anyone else do it. You have to be the one."

"Okay," I say, still trying to sound lighthearted, but now very much more concerned.

Abby's in the war room, surrounded by three-inch black binders. We, or rather she (and I'm sure an army of others—temps, paralegals, secretaries, mailroom guys), have prepared about thirty of these witness binders. Each has the witness's name written on the spine in large letters and inside is an outline of the points to be covered in the examination, followed by the exhibits we'll need to introduce into evidence through the witness, each designated with a numbered side tab.

"Well, good morning to you," Abby says, her face lighting up.

"You too," I say. "I just had the strangest call with Pavin," I say, a bit abruptly, I realize, because Abby's smile recedes.

"Isn't every call with him the strangest call?" she says, morphing into work mode.

"This one was in a special category. He said we need to focus on tape 17. What's on that one?"

"Alex, I'm listening to the tapes, not memorizing them." She says this with a nervous laugh suggesting she's worried she missed something important. "Anyway, since when is Pavin doing us favors?"

"That's one of the things that made the call so strange. And get this, he made a point to emphasize I had to be the one who listens—not you."

"Well, that does wonders for my ego," Abby laughs again, as she starts clicking through the electronic files on her laptop.

"Pavin must be worried Ohlig will have an appellate claim for ineffective assistance of counsel if we—I should say I—am not aware of what's on tape 17."

"I don't have tape 17 on the system," she says, now looking even more concerned. "I didn't upload every tape, just the ones I thought had relevant information. I have an index of what's on all of them, though." She pulls out a yellow legal pad from a stack that is sitting beside her and begins furiously flipping the pages.

"Finally," she says in an exasperated voice. "Tape 15, 16, okay, 17." She stares at her paper, reading her notes silently before she's going to say anything. "That one is just Ohlig talking to his wife." She looks up at me. "According to my notes at least, there's nothing about Salminol on that tape."

"I thought that Ohlig's phone wasn't taped."

"It wasn't, but occasionally he took a call on a broker's phone, and that was taped."

"Do you have the tape here?" I ask.

"Somewhere," she says, already walking over to the boxes on the far wall, which are stacked up behind me. I help her lift the ones on top until she begins to rummage through the contents of a box marked July. After some digging, she pulls out a disk. "Here it is. It's dated July

10." She pauses, staring at the disk. "I'm almost sure there wasn't any business talk on it. I'm sorry if I missed something, but I really don't know what Pavin is talking about."

"Let's find out," I say, probably sounding impatient, because I am.

She walks back over to her seat at the table and places the disk in her laptop. "Do you want the headphones?" she asks.

I shake my head no, and then explain we should hear the tape together, which elicits a smile that thanks me for not having lost confidence in her. Then she presses the play button.

The tape begins with Agent McNiven sounding like Joe Friday on his most serious day. "This is Special Agent Gregory McNiven of the Federal Bureau of Investigation. The date is 10 July. The conversations on this tape will be from the phone number, 561 area code, 555-7592. This tape recording is pursuant to warrant." From there the tape trails off into the familiar static, until Ohlig's voice is heard.

"Hello."

A woman's voice is next. "Hi there," she says.

"See," Abby says, "it's a personal call between Michael and his wife."

I'm not listening to Abby. Instead, all of my senses are directed to the laptop emitting these sounds.

Ohlig speaks next. "Is anything wrong?"

"No," the woman says. "I know you're busy, but I just wanted to thank you again for last night." A slight pause. "For both times."

Ohlig chuckles. "Glad to be of service."

"Can you service me again tonight?" she asks in a husky voice, like she's channeling Mae West.

"It will be my pleasure to be of assistance," Ohlig says, apparently not so busy at work that he can't take some time out to talk about his sexual prowess.

"That's all I wanted to hear. Go back to work. I won't bother you again until tonight, but then I'm going to bother you a lot."

"I'm looking forward to it," Ohlig says.

"Michael," a slight pause, "I love you."

"I love you too," he says and hangs up. There's static for about ten seconds, and then McNiven's voice saying that this is the end of the recording and that it took fifty-seven seconds.

"Do you think that Pavin mixed up the number?" Abby asks. "Maybe he was thinking about another tape."

"No," I say. "This is the right tape."

"Then I don't get it. Why does Pavin think this is so important?"

"Because," I say with a sigh, "the woman on the tape isn't Michael's wife. She's my mother."

My mother was in love with Michael Ohlig, that much seems clear. It isn't hard to go from there to the idea that he promised to leave his wife for her, and my mother got caught in the oldest lie there is. By Thanksgiving she must have realized that, one way or another, either because Ohlig was going to stay with Pamela or maybe because he might go to prison, she was going to end up being alone, and she decided that just wasn't the way she wanted to live.

Anger consumes me, rushing in a thousand directions. How could she be so selfish? Or so stupid? How could I have not noticed that she was suicidal? Why didn't I go to Florida for Thanksgiving?

But there is a special place of rage where it is most warranted. Michael Ohlig is responsible for my mother's death.

# 31

I tell Abby I need some time to process and go back to my office. Once there, I shut the door and dial Ohlig's number. In as matter-of-fact a voice as I can muster, I tell him to come to New York on the next flight. I explain that there's something on one of the tapes that we need to discuss in person.

I can hardly imagine anyone else who would not be beside himself upon hearing, a week before trial, there was a problem with the case and he had to meet with his lawyer immediately. Ohlig's only response is to tell me he'll take an early flight out tomorrow morning and, barring traffic, he'll be at my office by one. He doesn't even ask me what the problem is, but at this point it would have been more surprising if he had expressed some concern.

I head back down to the war room, finding Abby once again amidst the binders.

"What did he say?" she asks, a smile revealing that she's proud of how well she knows me.

I could play dumb, but there's no point. "We didn't really talk. I told him I needed him to come up to discuss a recent development, and it has to be in person. You know him, he acts like it's nothing, as if I'm calling to set up a golf game or something."

"You want me in the meeting?"

"You know I do, but I think I should do it alone."

"Okay," she says, sounding a little disappointed.

"Where are OPM's phone records?"

"Maybe I can help. What are you looking for?"

"I'll tell you when I find it." A response designed to convey that I'd like some privacy.

"They're boxed over there," she says with a sigh, pointing to the far wall, adjacent to the wall where the box containing tape 17 was located. There are about twenty-four boxes lining the wall, six rows, each four boxes high. "Fortunately for you, we've put them in chronological order. What time period are you looking for?"

"What's the most recent we've got?"

"Through the indictment are in the boxes on the end. On top, I think."

"And after that?"

"We don't have any. Through the indictment is all that's been produced."

"And what if I wanted to see who Michael called more recently?"

"Like during our prep right before Thanksgiving, for example?" Abby clearly knows exactly what I'm thinking.

"Yes, like then."

"Can I make a suggestion?"

"Please."

"Don't go through his records. Check your mother's. Her cell phone will have a call log, both incoming and outgoing. See if she was the one who called Michael."

"Her cell phone is down in Florida," I say. "I could probably get someone to FedEx it to me, but I really don't want to wait."

"You're the executor of her estate, right?"

"Yeah."

"I bet you can get the phone records from the phone company."

At last, a reason to smile. "That's why you earn the big bucks. Thanks."

Sure enough, getting my mother's phone records is only slightly more difficult than accessing my own. She used the same carrier for both her cell and her land line, so I have to call only one phone company. I explained that my mother had recently died and I wanted to pay off her bills in full; however, before I made the payment, I needed to verify the charges. The customer service rep, a woman with an Indian accent, was more than happy to oblige me. She told me that if I emailed her the documentation indicating my appointment as the executor of my mother's estate, she'd email me back the phone records.

Less than an hour later, I'm in my office with the door closed reviewing the last phone calls my mother ever made.

I look at her land line bill first. It isn't itemized and contains only the overall service charges and an indication that she made forty-two local calls. That makes sense. On the rare occasion that my mother called me or anyone else out-of-state, she'd use her cell to avoid long-distance charges.

The cell phone records have what I'm looking for. November 23 at 4:52 p.m.: a three-minute and twenty-seven-second call to Ohlig's cell phone. The timing matches up with the call in our conference room because I remember that I was thinking at the time that Ohlig would have trouble getting a cab at five. The three-minute duration also seems to be about right.

She called Ohlig again at 5:35, no doubt to confirm he was actually coming to see her as he had promised. At 6:19, there began a string of one-minute calls, every fifteen minutes or so, which I assume were her compulsive efforts to reach him before the plane took off, but he must have already turned off his phone. She finally made contact at 9:07, a two-minute call.

I don't know why it simply hadn't occurred to me before that moment to check my mother's voicemail messages. Getting her password won't be quite as easy as obtaining the phone records, but it's not impossible either. Before contacting the phone company again, I decide to try a more low-tech solution. I dial my mother's cell phone number. I hear my mother tell callers to slowly leave a name and number at the beep so she can return the call as soon as she's able. Hearing her voice, a wave of sadness crashes over me.

I press the pound key, getting the prompt to put in her password, and then repeat. Sure enough, my mother never programmed a password. The default still worked.

She had only one unheard message. It was from me, a call I had forgotten I made. Thanksgiving day, at

11:49 A.M., according to the computer voice. "Mom, it's me. Just calling to wish you a happy Thanksgiving. I'm sorry about how things turned out this year. Next year Elizabeth, Charlotte, and I will definitely come down. Call me."

My mother never heard that message, and so it makes little sense I'm as upset as I am, but I wish I had said I loved her. When was the last time I said it to her?

She also had one saved message. My mother always claimed we were the same and, at least in this regard, we are. It's from Ohlig and more than two months old. I can only assume she saved it for the same reason that I save Abby's messages—to be able to hear it over and over again.

"I love you," he says. "Last night was wonderful. A dream I wished I'd never wake up from. I can't wait until we're together again, and not just for a few hours, or even a night, but forever and always."

## 32

A lex?" Abby is standing in my doorway. She closes the door behind her without my inviting her in. "I know this is very upsetting to you. Would it help if we talked about it?"

I sweep my arm, gesturing that she should sit down. Abby settles into my guest chair, her face full of concern.

"It's not just the affair," I say without further prompting, "although that would be more than enough. I just hope to God my father didn't know."

I'm about to tell her my theory regarding the connection between the affair and my mother's death, but stop just before the words come out. I don't want to tell Abby that sometimes affairs with married men end up that way.

As if she's reading my mind, she says, "This is a subject that will be aided by alcohol, don't you think? Let's get the hell out of here."

We agree to meet up at the bar at the Mandarin Hotel in the Time Warner Center. I don't make any comment about her selecting a bar on the top floor of the hotel, meaning there's little chance of someone seeing us who isn't also selecting a clandestine spot for a drink, and she doesn't say anything about my request that we not be seen leaving the firm together.

• • •

The hostess tells me that my party has already arrived, and instructs me to follow her. Abby has secured a table in the corner, by the window. Outside is a panoramic view of Central Park. She has a glass of white wine in front of her, nearly finished.

I've barely sat down before someone arrives asking for our drink order.

"What scotch do you have?" I ask.

He points to the list on the table, which actually sets out about six or seven different varieties, ranging in price from $20 to $250 a glass. I order the $20 glass. Abby says she'll have the same, and downs the rest of her wine.

When the waiter leaves, Abby leans close to me and says, "Alex, don't be mad at me for saying this, and I know that finding out about your mother and Michael is very upsetting to you, but parents are people too, you know? Don't be too hard on your mother without knowing what she was going through."

"I know, Abby. Believe me, I do. I mean, who am I to throw stones, right?"

She could pretend that she doesn't understand, but Abby doesn't insult me in that way. I half-hope that she's going to comment that I've stayed on the right side of that divide, but what she says makes clear that she considers that to be a distinction without a difference.

"I guess that's my point. Until you know what was going on with her, you really can't judge her. My parents had a very rocky marriage, and so I learned a long time ago that there's nothing lonelier than being with someone you don't love."

"Would you provide the same defense for Michael? Because I won't. I'm furious with him."

The second round passes quickly, our banter covering our favorite books (Abby surprises me with her love for *Wuthering Heights,* while she tells me that I'm nothing if not predictable for liking *The Great Gatsby*) and the fact that neither of us has seen a movie since the summer. When I hear myself asking for a third scotch, there's a sloppiness to my words. Also, the conversation has turned to superheroes, which reminds me of the first time Abby and I were out drinking.

"I have one for you," she says. I can tell by her smile she's pleased with herself. "I've been thinking about your theories about Batman, and I have a real problem with them."

"And what's that?"

"You claim that Batman is really Batman deep down, and he created Bruce Wayne as a persona, but that's not really who he is, right?"

"Yes, that is my thesis."

"Then riddle me this: Why is he Bruce Wayne at all? Why isn't he Batman twenty-four-seven?"

I want to come up with a quick and pithy response, but none comes to me. I'm not sure if it's because of the alcohol taking effect or she really has me stumped.

"Wouldn't people wonder where Bruce Wayne went?" I finally say.

"Maybe he died. Or moved to Memphis."

"Do you equate the two?"

"Have you ever been to Memphis?"

"Fair enough. But how's this—I think he keeps the Bruce Wayne persona to protect those he loves."

"Nice try," she says dismissively. "But who does Batman ever love? There's no female, unless you count Catwoman, and we both know that relationship isn't going anywhere. Face it, Alex, Batman is a loner. He might as well be Batman all the time."

"That's so sad," I say.

Perhaps I also look sad because Abby changes her expression too. Her smile recedes and she looks at me intently. She brings her face closer to mine, and then she kisses me. At first lightly, and then more deeply.

"Please," she moans, our lips still pressed together. "Please come home with me. It's time, Alex."

From the moment we enter the cab, we're kissing like teenagers. Neither the cab driver nor anything else matters. We don't stop until the cab does, at which time I pull out a crumpled twenty-dollar bill from my pocket to pay a fare that is less than half that, and slam the door behind me.

Abby's building has no doorman. She unlocks the front door without looking back, but I scan the empty street to make sure no one sees me enter.

As soon as we cross the threshold we're kissing again,

my hands running down Abby's body. Without saying a word, Abby breaks our embrace and takes my hand. I know this is really happening, but there's a part of me that feels like tomorrow I will awake to realize it was all a dream.

Abby does not turn the light on in her bedroom. She steps out of her shoes and for the first time she seems small to me. My lips leave hers and I begin kissing her neck, working my way down to her now bare shoulders. When she lets out a gentle sigh, I know my life will never again be the same.

I want this moment never to end, and knowing that's impossible, I want to remember every detail—the smell of her hair, the way her breasts feel in my hands, the softness of her lips—so that when we're not together, I can relive it.

As I'm about to enter her, I hesitate. I'm not exactly sure why, to freeze the moment perhaps, a way of marking before and after. Or perhaps it's to remind myself that I could stop.

She shudders, and let's out a cry that is unmistakably of pleasure. We move slowly for a few minutes. Her breathing, short gasps, increases in intensity and speed as we do.

I know she's close, and I slow down to hold her off.

"What?" she says breathlessly.

"Can you go on top? I want to be able to see you better."

She doesn't answer, at least not verbally, but rolls around my body until she stretches over me. Her palms flatten on my chest and she begins to rock slowly; within seconds we're again at full speed.

"Abby," I whisper.

She opens her eyes and smiles broadly. She looks absolutely radiant. I'm about to say something else, but she closes her eyes again. Her head rolls back on her shoulders, and she swings her hair around like a lasso. I can feel her tighten around me, which is followed by a short shriek, and then a longer wail.

She goes on for longer than I could imagine. When she finally subsides, it's my turn to experience that exhilaration, and I release into her. The moment I do, however, I'm consumed with shame.

I could blame the alcohol, of course, but that would only be partly right. I knew it was heading in this direction, and I could have stopped it, but I didn't. And not just when I ordered a third round, but from the very beginning—the late night messages, the intimate talks, the dinners, the shared rides home and the voicemails. Every day the voicemails. I had thought maybe I could have the affair without the sex, as if that was somehow better, rather than worse. At least now there's a clarity to my actions and I can no longer hide behind the technicality that I haven't broken my marriage vows.

I start to get dressed, searching in her covers for my underwear, when Abby asks me to stay. "It's not even eleven o'clock," she says. "You normally don't get home this early."

I'm not going to be convinced, however. I can't wait

to get out of her apartment and to somewhere safe. The irony is not at all lost on me that for months now, Abby has been my safe haven from the troubles in my life. Now, in one fell swoop, I've made being with her the most dangerous place of all.

Rather than join Elizabeth in bed, when I come in to the apartment I go directly to the Pink Palace. Charlotte sleeps without a blanket, often on her knees with her backside in the air. I can't imagine how she can be comfortable that way, but she's snoring lightly, completely at peace. Belle the bunny's ears peek out from under her arm.

I sit at the corner of the bed and stroke Charlotte's soft curls. It was a bargain, I tell myself. One time. One time only, and then I'd know. What I was missing. What I longed for. I won't need to do it again because I'd have that memory to fall back on. Rather than repeat the act, I'd just remember it again, and it would be like being with her.

First I thought Abby and I could be lovers without making love. Now that that's failed, I take solace in thinking we can go back to the way things were before. I know it's another lie, but I'm praying I can make it come true.

33

# 33

**I**s something wrong?"

I had hoped to get out of the apartment before Elizabeth woke up. Six o'clock turned out not to be early enough.

I'm almost fully dressed. All that remains is for me to fix my tie and grab my coat and I would have made it to freedom, but now I'm going to have to engage her.

"No, why do you ask?" I say.

"You seem a little stressed."

"You can tell that by the way I'm tying my tie?"

"I heard you come in last night, but you went straight into Charlotte's room. Now you're leaving at the crack of dawn. It doesn't take a mind reader to recognize that something's going on with you."

"I've got a meeting with Ohlig this morning that I'm not looking forward to, that's all."

"Did something happen?"

There's no reason not to tell her about Ohlig and my mother. Their affair isn't covered by attorney-client privilege, and it would not only allow Elizabeth into my thoughts, something she complains I exclude her from too frequently, but also provide an explanation as to why I'm out of sorts this morning. I'm afraid to share with her my mother's infidelity for fear it reveals too much about my genetic makeup.

"Fruit of the poisonous tree" is the expression in the law. Once a piece of evidence becomes tainted, everything that flows from it is equally inadmissible. It's not a perfect analogy, but it works. If I tell Elizabeth about my mother, we'll start talking about the reasons people cheat, and that's not a discussion I want to have with her.

"Just the usual stuff," I say instead.

I access my voicemail within seconds of leaving my building. There's a message, and my heart lifts, hoping it's from Abby. It is. The computer voice reveals she left it just after we said good-bye last night.

"Hey you," her voicemail begins, "I already miss you. Your smell. Your touch. I can't say it was worth the wait because I've wanted you that way for so long, but God, it was amazing. Thank you."

I know that I've lost the bargain. I want her more than ever now.

I arrive at the office before seven, but it's already a buzz of activity. I want some quiet time, so I shut my door. I replay last night in my head, trying to experience it all over again, until I'm awakened from the fantasy by a knock.

"Come in," I call.

Abby opens the door. She has an unabashed smile, the very picture of joy. For the second time I feel a pang of shame.

"You're here early," she says. "I was going to leave

you a note, but this is so much better." Clearly, she is not suffering from the same hangover that I am, and I'm not referring to the effect the alcohol had on me.

"I had trouble sleeping last night, and so I decided to come in early today."

"That sounds like we should talk," she says.

"No, if it's okay with you, I'd just rather be for a little bit. We can talk later, if you want. But for now, I'd rather not."

"I'm going to make you a deal that I think you're going to like, Alex."

"Isn't the line that it's an offer I can't refuse?"

"If you prefer. Anyway, I can only imagine how you're turning inside. So, if you want to chalk it up to one of those *we-both-wanted-to-know-what-it-was-going-to-be-like* kind of things, and now we know that it was pretty damn spectacular, so we never have to go there again, I'm okay with that. Don't get me wrong, I'll be disappointed, but I'll live. I understand that you've got a lot of stuff on your plate right now, and the last thing you need is me making demands. Okay?"

This is more than okay. In fact, I can't imagine that she could have said anything that would have been of greater relief. She's essentially granting my greatest wish. We can pretend that last night didn't happen. I am having my cake and eating it too.

"I appreciate that, I really do. And you're right, things are a little . . . complicated right now, wouldn't you say? I mean, we're about to start a trial defending the guy my mother was cheating on my father with, and at the same time I'm cheating on my wife with you. This is going to be hard enough for me without pining for the next time we're going to make love. There's only so much my mind can take."

"Okay, Alex. Like I said, we can go at your speed. I'll keep my hands off you during the trial, and after that, you can tell me what you want this to look like. Deal?"

And that's how we leave it. We are once again lovers in every way other than the most defining.

A few hours later, Ohlig enters my office in the company of my assistant. I had earlier told the receptionist on my floor to have Ohlig cool his heels until I was ready for him. As power plays go, it was a little juvenile, but it apparently did the trick because Ohlig seems put out.

"What's with all the heightened security, counselor?" Ohlig says when he enters my office. "It's like the Corleone compound after Bruno Tattaglia got whacked. So now I've got to wait in reception?"

I've already decided not to engage in any small talk. As soon as he's seated, I begin.

"Michael, there's no way to say this without being straight up." I lean into him, the way he sometimes does with Abby to show he's totally fixated on whatever she's going to say next, and allow a long silence, waiting for him to offer something unsolicited. It gives me some professional pride that he's been trained too well to fall for such a trick. "I need to know about the relationship you were having with my mother."

Ohlig's expression is one I've seen before on

countless clients. It isn't surprise, shame, or embarrassment, but calculation. He's playing out in his mind whether he can pull off a lie or should come clean with the truth. I'd estimate that more than 90 percent of my clients who perform this calculus choose to lie.

"It's true, Alex. Your mother and I were, as you say, in a relationship."

I expect more, some type of explanation about how it began, or why they chose not to tell me. Anything. But he has answered the question in full and is not going to volunteer extraneous information; again, just the way I've prepared him to testify when he's cross-examined by Pavin.

"Why didn't you tell me? For Christ's sake, I'm representing you and you're having an affair with my mother? Michael, you flat-out lied to me."

"Not telling you that I was seeing your mother was not a flat-out lie. At most it was a sin of omission, and one she swore me to."

"You're giving me technicalities?" I say, my voice now rising. "At my mother's funeral I asked you when you'd spoken to her last and you made it seem as if you'd barely spoken to her in weeks. You spoke to her the day before she died! From my conference room, no less."

I see the same darting in Ohlig's eyes as before, the tell that he's still not sure whether to lie or not. But he must know that I couldn't make such a specific allegation unless I have proof.

"Yes. Your mother called me at your office. She said

she was going to be all alone on Thanksgiving and it was my fault. Well, yours and mine. The goddamn men in her life, as she put it. She was upset on the phone, I'm not going to lie to you about that. But I saw her that night and everything was good after that. I swear."

"You should have told me."

"With all due respect, what you were told about your mother's personal life was her decision, not mine. She didn't want you to know." He smiles as if to convey that we're still friends. "You may be my lawyer, Alex, but first and foremost you're her son."

Ohlig's delivery is smooth, as if he's been preparing this speech for some time, and I'm sure on some level he has. It's clear to me that when he questioned Abby about what phone lines were tapped, it wasn't because he was worried about something being incriminating on the tapes, at least not in a legal sense. He was concerned I'd find out about him and my mother.

"It's difficult to talk to you about this," he continues, "but if you must know, your mother was fine with what was going on between us. She understood that I wasn't going to leave Pamela. She was just happy for the time we were spending together. And as for my not telling you about us, like I said, that was her decision, but now I realize that was wrong on my part, and so I'm sorry."

I have no interest in his apology. "When did it start?" I ask, pointedly.

"Alex—"

"Just answer my question: Did it start before my father died?"

If he lies to me about this I'll know that he's likely lying to me about everything. Of course, the converse is not necessarily true—if he comes clean on this it just may be that he suspects I already know the truth, which, of course, I already do.

"As I'm sure you can understand, life can be complicated, and sometimes it gets messy, and we make choices and do certain things that, in hindsight, we probably shouldn't have."

"Not my question. It's pretty simple—before or after?"

"Before," he says quietly, breaking eye contact.

"Did he know?"

His eyes come back to meet mine. "No. He didn't know. Alex, I'm very sorry. I know that I was wrong to betray your father the way I did, and that's something I'm going to have to carry with me for the rest of my life. I deluded myself into thinking that if your father and Pamela never found out, then no one would be hurt. Your mother made me happy and I like to think that's how she felt about me."

"Right up until the time that she killed herself over you."

"What?" he says, sounding shocked by my allegation. "That's not what happened."

"Isn't it? Why else would she be swimming in the ocean alone? Did she give you her suicide note?"

I'm staring at him, my jaw clenched. If I were a different type of man, I would have already hit him.

"Alex, you have it all wrong." This he says calmly,

as if he's trying to soothe me. "Your mother's death was an accident. She had no reason to be upset with me. Things between us were fine. Believe me, if your mother was upset, especially if she was suicidal, I would have known about it. You know your mother, she's not the type to have kept that kind of sadness to herself."

"I'm not sure I can represent you," I say.

"Why not?"

"Are you serious? I have a pretty definite conflict of interest here."

"You can't just walk away from me, Alex."

"I don't owe you anything, Michael. I thought my father would have been pleased by the fact I was helping you, but if he knew what I know, he'd tell me to run for the hills."

"Well, maybe what I should have said is that I don't really have the luxury of letting you withdraw. I've got two million bucks with your firm, and otherwise I don't have a pot to piss in, now that every last nickel I have is frozen. My guess is you've spent most of the retainer already, and so whatever I get back—if your firm gives anything back—won't be enough to hire someone else of the caliber I need."

"Again, Michael, that's not my problem. You might have thought about that before retaining the son of the woman you were cheating on your wife with."

He takes a long breath, and then lets the air escape through his mouth. "Alex, have you ever asked yourself why I sought you out? Don't get me wrong, you're a top-notch criminal defense lawyer, but you don't need me to tell you that I could have retained someone else who would have been equally well credentialed. Hell, I might have even been able to get Aaron Littman's attention with a two-million-dollar retainer. So why do you think I picked you?"

I had wondered that, but frankly no more seriously in this case than I do whenever a client retains me. Even within the rarified air of $700 an hour white-collar criminal defense lawyers in New York City, there must be more than a hundred of us. There are probably five or six in Cromwell Altman alone, although Ohlig's wrong about a $2 million retainer coming close to getting Aaron's attention. It always seemed like a matter of happenstance more than anything else that someone comes to retain me. Usually it's because the client knows someone who knows me, either through a previous case or whatever connections people make. We share a dentist, or a friend went to college with me. More than once, the referral came from the parent of one of Charlotte's friends.

"Why don't you just tell me why, Michael?"

"Because I wanted someone for whom I wasn't just another case. I knew that representing me would be personal for you, and that's what I wanted. Because it is personal for me."

"Fair enough, but now it seems like you've gotten more personal involvement from me than you bargained for."

"Maybe, but maybe not. I know you're angry now, and I'd be too if I were you. But I think I know you well enough at this point to be able to make some judgments about the kind of man you are, and it tells me that you're still the one I want defending me."

That settles it. If Ohlig wants me as his lawyer, there's no way Judge Sullivan would let me withdraw, especially on the trial's eve. Still, I want him to know, in no uncertain terms, that things have changed between us.

"Big chance to take with your freedom, isn't it?" I say.

He smiles, as if to say that he knows I'm bluffing. "Remember that at your mother's funeral I told you that I think of you like family?" I do, but answer him only with a barely perceptible nod. "I meant that, and I still do. And, Alex, the thing about family is that family forgives. Maybe not right away, but in time, family always forgives. So, you ask me if I'm taking a big risk by putting my freedom in your hands? I don't see it that way. I have faith in you, as a lawyer and as a man. I know that as a lawyer, you will convince the jury that I'm innocent, and that, in time, as a man, you'll forgive me."

"Not guilty," I say.

"How's that?" he asks, not getting my point.

"The jury. The best they'll be able to do for you is declare you not guilty. Innocence isn't relevant here."

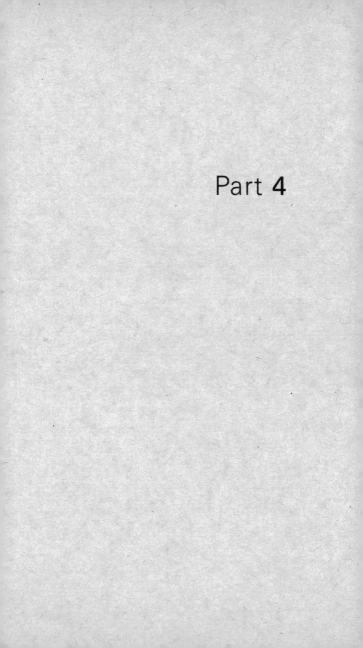

Part **4**

## 34

Judge Sullivan would have made a fine dictator. Everything in her courtroom runs on time. The trial of the United States of America versus Michael Louis Ohlig is no exception; it starts right on schedule.

There are probably sixty spectators in the gallery, a number I expect to be cut in half by tomorrow, but doubled on the day of the verdict. There are the usual court watchers, retirees mainly, who have decided that showing up to court every day is as entertaining as catching a movie, or at least that it's free. I also spot three court sketch artists. They work on spec, hoping to sell their work to the news outlets, or even to the lawyers as a piece of vanity art. Many of the rest I assume are reporters.

Aside from his wife, Ohlig is without any supporters in the audience. Some of that stands to reason, considering Ohlig's friends live in Florida and I've instructed his business colleagues to stay far away, or else risk the possibility they'll be easy targets for the FBI to question. Allison Shaw wanted to be here, but I put the kibosh on that one, fearing that the jurors might reach the same first impression about the nature of her relationship with Ohlig that I had.

Pamela Ohlig sits dutifully in the gallery's front row. Per my instructions, she's wearing nothing that costs

more than $500. Ohlig, too, is conservatively dressed—
dark suit, blue shirt, dark tie. As I asked, he's left the
Patek Philippe at home.

For my part, I'm wearing both the tie Elizabeth gave
me for my birthday and the cufflinks from Abby. Elizabeth said "nice cufflinks" when she saw me for the first
time today, and I told her that "I found them on eBay."

Judge Sullivan conducts the voir dire, the fancy
Latin term which literally means to tell the truth. Ety-
mology aside, in practice voir dire has very little to do
with truth; it is the process by which lawyers exclude
jurors that they think will decide against them. In some
courts, the lawyers are permitted to question potential
jurors, but for efficiency's sake, Judge Sullivan does all
the questioning herself.

The judge did permit the lawyers to submit questions to her in advance. We were sure that some of
those we proposed Judge Sullivan wouldn't ask because
she'd deem them to be too inflammatory, like "Do you
know of instances where the police have framed innocent people?" Others she'll ask, but they won't provide
us any more information than we can tell by looking at
the people who answer them.

The jury consultant we've hired, a woman named Leslie Newman, charges more per hour than I do. She's done
focus groups, polling, and psychological profiles in an
effort to ascertain the type of person most likely to acquit
Michael Ohlig. After all that work—and about $200,000
in fees—she's concluded our optimal juror is a non-
college-educated man, preferably under fifty years of age.

Her argument was one I'd heard before and, truth be told, is considered gospel by many: "The last thing I want is a jury that understands what's being presented to them," she said when we discussed the issue with Ohlig a few days ago. "I want a jury that's as confused as humanly possible. From confusion comes exasperation and then, eventually, someone will say the fact that they are confused is the very definition of reasonable doubt."

I couldn't disagree more. To the extent I have a cogent philosophy concerning picking juries, it's this: The stronger your case, the smarter the jury you want. It's pretty basic logic. If you want the jury to get it right, you need to pick jurors who are smart enough to understand what you're telling them.

I didn't voice any disagreement with Newman's approach, however. I could feel Abby's questioning look beside me, but she's kept her concerns to herself, at least for the time being.

Newman's only going to be at trial for the jury selection, so we've agreed she shouldn't sit at counsel table for the voir dire. She initially protested, but I won out by explaining that I didn't want the jury seeing that one day she's part of the team and the next she's gone. The smart ones will figure out we've hired a jury consultant, which is never good, and the less smart ones might think we've fired her, which would be worse, especially because she's African-American.

The compromise was that we would have a fairly rudimentary hand signal, the same one my fourth-grade

Little League coach used as the steal sign. If she touches her face, it means she wants to strike the juror. No facial contact means I'm being given the green light to put that person on the jury. Just in case she sneezes or accidentally touches her face, we've devised a cancellation system. Both hands on the face mean that the previous signal should be erased, and I should wait for a new one.

During jury selection, I follow the marching orders Newman hands down to a tee. I use our eight peremptory challenges to keep off the first eight college-educated people in the jury pool. The jury we end up with is exactly what Newman wanted—eight of the twelve don't have college degrees, and six of them are men. But of the four we couldn't strike, one is a retired Air Force colonel, and he should scare the hell out of Newman.

Pavin's opening is good. Better than good, in fact. He addresses the jury for nearly two hours, although the time goes by much faster than that, and he hits all the right notes. He tells the jury that the victims are people just like them, only that they had the misfortune of being called on the phone by someone who worked for Michael Ohlig. From there Pavin segues seamlessly into describing Ohlig's personal wealth. Even though I made Ohlig sell the vacation properties, Pavin has a way of describing what's left—the waterfront mansion in Palm Beach, the luxury cars (two Mercedes sedans, after Ohlig sold his Rolls), and the yacht (something Ohlig refused to sell)—as if merely possessing these things should be a crime.

After establishing Ohlig as a cross between Bernie

Madoff and the Grinch, Pavin lays out the evidence the government will present as if he's reading from a crime novel. He foreshadows the main event—the testimony of Eric Fieldston—whom Pavin describes as a surrogate son to Ohlig, and tells the jury that despite all of Ohlig's efforts to corrupt him, Fieldston's conscience could no longer bear the lives that were ruined, and he has now come forward to tell the truth.

I had thought Pavin would have trouble connecting with a jury because he's always so formal, but he turns out to be one of those rare lawyers who is quite a different person in front of a jury. He seems completely at ease, which permits him to create an intimacy that at times sounds almost as if he's addressing their concerns rather than making an argument.

My opening is less than fifteen minutes, with the focus entirely on reasonable doubt. When I've finished, I know my client is none too pleased.

Ohlig glares at me as the jurors file out for the day, and he doesn't even wait until we've left the courtroom before voicing his displeasure. "Alex, how could you drop the entire section about my testifying without consulting me?"

"You have to let me try the case," I tell him in a calm voice. "Just because I didn't promise the jury you'd testify doesn't mean you won't. It just keeps our options open a little longer."

When we're back at the office and alone, Abby sounds a similar note of displeasure with the way I opened the case. "I'm not second-guessing you, Alex," she says, although that's exactly what she's doing, "but first the jury selection and now this. What's going on?"

"What do you mean?"

"I mean that you knew Leslie's recommendation was not the right way to go, but you followed it anyway. And you've been telling me since day one that our only chance of an acquittal depends on Ohlig testifying, and now it looks like you're going back on that too."

"I didn't know Leslie was wrong; I just disagreed with her analysis. But Leslie's the jury expert, not me. If she thinks this is the way to go on the jury, it's not my place to disagree. As for Ohlig testifying, I'm still leaning toward putting him on, but Pavin's opening was stronger than I had anticipated, so I thought we needed some more leeway. Besides, you know that Aaron had strong views on this subject, so it's not as if I'm alone on this."

"It's me you're talking to, Alex," she says, seemingly more disappointed in me than angry at me. "Don't tell me that all of a sudden you've concluded that Leslie and Aaron are right. Lying to yourself is one thing, but don't think I'm going to be an accomplice."

"What's that supposed to mean?"

"It means that something is going on with you, and I'm not sure you're dealing with it the right way."

"Why don't you just come out and say it, Abby. You think that I'm throwing the case, don't you?"

"I'm not saying that, Alex. I'm really not. It's just that you have a pretty big conflict of interest and I'm worried about the decisions you're making."

"What's life except a series of conflicts of interest?" I say with a smile.

She doesn't smile back.

"Okay. Let me put your mind at ease. I fully understand my duty to represent my client zealously, and that's what I'm doing. You know better than anyone, litigation is an art, not a science, and reasonable people can disagree about strategy. That doesn't mean that I'm throwing the case, it just means we disagree."

I pause, trying to gauge whether Abby is on board. When I can't tell, I just ask, "Are we okay?"

"Yeah," she says, rather weakly.

# 35

It wouldn't surprise me if the Department of Justice manual requires AUSAs to open their cases by calling the FBI agent who handled the investigation because I've never been involved in a case where that wasn't what they did. I almost mouthed his name along with Pavin when he told Judge Sullivan that the government's first witness would be Special Agent Gregory McNiven.

McNiven can best be described as rugged in that everything about him is unfinished. He's wearing a dark blue suit, but it fits too snugly, probably because he bought it a while ago. My guess is that it's the only suit he owns, probably purchased when he joined the FBI, and now he pulls it out only when he's needed in court. He sports a lapel pin with an American flag, the only person outside of an elected official who still wears one.

On most trials, FBI agents act as the associate to the AUSA. A bigger trial may require more junior AUSAs, but in this one I'm sure McNiven plays Abby's role—the document reviewer, the fact maven, the sounding board.

The irony is that AUSAs and FBI agents have inversely proportional interest in white-collar cases. Although the AUSAs prosecuting terrorists or mob bosses have the better cocktail party stories, law firms look for ex-prosecutors who can defend the people they formerly sent to jail, and there aren't too many terrorists or busted mobsters able to pay a thousand bucks an hour for defense counsel. That means that AUSAs most covet white-collar work because it's the gateway to later riches at places like Cromwell Altman. The reverse is true for FBI agents, however. They join the Bureau to catch the real bad guys, the more violent the better. For them, being placed on a high-profile white-collar prosecution is akin to a cop being relegated to traffic duty.

Even though McNiven has probably testified in court at least a hundred times, Pavin nevertheless follows the textbook approach for direct examination—start by going through the witness's background to put the witness at ease, asking softball questions before getting to the hard stuff. It reminds me of Freeman's joke at Pavin's expense during the joint defense meeting—Pavin not only follows the book; he's also memorized it.

But this approach establishes beyond any doubt that McNiven is the real deal. In response to questions about his background, McNiven testifies that he graduated from Penn State on a ROTC ride, then served in Iraq, winning two medals for valor, and joined the FBI when his tour was over. He's been with the FBI for a little more than three years, serving most of his tenure in Organized Crime, which he refers to as "OC." He testifies that he was recently transferred to securities enforcement, omitting whatever infraction he committed to wind up in FBI agent purgatory.

McNiven's primary job as a witness is to explain to

the jury what was learned through the documentary evidence. "It is what it is" might be the silliest of all clichés, but when someone is testifying to what he's read in documents, the phrase is pretty apt. Nothing McNiven says from here on out is likely to be contested.

"Special Agent McNiven," Pavin says, "please tell the jury the number of shares of Salminol that OPM purchased."

"Approximately 185 million."

"What percentage of the company did OPM own at that time?"

"Approximately 27 percent."

"And Special Agent McNiven, how many of those 185 million shares did OPM own on the day that Salminol filed for bankruptcy?"

"None."

"Not a single one?"

"No, sir. Not one share."

"What happened to those shares, Special Agent?" Pavin asks this as if he truly has no idea.

"They were sold."

"Please tell the jury, Special Agent, the average share price at which OPM sold its position in Salminol."

Just as Pavin sprinkles his statement to the court with the words *your Honor,* he can't help but refer to McNiven as *Special Agent* at every opportunity. I'm tempted to make the point on cross-examination that every single FBI agent is a special agent—there's no one who's just a regular agent—which indicates that McNiven might not be so special after all.

"OPM sold at an average share price of $1.07."

"What was the average share price that OPM paid for those shares, Special Agent?"

"A little more than nineteen cents."

"Special Agent McNiven, were you able to calculate the total profit that OPM made on its Salminol purchase and sales?"

"$161,850,448."

Pavin lets the number speak for itself. After enough time has passed for the jury to recognize that Pavin considers this a strong point for the prosecution, he turns the witness over to me.

My cross is short, focusing on the only things I know McNiven won't fight me on. He concedes the share price of thinly traded securities—which he refers to as penny stocks whenever he can—sometimes rises quickly, but not before saying that such stocks are prime targets for illegal manipulation. He also has no choice but to acknowledge that Ohlig didn't sell his personal holdings of Salminol, suffering an almost $4.5 million loss, but he counters by making the obvious point that Ohlig's personal loss was more than offset by the enormous profit he earned through OPM.

When I'm done, Judge Sullivan dismisses the jury, reminding them to stay clear of the media and to return by 9:30 the next morning. When the jury has left, she says, "Counsel, anything else for us to do today?"

Pavin and I rise in unison and then say at the same time, "No," with him then adding the "your Honor" part.

"Very well," Judge Sullivan says. "Enjoy your evening."

I chuckle to myself. Perhaps Pavin will, but I know I won't. Today has not gone well, and I'm sure my client is going to tell me so as soon as he can.

Back in the war room after court, it doesn't take a mind reader to recognize that Ohlig is disgusted with me. It's of little concern to me, however. The client's ultimate opinion is invariably based solely on the result.

"My guess is that tomorrow Pavin will do a few of the OPM brokers," I tell Ohlig as he's getting ready to leave for his hotel. "They'll testify to the way the business ran, and my cross is going to be limited to establishing that they didn't know anything was wrong with Salminol. I figure they'll have to acknowledge that or else they'll be admitting their own securities law violations."

"Make sure you ask them if I ever told them to lie," Ohlig says. "They'll say that not only did I never do that, but that I said that one lie and they were out on their asses."

"I'm not going to go there." I say this firmly, not wanting to invite a debate on the subject. "Rule number one in cross-examination—don't ask anything unless you're positively sure of the answer. All we need is for one of these guys to say that they think you've sometimes crossed the ethical line and you're toast."

Ohlig glares at me, holding the stare for a good twenty seconds before speaking. "Does the truth matter to you at all? I guarantee that if you ask them whether I ever told them to do anything they thought was dishonest, they'd say I didn't."

I look in Abby's direction. She knows better than to disagree with me in front of the client, but by not meeting my eyes that's exactly what she's doing.

"The type of pressure the government has over them means they could say just about anything," I reply. "For all we know, Pavin could be threatening that he's going to bring a perjury indictment if they say anything he doesn't like."

"It sounds like I'm not going to add anything," Ohlig says, making little effort to mask his annoyance. "After all, it's not like what I think matters to you anyway, Alex. I'm just the guy who's going to end up in jail if you're wrong."

Elizabeth is awake when I get home. We've barely spoken since the trial began. In fact, we've barely spoken since Abby and I had sex, which was seven days ago (but who's counting). Some of that has to do with the late hours I've been keeping, which is par for the course when on trial, but it's also because I've been more than happy to avoid Elizabeth. I fear that she'll be able to see the betrayal on my face—not just for that one night, but of my continuing thoughts of Abby each and every day.

"You're up?" I say.

"I wanted to know how you were doing."

"Not good. Hopefully things will get better when we put on our case."

"I didn't mean about the case. How are *you* doing, Alex?"

"I'm not sure. It's harder than I thought. I really don't like him."

"Why? I thought you believed he was innocent. Did something happen to change your mind?"

Then I remember, I still haven't told Elizabeth about my mother's affair. I could tell her now, but I don't, for the same reasons I didn't tell her the first time.

"It's nothing specific," I stammer, "it's just that when his second-in-command flipped, I figured I must have been wrong about him." It's a lie, of course, but on the continuum of falsehoods I've told Elizabeth lately, it's a minor one.

"Well, no offense, Alex, but it's hardly a shocker that your client ends up being guilty after claiming he was innocent. I don't remember that ever upsetting you before, so why does it matter to you now?"

"Because in those cases I still wanted to win, and here I've started to believe that Michael Ohlig deserves to be punished for what he did."

# 36

A few years ago, I represented a twenty-two-year-old guy named Dominic Avallone who was arrested as part of what the Manhattan DA's office called "a major crackdown on Wall Street." The charge was securities fraud, but the underlying conduct was that he allowed his brokerage firm, a bucket shop called First Brooklyn Securities, to pay someone to take his Series 7 securities exam, the test that would-be brokers have to pass before dealing with the public. A Series 7 test is about as difficult as a driver's license exam, but it took only a few minutes with Dominic for me to realize there was no way he could have passed the test on account of the fact that he could barely read.

I tell this story because "Wall Street" is one of those terms that is awfully broad, ranging from the CEO of Goldman Sachs to guys like Dominic Avallone. More reputable brokerage firms may have their bad apples, but, by and large, their brokers are college educated, hardworking and honest. To become a broker at one of those places you not only need to get hired, which isn't easy given the competition, but then you also need to survive a somewhat rigorous training program. As you go down the food chain to lesser prestigious brokerage houses, the competition for employment is less and, oftentimes, so is the training.

OPM hired some brokers out of college, but most came from other walks of life. The training was little more than reading a twenty-seven-page manual, and it's likely no one ever actually did that.

The government's first witness on the second day of trial proves the point. His name is Lawrence Connors. He's tall and gangly, still much more a boy than a man, and is dressed in a double-breasted suit and clip-on red suspenders, as if he takes his sartorial cues from the movie *Wall Street*.

If McNiven's resume prepared jurors to hear from a man of integrity, Connors's background completely underscores just how unqualified OPM's brokers were to sell stock to the public. The point is driven home right off the bat when Connors explains how he joined OPM after being fired as the assistant manager of a Sbarro's at the food court in a Palm Beach mall.

Pavin takes Connors through the day-to-day activity of a broker at OPM. I've heard the same story dozens of times through the years—the morning meetings in which a voice on a speakerphone (often from the office next door) tells the brokers about which stock is to be sold that day, the dissemination of the "research" about the stock, which the brokers then use to develop a sales pitch, and the 3-by-5 cards identifying prospective customers—the "leads," as they're called—which are treated like gold, but are actually little more than the phone numbers for the senior citizens in the area.

"Was Salminol ever the stock of the day?" Pavin asks.

"Yes."

"For more than one day?"

"Yes. It was the stock of the day for more than a week," Connors says.

"Did you ever do any research yourself regarding Salminol?"

"No."

"So you didn't even run an internet search?"

"We didn't get the internet at the office," Connors says, which causes some titters in the gallery, although Connors doesn't seem to understand what they find amusing.

"Then how did you know what to tell the customers?"

"The research analysts told us what to say."

"How did they do that?"

"They would tell us over the phone, and sometimes they would hand out written materials."

"Did they hand out written materials with regard to Salminol?"

"No."

"Do you know why OPM didn't want to commit to writing what it was telling customers with regard to Salminol?"

"Objection," I say, "assumes facts not in evidence regarding the implication that OPM did not want to commit to anything in writing."

Judge Sullivan seems startled, undoubtedly because I've objected so infrequently. This was a no-brainer, however.

"I think you can ask a better question than that, Mr. Pavin," she says, a common judicial dodge to avoid having to rule.

"Thank you, your Honor," Pavin says. "Do you know why there were not written materials regarding Salminol, Mr. Connors?"

"No."

It's one of the reasons that I don't object much. There's really little point, other than to awaken everyone in the courtroom to the fact that something is about to be said that's damaging to your case. Here, all I've done is to get the jury to focus on the fact that OPM decided not to issue written materials on Salminol, and never explained why to its brokers.

"Did you ever meet any of the research analysts?" Pavin asks.

"No."

"Do you know whether they truly exist?"

"They would put their names on the top of the research reports."

"Is that the only reason you assume that these people existed? Because you read a name at the top of a piece of paper?"

"Yes," Connors answers, not even smart enough to realize how foolish he sounds.

I know that Pavin has left things out of his direct as little booby traps for me to step on during the cross. For instance, when I get Connors to confirm that Ohlig did not require that he or anyone else sell Salminol, he goes on to say that OPM offered four times the selling commission for it, so Ohlig didn't have to say it. The questions about the pitch go the same way.

"You decided what to tell prospective buyers, correct?" I ask.

"I took it from the research reports."

"No one ever told you what to say, did they, Mr. Connors? There was not a script you read from, correct?"

"No."

"And Mr. Connors, no one ever told you that you couldn't do your own research, did they?"

"No, but—"

I don't let him expand. It's litigation 101. Never let a witness gain control of the examination. I wanted a straight "no," and when I don't get it, I need to ask a more limited question.

"Did anyone at OPM ever tell you directly, Mr. Connors, you are not allowed to do your own research?"

"No, but—"

"Sir, the answer is simply yes or no," I say, anticipating that he was going to remind me that the OPM brokers did not have internet capabilities on their system.

I expect Pavin to object, but he doesn't. This can only mean that he's prepared Connors well enough to handle this on his own. Connors breaks eye contact with me and looks directly at Judge Sullivan. "I can't answer yes or no, your Honor. They told us that everything we needed to know about Salminol was in the written research, and I couldn't do my own research even if I wanted to because we didn't get the internet at the office."

By the time I tell Judge Sullivan I have no further questions, I wonder if more damage has been done on my cross than Pavin did on direct.

Ohlig looks at me as if there were no question about it.

The next witness is another OPM broker, a guy named Tom Pittman, who provides pretty much the same testimony as Connors. In all, Pavin has six OPM brokers on his witness list, and so when he says he wants to call a third one, I ask Judge Sullivan for a sidebar.

After we approach and Judge Sullivan nods in my direction, I say, "Your Honor, this broker's testimony is just going to be duplicative of what Mr. Connors and Mr. Pittman just said. The government has put every OPM broker on its witness list, but there's no reason for them to call additional brokers because their testimony is going to be duplicative of what the jury has already heard."

Judge Sullivan doesn't respond, but from her body language, I can see that she agrees. Just like anyone else, she doesn't want to hear the same thing over and over again.

Then Pavin lays down a trump card.

"Your Honor, we'd like to call one more broker witness. He's got something new to add."

"What is it, Mr. Pavin?" Judge Sullivan asks, sounding skeptical. Lawyers are a lot like children in that, no matter how much you give them, they always want one more.

"He's going to say that Mr. Ohlig offered him a bribe in order to change his testimony."

"Well, Mr. Miller," she says, peering down at me from the bench. "*That's* something different, wouldn't you say? Let's take a ten-minute recess and then you can call your witness, Mr. Pavin."

"You couldn't just send this one away on a Caribbean vacation?" I'm careful not to raise my voice too much because we're in one of the annex rooms right outside the courtroom and the walls are thin. "You had to go all out and *bribe* this one?"

Ohlig chuckles as if he's amused by the joke.

"There's nothing funny about this, Michael! What do you think you're doing? This is a *serious* crime you've committed. On top of which, I'm betting that Pavin is going to think I'm a co-conspirator. And call me crazy, but I'd rather not be indicted at this stage of my legal career."

"Can I offer something?" Abby says.

"I wish you would," Ohlig says, as calm as always. "I think Alex here is about to explode."

"Can't we keep the evidence out on relevance grounds? Bribing a witness"—Abby looks at Ohlig—"*allegedly* bribing a witness isn't evidence that Michael committed securities fraud."

"It is evidence of obstruction of justice, however," I say.

"So let Pavin bring those charges," Abby counters. "But we can argue that it isn't one of the counts of this indictment, and it's unduly prejudicial under Rules 404 and 608."

Ohlig responds before I can. "Abby, *you* make the argument. Maybe you'll have better luck on this one than Alex, since you, at least, seem interested in my defense."

"May we approach, your Honor," I say as soon as we reenter the courtroom. The jury hasn't been summoned yet, but I don't want to have this discussion in front of the press.

"What is it, Mr. Miller?" Judge Sullivan says, clearly annoyed that there's going to be a further delay.

"If we may approach."

"Come, but make it quick," she says.

As soon as we're beside the bench, I tell her that we'd like to be heard on the relevance of the prosecution's next witness.

"Didn't we already discuss this at the last sidebar?" Judge Sullivan says rather sternly. "Mr. Pavin has already proffered a theory of relevance that was accepted by this court."

"The relevancy objection we previously discussed concerned duplicative testimony," I explain. "Now that the government has identified the new area that this witness is going to address, we would like to be heard about why the testimony should be excluded under the Federal Rules of Evidence."

"Make it quick, Mr. Miller." Judge Sullivan sighs as if she's got somewhere else she's supposed to be.

"Actually, Ms. Sloane is going to address the court on this one."

"Let's hear it, Ms. Sloane."

"Thank you, your Honor," Abby says. "Without conceding the truth of what this witness will say, testimony about an alleged bribe isn't relevant to the crime at hand, but speaks to the commission of another crime, one with an extremely attenuated relationship to securities fraud. Pursuant to Federal Rules of Evidence 404 and 608, this kind of testimony is, at most, character evidence, which is inadmissible for the purposes of proving that the person acted in conformity therewith. To the extent the government claims it's impeachment evidence, it would still be improper at this juncture of the proceedings because Mr. Ohlig has not testified and therefore there's nothing to be impeached. Finally, if the government has evidence of the commission of another crime, they have an obligation to present such charges to a grand jury. They can't end-run that requirement by introducing the evidence now in this trial."

Abby is nothing short of outstanding. Perhaps it's because of the hold she has on me, but I can't keep my eyes off her. She's confident and in total control, and I'm embarrassed that it reminds me of how she was in bed.

"Your Honor, this is an issue for the jury," Pavin says when it's his turn. "If they don't believe the witness's testimony that Mr. Ohlig offered him money if he recanted, then so be it. But if they do believe it, then it certainly shows a guilty state of mind by Mr. Ohlig."

"When did you learn of this alleged bribe offer?" Judge Sullivan asks.

"I'm not exactly sure, your Honor."

And bingo—Judge Sullivan's expression leaves little doubt that Pavin just gave the wrong answer. If there's one thing she simply will not tolerate, it's the government not being straight with her.

"That tells me it wasn't yesterday, which is the only excuse that I would have tolerated from an Assistant United States Attorney for failing to raise this issue before trial. You go back and you tell the United States Attorney that he is *never* to send an Assistant to me that doesn't know precisely when evidence of a crime was discovered."

"Your Honor—"

"Don't even think about your Honoring me," Judge Sullivan snaps. "Tell me, Mr. Pavin, who is the government planning on calling after this next witness?"

"Your—" And then Pavin catches himself before finishing the phrase. "Our next witness is our expert. Unfortunately, he's not in the courtroom today. We had expected to lead with him tomorrow—"

"Stop right there, Mr. Pavin. You're zero for two and, to be blunt about it, I'm really quite fed up with you today. The very idea that you would not have your next witness present so that you thought I'd have no choice but to let you go with this one or else lose the afternoon—"

"That's not it—" Pavin is trying to get a word in, but Judge Sullivan won't let him.

"You listen when I'm speaking, Mr. Pavin. That's how it works. In case you forget that, ask yourself who's wearing the robe. Because that's the person who *always* goes first."

"I'm sorry, your Honor."

"Don't apologize, just do your job better. And, to help you out, I'm going to give you the rest of the day off to talk to your boss about what happened today in court. And then bright and early tomorrow morning, you can put on your expert."

No matter how much you hate your adversary, it's still hard to watch him getting his head handed to him by a judge. Not that Pavin doesn't deserve it, but I know it could just as easily be me the next time, and it probably will be.

"Abby, I really owe you," Ohlig says later, when we're heading back to the office. "How about I treat you to a very nice dinner. Ever been to Masa?"

Nothing but the best, or should I say, the most expensive, for Ohlig. I've never been to Masa, but I understand you can't get out of there for less than $400 a person.

"You too, Alex," he adds, although I get the sense that his invitation to me is hardly sincere.

"Thank you," I say, "but I should take advantage of the mini-vacation to prepare for Heller. Sansotta will be here by five."

Andrew Heller is the government's expert economist, and Paolo Sansotta is our counterpoint. Ohlig knows about this meeting with Sansotta, which is probably why he invited me to come along with Abby—he knew I'd have to decline.

"That leaves just you and me," he says to Abby. "Is it a date?"

She looks to me for the answer, but I'm doing my best to provide no hint. I could, of course, keep her from going simply by saying that she's needed for the expert prep, but that would concede that I think she'd otherwise go.

I could also push her the other way if I told her I'd be fine without her, denying her a polite decline. That, also, would cede too much.

"Thank you," she says, "but I need to stay here and help."

"I guess you're right," Ohlig says, without a smile this time. "I'd be in serious trouble if I didn't have you keeping Alex honest."

# 37

Abby and I meet with Sansotta for about an hour, but by six-thirty I tell them both that I'm ready to call it a night. Abby looks at me like I'm crazy but doesn't say anything until after Sansotta's left.

"So that's it?"

"Now that I have you keeping me honest, there's really nothing else for me to do."

I didn't intend for it to sound like I was taking my ball and bat and going home, but I suspect that's exactly what it sounded like.

"I'm sorry, Alex. But you know it's not my fault."

"I know, Abby. I didn't mean it that way. You did a great job today. You should be as proud of yourself as Ohlig is pleased with your work. I'll definitely be sure to mention it to Aaron."

"I hope you can tell that I'm not at all happy about this."

"There's no reason for you not to be happy. Angry clients are part of the job. I'd be concerned if he wasn't angry. At least with you on the team, he likes one of us."

"Then why are you leaving now?"

"I haven't seen Charlotte in weeks, and I thought this was an opportunity for me to cut out early."

"Okay," Abby says, although she sounds far from

okay. "I guess it's no secret that I miss being with you outside of the courtroom."

"Same here," I say.

The entire day in court washes away the moment I hear Charlotte's excited announcement that I'm home. Without any lead-in, she's talking to me as if we've been in the middle of a conversation.

"Gavin said that I wasn't allowed to play monster because that's a boy game and the girls have to play dress-up and princess, but I like playing monster sometimes. The other girls are scared, but it's not like there's a real monster, it's just one of the boys, usually it's Ryan, wearing a scary mask and screaming like this—*grrrrrrrrrrrrrrr*—and so it's not scary, and if you tag the monster you get to be the monster the next time."

"You go to an all girls' school; where do you play with boys?" I'm embarrassed to even be asking this question, given that it highlights just how much of my daughter's life is foreign to me.

"At sports, after school. There are boys and sometimes at the end, if we're good, they let us play whatever we want. And that's when the boys play monster."

"So did you get to be the monster?"

"Daddy, I just told you, girls aren't allowed to play monster."

"But I thought you wanted to play."

"I want to play, but they won't let me. Isn't that unfair?"

"That sounds very unfair."

"Do you want to play monster with me, Daddy? You could be the monster, but if I tag you, then I'll be the monster."

Elizabeth has up until now been standing quietly as Charlotte detailed the discriminatory practices of monster. "Sweetheart," Elizabeth says, "Daddy's probably hungry. After he has some dinner, then maybe the two of you can play monster."

"Then what should I do now?" Charlotte asks.

"Do you want to watch a little SpongeBob?"

Elizabeth often jokes that SpongeBob is like crack for five-year-olds. Sometimes she jokingly refers to an episode as a bump, as in, *Maybe I'll give Charlotte a bump of the Bob to chill her out.*

Charlotte is clearly pleased with Elizabeth's offer. In fact, I'm sure she views it as much more of a win-win than a compromise.

After the television is turned on, Elizabeth joins me in the dining room, and hands me a glass of red wine. A half-filled glass is already on the table.

"Is the trial over?" Elizabeth says with a sarcastic smile. She knows it's not but is asking why I'm home before midnight.

"The judge let us out early."

"So, how's it going?" she asks, after taking a sip of her wine.

"We're getting our butts kicked is how it's going. But Abby had a strong day today, so at least she's making Ohlig happy."

I'm exploring Elizabeth's face for some reaction to

my invocation of Abby's name. As usual my wife is difficult to read. Maybe because I want to push Elizabeth into some revelation about Abby, I begin to explain Abby's heroics. "So, Ohlig clearly bribed this guy to change his testimony. Of course, he doesn't seem the least bit concerned he's been found out, and it's now my job to make sure that, even though he's committed a crime, it's not put into evidence. I'm telling him there's no way, and then Abby comes up with this half-baked relevancy argument. Ohlig loves it, and he tells me that he wants her to make it. I say fine, and wouldn't you know it, Judge Sullivan ends up being pissed at the prosecutor over something else entirely and so she rules in our favor. That's justice in America. The one time we should definitely lose an argument, we win because the judge wants to send a message to the U.S. Attorney, probably as some kind of payback over something that happened in another case, maybe years ago."

"But it's good for you, right?"

"Yes. For today, it was good, but tomorrow's likely to be quite another story. First they're going to put their expert on, and then, after that, Fieldston is going to testify. He's Ohlig's number two and he's just going to bury us."

"You don't think that Ohlig's testimony will be enough for reasonable doubt?"

Once again Elizabeth's grasp of trial strategy is right on. I suppose being married to a litigator is the equivalent of at least two years of law school.

"It's the only thing that might. He's really quite

good. I guess it's true what they say: once you can fake sincerity, everything else is easy."

After dinner, I play monster with Charlotte, alternating between being the monster and the scared villager. At different intervals Charlotte tells me that I'm playing wrong, even though it doesn't seem to me that there are any rules besides running around screaming. After the game, it's bedtime, and I read her the same story I did the last time I put her to bed, which was more than three months ago, I think.

Elizabeth is watching television in bed. After I've returned from my evening ritual, brushing my teeth, taking my contact lenses out, and putting on my pajamas, I notice that she's wearing a nightgown. It's not one of the lacy things that I've bought her over the years for Valentine's Day, the kind that's intended to be worn once, and even then for less than five minutes. Rather, it's what I suspect some women wear to sleep every night, but Elizabeth prefers flannel pajamas, especially in the winter.

"Is that new?"

"No. I just don't wear it very often. Do you like it?"

"I do."

She looks beautiful, and the initial pang of desire I feel frightens more than emboldens me.

It feels like I'm cheating on Abby.

Abby might even ask me about it tomorrow, and the idea that I'd lie to her about whether I was sleeping with my wife just seems too ridiculous, even for me.

But I suspect that's what Abby was thinking when she questioned me about why I was going home early.

Why is it that my lust for Abby doesn't conjure the same fear? When I want Abby, it only makes me angry at Elizabeth, but the opposite isn't true. For some reason, I'm angry at Elizabeth now too.

"What are we watching?" I ask.

"It's a *Law & Order* rerun." Elizabeth laughs. "I'll switch it. I'm sure you've seen enough courtroom drama for a while."

"It's fine. I'm really tired, anyway. I'll probably be asleep before Charlotte."

I take my glasses off and put them on the night table beside me. Then I turn away from the television and shut my eyes, hoping that sleep takes me soon.

Elizabeth strokes my hair for a few moments, most likely an effort to remind me that there are other options besides sleep. The last thing I remember is that she lowers the volume to allow me some rest.

## 38

Sitting in the witness box, Professor Andrew Heller embodies what Santa Claus would look like if he taught at a New England prep school for boys, which is to say that he's approaching seventy years old, seemingly hasn't lost a single white hair, has a full white beard, and completes the look with tortoiseshell glasses and a rep tie with the Harvard colors. All pulled together on his six-foot-four frame, he makes exactly the impression the government is paying him to make—a cross between the beneficence of Mr. Rogers and the authority of God.

Direct expert testimony is like a professional basketball game—it's only worth watching the last two minutes. It takes Pavin almost an hour to go through Professor Heller's curriculum vitae, at the end of which the jury knows that he's won just about every prize there is to win in the field of economics. At last, Pavin's about to get to the good part.

"In your expert opinion, Dr. Heller, did Mr. Ohlig know Salminol was being propped up solely by OPM making a market in that security?"

Heller's not qualified to testify about what Ohlig knew, only what he thinks a reasonable person would know, and so I could object to the question. When I don't, I earn another of Ohlig's icy stares.

"He did," Heller says in a confident voice.

"And do you further have an expert opinion concerning Mr. Ohlig's state of mind regarding the value of Salminol at the time his company was selling it to the public?"

"Yes. Mr. Ohlig knew Salminol was about to go bankrupt, making its stock worthless. At the same time, he was directing his sales force to sell it as a can't-miss investment."

Pavin nods at the jury. They look back like an approving audience getting their money's worth.

"Your witness," he says without making eye contact with me.

My cross is as it's been with all the government's witnesses—short. I make the obvious points—Heller has no firsthand experience in trading, he has never met Ohlig, he knew nothing about Salminol until this case, and he's being paid for his testimony. Then I'm done and I sit down.


"Are you just going to bend over and let this continue?!" Ohlig says as we're packing up to leave for lunch.

Since Heller's direct began, Ohlig has looked like just sitting next to me has been a struggle. Now that we're out of the jury's presence he's having even more difficulty containing his rage. So much so that if we weren't in a courtroom with armed guards, I actually think he might take a swing at me.

"And what would you have me do, Michael?"

"Try putting up more of a fight."

"Trust me," I say, and as soon as the words pass my lips I realize that's the problem. "All objecting does at this point is signal to the jury we're afraid of what he's saying."

Ohlig stares daggers at me. "So you decide that the best way to defend me is to kiss Professor Father Time's ass."

"Michael, the guy's a Nobel Prize winner; we're going to have to rely on Sansotta to offset him." I should probably leave well enough alone, but I don't. "I know we've had a couple of bad days, but I can't change the facts."

"Well, thank you very much, *counselor*, for that sparkling legal analysis."

We're at a stalemate. All that's left is Ohlig's glare repeating what he has already said—he's not happy with the way this is going, and he blames me 100 percent.

"I've been telling you for weeks that Fieldston's the guy," I say. "He'll be the government's final witness."

"There are a few more people left on their witness list," Abby points out.

"Pavin's not going to call them. After lunch, he's going to call Fieldston, and then he's going to rest. Fieldston will testify that Michael knew he was defrauding his customers, and that's the last piece Pavin needs to convict."

"You better make damn sure he doesn't get it," Ohlig says, and then storms out of the courtroom.

On Thursdays, Judge Sullivan gives everyone a two-hour lunch break so that we can all catch up on our other work, returning phone calls and the like, during business hours. That means Abby and I are heading back to the office.

Before heading down to the war room, I stop back in my office to check my emails. There's an envelope on my chair. It was hand-delivered, with my address printed out on a plain white label. Inside there's a DVD that is equally nondescript; it could have been purchased at any electronics store. Taped to the disk is a card on white stock that contains only the printed message: "THIS MIGHT HELP."

I dial up the mailroom. A man with a heavy Spanish accent answers. I think he says his name is Jorge.

"Hi, this is Alex Miller. I received a package on my chair, but it doesn't have any return address. Do you guys have a record of when we received it?"

"Who's it from?" Jorge asks.

"I don't know. There's no return address or any markings. I was hoping you guys might have a record of where it came from."

"Hold on."

I wait a minute or two while Jorge yells in Spanish to others in the mailroom, apparently having forgotten to put me on hold. When he comes back on the line, he says, "I'm sorry, but nobody here knows anything about any package to you."

This isn't much of a surprise. It stands to reason that someone going through the trouble to make sure that nothing on the package can be traced back would be smart enough not to leave their name and number with the mailroom.

"Jorge, let me ask you this. If someone dropped it off with security downstairs, is it possible that they would have just sent it up to my chair?"

"They're not supposed to," he says. "All packages are to go through the mailroom. Ever since 9–11. If it's a bomb or something, I guess they want us guys to explode." He laughs, even though his analysis is probably correct.

I walk the disk down to the war room and wave it at Abby. "Look what I got."

"What is it?"

"Don't know. It was left on my office chair. No return address. The note only said that it might help. The mailroom has no record of any delivery to me. Whoever sent us this gift wants to be anonymous."

"Yeah, I wonder who," she says.

Abby pulls her laptop out of her bag and puts the disk in the drive. A few clicks later and we hear a woman's voice. I don't recognize who it is, but it's mature, confident, and if such a thing is possible to ascertain from sound alone, she's as sexy as hell.

I can't reach Ohlig on his cell, which might be because he's still in the courthouse, having opted to have lunch with Pamela in the cafeteria, another sign he'd rather spend as little time as possible in my company. With no other choice, Abby and I head back to court, disk in hand.

Sure enough, we find him in the cafeteria. "I'm sorry,

Pamela," I say when we approach, "but I'm going to need Michael for a moment."

It's no surprise that Ohlig doesn't ask what's so important. Of course, he wouldn't ask under any circumstances, but like Abby had already surmised, in this case he almost surely knows why I've sought him out.

We go upstairs to the witness room adjoining Judge Sullivan's courtroom. It's the only place in the courthouse where we can be assured of privacy. As soon as Abby closes the door, I get down to business.

"A disk was left on my chair when I got back from court today. We don't know who sent it. It's audio only. The whole conversation—at least the part that's on the disk—is less than two minutes."

Ohlig starts to say something, but I put up my hand like a traffic cop, directing him to stop. "Let's hear it first, Michael, and then we can discuss it." Without waiting for a response, I motion to Abby to play the recording.

We all listen. And I'll be damned if Ohlig isn't wearing his Cheshire cat grin even before it gets to the good part.

"This is good for us, right?" Ohlig asks when the recording is finished.

"Could be good, could be bad," I begin to explain. "Let's say it's not Fieldston on the tape. Then it looks like we're manufacturing evidence. Not the best foot to put forward in a trial that so far isn't exactly going our way, don't you think?"

"I'm willing to take that chance," Ohlig says matter-of-factly enough that I no longer have any doubt about the disk's origin, not that I had much before. God only knows how many times Ohlig has sent beautiful women wearing wires to make small talk with Fieldston in the hope that he'd spill something.

"Michael, I want to stress that this could easily go very poorly for us. For starters, if Fieldston denies that it's him, Judge Sullivan won't give us an inch to prove otherwise, especially after your brilliant bribery attempt. But even in the best case scenario, Fieldston is just going to say it's out of context and a lot of the discussion was edited out. We'll then be at his mercy, and at that point he'll be out for blood."

"Let him say whatever he wants. After the tape is played, no one is going to believe a word out of his mouth."

"Michael, the jury is going to assume you set him up."

Ohlig's face tightens, a look that reminds me of a clenched fist. "I can't believe that you're seriously thinking about not using this," he says.

"I hear what you're saying, but—"

"No. Don't give me the 'I hear what you're saying' bullshit. Say it straight out. You blame me for your mother's death, and now you're trying to even the score."

"That's not true," I say, almost too reflexively, like when a boxer tells the referee that he wants to continue without regard to the beating he's just received.

"Then tell me what it is, Alex, because when someone drops a bombshell in our lap like this, it just doesn't make any sense to ignore it."

"I'm just trying to lay out the negatives for you," I say. "I know you don't like to hear negatives, but it's part of my job to see the risks as well as the rewards."

"Okay," he says, this time more calmly. "Now it's my turn to say it—I hear you, Alex. I understand the risks. I still want to go forward with using the tape. Agreed?"

"You're the client," I say, fully knowing it isn't a direct response.

"Good," he says. "Sometimes you act like that's not the case."

# 39

Eric Fieldston approaches the witness stand without looking in our direction. Once in the witness box, he seems to be making a conscious effort to focus only on Pavin, as if to block Ohlig completely from his line of sight.

Fieldston has taken on the Ohlig persona, the way some people end up looking like their pets over time. Like Ohlig, Fieldston's hair is a little long, but well styled, and he's dressed impeccably, but without flash, as if he went to the Armani showroom this morning and bought whatever the mannequin was wearing.

From the beginning of his direct it's obvious that Fieldston has been very well prepared. His answers are all short and directly responsive to Pavin's questions. *Answer the question asked, and only that question* is rule number two of witness prep, right after *Tell the truth*. I once had a witness who took the instruction so literally that when asked if he could state his name, he said only *yes*.

Pavin gets the entire immunity issue out of the way early, making it clear that Fieldston goes straight to prison if he lies on the stand. Of course, Pavin omits that he will be the one who makes the determination as to whether Fieldston's lying.

When the preliminaries are over, Pavin goes right in for the kill.

"Mr. Fieldston, who directed that the stock called Salminol be sold by OPM?"

"That would be Mr. Ohlig."

"Was Mr. Ohlig aware that Salminol actually had no value at the same time OPM was selling it?"

"He was."

"Do you know why Mr. Ohlig directed this worthless stock be sold to the public?"

"Yes."

"Please explain to the jury why Mr. Ohlig made that decision."

"OPM acquired a huge block of Salminol stock. I think we paid around twenty cents, on average, so the total position was something like thirty-five million. I don't know precisely what happened to alert Mr. Ohlig to the fact that Salminol was going to crash, but I recall very clearly that he came into my office on March 23. It was first thing in the morning, before the markets opened, and he said there was bad news on Salminol, and we had to unload all of it, immediately."

"Do you recall what the price of the stock was at that time?"

"I do. The first thing I did after Mr. Ohlig said this was to check the quote. I did it while he was still standing there, in fact."

"At what price was Salminol trading?"

"Less than a dime and trending down."

"Then what happened in your discussion with Mr. Ohlig?"

"I said to him, if we dump it all now, we're going

to push the price down. I told him that we bought it at about twenty, so we could end up losing as much as three-fourths of our investment, which could have been more than twenty-five million."

"And what did Mr. Ohlig say in response?"

"He said, 'I don't want to take any loss on it. Pump it up and then dump it.'"

"Were those his exact words—'Pump it up and then dump it'?"

"Yes."

"And did you understand what he meant by that?"

"I did. He meant he wanted us to inflate the price by selling it to people who wouldn't know better and would pay more for it, and then once we had pumped up the price, to dump all of our shares."

"Is that what you did?"

"Yes."

"How much profit did OPM make on Salminol?"

"A hundred and sixty million, give or take."

"And what happened to the investors? The people to whom OPM sold Salminol?"

"They lost everything."

"Explain to the jury why that was the case."

"Because of the way we were pricing it, the investors were buying at more than a dollar, sometimes at a lot more, when Salminol was, in actuality, a worthless stock. As soon as we didn't have any more to sell, we stopped beating the bushes for buyers, and the stock went to zero. Simple supply and demand. There was never any real demand for Salminol because anyone who knew the truth knew it was worthless."

"Thank you, Mr. Fieldston," Pavin says, barely hiding a smirk.

On cross, I begin by going through Fieldston's history of friendship with Ohlig, highlighting all the help that Ohlig had given to Fieldston and his family through the years. Fieldston is more than happy to confirm Ohlig's generosity, full knowing that each time he acknowledges Ohlig's kindness, he buttresses his own credibility. By the time I've finished with this part of the cross, every juror must be wondering how Fieldston could possibly give such damaging testimony against a man who was like a father to him unless it were true.

I look up to Judge Sullivan. "Your Honor, may I have a moment to consult with my client?"

"You may have just a moment," she tells me.

All it takes to answer the question in my mind is one look back at the counsel table. Ohlig's expression leaves no room for doubt. If I don't use the recording, Ohlig will go to Judge Sullivan and maybe to the committee on professional responsibility too for that matter.

I turn back to the witness. "Mr. Fieldston, in exchange for the federal government giving you immunity, you were prepared to tell this jury whatever the government wanted you to, without regard for whether it was true or not. Isn't that right?"

"No, that's not right, Mr. Miller." Fieldston sounds as calm as he would if he were telling me the time. I always explain to witnesses, the hotter the questions get, the cooler your responses should be. Eric Fieldston is Mr. Freeze. "My testimony today is under oath, and it is completely truthful."

"Mr. Fieldston, haven't you previously admitted that you were going to lie under oath in order to protect yourself?"

He laughs dismissively. "No. I never said such a thing."

I turn around to Abby. Her laptop is already hooked into the speakers in the courtroom. She double-clicks.

*"Yeah, the feds really have me by the balls,"* the voice coming through the speaker says. *"They don't care about the truth. As long as I help them get the conviction, I get a free ride. You know, I don't care about the lying. I mean, who hasn't lied when they had to? But my boss, he just doesn't deserve it. He's always been good to me. I just don't have any real choice. It's him or me."*

Pavin is shouting objection before the recording is even finished.

"Chambers, both of you," Judge Sullivan says sharply.

We all walk back into a small room directly behind the bench. It's not actually Judge Sullivan's chambers, but a sitting room of sorts. "Why don't you set up here," she says to the court reporter. "I want to do this quickly."

The court reporter lengthens the legs on her machine and pulls up one of the chairs. She's ready in less than thirty seconds.

"Well," Judge Sullivan says with a disarming smile, "we were having such a nice friendly trial. Mr. Pavin, it's your objection, so please state it for the record."

Pavin looks like steam is about to come out of his ears. "Your Honor, we had absolutely no notice of this stunt. Mr. Miller never provided us with a copy of the recording during discovery, as he was obligated to do. On top of which there is absolutely no authentication of that recording. We don't even know whose voice that is." He pauses and takes a deep breath, as if he's trying to regain some of his composure. "For all these reasons, your Honor, we request that the court strike the recording in its entirety, and instruct the jury that it must be completely disregarded."

"Mr. Miller, any response?"

"This is impeachment material, Judge. We have no obligation to turn it over beforehand. In fact, if Mr. Fieldston had admitted that the conversation occurred, rather than lied about it under oath, we wouldn't even have used the recording. If it's not him, let him swear to that."

Judge Sullivan looks at Pavin and shrugs. "Your witness opened the door, Mr. Pavin. It seems to me that asking whether a witness is telling the truth or is just saying what it takes to save his own skin is pretty relevant stuff. If it's not Mr. Fieldston on the recording, I'm sure you'll be able to put that information before the jury on re-direct."

Pavin's shoulders slump. "Your Honor," he says, "I feel compelled to state for the record that neither I nor anyone from my office knew that Mr. Fieldston was giving potentially perjured testimony. We will investigate this matter fully and if it turns out Mr. Fieldston lied to us, we will prosecute him."

"Sometimes it's hard to tell the good guys from the bad guys, Mr. Pavin," Judge Sullivan says, and then, just to make it clear something like this would never have happened when she was a prosecutor, she adds, "Of course, sometimes it's the government who turns the good guys into the bad guys."

When we return to the courtroom, Fieldston is huddled with his attorney, George Eastman. That can only mean one thing—this is going to get even better for Ohlig.

When everyone's back in their place—Fieldston on the stand and me behind the podium—I continue the cross. "Mr. Fieldston, isn't it true you lied under oath in your direct examination when you testified you believed that Mr. Ohlig knew Salminol was a worthless stock?"

Fieldston looks over at Eastman, who is sitting behind me to my right, in the gallery's first row. "On the advice of my counsel," Fieldston begins with a heavy voice, "I respectfully refuse to answer that question and assert my rights under the Fifth Amendment."

A soft roar rises from the gallery. Even the uninformed know this is a major development. Eric Fieldston is essentially admitting his prior testimony was untrue. Like the old saying goes, the first thing you do when you've dug yourself into a hole is to stop digging. If Fieldston lies more, he makes it worse, but if he admits the previous lie, he's confessed to the crime of perjury. The only way for Fieldston to stop digging is for him to invoke his constitutional right against self-incrimination, thereby limiting the testimony that could later be used against him.

Judge Sullivan gavels twice and asks for quiet. "Do you have anything further, Mr. Miller?"

"No, your Honor. Just the standard instruction, please."

She looks toward the government's table. "Mr. Pavin?"

Pavin's between a rock and a hard place, and he looks as if he's about to be squished. He stands and, as always, buttons his suit jacket. "No objection, your Honor," he says with a sigh.

"Very well then," Judge Sullivan says, and spins her chair so she's now facing the jury. "Ladies and gentlemen of the jury, as you have just seen, Mr. Fieldston has asserted his constitutional right under the Fifth Amendment not to say anything that will incriminate him in the future. Although that is his constitutional right, you may infer that his assertion of this right means his testimony would, in fact, incriminate him. Some of you may think that's unfair, but it is the law, and it is your obligation to follow the law. If Mr. Fieldston were on trial, his assertion of his Fifth Amendment right could not be used against him. But it is Mr. Ohlig who is on trial here, and Mr. Fieldston's assertion of his right against self-incrimination can be used as evidence to help Mr. Ohlig."

She turns away from the jurors and, looking at me, says, "Anything else that needs to be accomplished with this witness?"

"No," I tell her.

"Mr. Pavin?"

"No, your Honor."

"Very well. Let's recess for the day. Ladies and gentlemen of the jury, you know the drill. Today was an exciting day, but please do not talk to each other about the case. No television, no newspapers, no internet. See you all tomorrow."

The moment the last juror leaves the courtroom, the judge makes her own exit. She hasn't been out of the room for more than ten seconds before Pavin is standing in front of our table.

"I need a word," he says. It doesn't sound like a request.

Given how poorly today's gone for him, I see no reason to rub it in any further. "Sure."

I follow him into the empty jury holding room. Pavin shuts the door behind us and looks me up and down with an expression that can best be described as one of disgust. "Oh, Mr. Miller, you're going to be so sorry you pulled this one."

"I don't know what that means, Christopher, but it seems like school-yard threats are at least two notches below what I consider to be your dignity level."

"If you knew what I knew, you'd understand all too well," he says, and then leaves me in the room alone with that thought now hanging over my head.

# 40

"No. No. No."

We're back in the war room, Ohlig, Abby, and me. Ohlig is reacting to my telling him that, in my professional opinion, after the government rests its case tomorrow, we should put on Sansotta, our expert, and then rest ourselves, without Ohlig taking the stand.

"We did very well today," I say, "but—"

"Before you bring in your doom and gloom," Ohlig interrupts, "let me just point out that you argued not to use the stuff that resulted in our doing so well today. Now you're telling me not to testify. Why shouldn't I just assume that you're wrong about that too?"

"Michael, I'll be the first to admit it, you were right about the tape and I was wrong. But that doesn't mean that I'm not right about this. I mean, what did you tell clients after you recommended a stock that went down when you had a second recommendation? There are thousands of decisions that go into a criminal trial. I never said I'd be right about every one. But you're paying me to be right enough of the time that you don't end up going to jail. So listen to me now."

He laughs, which is not at all the appropriate response. "Just so you know, I never recommended a stock that went down."

I decide to ignore the quip, mainly because if I were

to respond it would be to suggest that it's easy to pick winners when you're manipulating the stocks at issue. Instead, I smile, and continue on with my argument against his taking the stand.

"Michael, if you take the stand, Pavin's going to hammer you. He'll tell the jury that you hid one witness, attempted to bribe another, and hired a prostitute to record Fieldston. When you add it all up, the jury is going to conclude that this is not the conduct of an innocent man."

"I'll deny it. All of it."

"But they may have evidence to support it. Judge Sullivan will almost definitely let them put the broker you bribed on the stand. She may even let them put in the Popowski tape. And, last but not least, don't forget that if you deny it, there's the little matter that you'll be committing perjury!"

"Says you," he responds like a six-year-old. "He'll have to prove that too."

"Putting aside the perjury thing, their whole case was Fieldston. Now they've got nothing. Less than nothing actually, because their credibility is shot. With Sansotta's testimony, we'll have enough for reasonable doubt."

"No way," Ohlig says again. "This is not up for discussion. I'm testifying."

"Hear me out for a moment."

"Alex, don't think I don't know what's going on. Hell, even Abby sees it."

Abby casts her eyes downward. Her reflex aligns

her with Ohlig as much as if she had joined hands with him.

I turn away from her and toward my client. "Michael, after court today, Pavin pulled me aside and said that if I knew what he knew we'd be worried, or something to that effect."

"What does that even mean?"

"Your guess is as good as mine. It could be an out-and-out bluff. But it also could mean he has something we don't know about, just like we had on Fieldston, and he's just dying to use it. Maybe something on the tapes."

"Why would Pavin tell us if he had something? And if he did have something on the tapes, he would have already used it during his case."

"I don't know. Maybe you're right and he is bluffing. I know you're a gambler, but this is a lot to put on one bet, Michael."

"From day one, I told you I was going to testify, and you agreed that was the only way to get an acquittal," Ohlig says, an obvious sadness in his voice, a further sign he feels betrayed. "More than that, you agreed because you believed in me, in my innocence. And now . . ." Without finishing the thought, he turns to Abby and asks, "What do you think? If you were me, would you take the stand?"

"I don't know," she says quietly. "I really don't know."

She looks back at me; her face says that she, too, feels betrayed by me.

Ohlig locks his eyes onto mine. It's a struggle, but I manage to hold his stare.

"Alex, this is my life we're talking about. I don't know what you think happened between your mother and me, but you have to let it go. Not just for my sake, but for yours too. When this trial is over, I'm not the only one who's going to have to live with the consequences. So, you tell me: If it was you, if your freedom was at risk, would you go to the jury without letting them hear you swear you're innocent?"

"Yes," I tell him as if there is no doubt in my mind.

Ohlig's normally erect posture sags, signaling his concession. "You'd better goddamn be right."

# 41

The next morning, as expected, Pavin rests the government's case. As a pro forma matter, I move for a directed verdict—a judgment of acquittal on the grounds that the government's case is legally insufficient to support a guilty verdict—which basically means that no reasonable juror could vote to convict based on the evidence presented. Needless to say, Judge Sullivan denies the motion without a moment's hesitation, and then she asks me to call the defense's first witness.

I call our expert, Paolo Sansotta.

Because we were second in the expert sweepstakes—the prosecution had Heller locked up before Ohlig even knew about the investigation—our expert witness is the second best. He's got a Nobel too, of course, and has won all the awards Heller has, so his weakness has nothing to do with his expertise or intellectual fire-power.

The problem with Sansotta is purely superficial, but that's really what matters most in a trial. He's younger than Heller by about thirty years, and although in some quarters that might make him seem more impressive, usually jurors like their experts with gray hair. The bigger problem is that Sansotta is from the Wharton School by way of Italy, and he speaks with a trace of an Italian accent, English being one of six languages he's mastered. As impressive as that is, an American jury is likely to think that anyone who speaks with an accent is less smart than someone who speaks without one.

Sansotta rebuts each point Heller made, telling the jury that an expert cannot determine what was in Ohlig's mind, that it's not uncommon at all for one firm to push a thinly traded stock, thereby causing the price to rise, that part of the attraction for investors in low-priced stock is the possibility of quick and large gains, and that also means that there is a possibility of quick and large losses.

Pavin's cross lasts little more than an hour and, as was the case when I questioned Heller, it does little damage. Unless all twelve people in the jury box have their own Nobel Prizes in economics, I don't see how they can conclude guilt beyond a reasonable doubt based solely on the testimony of the experts.

"Next witness?" Judge Sullivan says, without any indication that she's expecting the response she's about to receive.

"Your Honor, the defense rests," I say, as if I'm making a triumphant pronouncement.

Closing arguments follow, rehashing the points made originally during openings. Shortly before six, Judge Sullivan gives the case to the jury to begin their deliberations.

Only the lawyers have reason to celebrate the beginning of jury deliberations. For us, the case has ended, but for the client it has really just begun. Rather than rub that point in with Ohlig, I tell him that Abby and I still have some work to do to be prepared in case the jury has some questions, so he should go back to the hotel and get some rest.

As soon as Ohlig leaves, Abby asks, "What work could we possibly do now? We can't guess what questions the jury is going to ask."

"I know. I thought we could go out and get a drink, just the two of us. I know you're angry with me, and I figure if Michael's convicted, that's going to get worse, so this may be my last opportunity."

"Opportunity for what?" she says with a lascivious grin.

"To win back your affections."

Abby selects Cesca, which I know is her favorite restaurant. It's on the Upper West Side, so it's a good choice for me because I'm much less likely to run into someone Elizabeth or I know. It's also close to Abby's apartment.

The restaurant is busy and loud. I can't help but scan the tables as the hostess leads us to ours, confirming that I don't recognize any of the other diners.

"You seem nervous, Alex," Abby says when we sit down. "Relax, okay? We're two colleagues having dinner together. No one is going to call the police."

It unnerves me sometimes that Abby seems to know exactly what I'm thinking, but then I realize it's possible that I'm wearing my feelings on my sleeve to such an extent that anyone could be so prescient.

When the waitress asks if we would like to order a bottle of wine, Abby nods in my direction and says, "I'm game if you are."

I order an expensive bottle of Amarone, telling Abby that Ohlig would definitely approve of the selection, and then joking that he might have a different opinion on my decision to charge this meal back to him. She laughs, but as she does so I detect a hint of nervousness on her part, something I might have noticed earlier had I not been so uncomfortable myself.

"Everything okay with you?" I ask.

"Yeah," she says halfheartedly. "How do you think it's going to turn out?"

"You've been watching the same trial I have."

"Sometimes I've wondered."

"What's that supposed to mean?"

"Maybe I should have asked you how you *want* the trial to turn out?"

"No reason to be subtle, Abby. Just come right out and ask me if I've thrown the case because I want Ohlig to go to jail."

"Okay. Have you?"

"Is this the next stage of our relationship? I tell you that I've committed an act that would get me disbarred?"

"Is that your way of saying it's true and you don't trust me?"

"No," I say and force a smile.

She smiles back. "No that it's not true, or no that you really do trust me."

"Both. Of course I trust you, *and* it's not true. I know that you would have made different calls than me. You would have put him on the stand, right?"

She nods. "Call me crazy, but when you were going on and on about how an acquittal in a state-of-mind case was virtually impossible without the defendant's testimony, I believed you."

"Anything else?"

"I was surprised that you didn't go after the brokers harder. And you knew as well as I did to argue relevance with regard to the bribery testimony."

"And I'll bet you ninety-nine times out of a hundred, Judge Sullivan lets him testify to the bribery attempt. We got lucky because Pavin pissed her off."

"Maybe," Abby says, not sounding too convinced. "But it was certainly worth the argument."

"Agreed, which is why we made it."

"*I* made it, Alex. I made it because Ohlig thought you wouldn't. He's talked to me about it, you know. He thinks you're setting him up. He asked me to tell him if I thought you were doing anything that was not in his best interest."

"And what did you tell him?"

She gives me another disappointed glare. One that I expect to be followed with the question *What do you think I told him?* Instead she answers me directly.

"I told him that you would never sabotage a client, that you were committed to his innocence and that I had absolutely no doubt every decision you made was solely because you thought it was the best way to achieve an acquittal."

"Thanks," I say.

"Don't thank me, Alex. Tell me it's true."

As always, our dinner conversation is easy, equal parts flirtatious banter and deep insights about ourselves that we share as if they're precious gifts. When the waitress asks if we've saved any room for dessert, Abby asks that she give us a minute.

"I'd like dessert, but not here," she says, looking at me so intently I feel as if I can't move.

"Where then?"

"Mmmmmmmm," she purrs. "Here's a hint. It's close by, and I promise it will be delicious."

She reaches across the table and takes my hand. Even though I'd already ascertained that I didn't recognize any of the other diners, I scan the room again out of reflex. Abby holds my hand tighter and guides it off the table and into my lap, so that our hand-holding is out of public view. She takes the opportunity to glide her hand over my pants.

"At least I know you're thinking about it," she says, a reference to my erection.

"If it's the place I'm thinking of, I've been there before and loved it."

"So, shall we?"

"I wish I could," I say, "but not tonight."

"Okay," she says softly, letting go of my hand.

"Don't be upset," I say, more out of reflex than anything else because Abby doesn't look upset.

"I'm not," she says. "I know you want to, Alex. If

you didn't, that would upset me. And I know you're conflicted, and if you weren't, well then you wouldn't be you."

I smile and nod. As usual, she's read me exactly right.

"Anyway, when I'm in bed alone tonight, in my mind at least we'll be together. It just won't be as good as when you're actually there."

"I'm going to have those same thoughts tonight," I say.

"I know you will," she says.

# 42

The next morning, after Judge Sullivan takes the bench, she calls in the jury solely so she can send them back out to deliberate. When the last of them exits, Judge Sullivan gives us all permission to leave the courtroom, telling us that she'll send word if they reach a verdict or have any questions.

"I'm going to get some coffee," Ohlig says to me. "Is it okay if I do that?"

"Sure," I tell him. "Just don't leave the building."

"If I haven't run yet, I'm not going to, Alex."

Since the trial ended, Ohlig hasn't once asked me to handicap the outcome. At first I thought that was because he's still playing his role as Mr. Cool, but I've come to believe it's more that he no longer trusts me to give him an honest answer.

At six-thirty, Judge Sullivan takes the bench.

"It looks like we're not going to have a verdict today," she says. "I'm inclined to let the jurors go for the weekend, unless either side wants to be heard on the issue." Pavin and I tell her that we do not. "Okay, then, let's get the jury back here and I'll dismiss them."

Judge Sullivan's clerk, a woman likely no more than a year out of law school, who usually sits below the bench, walks over and whispers in the judge's ear. It must be something amusing because Judge Sullivan is all smiles.

"I spoke too soon, apparently," the judge then says. "It seems that the jury has just reached a verdict on all counts."

Although the timing is coincidental, it's not that surprising. Jurors often reach decisions at the end of the day, when they realize that if they don't they have to come back for another day. That impetus is twice as great on Friday afternoons. I've never studied it, but I bet that most verdicts are reached at that time.

If I'm agnostic about the ability to predict a jury's verdict during voir dire, I'm a hardcore atheist on the subject of whether there are any tells regarding the jury's conduct during deliberations. I don't subscribe to any of the theories you hear on television, even though I have colleagues who swear that they've experienced them all firsthand. I don't believe you can read anything into the evidence the jury wants to see while deliberating; and when they ask to have a portion of testimony re-read it's impossible to know if that's because they're going to base their decision on that testimony, or they see it as an indication that the witness was totally unbelievable.

I've also heard a million theories about predicting the verdict based on the time the jury spends deliberating. Some people will tell you a quick verdict means an acquittal because juries are more sober about convicting and like to make it seem as if the decision was hard to reach. I've heard just as many others claim that a quick decision usually results in a guilty verdict because the longer the jury is out, the more it shows they have some reasonable doubt, or that they aren't unified.

As far as I'm concerned, it's all wishful thinking. I've seen juries deliberate for an hour and come back with a guilty verdict, and I've seen them deliberate for two weeks and return the same verdict. Same thing with acquittals. There's no rhyme or reason, and trying to make believe you can discern one is no different than whistling by a graveyard. It may make you feel better, but that's all it does.

Even though I don't believe it foreshadows anything, I can't help but look into each juror's eyes as they file into the courtroom. The old saw is that jurors who look away from the defendant have voted to convict and those who make eye contact are acquitting. In this case, some of the jurors look right at Ohlig, others look at the floor, still others look at Pavin, and one walks in with his eyes fixed on Judge Sullivan.

When all the jurors are seated in the jury box, Judge Sullivan says her line: "Has the jury reached a verdict?"

The Air Force Colonel, the one that frightened our jury consultant most during voir dire, rises. He has been chosen as the jury foreman. This probably doesn't mean anything other than that he volunteered for the job, and it's even possible he was selected after the verdict was reached, which sometimes happens. Nevertheless, it could also be an indication that he was a leader in the jury room, which, at least according to our jury consultant, would be very bad news for Ohlig. I'm sure Ohlig is thinking the same thing.

"We have, your Honor," he says.

"Please approach the bench, Mr. Foreman."

The foreman walks to the bench and hands the judge a piece of paper with the verdict. This gives everyone in the courtroom one more chance to try to read the tea leaves in the judge's expression. Like every other judge I've ever seen, Judge Sullivan is completely impassive as she looks down on the page she's been handed, and even if she danced a jig or started sobbing, I still wouldn't know which way that cut.

"Thank you," Judge Sullivan says after reading it.

As the foreman walks back to the jury box with that precious piece of paper in hand, I remember that this is a multi-count indictment. That means if he starts delineating the verdict by counts at least one must be a guilty verdict, even if the top count is a not guilty. Otherwise he'd say—"with regard to all counts"—or words like it. Conviction on just one of the lesser counts could still put Ohlig in jail for more than a decade.

The foreman is back in his spot, and Judge Sullivan is finally going to bring the theatrics to an end. "Will the defendant please rise," she says.

Ohlig and I stand. I've actually thought about letting him go it alone, but even my anger has its limits. I make it a point not to put my hand on his shoulder, however. He's flying solo here, and he should know it. As if he feels the solitude, he looks back at his wife.

"Mr. Foreman, what is the jury's verdict?" Judge Sullivan asks.

He waits a beat, perhaps to savor his moment in the spotlight. "On the first count of the indictment, violation of section 10(b) of the Securities and Exchange Act of 1934, we, the jury, find the defendant not guilty."

There is a roar in the gallery and Ohlig's posture slackens. He even grabs my hand with his fingers. He must not realize that the jury is going to offer a separate verdict for each count.

The foreman's voice cracks through the gallery's chatter. "On the second count of the indictment—" And then he stops, looking up from the sheet he's holding and toward Judge Sullivan. "Your Honor," he says, breaking the rhythm in the room, "do I have to read each count separately? We've voted not guilty on all of them."

I have absolutely no idea what, if anything, Judge Sullivan says in response. The gallery erupts, and then I feel Ohlig's embrace. "You did it! You did it, Alex!" he says over and over again in my ear.

I push against him and he releases his grip. Given his state of euphoria, I doubt Ohlig even notices that I've broken away somewhat abruptly. He has already put the bear hug on Abby, and I'm sure he's squeezing her even tighter than he did me. From Abby he moves on to his wife, embracing her over the wood divider separating the gallery from the counsel area.

I can't help but wonder if Pamela knows about Ohlig and my mother. I assume she doesn't, for if she did I can't imagine her being so supportive. Then again, perhaps she's forgiven him. The moment my mind flashes on that possibility, I wonder if Elizabeth would forgive me, which, in turn, gives way to whether I'd want to live in a marriage with that kind of debt. But maybe that's the quid pro quo. They forgive, and you acknowledge that you betrayed someone who loves you enough to forgive the betrayal, in the hope that you can become worthy of that love.

Out of the corner of my eye, I see Pavin approaching. I expect him to offer his congratulations, but he steps past me.

"Mr. Ohlig," Pavin says, and as he's doing so I become aware for the first time of the four large and rather hard-looking men standing beside him.

I can't believe Pavin is actually going to arrest Ohlig for obstruction of justice right here, in open court. Even for someone like him, this seems a bush-league move.

Ohlig hasn't even turned toward him, but Pavin continues, "These gentlemen are United States marshals. They are here to place you in federal custody and accompany you to Florida where you will be placed under arrest for the murder of Barbara Judith Miller."

Though I understand the string of words that Pavin has just uttered, I can't yet make sense of them.

Ohlig seems as much at sea as me, but the reality sinks in the moment the light reflects off the silver bracelets held by one of the marshals. Ohlig actually slaps the handcuffs away, but I have awakened enough to call out his name. That's all I need to say for his shoulders to slump and his hands to drop to his sides. He knows what's happening now.

In one pirouette, the marshal turns Ohlig around and handcuffs him behind his back. When the marshal spins him again, Ohlig and I stand face-to-face. His eyes are deep with despair, as if in one moment everything has been revealed.

"Alex," Ohlig says, but he stops short of saying anything else. I suspect that he was going to ask for my help, and then thought better of it. Maybe because he knows that under the circumstances there's nothing I can do.

Maybe because he knows that under the circumstances there's nothing I will do.

## 43

I'm really sorry," Abby says as soon as Ohlig clears the courtroom.

"You and me both. Just when you think the worst of it is that your mother was cheating on your father and now you're defending the guy she was cheating with, you find out that you've actually been defending her murderer."

I say this with a weak smile. She reciprocates with one of her own. As always, just the sight of it pushes me off balance.

"Let's get out of here," she says. "Wherever you want to go. Drinks. My place. My place and then drinks. Drinks and then my place."

I appreciate her effort to comfort me, but I decline. "I think I should stay here a little longer and see if I can get some information. Why don't you head back to the firm, and I'll catch up with you later."

"Are you sure? *I'm* more than happy to wait with you here."

"I've got some things I need to do," I say, realizing that there's likely no reason to be cryptic, as I'm sure Abby knows that I'm going to call Elizabeth. "I'll stop by your office as soon as I get back to the firm."

"Why don't we meet at Tao," she says. "I don't feel like going to the office and answering a lot of questions."

Tao is a bar on the corner of 58th and Madison. It's a large, dark space that serves strong drinks.

"Okay." I look down at my watch. "Can you give me another forty-five minutes here, and then another forty minutes or so to get uptown?"

"Take as long as you like, but I can't guarantee I won't be drunk by the time you show up."

Just as Abby starts to walk away, a woman in her early twenties, whom I'd presumed was one of Judge Sullivan's clerks based on the fact that she periodically whispered things in the judge's ear during the trial, approaches me. "Judge Sullivan would like to see you in her chambers," she says.

I could ask what she wants to see me about, but judicial requests, like those from Aaron Littman, can't be declined without damage to your career, so I simply follow her. When I enter the judge's chambers, I see that Pavin is already there. Next to him is Gattia, the deputy from the Palm Beach Sheriff's Department.

"Thank you for coming," Judge Sullivan says. She's not wearing her robe and is attired in a cream-colored silk blouse and black pants. "Now that the case is over, I don't have any obligations regarding ex parte communications, so I took it upon myself to talk to Mr. Pavin and the fine gentleman from the Palm Beach Sheriff's Department so I can better understand what just happened in my courtroom. Once they explained it to me, I thought that they owed you an explanation too."

"Thank you, your Honor," I say.

"No need to thank me. Also, I would be remiss if I didn't tell you that you tried a fine case. I've already told Mr. Pavin the same thing. It was a pleasure having both of you appear in my court."

"Thank you again," I say. Pavin, for once, is quiet, and just nods.

"So," she says, shifting her attention to Gattia, "Mr. Gattia, why don't you tell Mr. Miller what you just told me."

He doesn't hesitate. "Mr. Miller, as I just finished telling the judge, Michael Ohlig has been charged with your mother's murder. Unfortunately, I'm not at liberty to go into the full extent of our evidence, but you will be contacted by the assistant district attorney handling the matter. Her name is Morgan Robertson. Perhaps she'll be able to answer your questions."

"I didn't even know you thought my mother was murdered."

"We apologize for that, but given your relationship with Mr. Ohlig, we thought that was for the best."

"What can you tell me about the evidence?"

"That it's very strong," Gattia says. "There's the affair, of course, which I understand you're aware of from the tapes." I nod, closing my eyes in a semi-wince. "But we also have evidence that he was the last person to see your mother alive. We can put him and your mother near Ohlig's boat on the day she died. I wish I could tell you more, but I'm sorry to say that I can't. I've probably already told you more than the ADA would have liked. But she told me that I could say that our evidence is strong enough that she suspects Ohlig will take a plea."

Judge Sullivan apparently waits to see if I have anything more to say because after a few moments of silence, when it is clear that I don't, she says, "Mr. Miller, I want you to know that I did not have any advance notice that your client was going to be arrested. My understanding is that a deal was reached between Fitz"—a reference to the U.S. Attorney for the Southern District of New York that those who consider themselves to be his friends use—"and the District Attorney down in Palm Beach. Apparently, to avoid tainting me, the decision was reached to get approval through the chief judge. Which was probably wise because I can tell you right now, I would not have permitted that kind of spectacle to go on in my courtroom."

"Again, your Honor, on behalf of my office, I apologize," Pavin says, still groveling. I can't really blame him. Even though the Southern District of New York has more than forty federal judges, the U.S. Attorneys' Office can't afford to make an enemy of even one of them.

Judge Sullivan's expression makes it clear that no one is going to get off that easy. "Mr. Pavin, that is a discussion best had between Fitz and me, and not one that we need to waste Mr. Miller's time on."

In the cab on the way to Tao, I call Elizabeth. She had left several messages on my cell phone.

"I've been calling you non-stop," she says even before

saying hello. "Ever since I read on-line about the verdict and then that Ohlig killed your mother. Is it true?"

"I'm sorry I couldn't call you sooner. You're not allowed to bring cell phones into the courtroom. I didn't see you called until I left, which was about thirty seconds ago."

"I'm not mad, Alex. I'm worried about you. Are you okay?"

"How am I supposed to be? I just saved my mother's murderer from prison."

"Come home, Alex. We can talk about this in person. I won't pretend that I can understand what you're going through, but I'm here to listen."

"Thank you," I say, sounding more pro forma than I should. "I have some things I need to do first, unfortunately."

"Like what? I would think that, today of all days, the firm would go a little easy on you."

"Don't be mad at me, Elizabeth. As you said, today of all days. I need to talk to some people at the firm about what happened. They're not going to want to wait until tomorrow. There might be press inquiries." This is a red herring. As a rule, Cromwell Altman never comments on the record regarding any matter. "I'll try not to get home too late."

As I hang up the phone, I realize that I've become a very proficient liar. Like everything else, I suppose, practice makes perfect.

## 44

Tao is a cavernous place. There's a large bar area on the street level and tables upstairs. The hostess downstairs is a slim Asian woman wearing a bright blue silk kimono.

She leads me up the stairs and toward the back of the darkly lit room. Abby breaks into an easy smile when our eyes meet. I try to smile back but must not do a very convincing job.

"Not much to celebrate, I guess," she says as I take my seat.

"Can I get you a cocktail, sir?" the hostess asks.

I look to see what Abby's drinking, but because it's so dark I can't even tell what color it is. "I'll have whatever she's having."

"It's a mojito," Abby tells me.

"A mojito," I say to the hostess.

"Like I said," Abby continues when the hostess leaves, "you don't look like you're much in the celebrating mood."

"I'm not really," I say.

"Did you find anything out?" she asks.

"After you left, Judge Sullivan had me back to her chambers and I had a brief discussion with her, Pavin, and the guy from the Palm Beach sheriff's office that I met right after my mother died. He said that they have a witness who places Ohlig with my mom the day she died, near his boat or something like that. That and the affair. I think there was some more too, but I wasn't following all that well." I chuckle slightly, even though I know it's inconsistent with the tone I've set. "If you can believe it, he told me, with a straight face no less, that the Florida DA thought when they laid out all the evidence, Ohlig would take a plea."

This makes Abby smile. She truly is a beautiful woman, and my mind flashes on my conversation with Paul at Aquavit when he said that Fleming had given Abby to me. That was what, a little more than four months ago? Part of me wants to go back to then, before I came under her spell, but I know that's impossible. I take some comfort that it's only part of me with that desire.

"Did you talk to him?" she asks.

I think she means Ohlig, rather than the Florida prosecutor. I'm less certain whether she wants to hear what Ohlig has to say for himself or is concerned about how he's holding up.

"No. I don't think I even asked to, but if I did they must have told me that no one can speak to him until he gets back to Florida. You know, it was all a little bit of a blur and I honestly don't remember." My voice trails off, indicating that I have nothing else to say on the subject.

The waitress places my mojito in front of me. "Are you two ready to order?" she asks.

Abby says she's ready, but I ask the waitress to give us

a few more minutes. I'm not sure either of us is going to feel like eating after I've said what I came here to say.

After the waitress walks away, I raise my glass. "Thank you for all your work on the trial. Michael Ohlig was very lucky to have you. You did an outstanding job."

She meets my glass with her own. "Thank you, even if we both know that you're full of it." After she's taken a sip, she adds, "Alex, I know that this is really hard for you, but you should be very proud of the work you did for him. It was a very difficult case to win, and you tried it brilliantly. Just brilliantly. You were right at every turn and, as you know, I doubted you on some of it. All I can say is that I'm really embarrassed about that now."

Like me, and maybe all litigators, Abby is very precise in her language. In this instance, however, I'm not sure what she's embarrassed about. Perhaps it's her way of saying that she thought I was throwing the case and now thinks I wasn't. Then again, it could be as simple as her saying that she would have put Ohlig on the stand and she now thinks that I was right about keeping him off.

Trials are like sporting events in this way. A successful outcome seemingly validates every move leading up to it, as if any other decision would have changed the result. In hindsight, the decision to pass on fourth and four that gets the first down is considered the only option that would have worked, although in an alternate universe, a running play might have gone for a touchdown. Same goes for the Ohlig trial. Who's to say that if I had opened by telling the jury that Ohlig was going to testify and then closed the defense's case after he looked those jurors in the eye and, in his most sincere voice, swore to them that he had done nothing wrong, the jury wouldn't have still voted to acquit? Maybe they would have been even more certain of his innocence. You can never tell what was down the road not taken.

In trials, as well as life.

"Abby," I say, with far too heavy a voice as I'm looking down at my drink. "I can't do this anymore."

She reaches across the table to take my hand. "Alex, I know what's going through your mind. Believe me that I do. But we make each other happy. Don't throw that away."

"You don't know." I say this sharper, more angrily, than is warranted, and then try to take it back. "What I mean is that you couldn't know. No matter how strongly I feel about you, this just isn't what I want for my life."

"Then what do you want?"

"To be someone who doesn't cheat on his wife."

"But you are who you are, Alex," she says without judgment, as if it is uncontroverted fact. "You've been cheating on Elizabeth for months now. And not just the time we actually made love. You cheat on her every time you'd rather be with me than with her."

"Forgive me for saying this, but it really doesn't have to do with you. I have a family and I need to deal with them first."

Abby begins to cry. I'm embarrassed to say it makes

her look even more beautiful. My impulse is to comfort her, to tell her it's all going to be all right, that she's better off without me, all of which I believe to be true, but which I also know will sound patronizing. I reach over and put my hand on top of hers, but then she pulls hers farther away.

The moment I step into our apartment, Elizabeth offers me her best smile. When I don't smile back, hers drops away, replaced with a look of concern. I don't deserve her sympathy, of course, at least not because of how I look, which is more a result of my just ending things with Abby than the circumstances surrounding Michael Ohlig.

Then again, the two are not totally disconnected.

"Talk to me, Alex," she says.

"What's there to say?"

"Maybe we should try something new for us, Alex. Maybe, just this one time, we should talk to each other honestly."

"Okay," I say, dragging out the syllables to feign that I have no idea what she's referring to. "What is it that you want to tell me? Or is there something you want to ask me?"

She frowns. "Alex, sometimes you act like I don't have a clue about what's going on. Your father's best friend—the man who introduced your father to your mother—has been arrested for your mother's *murder*. Certainly you must have some feelings about that."

"What do you want me to say?"

"The truth, or something else even," she says with another smile. "Anything that lets me in a little bit."

"Michael Ohlig and my mother were having an affair. I'm not sure how long it was going on, but I know it started while my father was still alive. My mother must have ended it right before she died, or maybe Michael ended it and she was threatening to tell his wife. Either way, he killed her for it. I suppose if I'm being totally honest about it, my mother shares the blame."

Elizabeth sometimes has the type of concentration you can see, and she shows no hint of surprise at this disclosure, as if she's known about it all along.

"You knew, didn't you?" I say, probably too accusingly. "About the two of them."

"Let's say I had my suspicions. Not that she was involved with him, but I suspected that your parents' marriage wasn't as happy as you thought."

"Why didn't you tell me?"

Even though I say this with anger, she responds soothingly. "Alex, let's not start about what we choose to tell each other."

My reflex is to ask her what she means, but I know better. She might actually tell me, and that would take us down a path I'm not prepared to travel. Instead, I go in the other direction, sending my own signal that maybe Elizabeth should be wary too. "If my father made her unhappy she should have left him."

"No one makes someone else happy."

This is something of a credo with Elizabeth, the idea of taking responsibility for your own happiness, or misery, as the case might be. But she has said this with a vastly different voice than in our last few exchanges. It's still gentle, but now is characterized by a definite inward resolve.

Elizabeth takes my hand in hers. For the life of me I can't remember the last time we've held hands.

"Alex, I really don't think that Michael Ohlig made your mother very happy. Do you?"

# 45

The first day back at the office is excruciating. Amidst trying to catch up on the emails and voice-mails I'd ignored during the trial, and taking awkward congratulations on the trial, I can't stop myself from thinking about Abby. I begin the day checking my voicemails and end it the same way, but for the first time in months, there are no messages from her.

The next day is exactly the same.

The silence is double-edged. It hurts that Abby appears to be weathering the separation better than I am, but it would be worse if she weren't. At least that's what I keep telling myself.

All the litigators at Cromwell Altman meet on the last Wednesday of every month. Someone, usually a more junior lawyer, is tasked with the responsibility of giving a presentation, either about a case the firm just won (or, in rare instances, lost), or some developing area of the law. This month, the meeting was pushed up because most of the lawyers take off the week between Christmas and New Year's.

The meetings are held in the partners' dining room because there are enough seats for most of the litigation department, at least the half that shows up. It looks more or less like a five-star restaurant. Tables of two, four, and six seats, each with a white linen tablecloth and fine china place settings. A buffet is laid out along the back wall of the room.

Partners are encouraged to sit among the associates. The firm thinks of it as a way to bond, but it actually just makes the meetings that much more uncomfortable for everyone. Everyone except me, I should say. Since September, I've always sat with Abby, normally at a table for two.

David Geyser is the chairman of the litigation group, a figurehead position because it's well known that Aaron's the one who's really in charge. Pretty much all David Geyser does as chairman is make sure the litigation meetings start precisely at noon and end exactly at one. It's actually something he's quite good at.

I purposely arrive fifteen minutes late so I won't have the awkward moment of either choosing not to sit with Abby if she got there before me, or seeing her select a seat away from me if I'm the earlier arrival. I enter quietly, taking a seat at a table in the back. It doesn't take more than a few seconds, however, before I spy Abby sitting in the middle of the room. She's the only associate at a table of four male partners, one of whom is Aaron Littman.

When our eyes meet it's the first time since Tao. She smiles at me, but it's different from the smile I'd become so accustomed to seeing. It's uncertain and without the confidence she normally projects.

I smile back, as broadly as I can, and then her expression morphs into the glow that I've missed so much.

She flutters her fingers at me in a wave, and mouths "Hi." I nod back at her and mouth "Hello."

Meanwhile, Geyser is standing in the front of the room behind a podium that bears the firm's initials—CARW—in large letters. As long as I've been at the firm, there's been speculation that Aaron Littman's name was going to replace Franklin White's on the letterhead, a move that would make sense given that White was at Cromwell Altman for only a few years back in the 1970s, and was given a place on the masthead only because he was formerly a judge on the Federal Appeals Court. The firm thought it would provide some cachet during the recession at the end of that decade. The running joke is that the reason the name change hasn't happened is because no one wants the firm to be known as CARL.

Geyser is talking about Aaron's representation of a cable company against one of the phone carriers, which *The American Lawyer* magazine had opined was the biggest stakes litigation in the country this year; it settled sometime during the summer. That's when I realize that this is the final litigation meeting of the year, which is when Geyser does his year-in-review, going through the department's highlights over the past twelve months.

With the exception of mentioning Aaron's case first, Geyser is apparently going in chronological order because next he discusses a pro bono death penalty case from January, followed by an SEC insider-trading case that was filed in February. Six more cases follow, all of them resulting in successful outcomes. To hear Geyser tell it, Cromwell Altman is more successful than Perry Mason.

With about five minutes left before the hour is over, Geyser says, "And last, but certainly not least, just last week, Alex Miller and Abby Sloane obtained an acquittal of OPM CEO Michael Ohlig in a securities fraud trial."

Although he spared the other lawyers whose cases he discussed, Geyser says, "I see you, Abby, but where's Alex hiding?" I sheepishly raise my hand. "There he is, way in the back. Why don't you stand up, Alex. You too, Abby. Stand so we can all recognize the fine work you did in this case. You've made Cromwell Altman proud."

I rise, and then Abby comes to her feet. Our colleagues in the litigation department are clapping.

"Well done, both of you," Geyser says. His voice rises above the applause, although with the microphone in front of him it sounds as if he's yelling. "This was a spectacular year for our department and the firm. I have every expectation that next year will be even better. From my family to you and all of yours, have the happiest of holiday seasons and a joyous New Year."

When the applause begins to die down, Geyser adds, "Our next meeting will be on January 7, at which time we hopefully will have an announcement that a new partner has joined our ranks."

He doesn't mention Abby by name, but everyone knows it'll be her. The other two litigators of her vintage have already been told that they're going to be

passed over, their names not even being put up for
consideration, which makes Abby the litigation department's sole candidate. At this juncture, particularly
with her sitting next to Aaron, I doubt you could find
anyone to take odds against her making it.

There's usually some mingling after the departmental
lunch, but I get out of there as soon as I can. I'm just
not ready yet to make small talk with Abby, or even to
discuss Geyser's seeming endorsement of her with any
of the others.

I suspect our encounter at the lunch has emboldened
Abby because we run into each other the next day in
front of my office. It's not quite a chance encounter,
however. As I'm returning from the men's room, I find
her leaning against the door frame to my office, waiting
for me.

"Hey stranger," she says. "Long time, no see."

I don't know what to say. Taking pity on me, Abby
says, "Mind if we talk in your office?"

"Sure," I say, gesturing that she enter. I want to tell
her to shut the door, but I know that would be a mistake.

"So, how much did you have to pay Geyser?" I say as
she takes a seat, doing my best to keep this encounter
on a lighthearted plane.

"I know. It was a little embarrassing. After he said it,
I said something to my table like, 'God, if I don't make
it now, I'll never be able to show my face around here,'
and then Rick Rubin says, 'Don't worry about it, Abby.

If you don't make it, you'll be pushed out so you won't have to show your face around here.'"

"He's such a horse's ass."

"Aaron put him in his place, though. He looked right at Rubin and said, 'That's true of partners too, you know. It's not a lifetime position.'"

I chuckle lightly, a jealous pang hitting my stomach at the specter of Aaron coming to Abby's rescue. "So, what are you doing trolling 56?" I ask.

She looks flustered for a moment. "I've got a meeting."

"Who with?"

"Aaron, and a cast of thousands, of course."

"That's a good sign," I say. "I mean, if Aaron has brought you to a case less than two weeks before the partnership vote, there's little doubt that you're going to make it."

"I suppose," she says. "Truth is, my meeting doesn't start for another few minutes. I came up early because I wanted to see you."

"Here I am," I say, feeling foolish for saying it, but not sure what response would be more appropriate. Should I tell her that I miss her with every fiber of my being? What good will that do unless I want to end up in bed with her, which, while true, is something I'm trying my damnedest to avoid.

"How are you doing?"

"I'm good." I try to punctuate the point with a smile.

"Good for you," she says without a smile, and

somewhat bitterly, I think. "Unfortunately, I'm not doing so good." She lowers her voice. "I really miss you, Alex. It's so hard coming to work and not having you there to talk to. I mean, putting aside everything else, you were also my best friend."

I want to say that I miss her too. Actually, that's only partly true. What I actually want to do is lock my office door and take her in my arms. But I know that's only going to make things that much worse.

"It'll get easier."

The moment I say this I realize how patronizing it sounds. I should have been honest and told her that it's been torture for me too, that I think about her every minute of every day. But the opportunity is gone now.

Abby clenches her jaw, an effort to hold back tears, I think.

"Thanks for the advice, Alex," she says curtly. "I've got to go."

She bolts to the door and I take off after her, stopping once I enter the hallway. I can't yell out to her, and so I watch her recede from view, as she enters the women's restroom without looking back.

It is then and there that I decide I'm going to take the rest of the year off. I'd rather not encounter Abby again until I have my sea legs.

## 46

Growing up in a Jewish household, I longed for Christmas but couldn't have it. At least not directly. My parents were not religious people, and so they had no objection to my watching Christmas shows on television or participating in my friends' annual rituals, but they drew the line at having a Christmas tree of our own or giving out presents on the 25th.

After Elizabeth and I were married, I threw myself into Christmas with the zeal only a convert possesses. I wanted to get the biggest tree, and that first year I must have spent five hundred dollars on ornaments, much to Elizabeth's amusement. "Most people just wait until they're fifty percent off the day after Christmas and stock up then," she laughed at me.

I'm more excited about Christmas this year than ever before. Charlotte didn't seem to grasp the concept of presents the first three holiday seasons. Last year she was excited about it for the first time, but really couldn't recall it from the year before. This Christmas, however, she remembers last year's, so she knows what to expect, and she doesn't have the slightest doubt about the existence of Santa Claus. By next year, I suspect that will no longer be the case.

In front of the window in our living room is a seven-foot Douglas fir that is half-decorated. Charlotte insisted we stop putting ornaments on and pick what's going to go on top of the tree. She has a theory that what ultimately goes on the top of the tree will impact the subsequent placement of ornaments.

I'm on a step stool, holding the winged fairy in place. Charlotte is eyeing it with a squint. She has already rejected the snowflake, and she's deciding between the fairy and the gold star when the phone rings.

Elizabeth doesn't like making phone calls or receiving them. She carries a cell phone but almost never answers it. *No one ever has anything to say that can't wait,* she's told me on several occasions when our phone is ringing and she doesn't move to get it. *It would be rude for me to stop talking to you and start another conversation with someone else who was in the room, so why is it any more polite if that person doesn't even have the decency to visit us?* Like a lot of things Elizabeth says, there's some pretty convincing logic at work, and yet I also know it's a bit twisted and off.

"Can you answer the phone?" I call out to her. She seems annoyed by my request, but nevertheless walks over to pick up the receiver.

"Hello. Oh, hi, Joan. Yeah, he's here. Hang on a second." She pulls the phone away from her face. "Alex, it's your aunt Joan."

I climb down off the step stool and take the phone out of Elizabeth's hand. For some reason, I know it's a call for which I'll want some privacy, and so I walk to the bedroom even before saying hello. I sit down on the corner of my bed.

"How are you, Joan?"

She doesn't answer. Instead, she says, "I don't know if I should tell you this, Alex, but it's been making me crazy, and I . . . I just think you deserve to know, especially now."

"Okay," I tell her, although I'm not sure that it's actually better to know the truth than not to know it in all instances.

"Well, it's about your mother." I expect her to come out with it, but she hesitates. "It's about both your parents, actually," she finally says.

"Okay," I say again, now concerned.

"I don't know how to say it."

"Please, Joan, just spit it out. It's okay."

"Alex, your father believed that your mother was having an affair."

Goddammit. He knew. The one piece of solace I had taken through all of this was false. My father knew.

"What did he say?" I ask quickly.

"You knew?"

Joan sounds surprised, which makes sense. She had no reason to believe I'd learned about my mother's affair with Ohlig during the trial.

"I knew she was having an affair with Michael Ohlig. It came out during my representation of him. I didn't know my father knew about it, though. How did you find out?"

"Your father actually told me. Well, not exactly. What he said was that your mother was in love with someone else."

"He actually used that term—'in love'?"

"Yes." I can hear sadness in her voice. This couldn't have been easy for her to share.

"Thank you," I say.

"There's more, I'm afraid."

"What?"

"Please don't be mad at me, Alex."

"Joan, just tell me."

"Okay. Okay. She told your father about this on the day before he died."

She doesn't say anything more, and so I press her, as I would a hostile witness whom I suspect is holding back on me. "Joan, please just tell me what he said. I want to know all of it—what he said to you and what you said to him," I say, using a common lawyer formulation for questioning witnesses in a deposition.

I can actually hear her sigh, as if she's gathering strength for what is to follow. "The day before your father died, he called me. He sounded very upset and asked me to come over because he didn't want to be alone and he didn't know who else to call. When I got there, I could tell that he'd been crying. He reminded me of a little boy. Lost and scared. I asked him what was wrong and he just came out and said that your mother was in love with someone else. I asked him what happened, why he would think that, and he said that's what your mother had said to him." There's a long silence before she says, "I wanted to tell you at your father's funeral, Alex, but then I thought about it more and I decided maybe it was better that you have the best thoughts possible about your parents. But after that man was arrested, and it was in the newspapers about him and your mother, I thought you'd want to know. I hope I made the right decision."

My father knew that my mother was in love with someone else, and the next day he was dead. My mind flashes back to the rabbi's words at my mother's funeral, and how wrong he was. It was my father, and not my mother, who died of a broken heart.

I don't remember saying good-bye to Joan, although I doubt I just hung up on her, but a moment later the phone is beside me on the bed, my head is in my hands and I'm sobbing. It feels almost like I've lost him again.

"What is it?" Elizabeth says in a whisper as she enters the room. She sits down beside me and places her hand on my back, rubbing in a circular motion, the way we do with Charlotte when we're trying to comfort her.

Elizabeth is a patient sort, and so she doesn't ask me again, even though a good thirty seconds go by without an answer. Finally, catching my breath, I say, "He knew. My father knew about my mother and Ohlig."

"Is that what your aunt said?"

"Yeah."

I straighten up and wipe the last tear from my eye. Looking into Elizabeth's face I see only concern, and just like I was when I came home after breaking it off with Abby, I'm jarred by just how unfair this is—her comforting me about my father being betrayed by his wife.

"I'm so sorry, Alex."

She still doesn't know the worst part, the part that really pushed me over the edge—my father found out the day before he died. Could that really be a coincidence?

But then something else occurs to me, a fact I'd overlooked. My initial premise was that my mother told my father about Ohlig only because she was leaving him. But that made sense only if Ohlig was going to leave his wife too. Then why didn't they finish the plan? Why weren't they openly together?

Because my father died, I realize. The ultimate ironic twist—my father's death kept my mother and Ohlig apart. Now they'd have to wait. After a respectable period, they could tell everyone how, in their mutual grief, my mother turned to my father's oldest friend for comfort, and he toward her and, though no one planned on it happening, they fell in love. And then they could live happily ever after, the end.

Then, come last Thanksgiving, my mother must have assumed that enough time had passed, but Ohlig apparently had second thoughts. A lot had certainly happened since my father's death, not the least of which was that Ohlig was about to go on trial for securities fraud. He must have told her it wasn't the time to leave his wife. Maybe they had that discussion before and she was tired of his excuses. My mother must have threatened to tell Pamela, and that bastard couldn't risk that the truth would come out.

"What is it, Alex?"

Elizabeth's voice startles me.

"Nothing. I'm just trying to process it all."

# 47

"'m very glad this year is over," I say to Elizabeth as we're sitting on the couch preparing for the ball to drop in Times Square.

"What did the queen call the year that Diana and Charles divorced and the castle burned down?" she says. "Annus Horribilis or something?"

"I wish the worst thing that had happened to me this year was that our house had burned down."

"That's the great thing about New Year's, Alex. A chance to close the book and write a new one. Anyhow, it wasn't all terrible this year."

Elizabeth says this while looking down in her arms, where Charlotte sleeps soundly, curled up like a kitten. Charlotte is still wearing those ridiculous eyeglasses that they sell on the street corner for a dollar, the ones with the year serving as the eye holes.

Elizabeth had offered that we go out tonight. The mother of one of Charlotte's friends, a woman whom Elizabeth has become friendly with through playdates, was having a party. I wouldn't have been interested under the best of circumstances, but when I found out it was black tie, I told Elizabeth I'd much rather welcome in the New Year wearing my pajamas. She said that she was actually thinking the same thing.

"What do you think of the picture over there?" I say,

pointing to the Scary Lady, who has taken up residence in the dining room.

Two days ago, I'd picked her up from the framer, who had given her a makeover with a cherrywood frame and off-white matting. The guy in the frame store told me that the lighter border would make the colors brighter.

"The new frame is nice," Elizabeth says.

It's not lost on me that the compliment is for the frame only. "We can take it down if you'd prefer."

"No. If it makes you happy here, that's fine with me."

Ryan Seacrest is on TV, introducing this year's group with the hot song. I've never heard of the band or even the song for that matter. It seems that this year, or at least the second part of it, I've lived outside of the world, as if nothing happened that didn't happen only to me. I haven't been to the movies or read a book. Where did the year go?

"Did you make any resolutions?" I ask Elizabeth.

"I did," she says coyly, almost flirtatiously.

"Care to share?"

"You know that if I do, they won't come true."

"That's only birthday wishes, and maybe for a shooting star. It doesn't apply to New Year's resolutions." I say this with an air of seriousness, as if this is an expertise I possess, the knowledge of the distinction between resolutions and wishes.

"Nothing that extravagant," Elizabeth says, apparently having been convinced that resolutions can be shared without losing their potency. "Just to be happier."

"Just to be happier." I'm not sure whether I'm repeating her resolution or trying it on for size myself. "Just like that?"

"Why not? I could say I'm going to lose twenty pounds or learn Chinese, but I know I won't do either of those things. I think being happier is a more lofty goal anyway."

"You should put in an order for me on that one. You know, happiness for two."

She sends me the look that says things are about to become more serious. "Only you can make yourself happy, Alex."

"I know. I know." Even as I agree with Elizabeth, I'm still far from certain that Abby didn't have this right when she offered the opposite opinion.

Elizabeth gets up from the sofa while still cradling Charlotte and walks toward the Pink Palace. From the couch, I can see into Charlotte's room and watch Elizabeth pour our daughter into bed, bringing the covers up to her shoulders. Elizabeth reaches into the toy bin and pulls out Belle the bunny, gently tucking it under Charlotte's arm before kneeling beside the bed and kissing Charlotte's forehead.

Elizabeth returns to the couch and adopts a very similar pose to Charlotte's, curling her body and tucking herself under my arm. I begin to stroke her long hair with my palm, causing Elizabeth to make a purring sound to indicate her appreciation. There have been numerous moments like this over the past few months when I've wondered what happened to us. How did we—maybe I should say *I*—get here? I never have an answer.

"What about you?" Elizabeth says, startling me for a moment.

"What about me what?"

"Resolutions. You're a pretty big list maker. I bet you have some good resolutions."

"Nothing really," I lie, *really* giving it away, I'm sure.

"C'mon, Alex. I told. Now you tell."

"I kind of like the whole be-happy thing," I say looking into her face. "It wraps up everything so well."

"No fair. You can't steal my resolution."

"I can't be happy?"

"Okay. You can *borrow* that resolution, but how about a new resolution we can share?"

"What do you have in mind?"

"We should try to have more spontaneous, shall we say, *intimate* moments in the new year."

"That's a resolution I can get behind."

"Alex!" she laughs.

"Sorry," I say, realizing the joke. "I mean I fully support the sentiment."

Without another word, Elizabeth pulls her T-shirt over her head. She's not wearing a bra, and she presses her breasts against my chest. I pull back a bit to remove my own shirt, and then our bodies come together again.

We are as one on the couch, just like it used to be, when I hear the honking horns from the street and the screaming from the party down the hall indicating the arrival of the new year. Elizabeth opens her eyes and stares into my face inches above her.

"Happy New Year, Alex," she breathes.

"Happy New Year, Elizabeth."

"This is going to be a better year," she says, her eyes sparkling. "I promise. I really promise. Please don't give up on us."

# 48

For a city that never sleeps, just before nine in the morning on January 1st is pretty dead. I would wager that half the people I see on the street have not been home since yesterday, continuing their New Year's Eve revelry well into the sunlight. Even if they had been to bed, it most likely was not their own, and they must have hightailed it out of there as soon as they woke up.

On a normal workday the Cromwell Altman lobby teems with people, each one racing to make the elevator as if another one will never arrive. Today it's eerie how deserted it is. Some of that is understandable given the holiday, but I'm surprised I haven't overlapped with at least one or two of my partners.

I check my watch. It's five minutes to nine. Prime time for arrival.

The Cromwell Altman partnership has met every January 1st since 1885 to vote on whether to enlarge its ranks. In addition to Abby, three corporate associates are up for partner this year, one of whom apparently has enough backing to make it, although it may be close. The other two have already been declared dead on arrival. With Aaron's backing, Abby is considered a shoo-in.

I've never had any doubt that when the time came I would vote for her to make it. Of course, I realize it might be better for me if Abby simply vanished off the face of the earth, but even if I could derail her, which is highly doubtful considering Aaron's backing, I know myself well enough to realize that I'm not constitutionally equipped to handle the guilt of ruining someone's career.

There's another reason as well, one far less noble: I'm still not over her, not completely. I want her to stay at the firm so that I can maintain some type of connection. Even if we're not going to be lovers, at least I'll be able to still see her from time to time.

The front desk of the building's lobby is manned during business hours by as many as six security guards. Even on weekends there are usually two. Today a lone guard, the poor guy who has to work on a national holiday, sits behind the marble station. I've probably walked by this same guard three times a day for the past seven years at least, but I don't have the first clue as to his name.

"Happy New Year," I remark as I walk by, not making eye contact. I fumble for my wallet, which contains my building pass, and then slap it outside against the turnstile and proceed through, only to make hard contact with the gate. When I again touch the pass to the turnstile I hear the same buzz and this time also see the red "STOP" beside the gate.

The few times this has happened over the years, I've walked over to the front desk to explain that my ID was not working. Now I'm afraid I'm going to be late, and seeing that we're the only two people in the lobby, and he must have heard the buzz of denial as clearly as me, I call out to him.

"Hey, my pass isn't working. Can you let me through?"

"I'm going to need to see some ID," he calls over to me. "You're also going to have to sign in."

I let him know my displeasure with an exaggerated sigh, the kind that says I can't believe how so little power can go to someone's head. I walk over to him and put my wallet on the desk, removing my building pass and driver's license from the sleeve.

The guard examines the pass as if he's never seen it before, despite the fact that I'm quite sure he's seen more building passes than any man who has ever lived. He next looks down at the desk. I follow his eyes, but the barrier at the desk curls upward to block my view of what has captured his attention.

All of a sudden, I comprehend what's happening. I don't even hear the guard explain it. His words are drowned out by my own, although mine are in my head only.

"I'm sorry," I say. "I don't understand."

The better explanation is that I haven't been listening. I'm sure what he said is fairly simple to comprehend.

"Mr. Miller, someone will be downstairs at approximately nine o'clock to discuss the situation with you." He looks at his watch. "Please have a seat in reception."

Revoking my building pass and denying me access to my office is something that could only be done at the highest level of the partnership. My mind races with the possibilities, but there's really only one—Abby has filed a complaint against me.

If a client called me from the lobby of his office

building and said that his partners had locked him out of a partnership meeting, my advice would be for him to get the hell out of there immediately—do not pass go, do not collect $200—and come directly to my office without talking to anyone. And then he'd say: *But if I do that, they're definitely going to think that I did something wrong and they'll fire me.* And I'd respond: *They wouldn't be treating you like this unless they had already decided to fire you.*

The Cromwell Altman delegation selected to address me arrives in the lobby at precisely nine. It's comprised of Aaron Littman; Jim Martin, the head of the corporate group, whom I probably haven't spoken with for more than ten minutes in the twelve years I've been at the firm; and Paul Harris, whose presence on this team is undoubtedly to provide a friendly face to keep me calm.

Standing behind them, making it difficult to see him, is Ron Kantner, the firm's HR director. His presence confirms what I had already surmised—I'm about to be fired.

Paul steps into the lead as they approach. I wonder if this is choreographed. Then again, perhaps this is what friends do to cushion the blow.

"Hello, Alex," he says, extending his hand as if we were greeting each other at a funeral.

"What's going on?" I ask, although he knows that I know.

He shakes his head and looks to Aaron. I'm about to be on the receiving end of what I've seen Aaron do so many times before—impart bad news in a way that's designed to make the recipient feel lucky to be receiving it.

"Alex, I'm very sorry that it's come to this, but the partnership has voted to reformulate. We all wish you the very best in your legal career."

"I don't understand," I reply.

Aaron has faced down many more liars than most people, and I'm not as proficient as those who do it every day. He sighs deeply. The look on his face is classic Aaron—the one he gives at the point when clients profess their innocence.

"Alex, I was really hoping you would spare us the discomfort of going over what we all know." He says this solemnly, as if it's going to pain him to explain why my career is over.

"I'm sorry," I say, immediately kicking myself for apologizing to him, "but you're going to have to. I really don't understand why you're firing me."

Aaron sighs again, this time even deeper. "Very well. Why don't you have a seat." He motions that I sit down on the leather sofa where I was waiting for him. Aaron sits across from me but Martin, Harris and Kantner remain standing. When I'm in position, he begins, "Human Resources received an anonymous call via the sexual harassment line reporting that you were involved in an inappropriate relationship with Abby Sloane. As you know, we have a duty to investigate all such allegations, even the anonymous ones. We reviewed your emails and voicemails and they left no doubt that there was an intimate relationship between the two of you, which, as you also know, is improper and grounds for immediate termination."

The lawyer in me knows not to admit anything, even just to argue that Abby and I had sex only once. That means there's no way I can defend myself but to deny the charge outright—a futile gesture if they've actually listened to my voicemails or read my emails.

Although it shouldn't matter, that Aaron used the term *intimate*—not *sexual*—to describe my relationship with Abby has taken some of the wind out of my sails. I'm sure he thought the two terms were interchangeable and made the word choice based on decorum, but it makes his charge accurate, whereas otherwise there would be room for debate.

"What about Abby?" I say, just to fill the void because I know the answer.

"She's been elected to the partnership," he says, as if there is no inconsistency at play. Needless to say, it would compound the problem if Cromwell Altman penalized Abby in any way. I'm only glad she made it on her merit, because if she hadn't, your conduct would have put the firm in an untenable situation. Even so, her elevation is always going to be tainted with the idea that the firm had no choice but to make her partner in order to avoid a lawsuit."

Aaron moves slightly to the side, allowing Kantner's bald head to stick through. It's his turn now, like the guy who reads the disclaimers at the end of the commercials.

"Mr. Miller," he says, "we'll be boxing up and sending to you all of your personal items. After you sign a release, the firm will send you your final paycheck for the year and whatever year-end profit you're entitled to."

I spent nearly thirteen years at Cromwell Altman and billed more than 30,000 hours, and this is my good-bye. I'm being treated like a criminal, locked out and not even permitted to retrieve my photographs.

At least, I'm going to be paid for the year, which will provide some financial cushion. But the firm really had no choice about that. For starters, I'm owed that money under the partnership agreement. But what probably carried the day was that the last thing Cromwell Altman wants is a public lawsuit centered on partner compensation. Besides, the fact that they're going to require that I sign a release (and confidentiality agreement, I'm sure) before they pay me a penny of what I've earned leaves little doubt that they consider us to be enemies now.

After what is less than a minute, and feels like a blink of an eye, Aaron stands and extends his hand to me. "I look forward to continuing our relationship, Alex. Being your partner was enriching for me, and I hope that remains true, even as your ex-partner." The use of the term *ex-partner* strikes me as unnecessary and, in a way, just cruel, bringing home the finality of this decision. Then again, that was probably the point.

They are about to walk away—in fact, Martin is already heading toward the elevator—when Aaron turns back to me. "One more thing," he says. "I know you're enough of a professional that there's no need to say this, but Abby has specifically requested that you not contact her. She's understandably very upset. No one wants to make partner this way."

All at once, my entire being becomes consumed with the same thought. Not that I am unemployed; or how I'm going to explain this to Elizabeth; or even whether this will cause the end of my marriage.

I wonder why Abby would do this to me.

Even though it's close to freezing outside, I walk the more than twenty blocks back to our apartment, each step of the way wishing I had somewhere else to go. The walk gives me time to play out in my head different ways to tell Elizabeth, but no version sounds better than any other.

When I turn the doorknob to the apartment, I have no idea what I'm going to say, or even if I'm going to tell her. What awaits me inside, however, is even more surprising to me than the end of my career—Elizabeth is painting.

The easel I bought for her thirtieth birthday is set up in the living room and the paints that were included with the gift are on the coffee table.

"You're back earlier than I expected," she says, relaxed in a way I haven't seen in some time. "Last year, didn't it go all day? Isn't it some type of ridiculous firm tradition where you make them bend over and ask, 'May I please have another?'"

I don't even force out a smile. "You're painting?"

"You make it sound like you found me here with another man. Yes, I'm painting. You do remember that I did that once, don't you?"

"I'm just surprised is all. When was the last time you painted?"

"Why should that matter? I'm painting now. See, this is one New Year's resolution I've already kept. That bodes very well for the ones we discussed last night."

She has said all of this while looking intently at her canvas, which is probably the reason her lightheartedness has continued for so long. Elizabeth finally looks up at me to finish the thought. "Anyway, being a painter is like being president—even after you stop doing it, you still retain the . . ."

It has taken her this long to read me. But when our eyes meet there is no longer any doubt. She knows that something is horribly wrong. Lying is not an option.

I just tell her.

Short declarative sentences, without emotion.

I had sex with Abby Sloane. Once. Right after my mother died. She told the firm. They fired me. I'm sorry.

I'm very, very sorry.

When I'm finished Elizabeth doesn't say anything, at least not at first. She looks mainly at the floor, as if she's too disgusted with me to meet my eyes.

Elizabeth prides herself on remaining in control. I've never seen her lose it, not even with Charlotte, giving her a far better track record than I have.

"Is it over?" she finally asks.

I find the question odd, especially considering I'd already told her that it was only once and it had been Abby who'd gone to the firm with the disclosure that led to my termination. Then again, maybe she's asking about my feelings, which I had not addressed in my short mea culpa.

"Yes, it's over," I say.

Elizabeth takes a very heavy breath. It's obvious how hard she's working to keep it all together. Every muscle appears rigid.

"So, what am I supposed to do now?" she asks.

"What do you want to do?"

"I want to hurt you. I want to cause you to feel pain like I'm feeling right now, so you know how it feels to be betrayed. Betrayed by someone you thought was there to protect you. To feel like your entire life is coming to an end."

There is a fury to Elizabeth's words, so much so that I wonder if she might lash out at me, or even spit in my face. I'm trying to meet her eyes, but even that is too difficult, and I hang my head in shame.

When she hasn't said anything for a few seconds, I again say, "I'm sorry." I realize too late that I should have said that I loved her.

Her rage gives way to tears, although I can tell she's trying her best not to be swept away by that emotion. "I guess that's the best you can do for now," she says.

"I'll try harder. I promise I will."

"There's only one condition I have for not throwing you out right this minute." She pauses, as if she wants me to ask what it is, but I don't, afraid to say anything. "Promise me you won't call her or email her. That you won't see her under any circumstances. Ever. I want to know that it's just us. That it's completely over with her."

"Okay," I say weakly, deciding it was best not to mention that Abby, apparently, has no interest in speaking with me.

"Do you love her?"

It's not the first time I've entertained the thought, of course. And, most of the time I considered it, I concluded that my feelings for Abby must be love. What else is it when a person consumes your every thought, when just being in her presence makes you happier than you ever thought possible?

But if it was love, I wouldn't have ended it, I tell myself. Maybe it was lust. Or longing. Or just loneliness. No matter what I once felt, however, I can honestly say that I'll never feel it again for her. Not after what Abby did. Isn't that what's most important now, anyway?

"No, I don't love her," I answer.

Elizabeth doesn't seem the least bit pleased by my answer, which is hardly a surprise. I wonder if she wouldn't have found it somewhat redeeming if I was in love, elevating the betrayal above the pursuit of mere physical pleasure. More likely, nothing I say is going to make her any happier, and I should respect that.

"I guess the more important question is whether you still love me. Do you, Alex? Do you love me?"

Part **5**

# 49

All the while I was at Cromwell Altman, I dreamed of what it would be like not to work. In those fantasies, I went to the gym every day, took long walks in the park, picked Charlotte up from school, and read the great books I missed in college.

In the month since I was so unceremoniously sacked by Cromwell Altman, the reality of my unemployment has proven to be far different. With nothing to do all day and a wife who appears disgusted by the sight of me, I have difficulty finding a reason to get out of bed. When I gather up the strength to do so, I rarely leave the apartment, spending my days watching a lot of bad television and scarfing down junk food. Every so often Elizabeth tells me to get out because she wants some alone time, in which case I go to the Starbucks on 79th and Lexington and wonder why the other patrons don't have jobs to go to, and if they're just as depressed as me.

It is therefore hardly a surprise that Elizabeth is confused when I emerge from our bedroom at 9:00 A.M. wearing a business suit, a white collared shirt, and a tie. Elizabeth is in running clothes, but it's difficult for me to tell if she's coming or going. If it had been two weeks ago, I would have said going, as she was obviously looking for any excuse not to share the same space with me, be it in the apartment during the day or our bed at night. In the last week or so, some of that coldness has thawed. Twice we've had breakfast together and a few nights ago we watched a movie on pay-per-view. The bedroom is still off limits to me, which in some ways is just as well.

"I have that meeting with Clint Broden," I say. When it looks as if the name means nothing to her, I add, "the guy representing Michael Ohlig. I told you about it last week."

At Cromwell Altman, we referred to his kind as a television lawyer. The guy who either has the celebrity client of the day and is trying the case in the press, or is otherwise pontificating on television about someone else's case.

I had read that Ohlig retained Broden to represent him in my mother's murder trial, and so Broden's call last week had not come completely out of the blue. It made perfect sense that Ohlig opted for Broden this time around. In his last trial, he was being accused of corporate crimes in federal court, in a case that demanded the review and understanding of millions of pages of documents, and so he went with a white-shoe corporate law firm. But a murder trial—especially, I imagine, one in Florida—is more like a street fight than a chess match, and Clint Broden is the legal world's equivalent of the ultimate fighting champion.

"I didn't think you were actually going to go," Elizabeth says, sounding suspicious, as if I'm making up the entire meeting as a pretext to be somewhere else. Under the circumstances, I don't begrudge her this paranoia.

"I'd rather not, but Broden played on my professional obligation. Apparently, I have a fiduciary duty to bring new counsel up to speed about the prior representation."

"Even when the client in question killed your mother?"

"I made that point to Broden. I guess the real reason I'm going is because I have a morbid curiosity about the whole thing. Like rubber-necking at a traffic accident. I know it's best for me to let it go, but I want to know what the evidence looks like, what Ohlig's defense is going to be." I look at Elizabeth to see if she's getting any of this.

"Do you want to talk about it? It's okay if you don't."

This is the way we've been communicating lately. There's an exaggerated formality between us, characterized by each of us offering the other multiple-choice options on even the most trivial of matters. *Would you mind if I watch television with you, or would you prefer some quiet time?* Or, *I'd like to take Charlotte to school tomorrow morning. Are you okay with that, and if so, can you pick her up?*

"When it's over, maybe," I say, careful to add, "Thank you."

When I arrive at Broden's office, I am greeted by one of the most beautiful women I have ever seen. She identifies herself as his receptionist and directs me to have a seat.

The office is opulent in a way I have never seen in

even the largest of law firms, complete with its own panorama of Central Park that rivals Cromwell Altman's view. As I wait in reception, I peruse a large, leatherbound book without a title that rests on an antique end table. It is a map of sorts, identifying the artwork that hangs in the office, the artists, and where each piece was purchased. On the matching end table is a second book, this one listing the same information for the artwork that hangs in Broden's Miami office, which he maintains to service his large percentage of clients in the drug-trafficking trade. The price of each piece of art is omitted, of course, but the message is clear: Broden's clients spare no expense in retaining him.

"Hi, Alex. Clint Broden," he says as I'm flipping through one of the books. I stand and shake his hand.

Broden is a small man, not more than five and a half feet tall and a hundred and sixty pounds after a full meal. But there is a heft to him that signals he's a man of wealth and taste, as Mick Jagger so aptly put it. He's known for dressing with some flash, and for this meeting he's wearing a contrasting white collar on his blue striped shirt, oversized gold cufflinks, and a large watch ringed with diamonds. I normally don't even register the eye color of the men I meet, but there is something penetrating in Broden's stare, such that I immediately feel pulled in by his ice-blue eyes.

He leads me toward his private office, and as we're walking he lobs his first surprise. "Michael is already here," he says.

I stop short. I knew that Ohlig had made bail, so

that's not the reason I'm surprised he's here. After Ohlig showed up for trial in the securities fraud action, which posed the risk of life in prison, Broden was able to convince the Florida judge that it was foolish to think Ohlig would consider fleeing, even though the death penalty is a possible outcome this time. I wonder if it's Broden's pull with the state judge or Ohlig's money that has allowed him to keep his freedom. On the other hand, I have no doubt that Ohlig isn't actually a flight risk. Running would admit guilt, and I'm now convinced that he's just not built that way.

What surprises me, however, is that this is the first I'd heard that I'll have to face Ohlig. I don't think the bait-and-switch was by happenstance.

"On the phone you told me this meeting would be just the two of us," I say to Broden. "'Lawyer-to-lawyer' was the phrase I believe you used."

Broden smiles at me, a look that says that he wasn't trying to be deceptive. "As you know, perhaps better than anyone else, sometimes Michael has his own agenda."

With that he extends his arm to open the door to his office.

Broden's office is the size of at least three partner offices at Cromwell Altman—larger than Aaron Littman's even—and reminds me of the drawing room of a mansion on Fifth Avenue. The furniture is rich in color and texture, deep brown leathers mixed with red velvets and blue silks. The desk is enormous and strikingly modern, without even a scrap of paper on it. Two flat-screen televisions adorn the wall opposite the park, and between them is a large working fireplace, flames crackling inside. The art book in reception and my introductory art classes in college have already prepared me for the fact that the most valuable pieces reside here, including a large Miró that had only recently been purchased at Sotheby's.

Ohlig sits in a high-back leather chair beside the fire. He looks at me smugly, and I can't help but think that he should be wearing an orange jumpsuit and not the bespoke gray flannel number he's sporting.

Broden points to the chair closest to Ohlig, but despite the seating plan, I select the chair farthest from him, deliberately offering Ohlig a sneer as I pass. Broden settles into the chair between us without saying a word, as if everything is still going exactly according to plan.

"Thank you again so much for coming in, Alex," Broden says as he arranges himself in his seat. "It would have been easy for you to ignore me, so I want to start off by telling you how much I appreciate your agreeing to meet."

It doesn't escape me that Broden is prefacing his comments as if I'm doing him a personal favor that has nothing to do with Michael Ohlig. He wants this to be between him and me because that way there should be no bad blood. I imagine he pointed out to Ohlig several times the disadvantages of his presence at this meeting, and his client simply overruled him. In this way, Broden is right—I do know all too well the challenges Broden faces in representing Michael Ohlig.

"Ground rules?" Broden says, his inflection making it sound like a question. I nod, telling him that the floor remains his. "I've asked Michael to be here today." He stops and catches Ohlig's eye. "Actually, I misspoke. *Michael* asked me if he could be here today. I agreed, with the following proviso: he will not speak, and you should infer nothing by his silence. He is aware that you no longer represent him, and therefore that certain aspects of this meeting will not be subject to the attorney-client privilege."

"I understand the parameters of the privilege," I say, deliberately sounding annoyed by Broden's lecture, although I would have given exactly the same one were I in his shoes. "What I don't understand is what you want from me."

"A fair question," Broden says with a smile that, despite my knowing better, I find disarming. "Before answering you, I'd like to make one more point." He looks to me, as if he's waiting for my permission to make this very important pronouncement. This time I offer no encouragement.

"Thank you," he says, either because he views my silence as acquiescence or that's the way he had scripted it, assuming I'd say something to signal my assent. "Michael has asked me to say in no uncertain terms that he's eternally grateful for all you did for him in the OPM trial. He knows that he owes his freedom—his life, actually—to your skill and dedication. And he feels absolutely terrible that things have turned out the way they have. He's also aware of what happened at Cromwell Altman, and he is very sorry for your setback, and is confident you will land on your feet. *But*"—Broden puts a strong emphasis on the word, as if he's addressing a jury—"Michael is completely innocent of these new charges, and he once again needs your help to make sure that a gross injustice doesn't occur."

"Completely innocent," I repeat. "It's not like I haven't heard that from clients before, right?"

"Maybe," Broden concedes, "but I believe him. And from what he tells me, you believe him too."

"What is that supposed to mean?"

"That you know he didn't kill your mother."

"Well, that's news to me, Michael," I say, annoyed at this construct of Broden as interpreter.

Broden shakes his head at Ohlig, the non-verbal cue that he shouldn't rise to my bait. "Michael is certain your mother . . . forgive me for saying this, Alex, but your mother was not murdered by anyone. It will be our defense at trial that your mother took her own life. It's the only conclusion consistent with the evidence."

"You mean other than that your client's a murderer?"

"Please, Alex," Broden says soothingly, "let's keep this on a professional level. I know that's asking a lot given how hard all of this must be on you, but I think it will be best for everyone if we all refrain from personal attacks. I understand that, at first, you also believed your mother took her own life. Given that no one knew your mother better than you, it's important we place before the jury your initial assumptions about her death."

So this is why I'm here. For them to see how hard a line I'm going to take on this issue.

"Well, that's just not true." I say this firmly, looking first at Broden, and then at Ohlig. "In fact, I recall him saying that he was positive that she did not kill herself."

"So, you were discussing the possibility of suicide," Broden says, "and, at that time, before the evidence was known, Mr. Ohlig said that he did not believe it was a suicide."

This is why smart people don't meet with the other side's lawyer before trial. "No, that's not the way I recall it at all," I say.

"Michael told me that you and he discussed the possibility that your mother committed suicide on at least two occasions," Broden replies. "First, you said it at your mother's funeral. Pamela Ohlig corroborates this account. The second time was when you met privately with Michael after you learned of his romantic involvement with your mother."

I laugh. "So, Michael told you I said that my mother killed herself, and then to prove the point you tell me that his wife says so, too. *That's* what you've got?" I laugh again, louder this time. "Very compelling stuff." Then, turning to Ohlig: "You know, Michael, if you're going to lie, go all out, man. Why not just say that *I* confessed to killing my mother?" They both look at me grim-faced. "Well, I hate to disappoint you guys, but I never thought my mother killed herself and I never said anything of the kind to Michael, as he damn well knows."

"It's not just Michael and his wife," Broden says, playing what must be his trump card. "We have another witness who will testify you said the same thing."

"Yeah? Who?"

Broden looks at Ohlig. This must have been a point they previously discussed, whether to divulge this bit of intelligence. Ohlig closes his eyes slightly, which is apparently enough of a signal for Broden.

"We've spoken to Abigail Sloane," Broden says without emotion. "We know that there's some history between the two of you, and we have no interest in exploiting that, but she told us that you initially thought your mother took her own life."

"You have a hell of a lot of nerve, you know that?" I say to Ohlig, making no effort to hide my anger. "How do you sleep at night, anyway?"

This is enough to break Ohlig's silence. "It's not me, Alex. Your mother did this and you know it."

"All I know is that I hope you get the death penalty so I can be there when they stick the needle in your arm!" I'm suddenly leaning forward and shouting, surprised that I've lost control in this way.

Broden tries to restore calm, putting his hand on Ohlig's leg to stop him, while turning to me to respond to my charge. "Alex, we don't want to call Abby as a witness, but if you won't admit that you believe your mother's death was suicide, we're going to have no choice."

I doubt Abby would be allowed to testify about what I told her because it's hearsay, but stranger things have happened. And, if I denied the conversation and she testified it occurred, there are perjury risks in it for me.

"Okay, we're done here," I say, getting up from my seat, which causes Broden to do the same. I take a juvenile pleasure in using my height advantage to stare down at him. To his credit, Broden gives no indication he's the least bit intimidated. "Do what you have to do, Clint. But I'll tell you this. If I see Abby Sloane anywhere near that courtroom, I will bury you. That is a promise. I'll testify that Michael confessed to me, and the only reason I didn't come forward was I had concerns it was privileged, and have since been told otherwise. So why don't you think about that."

Broden knows better than to respond. The meeting has deviated from his script, and he isn't going to bring it back. The only thing he can do now is let me leave without making matters worse.

Ohlig, however, is not as well disciplined. "She was right about you, Alex!" he calls out harshly to me as I reach for the door. "Your mother said it to me time and time again—you're just like her!"

# 50

When Elizabeth first suggested that we go to marriage counseling I resisted, claiming it was not a good time to be spending money considering that finding employment has been much more difficult than I ever could have anticipated. Most law firms, it seems, would rather hire an alcoholic than someone fired from his last job for anything having to do with sex. Elizabeth correctly pointed out that counseling would be much less expensive than divorce lawyers, and it's not as if I didn't have a large year-end check, so we could afford it.

Our counselor is named Howard. He's in his mid-sixties, maybe even older than that, which I find reassuring, and he has a warm way about him. Elizabeth is convinced he's gay, which might be right, even though I think she's reached that conclusion on the flimsiest of evidence—he wears a bow tie and, she claims, never looks at her breasts.

The day after I met with Broden, Howard opens our session with a question: Which fictional person does your spouse remind you of? He tells us that he used to limit the inquiry to literature, but eventually found that too difficult for his patients, so now he's open to television or movie characters, cartoons, whatever the hell you want.

The first character that pops into my head is Scarlett O'Hara, perhaps because I know *Gone With the Wind* is Elizabeth's favorite movie. I know not to go with that choice, however. Elizabeth will say that I must think she's spoiled or looking for a man to save her, neither of which I actually believe. But, as Howard would say, the fact that my first thought is Elizabeth's reaction, and that I then alter my response to fit what I think she wants me to do, is more telling than whatever I actually say.

My mind next runs to stories I read with Charlotte, which must account for more than 80 percent of the reading I've been doing these days. I choose Belle from *Beauty and the Beast*. In my mind, this sounds like a good choice because I can describe Belle in the words equally applicable to Elizabeth—very smart, beautiful, protective of her family, and strong willed.

"You left out that she loves a monster," Elizabeth says with a self-satisfied smile, pointing out the rather obvious flaw in my selection.

"Well, perhaps it's not a perfect analogy," I laugh.

"Let's explore that for a moment," Howard suggests in his soothing way. "What do you make of the fact that maybe Alex thinks he's not the same on the inside and the outside?"

"I guess I'd have to say that I didn't know he thought that way," Elizabeth says.

"Do you, Alex?" Howard asks.

"I think everyone is a little like that, right? I mean, who's exactly the way the world sees him? But, I don't think you should read too much into what I said. I was talking about Elizabeth, not me."

I suspect that Howard isn't done with his analysis of my selection, but he can tell that I am, at least for the moment. He turns to my wife. "Your turn, Elizabeth."

"This is easy for me. Batman."

"Interesting," Howard says, "because he's another person who is not who he appears to be. It's as if there's a theme here. So, why Batman, Elizabeth?"

"For starters, Alex lost both his parents this year and, like it was for Bruce Wayne, I think it's been life altering for him."

I nod, waiting for Elizabeth to get to something meatier. Apparently Howard is too because he says, "What else?"

"I think Alex is lonely, but it's a loneliness that he's created for himself. There are people around him who love him, and yet he pushes us away."

"Talk to Alex," Howard says, a common refrain.

Elizabeth turns a quarter toward me. "You know how we once talked about how Superman was more like Clark Kent and Batman was really who he was inside, and that he *created* the Bruce Wayne persona, not the other way around?"

I nod back to her, even though I don't recall having shared my theories on the subject with her. I certainly remember when Abby and I talked about it, however. It is a sad reminder of where my focus has been lately. Each conversation with Abby remains clear as could be, and yet I can't recall much of anything Elizabeth and I have discussed in the last six months.

"Well, I was thinking that there was another pretty big difference between them. Superman is always Superman. He can't not be because he's got those powers whether he's Clark Kent or Superman. But Batman, he could *choose* not to be Batman if he wanted. He could just decide not to put on the costume. He could stop what he's doing, get married, and have a regular life."

"Maybe Batman could go to therapy," Howard suggests. "Or couples counseling, with Lois Lane."

Elizabeth smiles at me, a private joke that she knows Howard has mistakenly referenced Superman's girlfriend. I smile back that I recognize the error too.

She's right, however. They both are. I don't have to be the person I've always been. I could choose to be different. I could try to work harder at my marriage and take better care of the people in my life who love me.

It's not a foolproof plan, of course. There are some things that just cannot be bent to your will, and a happy marriage is one of them. But I certainly loved Elizabeth once. It's not impossible to think I could recapture that feeling, or recognize that it's matured into something equally satisfying.

At the very least, I'm determined to try. I only hope it's enough.

On Valentine's Day, my personal items from Cromwell Altman arrive in a single box. I'm sure it took no more than a half hour for someone to box it up, but the six-week delay just further reinforces how low a priority I am for the firm. Then for a moment I wonder whether the timing was intentional, someone's idea of a joke, but decide that I had it right the first time—no one at Cromwell Altman gives me a second thought, not even to have a laugh at my expense.

To add insult to injury, there's not even a cover note. At least they didn't make me pay for the delivery, I think to myself.

As I look through the accumulations of my professional life, I can't believe how few of the items that surrounded me every day actually belong to me. There are four photographs—two of Charlotte, both from when she was a baby, a wedding photo of Elizabeth, and a picture I took of Elizabeth and Charlotte three years ago during our vacation to St. Maarten. It never occurred to me how out of date the photographs are, or that I didn't keep a picture of Elizabeth and me in my office, although now I wonder why that was without arriving at a satisfactory answer.

At the bottom of the box is the Batman cup that I used for pens, which reminds me that the Cobblepot for Mayor poster hasn't been returned. I'm assuming that it will come separately, and I hope that I don't have to call Kantner to get it back; or worse, that they'll claim it's firm property by virtue of its hanging on the firm's walls.

"Is it what I think it is?" Elizabeth asks when she sees me holding the Batman mug.

"Afraid so," I say. "The nose on the Caped Crusader

is chipped." I hold the mug up. "Apparently it was too difficult for someone to put some bubble wrap around it." I expect some type of reaction, but when there isn't any, I add, "I can fix it pretty easily, though. A felt-tip black pen should do the trick."

"I'd prefer it if you throw it all away," she says. "I don't want any reminder of that place in our home."

## 51

As Deputy Gattia told me that day with Judge Sullivan, the Florida Assistant District Attorney assigned to prosecute Michael Ohlig is a woman named Morgan Robertson. I learned by googling her that she's a native Floridian who stayed in-state for college and law school. She went to the DA's office right after graduation and never left, her tenure approaching twenty-five years.

"I hope you didn't have any trouble finding the place," she says. "I still get lost every time I visit your fair city."

We had spoken by phone a few times, but with Michael Ohlig's trial now only a month away, she's come to New York to meet with me. Even though she hasn't shared the reason for her visit, I have a pretty good idea what she wants.

We had agreed to meet at the New York District Attorney's Office in lower Manhattan. She's right that it's a hard place to find. It has a vanity address of One Hogan Square, named after Frank Hogan, a legendary New York DA. The office is attached to the Criminal Court building and is accessed through a side entrance off Centre Street, so it's a real pain to find if you don't know where to look.

"I've been here before," I tell her.

"I thought your practice would be exclusively on the federal side of the street," Robertson says. "Good to know that Cromwell Altman gets down in the muck with real criminals, too."

It doesn't take me long to conclude that Morgan Robertson is a type—the hard-ass, professional prosecutor. She reminds me of Wednesday from the Addams family in that she has a very pale complexion and jet black hair, although hers is styled in a professional bob and not braided pigtails. All of this is topped off with a dark, conservative suit paired with an even darker shirt under it. She's probably in her late forties, and she's not wearing a wedding band. The predominant first impression she makes is that she's all business, which is accentuated by the fact that she doesn't smile at what I assume to be the joke she's just made.

"I'm glad to know you don't believe white collar criminals are criminals," I say. "I know quite a few AUSAs who would disagree with you. But I've actually had a few cases with the DA's office too. Usually the business crime unit."

"John Payton's group?"

"Yeah," I say, not hiding too much that I think Payton is an absolute imbecile.

"Agreed," she says, and for the first time smiles at me. As if she can tell a prosecutor's smiling in friendship is not something I'm accustomed to, she says, "We're on the same team on this, Alex. There's nothing I want more than to see Michael Ohlig pay for his crime."

"That makes two of us," I say.

"Good. You'll be pleased to know that we have a strong case against him. We can put him on his boat with your mother on the day of the murder. On top of which, the coroner's report said your mother had sleeping pills in her system at the time of her death, and an order was put in for this same brand of pills through a Canadian pharmacy, and was paid for with Ohlig's credit card. I originally thought that after we laid it out for him, Ohlig would take a plea, which is why I didn't reach out to you sooner. But now it appears that we're heading for trial, and so I'm here to ask for your help to make sure that your mother gets justice."

"I'm sorry, but I still don't see what I can add to the case. I didn't even know they were having an affair until after she died."

"Alex, you're the living reminder to the jurors that your mother isn't just a name, but a real person whose life was tragically cut short. That she left behind people who loved her. I want you in the courtroom every day of the trial so the jurors never forget that. And then, after we get a conviction, you'll need to give a victim's impact statement in the sentencing phase."

This shouldn't surprise me, but the idea that I'll have to testify in furtherance of putting Ohlig to death is sobering, despite what I said in anger during my meeting with him and Broden. As I understand Florida law (also from Google), in a death penalty case, after the defendant is convicted, there's a second trial regarding the sentence. The prosecution's case is usually based on the victim's family pulling the jurors' heartstrings, and some psychologists talking about how irredeemable the defendant is and how he'd be a danger to society if he isn't put to death. Then the defense goes the other way, the defendant's relatives beg for mercy and the shrinks claim mitigating factors—normally remorse, bad childhood, etc.—that make the defendant's life worth preserving.

"How long will it last?" I ask her.

"We've told the judge we estimate the guilt/innocence phase will take a month, so—"

"So you figure a week?" I say with a smile.

"Give or take, yes," she says, returning the smile. "And then the sentencing phase will be only a day or two, at most."

"Okay. If you really think it's necessary, I'll be there."

"I really think it's necessary." This is followed by a pregnant pause, which tells me there's more to come. "I'm also going to need you to testify."

"About what?"

"Ohlig's defense isn't a state secret. He's going to claim that your mother took her own life. I'd like for you to tell the jurors you knew her better than anyone, and she didn't commit suicide."

Of course, I already knew this, and I wish that he would mount another defense—any other defense—but, as they say, you have to play the cards you're dealt.

"Okay," I say, "I'll tell the jurors I knew her better than anyone else and I don't believe she committed suicide."

"You sure?"

"Yes." I think I've said this without equivocation, but Robertson looks like she's not sure I'm up to the task. "What's the problem?" I finally ask.

"No problem—assuming you're telling the truth. But Clint Broden told me that you initially believed it was suicide."

"I would have figured you'd be experienced enough to know better than to believe what a defense counsel says."

She doesn't smile, but instead looks at me even more closely. I imagine it's the same look I've given many a witness who I believed was lying to me.

"You ever see Broden do a cross?"

"Once. In law school. They played a tape of his cross of Senator Carmichael."

"Ah, the 'this is not the Senate, it's a place of justice and honor' speech," she says, quoting Broden's most famous line from the examination.

"That's the one."

"I've been up against Broden a few times. He's the only lawyer I know who is actually better than his reputation. He's the best cross-examiner I've ever seen, hands down."

"Is this supposed to make me a more confident witness?"

"No. It's supposed to make you a less cocky one. I've seen Broden get the truth out of hardened criminals, guys who have beaten polygraphs. You don't strike me as a guy who's that experienced a liar, so don't try to start now."

"You'd be surprised," I say.

"What's that supposed to mean?"

"Nothing. Just trying to be funny."

When I return home, Elizabeth is cooking dinner. It smells like she's making chili, or at least something with cumin in it.

"Are you going to be the star witness for the prosecution?" she asks as I approach her in the kitchen.

"Looks that way. The ADA wants me to attend the entire trial, which means I'm going to have to be in Florida for a week, maybe two. On the bright side, at least I'm not going to have to miss work."

Thankfully, Elizabeth has not seen the need to rub salt in my wounds by complaining about my unemployment. Based on the head hunter discussions I've had, it will likely be a while before I land a job, and when I do, I won't earn anywhere near the kind of money I was raking in at Cromwell Altman. On the other hand, most of the firms that would hire someone like me aren't going to demand 2,500 hours of work every year. For Elizabeth, that is more than a fair trade-off.

"You know, the trial probably won't start until Charlotte's done with school," I say. "Maybe you'll want to come down with me."

She gives me a soft smile, one that suggests she thinks I'm trying too hard. "Let's see what happens," she says.

By now the worst of it has seemingly passed. Elizabeth

and I are getting along well, even enjoying each other's company. I have not only been permitted re-entry into our bed, but Elizabeth has also been trying to make good on her New Year's resolution, concluding that some of our marital discord was due to a lack of physical intimacy. Howard, our marriage therapist, strongly endorsed the sentiment, and so Elizabeth and I have made love more in the last month than we did in the entire past year.

I welcome Elizabeth's efforts and am trying my best to reciprocate, but I find myself reflecting regularly upon whether I'd thought about Abby that day, and then realizing that the question supplies the answer. And, of course, it's difficult to be intimate with Elizabeth, a woman I've made love to for the past fifteen years, without comparing it to the one time I was with Abby, no matter how often I tell myself that no lover of long standing could win such a competition.

Elizabeth tastes whatever is in the pan and puts the wooden spoon back in the pot. "Can I talk to you for a moment?"

"Okay."

"Let's sit down," she says, and starts to move toward the dining room. Despite the fact that I believe everything is on the right track, I'm shaken by her need to tell me anything of such import that it requires sitting.

My concern increases with each moment Elizabeth doesn't seem to know the right way to begin.

After a few moments of this silence, Elizabeth begins to look as if she's going to cry, and my inner alarm grows to the point where I can feel tears well behind my own eyes. When I look more closely, however, I see that I've misread her. I can't explain how, and I'm not a believer in clairvoyance, but I know what she's about to tell me.

"I'm pregnant," she says, smiling, but in a cautious way.

Another baby was once a constant topic of conversation, but it hasn't been raised by either of us in a very long time. More than that, the very idea of Elizabeth becoming pregnant seems impossible. We were taking proper precautions, although I know that's never foolproof.

"That's . . . amazing," I finally say. "I'm so happy."

"Are you sure? I know it's not something we planned, and I know that the timing could hardly be worse."

She's right, on both scores. And truth be told, panic is the actual emotion I'm feeling, rather than happiness. I'm ashamed that my first thought is that it feels like I've re-enlisted in the army right before I was up for a discharge. And then a different sensation begins to take hold, as if this unplanned event is a sign that things are going to get better. I know from firsthand experience that children make marriage harder, not easier, but I can't help but see the possibility of another child being an opportunity for me to start anew. I don't have to stay with Elizabeth just because we're going to have a baby, but I can choose to do so. And I can be a better father, not just to this new life, but to Charlotte as well.

Is that even possible? Can you make yourself a better husband? A better person?

And then I realize that I've made myself a worse one—a distant father; an unfaithful husband; a liar— by the choices I've made. It seems only fair that different choices could make me a better person.

What if Batman went to therapy? He could stop being Batman, couldn't he?

"I'm very happy," I tell her, and pull Elizabeth into my arms. At that moment, feeling her exhale, I realize that, for the first time in quite a while, I'm optimistic about the future.

Part **6**

## 52

Michael Ohlig's trial for my mother's murder begins the second week of July.

Felony trials in Palm Beach County take place in the criminal court complex, which, without irony, is located on Gun Club Road. The building is one of those architecturally anonymous concrete structures that could pass for a suburban mall if only there were a movie theater attached to it.

A murder trial of a multi-millionaire is a relatively rare phenomenon, even in Palm Beach, and the gallery is filled to capacity, which is about a hundred spectators. The counsel tables and the jury box are empty, however, which I've always found a little eerie, like a riderless horse at a funeral.

As the prosecutor Morgan Robertson requested, I'm in attendance from the start, dutifully sitting in the gallery's first row, right behind the prosecution's table. Pamela Ohlig sits just across from me, behind the defense's table, but she never looks in my direction, not once, the surest sign she knows I'm here.

Clint Broden and Ohlig enter the courtroom together. Broden extends his hand and a warm smile, but Ohlig can't even force himself to put on that much of a show. He looks right at me, however, unflappable as always, his glare telling me he's not the least bit intimidated by my presence.

Ohlig is wearing what looks to be the exact same blue suit, light blue shirt, and dark blue tie that he wore on the opening day of our trial, but Broden apparently doesn't impose the same prohibitions with respect to client jewelry as I do—Ohlig's wearing his Patek Philippe, and I'd already noticed that Pamela looks more like she's attending the Oscars than her husband's murder trial. Of course, Broden is more flamboyantly dressed than either of them—dark, double-breasted suit with purple pinstripes, a pink shirt with contrasting white collar, a bright red tie, a diamond Rolex, and a gold pinky ring.

The judge's name is Hector Rodriguez, but to look at him you'd never guess he's Hispanic. He's lighter featured than most of my father's side of the family, and he has blue eyes. Robertson told me that he was head of the Florida Commission on the Death Penalty and a former Republican nominee for State Attorney General before being appointed to the bench, neither of which bodes well for Ohlig.

Unlike Judge Sullivan who handled voir dire herself, Judge Rodriguez plays a supporting role during jury selection, allowing the lawyers to ask the questions. This allows Broden to immediately establish control of the courtroom.

He's got a folksy manner, which I know to be a complete act, but it enables him to treat each juror like a guest in his home, so much so that I'm surprised he doesn't offer any of them tea and cookies. The contrast with Robertson's more businesslike demeanor is stark, and I'm immediately nervous that she's in over her head.

The accepted wisdom at Cromwell Altman was that Assistant United States Attorneys are about twenty IQ points smarter than their counterparts at the DA's office. Federal prosecutors get paid more than local ones and are more desirable in the private sector, which leads to the U.S. Attorney's Office usually attracting the better candidates. I've tried not to let this preconceived prejudice color my views of Robertson, but so far it seems to be right on.

I'm sure both sides had their jury consultants hidden among the spectators, but it doesn't take an advanced degree to know what each is looking for in a juror. Broden wants men, likely of any race, the older the better. Anyone who will identify with Ohlig and sympathize with his plight is a possible vote for acquittal. Even those who think that Ohlig's guilty may still vote to acquit if they can understand why he would have done it.

Robertson tries to put as many older women on the jury as she can. Twelve of my mom would work out best for her. There's some risk in that strategy, which I'm not sure she sees. First, statistically speaking, older women are usually the most cautious when it comes to convicting, likely the only group that takes the reasonable doubt instruction to heart. The bigger problem is that those same statistics point out the rather sexist conclusion that in the jury room, like in the living room, women, especially older women, tend to follow the lead of men. Maybe it's the same impulse that prevents them from exerting their will over the TV remote, but female jurors are known to defer to men who are adamant.

At the end of the selection process, the jury sworn to faithfully adjudicate Michael Ohlig's fate can easily be split into equal parts of older men, older women, and jurors neither side could avoid. It's a classic situation where no one is happy.

Neither opening statement contains any surprises. Robertson lists the evidence in a dry manner, but when it's all out it sounds pretty compelling. She lays the cornerstones that the prosecution always tries to establish—means, motive, and opportunity—and tells the jury that witnesses will place Ohlig with my mother on the day of her death, not far from the place where she drowned. She also has some evidence that he drugged her, although she's vague enough about this in her opening that I suspect she knows it's not rock solid. As for motive, she's going to argue that Ohlig killed my mother to prevent her from telling his wife about their affair, thereby avoiding a costly divorce.

Broden is a much more captivating speaker, making his points with a modulated voice and sweeping arm gestures, but the substance is pretty basic—no one except my mother could know the events that led to her death, and it's unfair for Ohlig to have to prove what is unprovable; namely, that he did not commit murder.

After an hour or so, Broden pulls a stunt I've heard he's done before, although I always thought it was apocryphal. He walks over to the prosecution table and asks Robertson if he can pour himself a cup of water from the pitcher in front of her. I notice that defense counsel table has no pitcher on it. This must be because Broden has removed it, as I'm positive that the court-house cleaning people who are charged with placing the water pitchers have no agenda. The point, however, is to show the jury how much the prosecution controls in the process, right down to denying the defendant and his counsel a simple cup of water.

Before concluding his opening, Broden goes where I did not during the New York trial. He promises Ohlig will testify.

"Ladies and gentlemen of the jury, you will hear from several witnesses who claim to have firsthand knowledge of certain *facts*"—and Broden air quotes the word—"and you will hear from certain people who claim to be experts"—this, too, earns air quotes—"but the only witness who really matters in this case is Michael Ohlig. He is going to take the stand and tell you he is innocent. I am confident that you will believe him."

After court, I go back to the hotel. It's closer to the courthouse than my parents' home in Boynton, but that's not why I decided to stay here. There are enough ghosts in the courtroom, and I figured there was no need to face even more after court.

The first thing I do is call home. Elizabeth sounds

happy to hear from me, and that's enough for my loneliness to lift.

"How did it go today?" she asks.

"It's hard hearing the evidence laid out. And, no big surprise, during his opening Broden promised Ohlig's going to testify."

"Did he give any hint of what Ohlig's going to say?"

"Broden didn't come out and say it directly; I think he's trying to keep all his options open. But when push comes to shove, he's going to say that my mother killed herself."

"Then it's a good thing you're there to tell them that didn't happen."

I move the topic away from my expected testimony. "Broden's something to see. He's really got them eating out of his hand."

"And how's the prosecutor, what's her name, Morgan?"

"She's fine. A little on the stiff side, but she makes up for it with absolute certainty that Ohlig's guilty."

"You say it as if you lack that certainty."

"I think it's more complicated than that."

"What's complicated about whether he's guilty or innocent?"

I smile, which I know is lost on her over the phone. If only things were that simple, I think to myself.

# 53

Robertson's first witness is the sheriff of Palm Beach County, Richard Brunswick. He looks like a cop undergoing a makeover that's still in progress. There's a certain amount of polish to him, the snug-fitting suit and the pocket square that matches his tie, but they are at odds with the used-car salesman mustache and large pot belly that hangs over an alligator belt.

His answer to Robertson's first question—"Are you currently employed?"—clarifies the inconsistency.

"Since my election in 2007, I have served as the sheriff of Palm Beach County. Before that, I was a career law enforcement agent here in Palm Beach."

I should have guessed. Richard Brunswick is a cop turned politician.

Just as Special Agent McNiven did during the securities fraud trial in New York, Sheriff Brunswick is going to lay out the prosecution's case. Robertson has already told the jury in her opening statement that eyewitnesses and experts will follow, but Brunswick will give the narrative into which the evidentiary pieces will fit.

Brunswick has a confident air about him without being too smug, not an easy balance for either a cop or a politician to master. He recounts his rise through the department, during which he seems to have held every position in law enforcement from crossing guard right up to chief of police. When there was nowhere higher to climb within the department, he was elected sheriff.

This is Brunswick's nineteenth murder case, he tells the jury, the fourth since he's been sheriff. This seems like a lot to me, which I imagine is why Robertson sought to bring this issue to the fore, so the jury won't think he's a small-timer in over his head.

Robertson takes Brunswick through the investigation chronologically, careful to touch on each of the points she made in her opening. Early on she plays tape 17, the one I first heard during Ohlig's New York trial. The one that started all of this, at least for me.

Tapes are catnip for a jury. It's the only time they get to hear the actual truth and not the testimony of well-coached witnesses. I understand from Robertson that there was a hearsay skirmish over this one, but because it's Ohlig's voice, the recording is admissable as a party admission.

Even though by now I've heard the tape at least half a dozen times, the sound of my mother's voice pledging her undying love to a man who is not my father still touches the same nerve it did originally. I can feel the jurors looking at me as they listen, and I oblige them by wiping my eyes, even though there are no tears.

"It is the theory of the defense," Robertson tells Brunswick as if he doesn't know, "that Mrs. Miller committed suicide—"

Broden objects, rightfully. This was a poorly worded question on Robertson's part.

"Your Honor," Broden says, "the defense doesn't

have theories. The defense is only obliged to point out that the government's theory of murder is not believable beyond a reasonable doubt."

"He's right," Judge Rodriguez says to Robertson. Even he looks a little disappointed with her. "Try to rephrase."

"Sheriff Brunswick, did you consider that Mrs. Miller committed suicide as a possible explanation for her death?"

Robertson actually looks over her shoulder at Broden, I assume to see if he's going to object. When he doesn't, she looks back at her witness.

"Believe me," Brunswick says, "I'm in no hurry to declare something a murder if it isn't. I know that the defense has claimed this might be a suicide, but that just isn't consistent with the evidence."

Broden could object and seek to strike Brunswick's answer, but he's smart enough to know not to dwell on this issue. He's made his point that it's not the defense's burden to prove suicide, and he's content to leave it at that.

"Why is that?" Robertson asks.

"For starters, there's no suicide note."

"In your experience, Sheriff Brunswick, do most people who take their own lives leave a note?"

Broden objects. This is an area in which the experts will fight it out later. Robertson has already told me that each side lined up a psychologist with differing views on the subject.

I expect Judge Rodriguez to leave the question for

them, but he lives up to his reputation as a prosecution-oriented jurist. "Mr. Broden," he says, "I believe that the experience of the county's leading law enforcement official is relevant here, and so I'm going to allow it."

It's a nice feeling being on the other side for once. Judge Rodriguez's ruling is probably wrong—after all, how many suicides has Brunswick actually dealt with, and how would he know how many he's missed?—but it's a tremendous boon to the prosecution.

"I've never seen a suicide that didn't leave a note," Brunswick says. Largely because I'm sure Robertson has informed him that statistically that's not accurate, he qualifies his answer by adding, "I'm aware that some have existed, of course, but I believe that they are the narrow exception."

After this detour into a subject matter he has nary any experience in, Brunswick goes on to sturdier ground, as Robertson focuses on the sleeping pills, which are a lynchpin of proving my mother was murdered.

"Sheriff," Robertson says, "please tell the jury about the quantity of sleeping pills found in Mrs. Miller's system."

"Yes," he says. "We found approximately 40 milliliters of a drug called Ambien. That quantity is inconsistent with Mrs. Miller voluntarily going swimming."

"Objection," Broden says again, although I can tell he knows it's not going to fly. I suspect he's trying to lay the groundwork for the jury to see what an uphill battle a defendant faces, a variant on the no water at counsel table theme.

"What is it, Mr. Broden?" Judge Rodriguez asks.

"Once again, this witness is a police officer. He has no training whatsoever in forensics or medicine, and therefore his views about sleeping pill quantities should be stricken."

"No. No." Judge Rodriguez says, shaking his head. Then he turns to the jury. "Ladies and gentlemen, Mr. Broden is correct that Sheriff Brunswick is not a doctor or a scientist or, for that matter, an Indian chief. He is, however, the sheriff of this county, and by virtue of that, he has been involved in more criminal cases than anybody else in this courtroom. It is for that reason, and only that reason, that I'm permitting him to testify about these subjects. The prosecution and the defense may call to the stand later other people who are more expert in these particular areas. If—and I'm not saying that this will happen, but *if*—any of those experts disagree with Sheriff Brunswick, then I leave it to your good judgment to decide whom you should believe."

Broden should now know where he stands. The judge is going to allow Sheriff Brunswick to serve as the master of ceremonies for the prosecution's case, and he's telling Broden to back off.

"Is that what led you to believe that Mrs. Miller's death could not have been an accident?" Robertson asks with the same wide-eyed expression she used for the question regarding how Sheriff Brunswick rejected the suicide angle.

"Your Honor, is it too much for the defense to ask that Ms. Robertson not lead her own witness to discuss what caused him to believe anything?" Broden asks with obvious contempt.

Broden scores with the gallery, if not the judge. "Mr. Broden, if you have an objection, please make it without playing to the crowd." Judge Rodriguez waits a beat. "That's only permitted for the judge." This quip earns a larger laugh, which Broden acknowledges with an exaggerated bow of his head.

"Would you like me to repeat my question, Mr. Brunswick?" Robertson asks, looking only too eager to move away from the banter going on between the judge and the defense counsel.

"No, I remember it. You asked why we concluded that Mrs. Miller's death was not an accident. As I previously testified, the amount of sedative—the sleeping pills—almost conclusively meant that her drowning was not an accident. These pills must have taken effect within an hour or two of her death. Our conclusion was that her murderer"—and then Brunswick points—"Mr. Ohlig, drugged Mrs. Miller so that he could later throw her overboard to her death."

You could almost feel Robertson ticking off the points she wanted to present through Brunswick. First, establish that it wasn't a suicide, but murder. Then show that Ohlig did it. If that was her plan, she was halfway there.

"Did you consider any other possible suspects in this murder?" she says, emphasizing the last word.

"Of course. The first rule in law enforcement is that everyone starts off as a suspect, and then you eliminate the ones who couldn't have done it. You don't do it the other way around."

"What ultimately caused the police to conclude that Mr. Ohlig was guilty of this murder?"

"There were several factors. First," he touches his two index fingers together, as if he is counting the reasons on his hand, "we learned that the sleeping pills in Mrs. Miller's system were purchased by Mr. Ohlig, which, of course, raised suspicions. Mr. Ohlig denied any involvement in the purchase of these pills, which we knew was untrue based on the credit card statements and the mailbox where the pills were delivered. That mailbox was the second reason," he says, this time touching two fingers on his right hand against the index finger of his left. "Third, Mr. Ohlig was engaged in a long-running affair with Mrs. Miller that he had just ended, which apparently upset Mrs. Miller sufficiently that she demanded to see him at once." Three fingers now touch his left hand. "Mr. Ohlig lied about the last time he saw Mrs. Miller, claiming it was weeks prior when, in fact, it was the morning of her death." Just as Brunswick is running out of fingers, he says, "Finally, we had an eyewitness who put Mr. Ohlig at the scene of the crime with Mrs. Miller—on his boat shortly before the time Mrs. Miller went into the water. All in all, the evidence of Mr. Ohlig's guilt is overwhelming."

"Thank you, Sheriff Brunswick," Robertson says. "No more questions, your Honor."

I can tell from the outset that Sheriff Brunswick

isn't going to fare well against Clint Broden. There's a swagger to Brunswick that you love to see when you're a cross-examiner. It's like someone pulling out a knife when you know you have a gun.

"Sheriff Brunswick," Broden begins, "I'm going to ask you some questions that are a little different than the ones the prosecution just asked. In my questions, I just want to know what you know firsthand. I'm not interested in what other witnesses told you—or what Ms. Robertson here told you. Okay? I only want to know what you know."

The point made that Robertson overstepped, Broden proceeds to show Brunswick exactly who's in charge. I have the sinking feeling that, despite the fact that the questioner always controls the examination, Brunswick might actually think he's running the show.

"Sheriff, did I hear you correctly that the presence of sleeping pills in Mrs. Miller's system is what made you conclude Mrs. Miller was murdered?"

"That's right."

"Why didn't you conclude that she took these pills herself, as part of a suicide?"

"Like I testified before, because there was no suicide note, and no evidence of her being in a suicidal state of mind."

"You're not a psychiatrist, are you, Sheriff?"

"No."

"And you're not a psychologist?"

"No."

"Do you have any training whatsoever that gives you

insight into recognizing when a person is in a suicidal state of mind?"

"As a law enforcement officer of twenty-seven years, I do."

By sparring with Broden, Brunswick is only making it harder on himself. Robertson should have prepared him better, but it's also possible that he was one of those witnesses who just wouldn't take instruction.

"Did your twenty-seven years of law enforcement experience teach you that the sudden death of your husband of thirty-five years doesn't make you depressed?" Brunswick doesn't answer, but blinks uncomfortably. "Sheriff, you need to answer, so the jury can understand how your twenty-seven years of law enforcement experience prepared you to offer the psychological evaluation that even though Mrs. Miller's husband of thirty-five years had just passed away, she wasn't depressed."

"Well, she was having an affair with Mr. Ohlig, so I don't know how upset she was about her husband's death." Brunswick is smiling, and that only makes it a thousand times worse. It's bad enough when the defense puts the victim on trial, but at least that's their job. No one wants to see the police impugn the dead.

Broden can probably smell blood in the water now. "And did your twenty-seven years of law enforcement training lead you to conclude that the death of Mrs. Miller's husband while she was cheating on him was insufficient to cause her to take her own life out of remorse or guilt?"

Brunswick doesn't answer at first, but at least he's not smiling.

"Is that your expert psychological opinion, *Sheriff*?" Broden emphasizes the last word, telling the jury once again that Brunswick is a long way from having expertise in this area.

"I don't know," Brunswick finally says.

"Think about how justice would have been better served if you had just admitted that you didn't know at the outset."

Robertson objects, but by now there's no point. The question didn't call for an answer, so the fact that Judge Rodriguez sustains it makes no difference.

"No more questions," Broden says, turning his back to Brunswick and walking toward the counsel table. But then he wheels around again. "Actually, if I may, your Honor. One more thing, Sheriff." He pauses, long enough that I'm sure he's scripted this moment and the preface was all for effect. "Did your twenty-seven years of law enforcement experience provide you with expertise as to how you would force four sleeping pills down the throat of a woman to murder her?"

Brunswick's eyes widen, as if he's looking for Robertson to rescue him. "We believe that Mr. Ohlig put the pills into something she ate."

"Can we conclude that the only evidence you have for that claim is your twenty-seven years of law enforcement experience?"

Judge Rodriguez puts an end to the massacre. "I think you've made your point, Mr. Broden."

It didn't require twenty-seven years of legal experience—or even twenty-seven minutes of it—to know that the trial had not gotten off to a good start for the prosecution. Robertson is going to have to step up her game if Ohlig is going to pay for what he did to my mother.

## 54

On the second day of the trial, the prosecution calls Gary Dillon, an employee of the Palm Beach Yacht Club where Michael Ohlig is a member. Dillon doesn't seem old enough to vote and looks scared as can be.

"Mr. Dillon," Robertson says, using her stern teacher voice, even though a more soothing tone would be more appropriate considering Dillon is her witness, "did you see the defendant"—and then she points at Ohlig—"on Thanksgiving morning of this past year?"

Broden motions for Ohlig to stand. It's a nice touch, conveying to the jury that he doesn't fear the identification, although why he doesn't fear it is less clear. If Ohlig was with my mother on a boat that morning, it goes a long way to proving he drugged her and then threw her into the ocean.

"I did."

"Approximately what time?"

"Early."

"What's early to you, Mr. Dillon?"

"I don't know. Around seven. I start my shift at seven, and I saw him just after I got there."

"How do you know it was Mr. Ohlig that you saw?" Robertson asks.

"I'd met him before."

"How can you be certain the man you saw on that day was the same man you'd met before and knew to be Mr. Ohlig?"

"We had a nickname for Mr. Ohlig at the club—the Silver Fox. Some of the guys called him Foxie for short," Dillon chuckles. "I remember thinking that it was funny that I was seeing a fox on Thanksgiving."

"Was he alone?" she asks.

"No, he was with a woman."

"Did you recognize the woman?"

"Not really."

"Please describe her to the jury."

"She had blond hair, really light like. She was tall."

"How old was she?"

"Mid-fifties, I guess."

Of course, that description would cover a large portion of the female population of Palm Beach, but then Robertson hands Dillon a photograph. The jurors sit up, taking special notice of what is about to happen.

The picture that Dillon is studying is one I provided to Robertson. I originally gave her a photo of my mother with Charlotte, but Judge Rodriguez ruled that was gilding the lily. The photo Judge Rodriguez allowed was taken by my father the last time I saw him alive, which was when we visited over Passover.

Dillon is studying the picture as if he's never seen it before. In actuality, he's likely seen it more than twenty times, the last of which was probably right before Robertson called him to the stand.

"Mr. Dillon," Robertson says, "is the woman in this

picture the same woman you saw with Mr. Ohlig at the yacht club on the morning of Thanksgiving?"

Dillon swallows hard. "Yes," he says, not quite as a question, but certainly not as emphatic as you want your witnesses to make identifications.

Robertson passes the witness, looking relieved to have finished the examination. As Broden stands to begin his cross, all I can think is that I'm glad I'm not Gary Dillon.

"Mr. Dillon," Broden begins, "do you consider your-self someone who has a better-than-average memory?"

"No. I'd say it was average."

"Me too," Broden says, his smile suggesting that there's no reason for Dillon not to trust him. "Mr. Dillon, do you recall what Foxie was wearing Thanks-giving day?"

"Not everything, but typical stuff to go sailing."

"Was he wearing sneakers or boat shoes?"

"I don't remember that."

"But it was one or the other, right? I mean, he wasn't wearing work shoes."

"Yes. It was either boat shoes or sneakers."

"And, Mr. Dillon, I assume you recall he was also wearing a hat, you know, because of the sun on the water?"

"Yes."

"Did the hat on this person you think was Foxie hide his hair?"

"Oh no," Dillon says, as if he's proud of himself for anticipating the trap that Broden had been setting. "I remember very clearly that I could see his hair. That's how I knew it was Foxie."

"Mr. Dillon, about how long would you say that you looked at Foxie?"

"Not too long. I wasn't staring, but long enough."

"Maybe ten or fifteen seconds. Is that a fair estimate?"

"Maybe a little bit longer than that."

"I assume that Mr. Ohlig is not the only member of the club with gray hair, correct?"

"Uh-uh," Dillon says, beginning to sound much less sure of himself than he did during direct.

"In fact, I'm sure the only demographic in the Palm Beach club that's larger than gray-haired men is bald men. Wouldn't you say, Mr. Dillon?"

Laughter spills from the gallery, and even Judge Rodriguez seems amused. Dillon, however, looks like he doesn't get the joke.

"Mr. Dillon?" Broden asks.

"I'm sorry, sir, but I don't know what that word you used means."

The gallery has a chuckle at Dillon's expense, but Broden looks apologetic, despite the fact that I'm reasonably sure he used the word "demographic" to show the jury that Dillon isn't the smartest tool in the shed.

"My apologies, Mr. Dillon. What I meant to ask is whether there are a lot of gray-haired individuals at the club."

This time Dillon nods.

"And from time to time, is it the case that non-club members dock at the club? Just for the day?"

"Yes."

"And, Mr. Dillon, do these people sometimes have gray hair?"

"Yes, sometimes."

"And on a holiday, like Thanksgiving, is the dock more crowded with non-club members than on other days?"

"Yes. Non-club members will sail in for Thanksgiving or Christmas to visit family."

"Mr. Dillon, you feel like you got a good look at that hat, right? Otherwise you wouldn't have known it was Foxie, if you didn't see that hat and the gray hair underneath, right?" Dillon is nodding as Broden says this, having no idea that Broden's about to slam him. "So tell me. What color was the hat?"

Dillon gets the deer-in-the-headlights look that you dream about as a cross-examiner.

"Mr. Dillon, you saw Foxie for little more than fifteen seconds, and you're certain he was wearing sneakers or boat shoes and a hat that hid his hair, but not so much you couldn't identify him as Foxie—due to his gray hair—but you don't recall the color of the hat?" Before Dillon can venture a guess, Broden cuts him off. "Let's try something easier. What color hat were you wearing that day?"

Broden must know that Dillon wears different colored hats on different days or he'd never take such a gambit. "I'm sorry," Dillon sputters, "I've got a bunch of hats and I just don't remember which one I was wearing on that day."

"It was Thanksgiving day," Broden continues, now working at a rapid-fire clip. "What clothing were you wearing that day? Better yet, what was your mother wearing? How about anyone at your Thanksgiving dinner?"

"I think—"

"Mr. Dillon, please do not guess. I'm prepared to call your family members to testify whether you're right or not, and if your family is anything like mine, I bet someone took a picture that day, so we can confirm your recollection."

Robertson objects. "Your Honor, this witness isn't here to test his memory on what people wore on Thanksgiving. He's made an identification of Mrs. Miller, and Mr. Broden's questions should stick to the issues in this case."

"Mr. Broden," Judge Rodriguez says, "I think you made your point. Let's move on."

"Thank you," Broden says. "Mr. Dillon, the prosecutor wants me to ask you about your identification of the woman on the boat, so that's what I'm going to do next. You say that it's the same woman as you saw in the picture. The woman we all now know is Barbara Miller. First off, you didn't know it was Barbara Miller then, correct?"

"No."

"And you'd never seen Barbara Miller before, that's also correct, isn't it?"

"Yes."

"So are you absolutely sure that it was Barbara Miller you saw that morning—what, one, two, three, four, five, six, seven months ago? I mean, would you bet your life on it?"

"Objection," Robertson says, this time with a world-weary tone, as if to convey to the jurors that this is a complete waste of time. Unfortunately, I suspect the jurors have the sense that Robertson doth protest too much.

There's a silence in the courtroom as the lawyers wait for a ruling, but then Broden takes advantage of Judge Rodriguez's hesitation to drive his point home. "Your Honor, he can just tell us if he's certain or less than certain. So, I don't really know the basis of Ms. Robertson's objection."

Rodriguez looks the way Elizabeth sometimes does when Charlotte has exasperated her. I'm half expecting him to call a time-out and send both of them to their rooms.

The judge finally lets out a heavy sigh and then turns to Dillon, craning his neck to see the witness beneath the bench. "Sir, how confident are you that the woman you saw is the same woman in the picture? Very confident, or is this a case where you think it was the same woman, but you're not completely sure?"

"I don't know," Dillon says, and then, as if he's just caught Robertson's eye, he clears his throat, and adds, "I think it's her, which is why I said it was, but I'm not one hundred percent certain. I'm sorry."

Broden got what he wanted, and now it's time to rub salt into Robertson's wounds. "No need to apologize, Mr. Dillon," he says loudly. "All *I* want is your honest recollection," and then Broden stares at Robertson, accentuating the point that the desire for honesty above all else is not mutual.

After the Dillon debacle, the prosecution calls a representative from the Canadian internet pharmacy where the sleeping pills were purchased, and then the store manager of the Palm Beach Post-Drop USA branch where the pills were sent. Robertson gets from each what she needs, laying the foundation that the pills in my mother's system were purchased through the pharmacy and then shipped to the post office box under the name M. Ohlig.

On cross, Broden gets what he needs too—an admission from the pharmacist that anyone with access to Ohlig's credit card could have placed the order for the pills, including Ohlig, his wife, or even my mother. The Post-Drop USA representative acknowledges that they don't verify identity when someone opens a post office box. For the type of box that was opened under the name M. Ohlig, a key is given out at the time of purchase, which means anyone could have opened the box under that name, or any other, no questions asked.

As her last witness of the day, Robertson calls her expert, a shrink named Westwood. His testimony is brief, most likely because his opinion—that most people who commit suicide leave a note—is suspect, at least according to what I've read on the internet. Broden's cross is twice the length of the direct, but all he can do is sound incredulous at Westwood's testimony, because the psychiatrist doesn't yield an inch.

"How do you think we're doing so far?" Robertson asks as we're leaving court at the end of the day. She often uses phrases like "we" to describe the prosecution's case, her effort to give me some ownership of the mission, I suppose.

"You're getting the evidence you want in, and the jury appears to be engaged," I tell her, a little unenthusiastically. "The shrink was pretty good, and you did as well as possible with the pharmacy guy. I'm sure the jury believes that the pills my mother took were the same ones purchased with Ohlig's credit card. But I don't know if that's enough to conclude he was the one who bought them, or that he gave them to her. And neither the sheriff nor Dillon helped the cause much."

"Take it as a cautionary tale for you, Alex," she says.

"How so?"

"Your testimony is going to make or break our case, and I don't want Broden making you look like a monkey too."

"I'll be okay," I say.

"And just so there's no misunderstanding between us, I'm not asking you to lie. I don't know what happened with Dillon, but I didn't pressure him to make the identification, and the last thing I want is for you to think that I'm pressuring you. Understand?"

"Understood."

"Are you sure? Because I get a weird vibe from you sometimes." She stares at me, as if she's trying to read my thoughts. "So far I've spared you the perjury lecture because I can only assume you know it by heart. But, believe me, victim's son or not, if you lie up there I will prosecute you for perjury. Understood?"

"Yeah, sure. I understand."

## 55

My "I do" upon taking the witness oath sounds like a squeak. I'm not too surprised that I'm nervous. Part of my apprehension is because I've never testified before, but that's only part of it.

Robertson begins my examination the textbook way—asking questions about my educational background and work history. I tell the jury I'm unemployed, but quickly mention that I'd been practicing law for the past twelve years, in the hope that causes the jury to assume I've voluntarily taken time off. I know I shouldn't care what they think, but I still do. So much so that I've asked Robertson not to inquire about the reasons I left Cromwell Altman. I'm assuming Broden will be smart enough not to do so. After all, there's nothing in it for him to piss me off, especially concerning an issue that doesn't help his case.

After Robertson has finished going through my resume, she makes the transition to the facts at issue. "Mr. Miller, please tell the jury how you came to know Mr. Ohlig."

"I had heard his name throughout my childhood due to his role in my parents' first meeting, but then I came to represent him—"

"Objection," Broden interrupts. "Your Honor, may we approach?"

Robertson told me several times during prep that she'd be the lawyer and my job was only to be a witness. As a sign of how well I've listened, I'm not sure what was objectionable about Robertson's question.

After Robertson and Broden join Judge Rodriguez at the bench, the judge puts his hand over his microphone and leans away from me. This means that, just like the jury, I can't hear what's being said.

I can see Broden go first, and then Judge Rodriguez nods at Robertson, apparently to permit her a brief rebuttal. After she's done, I can see Judge Rodriguez rule, but I can't make out who won. Then, in his normal voice, the judge says, "Step back," followed by a flick of his fingers.

When we resume, Robertson begins a different line of questions—"Please explain, Mr. Miller, when you first met Mr. Ohlig"—which means that Judge Rodriguez sustained Broden's objection. It finally occurs to me that Broden must be trying to keep the jury from learning the facts surrounding my representation of Ohlig—or, more specifically, that he was the defendant in a criminal matter.

"Um, it was at my father's funeral," I say. "Mr. Ohlig"—Robertson instructed me to address Ohlig formally to convey to the jury that I have no affection for the man—"spoke to me after the service."

Then, without prompting, I decide to help Robertson out a little and send a message to Broden that he should be wary. "Mr. Ohlig asked me to represent him in connection with a criminal investigation—"

"Objection!" Broden shouts.

"Yes. Yes. Well, I think the cat's out of the bag now," Judge Rodriguez says, barely stifling a smile. "Ladies and gentlemen of the jury," the judge says, now looking toward the jury box, "the circumstances of how it came to be that Mr. Miller met Mr. Ohlig are not relevant here. The only crime for which you should concern yourselves is the crime for which Mr. Ohlig now stands accused. You may continue, counselor."

"Mr. Miller," Robertson says, "what was the nature of your mother's relationship with Mr. Ohlig?"

"They were engaged in a sexual affair." I say this matter-of-factly, realizing only after I say it that Robertson had wanted me to testify with as much emotion as I could muster.

"When did you first come to learn that your mother was having an affair with Mr. Ohlig?"

"When did I first learn about it, or when did it begin?"

"First tell us when you learned about it."

"It was when I was representing Mr. Ohlig. The government had produced wiretap recordings." I see Broden shift uncomfortably at my continued references to Ohlig's criminal prosecution, and I enjoy making him squirm. "On one of those tapes, my mother and Mr. Ohlig were discussing that they had recently had sex."

"What was said on that tape that led you to believe—"

"Objection!" Broden calls.

When we practiced this line of questioning during prep, I told Robertson that Broden would object. He was right on cue.

"Ms. Robertson already played the tape for the jury during Sheriff Brunswick's testimony," Broden explains. "There's no reason to question this witness about it because we all know what was said."

Judge Rodriguez nods. "I agree, Ms. Robertson. Let's move on."

"Did you confront Mr. Ohlig about the sexual relationship he was having with your mother?" she asks next.

"I did."

"Explain to the jury as best as you can recall, what you said to Mr. Ohlig and what he said to you in that confrontation."

"Your Honor," Broden says, now standing, "although the court has already ruled on this issue, please note the defense's continuing objection on privilege grounds."

"So noted, Mr. Broden," Judge Rodriguez says dismissively. "The prosecution may continue."

Robertson told me that the privilege issue has already been decided by Judge Rodriguez as part of the defense's *in limine* motion—the request before trial for the exclusion of certain evidence. Robertson wanted me to testify about the discussions I had with Ohlig about my mother, but Broden claimed any utterance between Ohlig and me was privileged. Judge Rodriguez sided with the prosecution, reasoning that my conversations with Ohlig about his relationship with my mother were not in furtherance of his seeking legal advice.

"Mr. Miller, do you need to hear the question again?" Robertson asks. "It concerns your conversation with Mr. Ohlig about his *sexual* relationship with your mother."

"No. I remember the question. Mr. Ohlig admitted to me that he had been involved in a sexual affair with my mother. This was after my mother had died, so I couldn't ask her about it."

"Let me focus you now on the day before Thanksgiving, the day before your mother's death. On that day, did you hear Mr. Ohlig speaking to your mother on the phone?"

"I did. The day before my mother died, I was meeting with Mr. Ohlig in my office when he received a phone call. After my mother died, I looked at her phone records and they showed that this call was from her."

"Please describe this call for the jury."

I'm able to say, "They were arguing," before Broden objects.

Judge Rodriguez doesn't need to hear the substance of the objection. "Mr. Miller, please confine your answer to what you heard and, if asked, to what you observed concerning Mr. Ohlig's demeanor. In other words, don't characterize it. Think of yourself as more of a video camera simply capturing what was observed, and less of a narrator."

I smile at him. The video camera analogy is one that

I've actually used when preparing witnesses. "I apologize, your Honor."

The judge then throws me a bone. "No need to apologize, Mr. Miller. We all know how difficult this is for you."

"Mr. Miller, let me ask you again," Robertson says, "what did you hear and observe during that phone call?"

"Mr. Ohlig appeared to me to be very agitated. He asked that I leave the room so he could have some privacy, but before I left, I heard him say that my mother should calm down. He said that several times."

"You say that it wasn't until after your mother's death that you learned this call was from your mother?"

"That's correct."

"Who did Mr. Ohlig tell you he was speaking with at the time?"

"He said it was his wife on the phone."

"So he lied to you?"

"Yes. He lied."

Robertson looks more than pleased with the way this is going. "Mr. Miller, did Mr. Ohlig lie to you at any other times about your mother?"

"He did."

"Please tell us about those lies."

"At my mother's funeral, I asked Mr. Ohlig when he had last seen my mother. He said that it had been several weeks. But I now know he was the last person to see her alive."

"Objection," Broden says, rising. "Mr. Miller's response assumes facts not in evidence."

Broden's right, and he's entitled to an instruction on this point, but Judge Rodriguez looks as if he's thinking this one over.

"Ladies and gentlemen of the jury," Judge Rodriguez finally says, "so far there has been no evidence that proves Mr. Ohlig was the last person to see Ms. Miller alive. Based on the evidence, you could conclude that he saw her late in the evening on the night before she died, and you are certainly within your rights to believe Mr. Dillon's testimony that it was Mr. Ohlig and Mrs. Miller who were out on a boat early Thanksgiving morning, in the vicinity where Mrs. Miller drowned. But no evidence shows conclusively that someone else did not see Mrs. Miller after that. Of course, the defense has not had their turn yet, so perhaps they will put on evidence which shows that someone else did see Mrs. Miller after Mr. Ohlig."

Broden has the look that I've seen before from criminal defense lawyers all too often. It's rare enough for a judge to side with you on something, and then when he does, it turns out to be worse than if he had overruled.

"Your witness," Robertson says, and gives me a wink.

It's a little bit of a point of honor to be cross-examined by Clint Broden, like batting against Mariano Rivera. Something to tell your grandchildren about. Broden has cross-examined everyone from a former vice president of the United States to the head of one of New York's five mafia families.

It is a tremendous surprise, and a little disappointing then, when Broden tells Judge Rodriguez, "The defense has no questions for this witness." After which, he turns to me and says, "Mr. Miller, on behalf of my client, please accept our heartfelt condolences for your loss."

And with that my testimony is over.

That evening, when I call home, Charlotte says she doesn't want to talk to me. "I'm busy, Daddy," she says, "here's Mommy."

"Sorry," Elizabeth says when she takes back the phone. "Don't take it personally, she's been in a bit of a mood all day."

"Anything wrong?"

"Not that I can tell. She probably just misses you. I know she's liked having you around so much over the past few months. She asked me if you're back at work, and I told her that you just needed to go on a trip. She said she hopes you don't go back to work."

"She won't say that when we're living in a box in Central Park."

"That's probably true, but you should be happy that your daughter enjoys you being home so much. Better than the alternative, right?"

"You mean like her not wanting to talk to me on the phone?"

"I think that's just her way of telling you she wants

you to come home. So, tell me. How did it go today? You testified, right?"

"Yeah. It's finished," I said.

"Was it how you thought it would be?"

"More or less." And then I realize that's not true. "Actually, much less. Broden didn't do any cross-examination."

"Why not?"

"He must have figured it wasn't going to earn him any points with the jury to call me a liar, and he decided just to get me off the stand as quickly as possible."

"So, what did you say?"

"What I told you I would. I talked about how Michael had lied to me at the funeral about the last time he saw my mother, and I talked about how they were arguing that day in my office, you know, the day before she died."

"They didn't get into the whole suicide thing?"

"No. Morgan had prepared me for that being the focus of cross, but for whatever reason, Broden decided not to go there."

"That's good, right?"

"I don't know. I've lost the ability to gauge what's good and what's not good about this. It meant that I got off the stand quicker, so it was good in that sense."

"What comes next?"

"I don't think Broden's case is going to last more than a day or two. He'll call the shrink tomorrow. That probably won't go too long, and my guess is Michael will testify after that."

"You don't sound good, Alex. Are you sure you're doing okay?"

"I didn't think it would be so hard. And, unfortunately, I suspect tomorrow is going to be the worst day of all." I pause for a second, and then amend the statement. "Actually, closing arguments will likely be worse. At least tomorrow I'll be able to see Robertson stick it to Michael a little bit."

# 56

As I'd predicted, the next morning, after welcoming the jurors back, Broden calls as his first witness his expert, a psychiatrist with a four-syllable Italian name, Favinelli or Fanarelli or something like that. He's on the stand for less than twenty minutes, during which he says the same thing in a half-dozen different ways—people sometimes commit suicide and don't leave notes. Robertson's cross is limited to getting the concession that sometimes people who commit suicide do leave notes.

After the shrink steps down, Broden says, "Your Honor, the final defense witness is Michael Ohlig." Broden proclaims this proudly, facing the jury, as if the defense's decision not to call other witnesses was somehow further proof of Ohlig's innocence.

Ohlig purposely strides to the witness chair. It reminds me of that very first time I saw him—the way his body communicated his complete and utter commitment to the task at hand. His "I do" upon taking the oath is far more assertive than my own had been. In fact, everything about him exudes confidence that he will be able to explain his innocence. As he told me and Abby more than once, he can be quite persuasive when he has to be.

And now he has to be.

Broden spends the better part of the morning detailing Ohlig's rags-to-riches story. The way Ohlig tells it, he's still a Master of the Universe, his narrative ending prior to the time that OPM started selling Salminol and the SEC shut the place down. I can only assume that Judge Rodriguez previously ruled OPM's collapse was off limits, thereby giving Ohlig free rein to put the lie of his continued success before the jury without fear of contradiction.

It's as much of an education to watch Broden do a direct as it was to study his cross-examinations. The method at Cromwell Altman on direct examination is cool precision, a minimalist style of interrogation, where the lawyer's goal is to be unobtrusive so as to allow the client to appear to be telling his story without a filter. On more than one occasion, I recall Aaron Littman saying, *If a juror knows what color tie I'm wearing, I haven't done my job.* Broden, however, is ever present as Ohlig testifies—he's the lion tamer to Ohlig's lion, the two working in tandem to paint a picture of events.

After lunch, Broden focuses on the day years ago in Central Park when Ohlig and my father met my mother. Michael Ohlig claims he fell in love with my mother that day in the park and yielded out of friendship to my father's claim of prior right.

"It must have been difficult for you, Michael," Broden says, sounding more like a therapist than a lawyer, "to wonder what your life would have been had you not stepped aside for your friend."

"I wondered about that for a long time," Ohlig says,

sounding almost wistful. I can only imagine the extent of coaching required to make Ohlig seem introspective. "But that stopped the moment I met my wife. It may sound hokey to some, but I knew then and there that my destiny was to be with Pamela."

"But you were unfaithful to your wife," Broden says, now sounding like a parent scolding a child caught smoking cigarettes.

"It's the greatest failing of my life." If I didn't know him better I would have thought Ohlig was going to cry. "I have absolutely no excuse. It was a mistake, and one for which I'm so very sorry. I have apologized repeatedly to Pamela. Luckily for me, I married a woman who is very understanding, and whom I certainly do not deserve. Pamela says she forgives me, but I feel like I need to prove myself to her every day."

I look over to the jury, wondering if they're buying what Ohlig's shoveling on them. I want them to be looking on with disgust, but, amazingly, they seem particularly engrossed by this fairy tale.

When you put a client on the stand, there's always the decision about whether to place the more damaging evidence before the jury during the direct, in order to blunt the force of the cross-examination. "Drawing the teeth" it's called. On television, to heighten suspense, they never do it, and so the viewer is given two starkly different versions of events. During direct examination you're taken hook, line and sinker by the testimony, but then on cross you learn what a lying dirtbag the witness really is. In real life, it makes much more sense to introduce bad testimony during direct examination in order to put the best face on it. This also has the benefit of creating a level of trust with the jury that you're not holding anything back. In the best-case scenario, the jury ends up being uninterested when the same information is brought up on cross with a more sinister slant because it feels like old news.

"Let's turn to some of the evidence we've heard from other witnesses in this courtroom," Broden says, preparing to lay this groundwork. "First, let me ask you the question straight out—did you kill Barbara Miller?"

Ohlig breaks eye contact with Broden and looks directly into the jury box. I can actually see his eyes move from one juror to the next.

"No. I did not." He says this in his most authoritative voice, as if he's daring the jury to disbelieve him.

In Broden's hands, the evidence against Ohlig seems insignificant. He didn't order the sleeping pills or open the post office box, and so he has no information about that. He wasn't on his boat that morning, but at home, in bed, so Dillon must be mistaken when he claimed to have seen Ohlig and my mother at the yacht club that day.

I wonder if the jurors realize that Pamela Ohlig's failure to testify means she wouldn't corroborate his story. Maybe she was out before him that morning and seen by others so she couldn't lie, even if she were so inclined. It's also possible that she could alibi him, and for whatever reason refuses to do so.

Ohlig admits to the phone call with my mother in

my office, but says that I must have received a distorted view having listened to only one side of it, and only the beginning of the call at that. "Barbara wasn't upset with me at all," he says earnestly. "She wanted to see me, and so I told her that we could meet that evening."

"Did Mrs. Miller ever threaten to tell your wife about the affair?"

"Objection," Robertson says, but it's a loser. What my mother said fits another hearsay loophole because it's not being offered for the truth. In other words, the issue isn't whether my mother was actually going to tell Ohlig's wife about the affair, but whether she made the threat to Ohlig—thereby giving him a motive for murder.

"Overruled," Judge Rodriguez says.

"She never said anything of the kind," Ohlig says definitively.

Getting the answer he wants, Broden quickly pivots to another topic. "Michael, how well do you know Alex Miller?"

The sound of my name brings a flush to my cheeks. I stare intently at Ohlig, and he stares back just as hard.

"I knew a lot about him," Ohlig says, shifting his focus back to Broden. "Both his parents were understandably very proud of him, and they would share his accomplishments with me. And then, as Mr. Miller testified, I had the privilege of working with him, at which time I was able to see firsthand that all his parents had told me over the years was true."

"Did you lie to Mr. Miller about the relationship you were having with his mother?"

"I can only answer that as yes *and* no. And by that I don't mean to sound clever, but it requires some explanation. Let me start by saying that I'm sorry for anything I've done that might have caused Alex even the least amount of pain. He is a very good man. As with my wife, I hope that someday Alex will find it in his heart to forgive me. And I'm very sorry to say that I misled Alex at his mother's funeral. I wanted to tell him the truth, and I would have, but Pamela was standing right beside me. So I told him that the last time I had seen his mother was a few weeks before."

"There were other times when your wife wasn't beside you, weren't there, Mr. Ohlig? Why didn't you tell Mr. Miller then about your relationship with his mother?"

"Barbara said—"

Robertson objects, again on hearsay grounds, but the objection is overruled for the same reason it was rejected before—the testimony is relevant for what Ohlig heard, without regard to whether my mother's statement was true.

"You may answer," Broden tells his client after the judge has ruled.

"Barbara didn't want me to tell him, and I respected her wishes."

Finally, at four-thirty, Judge Rodriguez asks Broden whether he'll finish the direct by the end of the day, or if he'd like to break early instead. This is a no-brainer for Broden—he wants to finish the direct and then let the jury sleep on it for the evening. In fact, I've gotten the feeling that he's been stalling for the last half hour just to choreograph the timing.

"I'm almost finished, your Honor. If you allow us to go until five, I'm sure I'll complete the direct by then."

Given the green light by the judge, Broden turns to the suicide angle. He approaches the subject gingerly, asking Ohlig if he has any understanding of what caused my mother's death.

"I don't know for sure, of course," Ohlig says. "I like to think it was an accident. As hard as it is to believe because we all like to think that such things just can't happen, it's possible Barbara went into the water and got tired or developed a leg cramp or just got caught in the undertow. But, although I hope to God that it isn't the case, Barbara may have taken her own life."

"Why do you say that?" Broden asks.

"Well, the coroner said that she had sleeping pills in her system. Now I don't know if that's true or not, but if it is, that would explain why she took the sleeping pills before going in the ocean. And I know that she was feeling depressed—"

"Objection," Robertson shouts.

"Grounds, Ms. Robertson?"

"This witness isn't qualified to opine as to the victim's mental state. He's not a therapist."

She should have let this one go, especially considering the leeway Judge Rodriguez gave her with her witnesses, Sheriff Brunswick in particular, and also me. Judge Rodriguez has little choice but to be consistent.

"Ladies and gentlemen of the jury," the judge says, turning to face them in the box, "Ms. Robertson is correct that Mr. Ohlig is not a health care professional. As a result, when he says that he thought Mrs. Miller was feeling depressed, you must understand that he's not making a medical diagnosis, but providing an opinion about what he observed. You can consider Mr. Ohlig's opinion the way you would any testimony about what a witness observes, giving it whatever weight you deem appropriate."

Broden knows enough to make as much as possible out of every victorious skirmish, so he continues on with the theme.

"On what do you base your opinion that Mrs. Miller was depressed?"

"First of all, how could she not be? Her husband had just died, and she told me many times—"

"Objection!" Robertson shouts, this time louder than before. "Mr. Ohlig is going to provide hearsay testimony."

"Mr. Broden, try it another way," says Judge Rodriguez.

"Michael, what did you observe Mrs. Miller's demeanor to be in the weeks leading up to her death?"

"She was very upset, crying a lot. She told me she had been praying for forgiveness—"

Robertson objects again, but she's a beat too late. Through what was hearsay testimony, Ohlig has already painted a picture of my mother as a woman on the edge.

"Mr. Ohlig," Judge Rodriguez says, "as I instructed Mr. Miller when he testified, please limit your testimony to what you observed, and not what Mrs. Miller said to you." He then turns to the jury. "Ladies and gentlemen of the jury, please disregard Mr. Ohlig's statement about what Mrs. Miller said to him, although you may consider his perceptions about her mental state."

After a few concluding questions, Broden passes the witness. He's done about as well as he could have with Ohlig, and I wonder if I would have done as well putting him on the stand in New York.

But then I remind myself, it's only halftime.

Just like in direct examination, most lawyers start cross with the easy stuff and attempt to gradually build momentum, with their questions becoming more pointed as the examination progresses. Robertson decides to go with the other school of thought—attack right from the opening bell.

"Mr. Ohlig, let me get this straight. You didn't kill Mrs. Miller?"

"No. I did not."

"And you were not on your yacht on Thanksgiving morning?"

"No."

"And Mr. Dillon is mistaken when he says he saw you there."

"That's correct."

"Because you were home at the time? That's your story, right, and you're sticking to it?"

"That's the truth."

"Did your wife see you in bed?"

This is a risky move because it invites Pamela Ohlig to reconsider her refusal to testify—assuming that's what's going on—but Robertson must feel it's worth the risk. She turns out to be right.

"My wife saw me asleep, but she's an early riser and leaves for her regular gym class at 6:30 in the morning. After that, she did some shopping for our holiday dinner, and so I didn't see her again until maybe one o'clock."

"In other words, Mr. Ohlig, no one can verify your story that you were in your house during the time that Mrs. Miller was murdered? That's what you're saying—or I should say, trying not to say—isn't it?"

"Objection," Broden says.

Judge Rodriguez doesn't need to hear more. "Ms. Robertson, please don't argue with the witness. Simply ask questions."

"My apologies," Robertson says, although a more insincere statement of regret would be hard to fathom. Then she turns back to Ohlig to get an answer to her question.

At first Ohlig doesn't say anything, but then he flinches. "That's right," he says, "no one can verify where I was after my wife left the house that morning until she returned at about one o'clock."

"And it's also your testimony that you never ordered the sleeping pills from the Canadian pharmacy that were charged to your credit card?"

"I did not."

"And you have no idea who did?"

"I assume it was Barbara."

"Ah, Mrs. Miller. You think she ordered them under your name."

"Yes. Yes, I do."

"So, is it also your assumption that it was Mrs. Miller who opened the PO box under your name where the sleeping pills were delivered?"

"It's the only conclusion that makes sense to me."

"And why—withdrawn. Is it your view that Mrs. Miller was trying to frame you for murder?"

He sighs, perhaps knowing that this isn't going to sound good. "It's one theory."

"Here's another theory, Mr. Ohlig—you bought the pills, you opened the PO box, you drugged Mrs. Miller, you murdered her by throwing her off your yacht on Thanksgiving morning, and you did this so she wouldn't tell your wife about the affair."

Broden has said objection three times during Robertson's speech, the last time followed by Judge Rodriguez shouting "sustained," but Robertson still finishes the sentence.

This time Robertson doesn't apologize. "Let's get back to how sorry you are about all this, Mr. Ohlig," she says with a sneer. "You previously testified that you're very, very sorry for cheating on your wife." Ohlig stares at her after this question. "Please answer audibly. I'm sure the jury wants to hear again about how so very, very sorry you are for breaking your marriage vows by having sex with your best friend's wife."

For a moment I wonder if Ohlig is going to flash the temper I'd seen from time to time, but he's too good a witness for that. "I didn't think you had asked a question, Ms. Robertson," he says matter-of-factly. "But, yes, I am sorry, and I have apologized to Pamela."

"And you are also very, very sorry for lying to Mrs. Miller's son—at Mrs. Miller's funeral no less—about the last time you saw his mother alive."

"I am."

"And you are also very, very sorry for lying to Mr. Miller about the fact that you were having sex with his mother at the time he was your lawyer?"

"Yes," he says, although this time with more edge to his voice, as if he's beginning to see that he's coming off far less sympathetic than he might have imagined.

Robertson makes the rest of her points crisply, like a boxer throwing more jabs than knockout punches.

"Mr. Ohlig, you and your wife have a combined net worth in excess of $50 million, is that correct?"

"It is substantial," he concedes. "I've been very fortunate."

"And it's true, isn't it, sir, that nearly all of that is in your wife's name?"

"For estate planning reasons, a substantial portion of my wife's and my assets are in her name, yes, that's correct. It also is very common among high-net-worth individuals."

"Common or not, you would have been in a hell of a lot of trouble if your wife divorced you?"

Robertson's less than precise question allows Ohlig an opportunity to counterpunch. "I would have lost the love of my life, if that's what you mean."

Robertson doesn't react, but instead goes on to her next question. "You don't deny, do you, Mr. Ohlig, that you didn't want your wife to find out about your affair with Mrs. Miller?"

Ohlig has no choice but to agree, or else he'd lose all credibility with the jury. "Of course," he says in a strong voice. "I did not want Pamela to know, that's true."

"And it entered your mind that if she found out about the affair, she might seek to divorce you."

"I didn't think that would happen, and it hasn't."

"That's not my question, Mr. Ohlig. Before your wife found out about your affair—before Mrs. Miller was murdered—did you think about the prospect of her divorcing you if she found out?"

"Fleetingly, perhaps."

"I'll take that as a yes," Robertson says. She hesitates a beat, perhaps because she's expecting Broden to object, but he doesn't. "And if she did divorce you, she'd get nearly every penny of the money, wouldn't she?"

"I don't know. That would be an issue for the lawyers to figure out."

"Oh come now, Mr. Ohlig. You're not telling this jury that the thought never crossed your mind that if your wife found out about your affair she might divorce you, and that would leave you with nothing. You're not saying that, are you, sir?"

"I can't say that I never thought about it."

She's done well with this part. I didn't expect Ohlig to give her what she wanted without a fight, but she got it in the end.

"No more questions, your Honor," she says, and then, as she walks back to counsel table, she smiles at me.

"Your Honor," Broden says when Ohlig is excused, "at this time the defense rests."

"Any rebuttal, Ms. Robertson?" Judge Rodriguez asks.

"We will have one rebuttal witness," she says.

"Very well," the judge says. "Given the lateness of the hour, let's pick this up Monday morning for rebuttal and then closing arguments." He pauses and then remembers to ask, "Ms. Robertson, who will the people's rebuttal witness be?"

"Alex Miller."

The moment Judge Rodriguez leaves the courtroom, I confront Robertson. "I thought I was done testifying."

"I wasn't trying to trick you, Alex," she says in a whisper. "I was hoping I wouldn't have to put on any rebuttal case at all. But I'm concerned Ohlig may have some people buying the suicide angle, and you're the only one who can contradict his testimony about your mother's mental state at the time of her death."

I wonder if there's something in my expression that leads to her next question.

"You up for this, Alex?"

"Of course," I say, trying to assuage her concern.

"Because this is it. You're going to need to tell the jury that you had no reason to think your mother committed suicide. If there's any reason you think you can't do that, tell me now."

"No reason. No reason at all."

To my great surprise, Elizabeth is sitting on the bed watching television when I get back to the hotel room. She's six months pregnant, and even though I saw her a week ago, she seems much larger now. She looks almost as if she won't be able to get any bigger, but I know from our experience with Charlotte that she's still got a long way to go.

"What are you doing here?" I ask. "And where's Charlotte?"

"She's with my mother. And I'm here because you sounded so sad on the phone last night that I thought you could use some moral support. I figure that closing statements are going to be difficult, and then the witness impact stuff. I just thought I might be able to make it a little easier on you." She pauses a moment. "I hope that's okay."

"It's more than okay. I can't tell you how glad I am that you're here. It was okay for you to fly?"

"Yes, the doctor said it was fine."

"And how are you feeling?"

"Great. Second trimester, nothing better than that. Although I've got to figure out how to get the baby on a schedule so she sleeps when I sleep, rather than using that time to practice her soccer kicks."

We found out during the first sonogram that our second child would be another daughter. I felt the slight pang of the Miller name not continuing, but only for a moment. The prospect of having another daughter was nothing to be disappointed about.

"I'm really glad you came down, Elizabeth. Thank you. I really missed you."

She kisses me, fully on the mouth, and I can feel her swollen belly rubbing against mine.

"Do you remember what one of the great benefits of the second trimester is?"

"I do," I say, knowing that she means that the sex is great.

"Good," she purrs, pulling off her shirt.

## 57

I'm no more relaxed for my return engagement to the witness chair than I was the first time. If anything, I'm a little more nervous, feeling as if the case now rides on my shoulders. The gallery is the most crowded it's been so far, having more to do with the fact that closing arguments are to follow than any interest in my testimony, but it still adds to the pressure.

Judge Rodriguez reminds the jury, and me, that I continue to be under oath from my prior testimony, so there's no need for me to be re-sworn. He asks if I understand, and I tell him that I do. With that, the judge tells Robertson to proceed.

"Mr. Miller," Robertson begins, "you have been called to give what is referred to as rebuttal testimony, which means it's limited to certain issues that have already been addressed in the trial. In this case, I only have one subject to ask you about—your mother's mental state at the time of her death."

"Okay."

"Mr. Miller, were you in the courtroom on the day that Michael Ohlig testified?"

"I was."

"Do you recall Mr. Ohlig testifying that he thought it was possible that your mother committed suicide?"

"I do recall him saying that."

"Do you believe that your mother committed suicide?"

I had given considerable thought to how I would answer this series of questions. Not to the actual responses, which I had little doubt about, but the tone I should convey. Matter-of-fact? Outraged by the suggestion? Surprised?

I go with matter-of-fact. "No, I do not."

"Did your mother leave a suicide note?"

"No, she did not."

"Did your mother ever—*ever*—say anything to you to indicate that she was suicidal?"

"No."

"When was the last time you spoke to your mother?"

"The day before she died."

"Please tell the jury about that last conversation you had with your mother."

"Objection!" Broden shouts. "May we approach, your Honor?"

Judge Rodriguez motions for the lawyers to come forward to the bench, and shifts his body away from me so that I won't hear what's transpiring. I have little doubt Broden is making a hearsay objection, the same one that Robertson made when Broden had Ohlig on the stand and asked about his conversation with my mother the day before she died—and Robertson will argue that a hearsay exception for state of mind is applicable, the same exception that Broden tried to use.

When the sidebar breaks up, Robertson says, "Mr.

Miller, what did you and your mother talk about during that last call you had with her?"

Judge Rodriguez overruled the objection and is going to allow me to testify as to what my mother told me on the phone. Like a running back that sees daylight, I rush as fast as I can through the hole the judge has opened. "My mother said she was very excited about spending Thanksgiving with her friends. She also said that she was looking forward to seeing my daughter, her granddaughter—"

"I apologize, Mr. Miller," Judge Rodriguez interrupts, apparently realizing his earlier ruling had been in error. "Your testimony should focus on what you said to your mother, rather than what she said to you. Ladies and gentlemen of the jury, I realize that may seem to you a strange distinction, but Mr. Miller is an attorney and will recognize that what his mother told him is hearsay, and therefore I cannot allow testimony concerning it."

"I apologize, your Honor," I say.

"No need to apologize, Mr. Miller," he says with a smile. "Just limit your response to what you said to your mother on that call."

Even with the judge's belated imposed limitation, I still had enough leeway to pour it on thick. "We discussed my daughter, my mother's only granddaughter. Her name is Charlotte and at the time she'd just turned five." I catch the eye of the two older women on the jury—both of whom are grandmothers according to the jury questionnaires they filled out before trial—and they're smiling. "I told my mother that Charlotte had recently confided in me that she was in love with a boy in her class."

This earns a modest amount of laughter from the gallery. Much more importantly, the two grandmothers nod with approval. That's enough encouragement for me to further gild the lily.

"I also discussed with my mother taking a visit to Florida with Charlotte and my wife. We talked about going to Disney World."

"The last conversation you had with your mother was inviting her to a vacation at Disney World with her granddaughter?" Robertson says, reemphasizing the point even though she must recall that I never mentioned such a conversation during our preparation.

"Yes."

"Mr. Miller, do you have reason—any reason at all—to believe your mother took her own life?"

"No. To the contrary, I know she would never do that."

This time I know Broden is going to question me. He's in the worst position possible for a lawyer—he's got to shake my testimony without looking as if he's attacking the victim.

Broden stands, folding his hands across his chest. As with all his cross-examinations, he has no notes. He walks deliberately to the jury rail, and then leans on it with one arm, careful that his back is not to any juror.

"Mr. Miller," he begins, "you just said that you had no reason to believe that your mother might have taken her own life." I don't say anything, following Robertson's prior instruction to answer only questions. "Do you recall that testimony?"

"I do."

"The thought never—withdrawn. Mr. Miller, isn't it the case that the police told you that your mother's death may have been a suicide?"

"No, the police arrested your client for murdering my mother. I take that to mean they thought she was murdered."

There are some chuckles in the gallery, but Broden doesn't seem the slightest bit ruffled. He looks at me hard and says, "The police ultimately decided to charge Mr. Ohlig with this crime, but that was not my question, Mr. Miller. I know it's difficult, but please try to listen to what I'm asking because it's very important. Can you do that for me?"

This last part is for him to show he's not without some power to make me look foolish too. At first I don't answer, but he repeats the question, which only highlights the point.

"Yes," I say, trying not to look too chastened.

"Thank you. Now, my question was whether anyone in the Palm Beach Sheriff's Office ever communicated to you that your mother's death might be a suicide."

"No."

"Never?"

"No. Never."

I'm trying not to break eye contact with him. Not an easy feat considering Broden looks like he's going to spit fire at me.

"Mr. Miller, you recognize you are under oath, correct?"

"I do. As you know, Mr. Broden, I'm a lawyer too. So I take the witness oath very seriously."

Clint Broden asks the judge for a moment and turns away, slowly moving back toward the counsel table. When he gets there, he leans over and whispers in his client's ear. After a moment, Ohlig breaks contact with him and focuses on me, actually squinting his eyes as if he's trying to read my mind. There's not much mystery about what the two of them are discussing, however.

Broden now has three choices. He could call Deputy Sheriff Gattia and ask him if the police ever seriously considered suicide a possibility, but considering that Sheriff Brunswick has denied my mother committed suicide, Broden's not likely to get Gattia to contradict the boss. Second option is to play the Abby card, but I'm sure he knows that I'll deny ever having such a discussion with her, and he's got to be concerned that if he starts down that path, I'll follow through on the threat I made back in his office to tell the jury that Ohlig confessed to me.

When Broden straightens back up and faces me, I know what he's decided to do by the fact his jaw is clenched. He's going to select the third option.

Still standing behind his client, Broden says, "Mr. Miller, I have no further questions."

Judge Rodriguez excuses me from the witness stand, but rather than take my usual seat in the gallery, I leave the courtroom. I've had enough testimony for the day.

Elizabeth must have followed me out, because a minute later she's joined me on the wooden bench in the hallway.

"Quite a performance," she says.

Elizabeth will leave it at that. Someone else would be more direct, asking me why I lied . . . about Disney World, about my suspicions that my mother took her own life, or about the sheriff's department's initial suspicions of suicide. I know Elizabeth well enough to know that she's not going to go there. She's said all she needs to on the subject, and she'll wait for me to tell her my reasons when and if I'm ready.

The jury files out a few minutes later, several of them nodding at me as they walk by. Robertson comes out right after that, looking as giddy as a schoolgirl.

"You did it, Alex!" she says. "Broden just rested, and by the way the jurors were nodding during your testimony, I think they're going to convict. Poor Broden, that son of a bitch didn't know what to do with you. You both go out and have a nice bottle of wine tonight—" She stops herself short, in recognition of Elizabeth's condition. "You have the wine, Alex. Elizabeth, you should stick with something healthy."

• • •

We take Robertson up on the suggestion and go to an Italian restaurant on Worth Avenue. It's the same place that Elizabeth and I once took my parents for their anniversary, maybe two or three years ago.

·"Do you think he's going to be convicted?" she asks me after our entrees have arrived.

"I don't know. Obviously Morgan thinks so."

"If he is, will he get the death penalty?"

"Hard to say. Morgan's going to ask for it, and even though it's not Texas, they're pretty liberal with giving it out here too. But it'll ultimately be the judge's call."

"How would you feel about that? About his getting the death penalty?"

"I try not to think about it, actually. I'm glad it's not going to be my decision."

She nods at me, without showing any hint of what she's thinking. But there's no need for her to say more.

I know she's thinking that it actually has been my decision.

## 58

Closing statements are the following morning. They track the openings, laying out the evidence. Robertson makes her case for murder, and Broden argues that the jurors must have some doubts about whether it could have been suicide.

Fictional courtroom portrayals usually show each side taking its turn. However, in real life, the prosecution gets a second bite at the apple during closing arguments, a rebuttal after the defense closes. The theory is that because they carry the burden of proof, they get the final word.

During rebuttal, for the first time all trial, Robertson seems at ease in the courtroom. "There is only one truth," she tells the jurors. "There's only one way that Mrs. Miller died. We have given you proof beyond a reasonable doubt that it's murder. The defense would like you to believe that it's something else, maybe suicide. But what it all boils down to is who do you believe: Mrs. Miller's son, Alex, an attorney of impeccable reputation who understands the importance of truthful testimony, or Michael Ohlig, a man who admitted to all of you that he lied numerous times to protect himself? You can only believe one of them. Alex Miller told you that right before her death his mother was making plans to see her granddaughter in Disney World. He swore to you that his mother would never—*never*—have committed suicide under any circumstances. It is even more inconceivable that she would do so and not leave a note to explain her reasons or just to say good-bye to her only child and only granddaughter. Do you believe him? Or do you believe Michael Ohlig, a man who was cheating on his wife with his best friend's wife? A man who lied to Mr. Miller not once, not twice, but several times? And why did he lie? Because, he said, he was afraid of his wife finding out about the affair. Well, if Mr. Ohlig would lie to avoid his wife finding out he was engaged in an affair, wouldn't he surely lie to all of you to stay out of prison?"

The jury is out for a day and a half. Thursday afternoon, they finally file into the courtroom with a verdict in hand. I remember the feeling I had sitting next to Ohlig the last time this happened. I'm just as uncertain about the outcome, again wondering if decisions I made played a determinative role.

Elizabeth squeezes my hand, and this, too, takes me back to when I stood beside Ohlig as he accepted judgment in New York. Then I resisted making any physical contact with him so he'd know he was in it alone. Elizabeth's gesture conveys the opposite. She's with me, she's saying. I caress the top of her hand, and think about how thankful I am that she's here. More than she knows.

The theatrics are the same as before: The foreperson, this time a young woman, rises and walks the note to the judge. When she returns to her spot, Judge Rodriguez calls for Broden and Ohlig to stand to accept judgment.

"Madame Foreperson," Judge Rodriguez says, "on the sole count of the indictment, murder in the first degree, how does this jury find?"

In a clear and loud voice, the young woman says: "Guilty."

Ohlig shows little emotion, as if he had expected this outcome. He shakes Broden's hand and then reaches over the gallery's railing to embrace his wife. Pamela is less stoic, tears visibly running down her face.

"Quiet, please," Judge Rodriguez says in a booming voice over what has by now become a fairly loud rumble from the gallery. "Ladies and gentlemen of the jury, this completes your duty for what we call the guilt and innocence phase of the trial. However, your service is not yet finished. In this state, when the prosecutor has obtained a conviction for capital murder, a sentence of death by lethal injection may be imposed. It is now your obligation to hear and evaluate the evidence as to whether capital punishment is appropriate in this case. Please be advised, however, that you will not render sentence. Your verdict is solely an advisory opinion for me to consider. I will issue the sentence, but I will consider your opinion seriously."

He pauses, surveying the mosaic of people in the jury box. "All right then," he says, "I'm going to give everyone the day off tomorrow, so the lawyers can prepare for the sentencing phase and so all of you in the jury can reconnect with your employers or families. But you continue to be under my jurisdiction, and you must return back to this courtroom on Monday at 9:30 A.M. And, of course, while you're away the same instructions that I've given you throughout this trial still apply. No talking to media or each other about the sentence."

The jurors begin their single-file procession out of the courtroom. When the very last of them has receded from view, Broden calls out, "Your Honor, we request that Mr. Ohlig be permitted to remain free on bail pending sentencing."

I can tell from the way Judge Rodriguez sighs that he's not even going to consider the request. "Mr. Ohlig," he says looking down from the bench, "as I'm sure your able counsel has already discussed with you, the presumption of innocence no longer applies to you. In the eyes of the law, you are now a murderer. As a result, I'm immediately revoking your bail."

This pronouncement causes the first sound to come from Pamela, a loud gasp, even though this can't truly be a surprise to her. As Judge Rodriguez said, Broden must have advised Ohlig that he'd be immediately taken into custody if he were found guilty.

During the trial, there have been one, sometimes two, court officers in the room. Now four uniformed guards approach Ohlig at counsel table, one of whom I can see reaching for handcuffs.

It's yet another moment of déjà vu. Michael Ohlig's pirouette as he's being placed into custody. The last time he looked at me with an expression which, at the time, I thought was contrition. This time, as he's being led from the courtroom in handcuffs, Ohlig stares at me with nothing but dead coldness in his eyes.

"This has got to be the worst celebratory dinner I've ever attended," I say to Robertson. Elizabeth has joined us at an Irish bar called Mick Michaelson, which is across the street from the courthouse. It's the kind of place with only burgers on the menu, but over a hundred different beers on tap.

"Sorry, the county of Palm Beach doesn't spring for lobster and Dom Pérignon every time we put a murderer behind bars."

I raise my beer mug. "Thank you," I say. "To a successful prosecution."

"I prefer to drink to justice being done," Robertson says.

"To that then," I say, taking a sip of my beer.

"I meant in the future sense. Like the judge said, we're not done yet."

I look at Elizabeth before saying anything. She nods, ever so slightly, telling me it's okay to respond as we'd discussed I would.

"I know you're not, Morgan, but I'm afraid I am. We're heading home tomorrow morning, and I'm not coming back."

"Alex, I need you for the sentencing phase."

"I'm sorry," I say in a flat voice, one that I hope gets across that she won't be able to change my mind.

"I don't understand. Family members are usually

climbing over one another to give an impact statement. I need you to be at the hearing to speak for your mother. But more than that, I'm sure she'd want you there to see that Ohlig pays for what he did."

"I'm sorry," I tell her again. "My mother would understand that I've already done enough."

## 59

True to my word, I returned to New York with Elizabeth before the penalty hearing began. Robertson called when it ended. "Dueling experts," she said, making a point to note that Ohlig didn't return to the stand. That wasn't surprising. Given that Ohlig wasn't going to admit to the murder, his testifying would only make the jury think that he lacks remorse. Robertson told me that Judge Rodriguez said he'd pronounce the sentence today at five. She promised to call me as soon as she could.

It's now a little after six, and I still haven't heard from Robertson. At 5:30 I started obsessively checking the internet for news of the result, but to no avail.

"Any news?" Elizabeth asks when I look up from the laptop.

"Not yet."

"Should we have dinner? Or do you want to wait?"

"No, let's have dinner. I think it's better if I pull myself away from the refresh button for a while."

"Charlotte, dinner," Elizabeth calls toward the Pink Palace.

Charlotte runs into the dining room. Climbing onto her chair, she asks what we're having for dinner.

"Noodles," Elizabeth tells her. "Your father and I are having salmon. You can taste it if you want."

"Blech," Charlotte says.

"That's not very polite," I tell her.

"Daddy, tell me again why Papa thought the Scary Lady looked like Grandma."

Like most small children, Charlotte likes repetition. She asks to play the same games, watch the same television shows, and hear the same stories over and over again. For the last few weeks, she's become fixated on the Scary Lady and asks about her nearly every time we sit down for dinner.

"Well," I say, staring up at my former nemesis, now peacefully hanging on the wall looking down at our dining room table, "Papa was in a flea market one day and he saw a picture on one of the tables. Do you know what picture he saw?"

"Was it the Scary Lady?"

"It was. And he looked at it and he thought it looked like the most beautiful woman he had ever seen. The woman in the picture had dark hair and beautiful blue eyes, just like the woman Papa loved."

"But Grandma had yellow hair." This is a point Charlotte always makes at this juncture of the story—that the picture doesn't look like my mother.

"When I was a little boy Grandma had dark brown hair, just like in the picture."

"But why did Papa think all those lines on her face was like Grandma? Grandma didn't have different colored lines on her face when you were little, right, Daddy?"

"That's right, sweetie. The picture *reminded* Papa of

Grandma even though it didn't look exactly like her. What type of picture looks exactly like someone?"

"A photograph."

"Right."

"But sometimes a painting can too," she says. "We saw a picture in school of a lady who was kind of smiling and it looked just like a lady."

"That's also right. But sometimes you draw a picture of me or Mommy or even yourself and it doesn't look exactly like us, right? It may not have hands or a nose, but I still know it's me."

The phone rings. It's a family rule not to answer the phone during mealtime, but Elizabeth jumps up at the first ring.

"Hello? Yes, he's right here," she says, and hands the phone to me, mouthing, "It's Morgan."

I walk into the bedroom for privacy. I don't even say hello into the phone until after I've shut the door behind me and am seated on the corner of our bed.

"Hi, Morgan."

"Did you hear?"

"I didn't. What did he get?"

"Life. No parole." She sounds halfhearted, to say the least.

"Congratulations."

"For what? It's losing, Alex. In Florida, that's the only other sentence that can be given in a capital case."

"I know. But it's a good result. You did a great job on this case, Morgan. I'll be eternally grateful to you."

"I wanted the death penalty," she says. "Maybe someday you'll tell me why you didn't."

By the time I return to the dining room, Charlotte's gone.

"I said she could eat in front of the television," Elizabeth explains. "I thought you might want to talk." Elizabeth places her hand on top of mine. "Is it what you thought?"

"Yeah."

"Are you—" She searches for the right word—I can almost follow her thought pattern. Happy? Pleased? "Satisfied" is the one she settles on.

"I think so. Most of all, I'm just relieved it's finally over."

Elizabeth draws closer to me and kisses me on the cheek, which is followed by a meaningful hug. As is her usual practice, she doesn't say what she's thinking, instead leaving it to me to decipher her thoughts. Sometimes I think of it like learning a foreign language—if I continue to practice, someday I'll be fluent.

I suspect she's questioning whether it's truly over, which, to misquote our former president, depends on what the meaning of the word "it" is. The Ohlig trial is over, but only in the sense that a verdict has been rendered and a sentence imposed.

Part **7**

## 60

The moment I walk through the large doors, the irony hits me. I've probably spent more time in courtrooms over the last year than I ever have before, and yet this is the first time I'm doing it as a lawyer in nearly a year. And the surroundings are anything but familiar.

New York Supreme Court, the majestic name notwithstanding, is actually a lower trial court (the highest court is the Court of Appeals). Cromwell Altman's cases were almost always in federal court, which has jurisdiction over federal crimes such as insider trading, securities fraud, and money laundering.

The distinction between state and federal courts is one that I didn't even know existed until I took federal procedure in law school. I remember Professor Thalstein telling us on that first day: *All the legal training in the world isn't worth a damn if you don't know what building to go to.*

Although there are jurisdictional differences, it's the stark difference in comfort level between the two venues that matters most to me. Federal courthouses were built by the United States government and a finer example of pork spending by Congress would be hard to find, right down to the fact that the two newer federal courthouses in New York are named after the United States senators that made possible a billion-dollar expenditure on a single building. No expense was spared in either of them, from the high-tech audio and computer linkages to the leather chairs and twenty-foot ceilings. By contrast, the state court-houses serving Manhattan couldn't be less impressive. They're spread among several buildings, none of which appear to have been renovated in the last fifty years. The courtrooms themselves are poorly lit, and even more poorly ventilated, freezing in the winter and like ovens in the summer. Behind each state court judge's bench is some type of quote—like *In God We Trust* or *And Justice For All*—and I've never been in a court-room in which every letter was still affixed to the wall.

Three weeks ago, right after Labor Day, a head-hunter introduced me to a small law firm called Peikes, Schwarz, & Selva. The firm has six lawyers—the three founders, who have some type of insurance-based cor-porate practice, an associate who helps them out with their deals, and a tax guy. They decided they needed a litigator and, at least according to the headhunter, they were impressed with my big-firm background.

A day after the call I had a one-shot interview, a far cry from the three times I had visited Cromwell Altman just to get my summer position. I met with Donald Peikes, Stephen Schwarz, and David Selva, en masse, in the firm's only conference room. We talked for close to an hour, about a 70-30 split between them asking about me and my asking about them. When they left, they sent in the tax guy, and after him the associate, each getting a separate fifteen-minute audience with me.

After I'd met everyone at the firm, Schwarz came back alone and made me the offer. He explained that it was an "eat what you kill" kind of place, but I had already been primed by the headhunter that my compensation would be about half of what I had been earning at Cromwell Altman.

I called back the next day and accepted the offer. Don Peikes told me that he was confident I would do well at the firm, and I said I was excited about the opportunity. In truth, the thing I liked best about them was that they didn't seem to care why I left Cromwell Altman.

My case is sixty-eighth on the docket. That means I'll be here at least all morning before I get my less than five minutes in front of the judge, and then he'll almost surely adjourn the motion so we can do it all over again in three months.

The lawyer on the first case on the calendar asks for a three-month adjournment because he's not prepared. His adversary tells the judge that this is the fourth adjournment request, but the judge responds that he shows only two prior adjournments, as if that made it any better, especially considering that each adjournment is at least two months. As the only sanction, the judge tells him that it is now being marked "final."

The judge listens to about three minutes of argument on the next case before telling the lawyers that he's heard enough to know that the case should settle.

He says he's going to hold the motion in abeyance while the parties meet with a mediator and gives them the same day to return to the court as he did the first case—three months from now.

"Next case," the judge calls out to his clerk.

"The People of the State of New York against Axion Chemicals," the clerk shouts out.

Unlike the prior two cases, which had one lawyer per side, this time a scuttle of lawyers rise in two packs and start to move from the gallery and approach the bench.

In the row in front of me are three not too well-dressed men, and my prejudices on these types of things lead me to assume they are the civil servant lawyers employed by the New York State Attorney General's Office. Out of the corner of my eye I see their adversaries, who are sitting closer to the front, and I swallow hard.

"Appearances," the courtroom deputy shouts. "Plaintiff first."

"For the People of the State of New York," the oldest of the shabby-suit contingent begins, and then rattles off some names.

"And for the defense?" the courtroom deputy asks in the other direction.

"Abigail Sloane of the law firm Cromwell Altman Rosenthal & White."

As the argument begins, I can piece together that it has something to do with an environmental claim the state had brought involving some type of illegal dumping. The Assistant AG says the case had only recently been filed and requests discovery from Abby's client before any adjudication on the merits. Abby argues for dismissal now, claiming that a recent decision by the highest court in the state reinterprets the statute on which the charges are based. The representatives of the AG's Office vigorously dispute that assertion.

The judge listens to about ten minutes of this back-and-forth, which is three times more than he gave to the first two matters combined. He says the issue is "interesting and complex," so he'll reserve judgment and file a written decision in the future. In state court, that means nothing will happen in the case for another six months to a year, which I'm sure is exactly the reason Abby filed the motion in the first place.

I use the transition between cases as cover to leave the courtroom. As I'm lying in wait in the corridor, I see the male colleague who stood beside Abby during the argument push the door open for her. She's saying something to him when she catches my eye.

My stomach is in knots, and I wonder if I'm going to be able to confront her without becoming sick. But as she approaches, those feelings dissipate, and I realize that I'm going to be able to go through with it.

It's been nine months since I last saw Abby. She looks harder than I remembered. She's still beautiful, of course—looks like hers don't vanish quickly. She's cut her hair short, which is ironic because I've let mine grow.

Abby actually jumps back a bit when I say hello, confirming that she hadn't seen me in the courtroom. She displays no hint of pleasure in this reunion. If anything, she seems annoyed that I still exist.

"Sean, do you mind going on ahead of me?" she says to her colleague.

Since I left Cromwell Altman, I'd composed a myriad of monologues in my head about what I would say to her if given the opportunity. Some were little more than rambling diatribes, filled with curses and promises that she'd rot in hell for what she did to me. In others I went even further, vowing some type of revenge, although I could never figure out exactly what form it would take. In my better moments, I took the high road, telling her about how happy I was with Elizabeth, and about our new child on the way—serving the revenge fantasy up cold, as the saying goes.

Now, in the moment of truth, I'm overwhelmed by the realization that nothing either she or I say is going to matter. For better or worse, we're both where we are, and we both know it's because of what she did.

"Fancy seeing you here," I say when Sean is far enough away not to be able to hear.

"What do you want?" she says, bitterness in every syllable.

"I want to talk to you. Given everything, that doesn't seem to be too much to ask."

"I don't want to talk to you, Alex."

"I can't believe you're still so angry. I mean, after what you did I should be the angry one."

"What *I* did?" she says, her voice rising to the point that I can feel the eyes of others in the corridor on me, as they turn to wonder what the commotion is about. "You have no idea, do you?"

I take a step back, but she holds her ground. At first her face screams her contempt, but then it slackens, and I now see in her eyes that she feels sorry for me.

"I didn't tell the firm about us," she says with a trace of pity in her voice. "Your wife did."

"Elizabeth? No, that doesn't . . . Aaron told me it was an anonymous call."

"It was, Alex. But then she called me. She told me she'd known for a while, and wanted to get you away from me. I told her that you'd ended it with me already, and that it had only been once."

"What did she say?"

"She said that . . . she said that she didn't care, and told me that someday I'd have a family and I'd understand, and I should stay away from you."

## 61

I go directly home from court, the trip reminding me of my walk home from Cromwell Altman on New Year's Day. Once again, my thoughts are consumed with what I'm going to say to Elizabeth.

My desire to confront her is powerful. Not only did Elizabeth ruin my career at Cromwell Altman, but she allowed me to believe it was actually Abby who had done it.

When I enter our apartment, Elizabeth is sitting at our dining room table. Her hands rest on her swollen belly. She's a little less than a month shy of her due date, but Charlotte came two weeks late, so I'm not expecting anything to happen for a while still.

She jumps up, startled that I'm home in the early afternoon. "Did something happen at work?"

I pause, simply to freeze the moment. I know everything will be different after I tell her.

"I saw Abby Sloane in court today." I wait a beat, trying to ascertain what Elizabeth looks like when she lies. Then, almost involuntarily, I deny myself the opportunity. "She told me it was you who told the firm about Abby and me."

I expect an apology, but Elizabeth doesn't offer one. To the contrary, she looks at me through defiant eyes, seemingly without any remorse for what she's done.

"Why, Elizabeth? You know everything I sacrificed to become a partner at Cromwell Altman. How could you feel justified to take that away from me?"

"That place," she says, unable even to bring herself to mention the firm's name, "made you lose sight of what's important—your family. Alex, I know it's hard to see it now, but I did what I did to protect our family. You included."

"How can you say that? I'm earning less than half what I did at Cromwell Altman. Who's going to pay for private school for Charlotte? For a baby nurse? For this apartment?"

"We'll be fine financially. It's not like you're working for minimum wage. You're still earning more than most people. A lot more. Besides, you know that I never cared about the money."

"You certainly spent it."

"I liked it. I'm not going to deny that it was nice having money. But it's more than a fair trade-off to have my family back. And, Alex, that's what happened."

That the ends justify the means is an often heard argument in criminal defense, and yet, with the exception of self-defense, it is almost never exculpatory. Rather than debate Elizabeth on this issue, however, I ask a different question.

"How long did you know about Abby and me?" I ask.

"I suspected for a while. I've seen you on trial before, but this time you weren't just working all the time—you seemed happy about it, like you couldn't wait to go to the office. Your parents died within months of each other and you didn't seem to lose a step, and that's just not normal, Alex. I figured something else had to be going on with you. Then after the trial ended . . . it was like a switch flipped. All of a sudden you announce that you're taking some time off, and I was really excited about it, but then you were walking around here in a trance . . . and no matter how hard I tried to talk to you about what was going on, whether it was the fact that Michael had been arrested or something else . . . I just couldn't get through to you. So . . . I checked your BlackBerry. Because yes, I think I have the right to know what's going on with my husband. And it's not like your password was hard to crack. I was hoping it was going to be *Elizabeth,* but I knew it'd be *Charlotte.*"

"I still don't understand why. Why go to the firm? Why not just tell me?"

"Because that wouldn't have worked, Alex. Maybe it would have been enough for you to stop with Abby, but that was never the real problem. That was more of a symptom than anything else. If you stayed there, in time, things would have gone back to being just like they were. And I don't mean the infidelity. I mean you wouldn't have seen what was happening to yourself. To us."

"So you made the decision that my career should be over? Just like that?"

"I know you want me to say that I'm sorry, but I can't. I won't. I did what I needed to do to keep our family together. You know the way we're always telling ourselves we'd do anything to protect Charlotte? This is *anything*. You owed it to Charlotte as well as to me to work harder on our marriage when things got tough. You don't just . . . fuck whoever you happen to be working with."

"So, that was my punishment for sleeping with Abby once? I lost my career? That seems a bit disproportionate, don't you think?"

"Don't insult me, Alex. It wasn't the sex. You know that. Even if you'd never slept with her, it would have been the same problem. She was your person, not me. Besides, I don't really know what proportion means in this context. 'Desperate times . . .'" She shrugs, leaving unsaid the rest of the quotation, about desperate measures.

Then she smiles. It's completely incongruous with the topic at hand. It's warm and loving.

"The main reason I can't be sorry, Alex, is that it worked. At least I think it did. I'm happy. You're happy. We're going to have a baby. You have a job that pays enough for us to live well. It's like Howard said, we just needed to get over that hump."

I suspected at the time that it was marriage counselor propaganda, but Howard told us that statistics show most couples endure at least one major crisis in their marriage, something significant enough to cause one or both of them to consider divorce. Those who survive it, he claimed, end up having happier marriages than those who never faced the test in the first place.

In my mind I can see myself storm out, but I don't know where I'd go, and after all Elizabeth and I have gone through, and with a baby coming, that doesn't make the most sense. It's more than that, though, that keeps me here. Cromwell Altman is all in the past, and my future sits in front of me, her hands on her belly.

"I love you, Alex," Elizabeth says, now crying. It's a heartbreaking sight, my nine-month-pregnant wife sobbing about her love for me. "That's why I forgave you for what you did—because *I love you*. I don't think it's too much to ask for you to do the same."

## 62

"Another one came for you today," Elizabeth says the following day, pointing to the foyer. I walk in that direction, stopping by the console table where our mail is deposited. It's on top of a small pile, as always in a flimsy, nearly transparent envelope. I know what it is even before seeing Ohlig's name and prisoner ID number in the upper-left corner.

Since his sentencing, Ohlig has written to me on a weekly basis, sometimes even more than that. The letters are always typed on an old-fashioned typewriter—apparently computers are not standard issue in maximum security—and errors are marked by x's blackening out the words underneath, often with handwritten words in pencil on the line above. They tend to be dated seven to ten days prior to when they arrive. I assume the delay is a result of the prison's review process, but I really don't know for sure.

The letters are all more or less the same. They usually start out by expressing how sorry he is, telling me that he knows he betrayed my father, and sometimes he includes my mother as another of his victims. In some he recounts anecdotes about my father as a younger man, or about my parents as newlyweds. I've always assumed he does this to convey that he has not always been such a destructive force, that there was a time when they all existed together quite happily.

Then he closes with a plea for my help.

Elizabeth long ago suggested that I stop reading the letters and just throw them away, but I never do.

I tear open the envelope, careful not to rip the letter inside, which I've done before on more than one occasion. It's a shorter one, as these letters go.

> *Dear Alex:*
>
> *I hope this letter finds you and your family well. I read about your new job (we get internet here, but only an hour a week). I don't know much about your new firm, but I know that they're lucky to have a lawyer of your XXXXXX caliber. My best wishes for success and happiness with them.*
>
> *Last week marked the fourth month of my incarceration. I wish I could report that it's getting better, but sadly I cannot. Like many inmates, I am trying to put my situation in a larger context, an effort to ascertain why God has chosen this path for me.*
>
> *I XXXXXXXX understand why XXXXXXX XXXXXXXXXXXXXXXXXXXXXXXXXXXXXX XXXXX you have not written back to me, but I hope that if I keep writing I will ultimately be able to appeal to what Abraham Lincoln once called the better angels of our nature. I hope it is not presumpXXXious for me to say that I believe I have some understanding of who you are inside, Alex. Not only because of*

*the time we've spent together, but also by vir-*
*tue of all that your mother and father shared*
*with me over the years.*

*We all lose our way at times. I did, and I*
*believe your mother did too. As I've written*
*before, I cannot begin to fully apologize to you*
*for my actions, but it will not stop me from*
*seeking your forgiveness.*

*Once lost, it hardly matters how you came*
*to be there, or even how long you've been lost.*
*All that matters is finding your way.*

*I believe, Alex, that like me, you have lost*
*your way. You know the right thing for you*
*to do, and yet for some reason you turn away*
*from that path. It is far from my place to*
*judge, and I can only hope that you find your*
*way before the false path leads you to the type*
*of self-destruction that befell me.*

Like all of his letters, it's signed, "Faithfully, Michael." Every time my eyes roll past the words, they give me pause. *Faithfully.* What does such a word mean to a man like Michael Ohlig?

Whenever I read his letters, I try to picture Ohlig in a cement block cell, banging out another letter on an old typewriter. What must be going through his mind, imprisoned for the rest of his life for a crime that I have long known he didn't commit?

## 63

A week or so later, while we're having breakfast, Elizabeth tells me that "something feels funny." Even though I suspect it's only nerves, Elizabeth insists that we go to the hospital.

We arrive at about ten and have a new daughter a half hour later. The doctor later tells us that it had been an emergency situation—the umbilical cord had prolapsed, and to add good measure, the baby had managed to wrap the cord around her neck, cutting off her oxygen supply.

"I probably don't see a situation like this more than once a decade," our doctor told us. "You have a miracle baby here. If you hadn't come to the hospital when you did, she wouldn't have survived."

With Charlotte, Elizabeth and I had an agreement not to settle finally on a name until after her arrival. Elizabeth was more new-agey than me about it, saying she wanted to make sure that the name we were selecting would fit the actual person, as opposed to the abstract notion of a baby. I told her that I couldn't imagine what made a newborn look more like an Amanda or a Natalie, but if it made her feel better to wait, that was fine with me. In actuality, we had decided on Charlotte Emily within a few weeks after Elizabeth's ultrasound revealed we would be having a girl, and after Charlotte's arrival, Elizabeth confirmed the name fit her sufficiently for us to put it on her birth certificate.

Elizabeth and I had a harder time selecting a name this time around. We knew we'd be having a second daughter, and Elizabeth again requested that we remain open-minded about a name until the baby actually arrived. Early on in the process, Elizabeth suggested we name the baby after my mother, but I demurred. One Barbara Miller was enough for my lifetime, I told her. I hesitated a little longer about paying some type of homage to my father, but ultimately concluded that the next generation should start without any connection to the failings of those who preceded them.

The name we had tentatively settled upon was Julia. However, last night Elizabeth told me that she had been thinking about a new name, but wasn't prepared to share it with me just yet.

As Elizabeth lies in bed holding our newborn daughter at her breast, I ask her if our baby is a Julia.

"I was wondering if you might consider a different name."

"Depends on what it is, I suppose."

"I've been thinking about it for a while, and then after what the doctor said . . ."

"You want to name her Miracle Baby?"

Elizabeth laughs. "Not exactly. How do you feel about the name Hope?"

"Hope," I repeat. "I like it." I touch our daughter's soft hair. "But that might be too much responsibility for a brand new baby to handle."

"She won't be hope for us, Alex," Elizabeth says, reaching over to take my hand. "We're going to be whatever we're going to be. But I'd like her to remind us both that great things are possible, even when they look the worst."

I take a deep breath, letting Elizabeth's sentiment wash over me. "Since it was your idea, I think you should be the first person to call your daughter by her name," I say.

"Welcome to our family, Hope," Elizabeth says, and kisses our newborn daughter's head.

## 64

Entering a prison is a sobering experience. Until you've done it, you simply cannot imagine how powerful the sound of a metal door locking can be.

I arrive at the Florida State Prison on a particularly humid day, despite the fact that it's late November. It's nearly a year to the day after my mother's death.

FSP, or Raiford, as it is sometimes called, is probably the most famous prison in Florida, partly because of the Lynyrd Skynard song about an escapee, but also because it was the last home of serial killer Ted Bundy. It's actually a prison within a prison, situated at the center of several other correctional facilities and housing approximately 1,400 of Florida's most dangerous convicts.

The woman in front of me in line is a paralegal from a local law firm. From what I can overhear, she's there to have the firm's incarcerated client sign some papers. The guard behind what I assume to be bulletproof glass tells the legal assistant that she can't go in.

"I'm sorry, honey," she says in a heavy southern drawl, "you just can't go into a maximum security facility wearing that."

"I dress like this for work," the paralegal says.

"This isn't work, honey. This is you going into a facility with over a thousand men inside who don't see many women. Call your office and ask them to send someone else, or come back wearing a sweater. If I can see any part of your bra through your shirt, you don't make it through the gate."

The paralegal steps out of line and looks at me like she's in an Orwellian state, but I can see the guard's point. It's precisely because the inhabitants of this institution refused to abide by the dictates of a civilized society that they must now reside in a place that imposes different standards.

"My name is Alex Miller," I tell the guard, slipping my driver's license through the small slot. "I'm here to see Michael Ohlig. I'm an attorney."

"From New York?" she says, looking at my license.

"Yes, ma'am," I say. "I sent paperwork over earlier in the week about my visit."

"This a legal visit?" she asks.

"Yes," I lie. Prison visitations are recorded, the exception being attorney conferences.

"You don't have any firearms on you, do you, Mr. Miller?"

She's serious, and so I don't make light of the question. "No, ma'am."

The large metal door buzzes and automatically slides open. After I step through I see that another door of equal size remains locked before me. Its buzzer doesn't begin to sound until after the first door has already locked, at which time the second door begins to open, permitting me to enter the prison.

Once Ohlig was sentenced to live the rest of his life in this facility, Clint Broden called me in a final effort to have me come to Ohlig's rescue. Broden told me some of the horrors Ohlig would experience at Raiford—sodomy, intolerable living conditions, gang domination. I maintained the same predisposition I had in his office, refusing to acknowledge that Michael Ohlig wasn't getting precisely what he deserved.

At a second checkpoint, a guard tells me I'll need to be accompanied before I'm permitted to proceed further, and he reaches for the phone to call for my escort. Once my guide arrives, he leads me through three more sets of double-locking doors until I'm finally deposited in the visiting center of the maximum security part of the prison. There it looks like what I've seen on television, banks of chairs against glass windows with telephones on either end.

"Which one?" I ask the guard.

"For an attorney visit, you're given more privacy. It's a separate room."

He walks me around the corner and leads me to a three-by-three room, furnished with only a single metal chair. On the other side of the glass is a similar-sized space with a similar-looking metal chair. My side smells like a high school gym locker room. I can only imagine the stench on the other side.

I wait for twenty minutes until I hear the clank as the door on the opposite side of the glass begins to open. A prisoner walks in and the door locks behind him. For a moment I think the guard has made a mistake by putting the wrong man in this room.

Michael Ohlig has aged considerably since the last

time I saw him on the day of his conviction. He's thinner, so much so that where he once had a certain power to his presence, he could now be described as drawn, almost gaunt, much the way a cancer patient looks during chemotherapy. His hair is sparser too, and cut shorter, not much longer than a crew cut. He smiles at me, but it comes out crooked, like a barbell that's too heavy, as if he can't summon the strength to balance it.

Ohlig's legs are shackled and his hands cuffed behind him. "Knees," calls out a deep voice from a man I can't see who's outside the closed door. Ohlig kneels, placing his handcuffed arms behind him and onto the ledge in front of a small metal door. The window slides open and two thick, hairy hands reach in with a key, unlocking the handcuffs. Ohlig quietly says thank you, a whisper really, and the window is slammed shut.

I've already reached over to grab the black receiver on my side of the glass from its holster, but Ohlig hasn't yet followed suit. Instead, he stares at me without movement. I wonder about the reason for this delay, but no explanation comes to me. Then he removes the phone on his side and takes some time wiping it down on the sleeve of his orange jumpsuit.

"You don't want to know the kind of stuff that ends up on these phones," he says to me as his opening line.

"Hello, Michael." I know better than to ask him how he's doing, having made that mistake once with an incarcerated client. "Do you know why I'm here?"

"I hope so." His voice is hoarse, even beyond the distortion of the phone.

It has been nearly a year since I took the Scary Lady in to be reframed. When I picked it up from the framer, the man behind the counter handed me a white envelope. My name was written on the front, and it was taped closed.

"Are you Alex?" the man in the frame store asked.

I nodded.

"This was in the backing," he said to me. "Sometimes people put things in frames for safekeeping—usually it's a description of the artwork or a reminder of where it was purchased, but some people have been known to put real valuables in there, like a deed or even cash."

I studied the envelope. "Did you open it?"

"It's sealed," he said, which meant that he probably had. That was one explanation for why it was taped closed. The frame store guy likely opened it thinking the Holy Grail was inside. When he recognized what it was, he must have realized he had to turn it over, and taped it shut. Then again, perhaps he's an honest man and didn't open it at all.

"Thank you," I told him, taking the envelope and placing it in my coat pocket.

"Aren't you curious what it is?" he asked.

"I know what it is," I told him.

I read the note twice in the park across the street from the frame shop, and then each day thereafter for about two weeks. But I haven't read it for nearly a year—not when I met with Clint Broden that first time, nor when I repeatedly swore under oath that my mother didn't take her own life, nor on the day Michael Ohlig was convicted of her murder.

Last night I opened it again.

I suppose I wasn't too surprised that my mother's suicide note didn't contain any apologies. That wasn't her way. The closest she came was to ask me not to let her decision to end her life deprive me of my own happiness.

She wrote that after Michael Ohlig she would never love again, and without love there was no reason to live. Somewhere, buried within a paragraph of rambling sentences, was the phrase: "I've reached the conclusion that my life is better finished now, on my own terms."—as if her life was like a good meal that, upon completing, she was now free to be excused from.

In another part of her letter she claimed it was at Ohlig's insistence that she confronted my father about her affair, and she could no longer live with the guilt of what that had wrought. She asked that I understand and wrote that it was her dying wish that I not do anything to interfere with her plan.

Knowing my mother, I wasn't shocked at her plan for revenge. As she said in the note, since it was Ohlig's fault she was going to end her life, she might as well take him down with her.

At first I regarded the note with almost Talmudic reverence, trying to parse the meaning behind the selection of every word, the nuance of each sentiment. Soon enough, however, I realized that even the most carefully drafted parts were not constructed with such fine attention to detail, and therefore my efforts to see more than the plain meaning were fruitless.

My mother's note left no doubt that her affair with Ohlig began shortly after they first met at the Central Park tennis courts, and continued, off and on, for the next thirty-six years. Even my father's meeting Ohlig at that bookstore, the one that supposedly triggered their reunion, was not a chance encounter.

No matter how it actually played out, it's an inescapable conclusion that Michael Ohlig was responsible for the deaths of my parents. His urging my mother to confront my father must have induced his heart attack, and then Ohlig's cavalier treatment of my mother caused her to take her own life.

He didn't act alone, of course. My mother was at least as culpable, if not more so, in both deaths, but as she wrote, she was suffering the ultimate punishment for her actions. Judge Rodriguez spared Ohlig that fate. Even if he is not guilty of murder, that seems to me to be much more of a technicality than an excuse.

I called Clint Broden last week, telling him that I'd be going to Raiford, at which time I also explained the purpose of my visit. He originally asked if he could meet me there, about a four-hour drive from his Miami office, but seemed relieved when I told him I wanted to do it alone. I'd told him I'd send him a copy of my mother's suicide note, and he said he'd immediately begin the process of freeing Ohlig.

I explained to Broden that I had only recently found the note, careful to reveal only as much as necessary so as to provide a sufficient shield against the possibility of perjury charges stemming from my testimony at Ohlig's trial. If Broden doubted the chronology I was suggesting, he didn't say it, apparently willing to leave to Ohlig, or maybe to karma, whether further payback was warranted.

It often takes more than a week for any news from the outside world to reach an inmate, so it's very possible that Ohlig has not been told anything about my visit. It's even likely Ohlig didn't know he had a visitor until the guards got him from his cell ten minutes ago, and didn't know it was me until he saw my face. But even if Ohlig had been surprised, I know him well enough not to expect him to show it.

I press the first page of my mother's note up against the glass. "They said that I could leave it for you, but I can't pass it to you now, and you likely wouldn't actually get it for a day or two."

He nods, indicating that he's fully aware of the prison procedures. "I'm sorry, Alex," he says. "My eyes aren't so good and I don't have my glasses. You know that scene from *Godfather III*. . . ." His voice trails off. I take it as a good omen that he's made a joke, even if it's a grim one about a murder at the end of the movie perpetrated by jamming eyeglasses into someone's throat.

I read him the entire letter in a slow and steady

voice. I practiced it out loud in the hotel this morning so I could make it through without breaking down. Ohlig didn't need the dry run. He's stoic throughout, staring straight ahead, looking like a passenger on a long flight.

"How long will it take?" he asks.

By his tone he could be asking about anything, but I know what he means. "It's not as easy as it should be, but Clint Broden has already started the process. He said he can't promise anything, but he hopes you'll be released within six months, maybe a year. But it could be longer."

I can almost see Ohlig's thoughts. Six more months, maybe more. If all goes well for him, his total prison sentence will be less than a year, but it will probably have taken ten years off his life.

"I don't know if you read my letters, Alex. . . ." I nod to indicate I had, but it doesn't seem to register with him. "I meant everything I wrote. I am very, very sorry for the suffering I caused you and your parents. I never wanted to be the person I became, and for the life of me, I just don't know how it happened. I did love your mother, but . . ."

He doesn't finish the thought, and I don't ask him to. There is no "but" that will explain away all that's transpired.

"Why now?" he asks. "Do you want something?"

Shortly after Ohlig's sentencing, Broden offered to pay me for providing proof that my mother took her own life. He phrased it in a lawyerly way, of course, so there could be no claim that he was bribing me, if such a charge could apply to paying someone to come forward with the truth. I told Broden I was insulted by the suggestion I was withholding such critical evidence of a man's innocence.

Ohlig's query reveals he's already surmised the most important piece of information—the part that I'm not going to admit—that I've known for some time that he was not guilty of murder. He's questioning why I'm changing that position now, and his logical deduction is that it must be for money.

"I want to be rid of you, Michael. To have nothing to do with you ever again. To leave you to live with what you've done, and without your sins becoming my own."

"I understand," he says quietly, leaving it at that. We stare at each other in silence, the same way we did when he first entered the room.

Of course, it has occurred to me. Seeing that photograph of my father and Ohlig as younger men first put the thought in my head. That's why I showed it to Abby in the first place, I suppose, even if it was subconscious: to get a second opinion. Once I considered Ohlig's paternity a possibility, it led me to various other connections—my height, my hair, and maybe most tellingly of all, my mother's life-long insistence that, at my core, none of my father could be found.

I can easily envision the drama of my mother's courtship, each of the three parties playing their roles to perfection. My father thinking that he had been truly blessed to find someone as beautiful as my mother, her playing both ends against the middle, hoping for Ohlig, but keeping my father interested as an insurance policy. And Ohlig, unable to resist being the cad, betraying his best friend for the affections of a woman who, despite what he claims now, probably meant little to him, at least at the time.

Who knows what happened when my mother found out she was pregnant. I'm sure she would have hoped this would cause Ohlig to marry her, but if she did, she didn't know him very well. That left her with my father, adoption, or abortion, and I suppose I should be pleased with her choice. Of course, it's also possible that she never told Ohlig, anticipating his likely response without having to ask. Even if this were the case, the timing of my birth would still have put Ohlig on notice of the distinct possibility that he was my father. I sometimes think that's why, of all the lawyers in New York City, he picked me to represent him. A last chance at some father-son bonding, perhaps.

There's at least one flaw in this scenario—Ohlig must have known that I was withholding evidence that would exculpate him for murder and yet he never once suggested I was committing a form of patricide. A cynic might say that he didn't know that I'd discovered her suicide note, or that he didn't tell me about the possibility of his parentage because he thought I wouldn't believe him, or that even if I did, it would anger me enough to ensure that I'd turn my back on him. It's also possible he assumed that I had already figured it out on my own, or that my mother had told me, and therefore there was nothing for him to add.

I even have one other theory—that Ohlig withheld the truth because after all he had done, he wanted to do the right thing, for once.

I could find out, of course. His DNA is now on file, and so it wouldn't take more than a scrape of my inner cheek to confirm whether we share a gene pool. But I don't want to know. I meant what I told him—I don't want to have any attachment to him whatsoever. Even more fundamentally, whether he contributed the sperm that fertilized my mother's egg has no real significance to who I am.

Of course, that only raises a more troubling question—Who am I? The man who cheated on Elizabeth? The man who violated my fiduciary duty to my partners by sleeping with a subordinate? The man who committed perjury to see Michael Ohlig go to prison for a crime he didn't commit?

I'm all of them, I know. But I take solace in, of all things, the phrase found in every securities prospectus, even the one for Salminol—*past performance is not indicative of future results*—to mean that I don't have to be only that man.

Although I recognize that our actions are not comparable, there's a symmetry to it all that I find comforting. Like when you first discover that the area of every circle is Pi R squared, and with that realization comes the belief that there's greater order to the world than you can see. Elizabeth and I both have reason to be angry, and yet we're both optimistic about the future. I do not forgive Elizabeth for what she did as much as I understand why she did it, and love her despite her worst deeds because I know that they do not define her. I'm almost certain she'd say the same thing about her feelings toward me.

Whether that's enough for a happy marriage remains to be seen, but it seems to be a good place to start. As Elizabeth said on the day Hope was born, we'll be whatever we're going to be, but at least we're both committed to our being whatever we're going to be together, to facing our difficulties instead of looking for an escape from them.

So far, I think we're on the right track. I recall how difficult the first weeks of Charlotte's life were, the sleep deprivation among other reasons that Elizabeth and I seemed to be forever sniping at each other, but during Hope's first three months Elizabeth and I are more in sync, and more forgiving of each other when we're not. Most importantly, when our children are asleep, and it's just the two of us, I remember why I fell in love with Elizabeth, and hold on to that thought like a life preserver, knowing what I saw then is still there.

Like my infidelity to Elizabeth, I can never absolve myself of the role I played in sending Michael Ohlig to Raiford, but I'm here now to limit the damage as best I can. And, like with Elizabeth, I don't forgive Ohlig for his betrayals as much as I understand them, and hope that he's committed to a different path now. Perhaps in time he'll feel that way about what I did to him, but that will be his decision.

I return the phone to its holder, and begin to step away from the glass divider when I hear a tapping. It's Ohlig, asking me for a final word.

"Your father," he says after I've put the receiver back to my ear, "he would be proud. Your mother always said how much you were like her, but in many ways, Alex, I think you are more your father's son."

# ACKNOWLEDGMENTS

My sincerest thanks to all the people at Simon & Schuster for making what I thought would always be just a dream into a reality. Ed Schlesinger took what I considered to be a finished product and made it better in more ways than I could have imagined, even improving upon my knowledge of Batman. Scott Miller of Trident Publishing has been a great advocate for my work. Without his help, my readership would have been limited to the friends and family listed below.

Ed Stackler was the very first person with any professional knowledge to suggest that I could someday see my work in print. I simply cannot credit him enough with not only shaping *A Conflict of Interest* to its present form, but giving me the encouragement to believe I could really be a writer. Although we've never met face-to-face (something I hope to remedy soon), I consider him a friend.

Heartfelt thanks also go out to all my friends who read earlier versions of *A Conflict of Interest,* and whose comments and insights made it a much better book: Matt Brooks, John Firestone, Anna Grzymala-Busse, Allison Heller, Margaret Martin, Debbie Peikes, Ted Quinn, Elisa Chiara Reza, Ellice Schwab, Lisa Sheffield, and Marilyn Steinthal.

I must single out Clint Broden, who not only read the manuscript more than once, but helped me with certain criminal procedure issues and lent his name to the effort. Although the character Clint Broden is not based on the real Clint Broden, the real Clint Broden is the finest criminal defense lawyer I know.

I owe the greatest debt to my family for their support and encouragement. My daughter, Rebecca, was always interested in hearing plot developments and making suggestions, and her sister, Emily, would often color pictures on the page opposite the one of what I was editing, making the process that much more enjoyable. Michael and Benjamin Plevin were both very good listeners and great promoters of my work to their friends' parents. Jessica and Kevin Shacter (and Molly and Jack) helped by reminding me how lucky I am to have them as my family.

Above everyone else, this book would never have been written without Susan Steinthal's support and encouragement. She read the manuscript more times than she could have imagined, correcting my grammar without making fun of me, and was always willing to talk about characters and plot, even when she would have preferred to play with the dog. For good measure, she even took my picture for the back cover. If it were just her contributions to the written words I would be forever grateful, but I am most appreciative of Susan's contribution to my life because without her love, nothing else would matter.